TORKIL DAMHAUG

MEDUSA

AN OSLO CRIME FILES NOVEL

headline

Se Meg, Medusa © Cappelen Damm AS, 2007, 2011
English translation © 2015 Robert Ferguson

The right of Torkil Damhaug to be identified as the Author of
the Work has been asserted by him in accordance with the
Copyright, Designs and Patents Act 1988.

First published in Great Britain in 2015 by
HEADLINE PUBLISHING GROUP

Published by agreement with Cappelen Damm AS,
Akersgata 47/49, Oslo, Norway

1

Cataloguing in Publication Data is available from the British Library

ISBN 978 1 4722 0683 1

Typeset in Granjon by Palimpsest Book Production Limited,
Falkirk, Stirlingshire

Printed and bound in Great Britain by Clays Ltd, St Ives plc

Headline's policy is to use papers that are natural, renewable and recyclable
products and made from wood grown in sustainable forests. The logging
and manufacturing processes are expected to conform to the environmental
regulations of the country of origin.

MIX
Paper from
responsible sources
FSC® C104740

HEADLINE PUBLISHING GROUP
An Hachette UK Company
Carmelite House
50 Victoria Embankment
London EC4Y 0DZ

www.headline.co.uk
www.hachette.co.uk

To M

TODAY I BECAME a thief. I've stolen before, but today I became a thief. People who know about such things say it's the autumnal equinox today so that's probably a good day on which to become a thief. Everything hangs in the balance before the darkness begins to take over. It wasn't planned. I only plan the most necessary things. The rest just has to take care of itself. I was passing a shop and a Dictaphone caught my eye. I stopped and went back and entered the shop. The boy behind the counter seemed dull and uninterested. I got him to go looking for something I didn't need. Then opened the box and stuffed the Dictaphone into my pocket. Not until I was back out on the street did I know what I would be using it for. And when you hear this, you'll know too. Because one day you'll hear exactly what I'm saying now. I don't know yet how it'll happen but I can see you in my mind's eye lying there, listening to my voice, completely unable to turn away. You can throw letters away, or burn them. You can forget about me and tell yourself I'm dead even though you know I'm alive somewhere out there. But you will hear my voice and then you'll remember everything you've said to me, and everything I've said to you.

Once you told me about those twins. You read so much and knew so much and wanted to share everything with me who hardly ever read. Was one of them named Castor? We were sitting in the classroom before the others came in when you told me about them. Castor and Pollux, that was their names. They were inseparable. And instead of going to heaven, one of them chose instead to go to hell, where the other one had ended up. To be with him. You've forgotten that you told me this but I don't forget.

This is a good Dictaphone. You can delete and change things and insert individual words anywhere you like just by pressing a few buttons. But I don't use them. I'm saying this to you, and you shall hear it exactly as it is, with no polishing and no frills. It's the thought of this that makes me feel calm and excited at the same time. That you will know what you have done.

1

PART I

1

THE WOMAN SAT motionless with her back to the window. Her arms hung straight down. Her pale grey face seemed frozen. She was dressed in green trousers and blouse, with a jacket the same colour loose over her shoulders. Her cheekbones were high and prominent and her eyes still greeny blue, but now the iris was narrowing inside a milky white rim. Outside, the wind lifted a bare birch branch behind her head.

Suddenly she glided her tongue over her teeth before opening her mouth and fixing her gaze on her visitor.

– I've been waiting all day, she said. – About time someone from the police could be bothered to turn up.

She stood up, tottered across the floor on her high-heeled sandals and checked that the door was closed behind him, came tripping back and sat down in the other chair, the one next to the writing desk. In flashes she still had that energetic way of moving, and she brushed a lock of her perm from her forehead with a gesture he knew well.

– The reason I have asked you to come . . . She interrupted herself, again went across the floor, opened the door and peered into the corridor outside.

– I don't trust anyone in this place, she declared, closing it with a bang that was perhaps intended to underline what she said. Back in the brown leather chair, she smoothed her trousers over her knees.

– I've been waiting all day, she said again, now in a despairing voice. – I've got a missing person to report. The police must do something soon.

Her visitor was a man in his forties. He was wearing a hand-made suit, with a pale grey shirt underneath it. It was open at the neck, not that this made him look any the less well dressed.

– I came as quickly as I could, he said, and cast a glance at the clock.

– It's about my husband, the woman went on. – He didn't come home last night.

– I see, the visitor answered, and sat on the side of the bed, directly opposite her.

– He's very particular always to let me know. But I haven't heard a thing from him. Now I think something terrible has happened.

She moistened her dry upper lip with her tongue and smiled bravely.

– Do you know what the worst thing is?

The visitor passed his hand across her shortish hair, obviously recently cut. He knew what was coming.

– The worst thing is . . . The woman groaned as she opened her eyes wide, as though afraid.

– Have you had enough to drink today? the visitor interjected with what seemed like genuine concern. – I think you're thirsty.

She didn't seem to hear what he said.

– The Gestapo, she whispered as her eyes filled with tears. – I don't think my husband will come back again ever.

The visitor remained sitting with his mother for almost three quarters of an hour. He poured her orange juice from a carton on the bedside table and she emptied two glasses. Having expressed her fear, she was finished with it this time around and opened a copy of *Allers*. It had been there on the table the last time he'd visited, a week earlier, and all the weeks before that. She didn't say another word, as though she was completely engrossed by this single page she happened to have opened the magazine at. Now and then she looked over in his direction, her gaze diffuse, a slight smile playing about her mouth; she seemed to have descended once again into that remote calm that spread through her more deeply with every passing week, killing off everything else. He'd remembered to buy *Dagbladet* on the way and now leafed through it. When there was a knock on the door and the nurse came in with her medication – a man with greying hair, possibly a Tamil – he quickly got to his feet and gave his mother a hug.

– I'll come back again soon, he promised.

– Judas, she hissed, her eyes transformed into glowing embers.

He swallowed his surprise, struggled not to laugh. She raised the half-full glass of juice, looked as though she were about to throw it in his direction.

– No, Astrid, the nurse scolded and took the glass from her.

She stood up and shook her fist.

– Brede is evil, she shouted. – It wasn't the Gestapo, it was Brede who shot.

The nurse got her down in her chair again. She continued to gesture with her arms.

– Twins, that's one too many kids, that is. But you wouldn't have a clue what I'm taking about, a Negro like you.

The visitor glanced at the nurse and shook his head apologetically. The nurse opened the dosage box.

– Negroes are from Africa, he said with a broad smile and handed her the juice glass.

She swallowed one of the tablets.

– Because you are Brede, aren't you? she said, peering in confusion at the visitor.

– No, Mother, I'm not Brede. I'm Axel.

He knocked on the charge nurse's door and entered the office. When she saw that it was him, she swung her chair round from the computer desk and gestured with her hand towards the sofa.

– Sit yourself down a moment.

She was in her thirties, tall and athletic, with a face that he found attractive.

– Mother seems much more disturbed these days.

The charge nurse gave a quick nod.

– She's been talking a lot about the war recently. Of course everyone here knows who Torstein Glenne was, but is there anything in all this about the Gestapo?

Axel pointed to the plastic plate of Maryland cookies on the table.

– Mind awfully if I take one? I missed lunch today.

He said no thanks to offers of coffee and blackcurrant juice, and was amused by the nurse's further attempts to make up for her initial lack of hospitality.

– It is true that the Gestapo were after my father, he confirmed as he munched away. – He managed to cross the border into Sweden at the last moment. But Mother knew nothing about it at the time. It was fourteen years before she met him. She was four years old.

The charge nurse struggled to fasten her smooth hair at the neck in a hair band.

– It's tremendously useful to know things like that. She's always very uneasy whenever there's anything about war on the TV. Recently we've had to switch off when the news comes on. By the way, who is Brede?

Axel Glenne brushed the biscuit crumbs from his lapels.

– Brede?

– Yes. Suddenly Astrid has started saying lots of things about this Brede. That he isn't to come here, that she doesn't want to see him any more and God knows what else. She actually gets quite worked up about it. When she's really in a state we have to give her a Murelax. Of course we don't know if this Brede really exists, so it isn't easy for the nurses to know what to say.

– Brede was her son.

The charge nurse's eyebrows shot up under her fringe.

– You have a brother? I had no idea. There's never been anyone else but you come to visit. And sometimes your wife, and the children.

– It's been more than twenty-five years since Mother last saw him, said Axel.

He stood up and rested his hand on the doorknob to indicate that the conversation was over.

2

FROM THE BACK seat of the taxi he called Bie again. She still didn't answer and he sent her a text saying he would be late. It was Monday, football practice and violin lesson. Bie was going out this evening, but she'd have time to drive to the violin lesson first. Picking up afterwards was his responsibility.

The ship's bell had already started ringing as the taxi turned into Aker Brygge. He had a few notes in his card-holder and paid cash, didn't have time to wait for the receipt, scrambled aboard just as the barrier was about to be lowered. He wouldn't be home until close on 6.30; Tom would have to go to practice by himself, if he could be bothered. He felt a twinge of guilt and send him a message too.

He knew a lot of the other passengers, perhaps even most of them. But this particular evening he made his way quickly through the salon and settled out on deck. It was warm for late September. A thin, creamy layer coated the sky above the fjord, the evening sun still visible behind it. He heard the echo of a voice in his thoughts: his mother calling him Judas. His mother thinking he was Brede, and being angry with him.

A group of men in dark suits were gathered around the peace torch at the end of the quay. One of them raised a hand as the ferry glided past, and from where Axel Glenne stood by the railings aft, it looked as though he were putting it into the flame.

The house was empty when he got home. Only now did he remember it was half-term holiday. On the kitchen worktop was a note from Bie. *Marlen is spending the night at Natasha's. Tom will be home before ten. Spaghetti in the microwave. Be back late. B.* Alongside she'd drawn a little heart, from which something red dripped. A tear maybe; it was definitely not blood she had in mind.

He sat down at the kitchen table, listened to the silence in this house in which he had grown up. He still got that feeling when he was alone here, a sudden urge to do something naughty. When he was a child, it might be to go poking around in the kitchen cupboard, or in the drawer of his father's bedside table, where there was always a magazine with pictures of nude women, or else to go up into the loft and do the most forbidden thing of all: take one of Colonel Glenne's pistols from the drawer in the box room where his uniforms still hung . . . Actually, Brede was the only one who dared do that.

After the spaghetti, he wandered out on to the terrace. The sun had set behind the hills above Asker. There was a touch of cold in the air; it was clear and sharp to breathe in. Bie hadn't replied to his message and he didn't know where she was, and this thought was calming: that she lived her own life and he didn't need to know what she was doing at every moment.

He sat down with his back to the empty house. It was full of their presence; he felt it even more strongly than usual. It was as though Bie were padding about in there, whispering to her orchids, or else was curled up on the sofa with a book. Tom sat playing in his room, the guitar plugged in to the little amplifier, and down in the basement Marlen was holding a meeting with Natasha and the other members of her club. Daniel was there too, even though it was now almost two months since he'd left for New York to study.

Axel was forty-three. He had always had the feeling of being on a journey. Was this his destination, this terrace with its view across the fjord to the distant hills on the other side, this presence of other people who were not there but who would presently enter the house and call to him, and when he answered they would find him out here, and he would hear in their voices that they were glad he was home? He would ask Marlen to show him her maths test, and when she asked him how he thought she had done, he would say, *Well, I expect you got over half of them right*, and she would nod and keep her lips pressed together and try to hold out as long as she could before telling him her result. And when she couldn't contain herself any more and was forced to tell him, he would shout out, *What are you saying? I just can't believe it*, so that she would have to run off and fetch her satchel and get the book out and open it for him, and he would shake his head in disbelief and ask how on earth she had managed it. And Tom would lounge in the door opening, *Hey, Dad*, and wonder why he hadn't been home to drive him to football practice so that he wouldn't have to cycle, but wasn't so bothered that he wouldn't ask him to come to his room and listen to a new riff with him, singing along in his hoarse adolescent voice.

He went inside and fetched a bottle of cognac and a glass. It was an unusually fine cognac, bought on a trip abroad. He'd been waiting for a special occasion to open it, and decided now that this sharp autumn evening, this Monday evening on the terrace, with the sky still high above the fjord, was precisely the right moment. He left the bottle standing, gathering the evening light to it. Sat and watched the boats down on the fjord, a container ship on its way towards the city, a few sailing boats. The psychiatric hospital was in a bay on the other side. He'd worked there about ten or twelve years ago; he needed the subsidiary training to complete his course as a specialist. A few years before that, he'd visited the place. Quite by chance, he'd heard that Brede was a patient there. It was not long after 17 May, National Day, he remembered. There were still a few leafy braided wreaths hanging on the doors with ribbons in red, white and blue. It was two days before his father's funeral, and that was why he had gone there, to try to persuade his brother to attend. The nurse who opened the door to him stood there gaping: *Jesus, has Brede got a brother?* And came back again a few minutes later: *Sorry, he doesn't want any visitors.*

Axel opened the bottle and poured cognac into the large tulip-shaped glass. The smell of corrosive caramel now mingled with the faint scents coming from Bie's rose garden. He'd never told Bie that he had tried to contact Brede before his father's funeral. Brede was part of a world he couldn't talk about to her. They'd been married now for twenty-something years. She still occasionally told him she loved him. It had always embarrassed him. He wasn't afraid to express his feelings, but he had never managed to believe she meant it. Bie admired him. She admired everyone who was strong, and ended up despising them when they turned out not to be after all. She felt as if they'd tricked her. It was the certainty that he would never disappoint her in this way that made her whisper these *I love yous*.

He raised the glass and let the evening light run out of it. As he was about to put it to his lips, his mobile phone rang. On the display he read the number of a colleague from work, and immediately he knew what it was about, because his colleague was on duty that evening. He smiled to himself at the sudden thought of downing the cognac in one so that he would be unable to cover for whoever was sick.

Instead he put the glass down and took the call.

3

ANITA ELVESTRAND CHANGED channels. She'd seen the film several times before but looked forward to catching the ending one more time. There was still a while to go, so she muted the sound, reached out for the chocolate on the table and broke off a row. Enough is enough, she decided, and wrapped the paper around what remained of the bar. She put two pieces in her mouth and tried to chew slowly, washed them down with a swig of red wine. She lifted the box of wine; it was still quite heavy, but she mustn't drink any more this evening. It was five past eleven. In less than nine hours she had to pick up Victoria. They were going to the dentist's together. If they smelt the wine on her, they would use it against her.

There was a knock on the door. Must be Miriam. No one else knocked on her door. Anita got up from her easy chair and walked out into the corridor. Miriam stood outside smiling, and no other smile could make Anita feel relieved in quite the same way. Apart from Victoria's, of course.

– I saw the light was on, Miriam said apologetically, as though *that* were necessary. She was wearing a denim jacket and a short skirt. A white blouse with a lace collar.

Anita opened the door wide.

– Would you like a glass of wine? she said, positioning herself on the threshold of the room, moving back just a tiny bit to let Miriam pass. Pass so close that Miriam's shoulder brushed one of her breasts and she could inhale the lovely smells from her hair and the skin beneath the clothes. A hint of smoke, too; Miriam had been somewhere where people were smoking, because she didn't smoke herself.

13

– A small one perhaps. I can't stay long. I have to be up early tomorrow.

– So do I. I have to take Victoria to the dentist.

Miriam watched her as she sat down. When something surprised Miriam, her thin eyebrows shot up and stayed there quivering for a moment before sinking down again. Anita couldn't take her eyes off her face. Miriam's eyes were almond shaped and dark, her thick dark brown hair gathered in braids at the temples and fastened at the back with a hair grip.

– You're allowed to take her to the dentist? Just a half-glass for me, please.

Anita filled it three quarters and her own to the top.

– In a fortnight's time she might be staying the night with me.

– How wonderful, Miriam beamed. Anita felt herself on the verge of tears but controlled herself. – Are you watching *Sleepless in Seattle*?

– I've seen it enough times, rasped Anita and turned it off.

– I like that film, said Miriam. – I like films where they get each other in the end. When you already know from the beginning, no matter how hopeless it seems.

Anita was about to make some sarcastic comment about *getting each other* but desisted. Miriam was ten years younger than her. She studied medicine and was terribly bright. There was something about her eyes; she always seemed interested in what Anita was saying, no matter how stupid Anita thought she was being herself. At the same time there was something girlish about her that was reinforced by the slight accent she spoke with, and Anita felt a desire to sit down next to her on the sofa and put her arms around her and hold her tight . . .

Miriam had had trouble with a difficult relationship, Anita knew that. Someone she was trying to finish with. Someone she felt so sorry for that for a long time she couldn't do it. That had been several years ago, at least before she moved into the upstairs apartment. Since then there had been no one, Anita was almost certain of that, though she could hardly understand why.

On the windowsill she found an Aretha Franklin CD and put 'Chain of Fools' on. She drank half her wine and felt it prickle in her chest. She couldn't bring herself to ask Miriam what she did about getting someone to sleep with, but it was okay to ask if she missed having a boyfriend.

Miriam sipped at her own wine, put it down and leaned back in the sofa, knees slightly apart.

— Imagine if there's a certain someone out there who was just meant exactly for you, she answered with a smile, — only he's married and has a family.

— You're not thinking of getting involved with an *impossible*, are you?

That was how Anita referred to anyone in the category of 'family man'. Not too hard to get hold of, a lot more difficult to digest.

Miriam had to laugh.

— No, I haven't . . .

She sat there looking out of the window.

— But what?

Anita realised she was being too intrusive; she mustn't push Miriam, mustn't use her up. She mustn't forget that Miriam was more of a helper than a friend. But she couldn't contain herself.

— You don't have to tell me, she said in a slightly hurt tone.

Miriam seemed to change her mind.

— Tomorrow I'm starting at a clinic in Bogstadveien.

— Sounds very exciting, Anita responded, a touch disappointed.

— I've met the doctor who's going to be my supervisor several times already. He gave us some lectures in the summer. I talked to him in the breaks. And after the lectures too.

— That's what I like to hear. Anita snuffled and wiped a drop of red wine from her lower lip. — And is he the one-and-only somewhere out there?

Miriam looked up at the ceiling.

— And he's the one you've got as your supervisor? That just has to be *fate*.

— I've helped things along as well. I swapped places with another of the students to get into the clinic. But you heard what I said. He's married and has three children. At least.

Anita burst out laughing. It was a long time since she could remember laughing like that.

– This calls for a celebration.

It was quarter to twelve. She wanted to fetch the latest photos she'd taken of Victoria and show them to Miriam, sit close beside her on the sofa and inhale the smell of her hair as she leafed through the album. She picked up the box of wine and was going to pour more wine but Miriam held a hand over her glass and stood up.

At the front door, Anita put an arm around her and gave her a hug. Miriam's cheek was almost as soft as Victoria's, and she felt an almost irresistible urge to put her lips to it and beg her to stay. Miriam extricated herself gently.

Anita stood there watching her as she disappeared up the stairs to her attic apartment. Miriam was an easy person to get to know. But at the same time Anita didn't know her. She seemed to be always happy, but there was something else there too, as though she was grieving over something. Grief was something Anita knew a lot about. So much so that she could sense it in others, even when it was hidden.

4

THE FIRST FEW hours on duty were quiet. Axel Glenne treated a few sore throats, stitched a few cuts, lanced a boil. After midnight he made a round of calls. Got an eighty-two year old with pneumonia admitted after an argument with a junior doctor, some kid whose voice had only just broken. A three year old with a rash and a temperature was also admitted. A woman who sat under her kitchen table howling and refusing to come out unless she was given Valium quietened down immediately when he told her she could have it her way.

At two twenty, Axel was sitting in the back of an ambulance that had been called out. He pushed aside the thoughts of what he had been dealing with earlier in the night and tried to piece together the few bits of information he'd been given to form a picture of what awaited him: a car that had left the road, possible serious injuries, perhaps even worse than that . . . Suddenly the image of his mother appeared, getting up from her chair, shouting angrily into his face, calling him Brede. He closed his eyes, heard his father's voice: *Brede puts himself on the outside. But you, Axel, you'll be someone who always pays his dues.* Brede truanted from school when he felt like it. He stole from their father's wallet. Not just small change, notes. He started a fire in a field that the fire brigade had to come and put out. Axel went along with him part of the way, but pulled out when things started to have consequences. His twin brother got punished. It had no effect on him.

Resistance fighter, war hero, high court judge: the honoured and much-decorated Colonel Glenne had a son who brought shame on his name. Axel's duty was to redress the balance. Show the world that the problem was not with the family. He soon discovered how easy it was, as though borne forward by invisible hands. His parents,

17

of course, but also teachers, trainers, then later supervisors and examiners, all seemed to share the same assumption: that Axel Glenne should be helped; he was a winner. He hadn't even had to fight for Bie. He met her at a student party. She was there with her boyfriend but spent the time talking to Axel out in the kitchen. For some reason or other she wanted to interview him for the student newspaper. When he was about to leave, she asked for his address.

The rear wheels of the car were up on the side of the road. One of the rear lights was still working. It struck Axel that it was encouraging to see it in position; perhaps it hadn't been going that fast. But as soon as the ambulance came to a halt and the scene was illuminated, he saw that the roof was squashed. He jumped out immediately, surgical bag in one hand, torch in the other.

– It must have flipped over.

The ambulance driver, a man named Martin, agreed. Sven, his partner, added: – At least once.

Three or four figures were standing further down the roadside in front of a parked car, its engine still running.

– Are you the people who rang?

– It was me, answered one of them, an elderly man with a woollen hat pulled down over his ears. – We drove past and saw it like that. There's someone inside. We couldn't get the door open.

Martin had clambered down into the ditch and was shining his torch into the car.

– One person trapped behind the wheel, he shouted up to Axel.

– Can we get inside without assistance?

Martin tugged at the door handle.

– Try the other one.

Axel jumped down and tried it. The car wasn't as badly damaged on this side, but the door was locked.

– The front windscreen is more or less gone, he shouted to Martin, and climbed up on to the bonnet. From the engine compartment beneath him came a hissing sound.

– We've got to cut the wires.

He shone the beam inside. A figure was slumped over the steering wheel. Axel reached through the shattered windscreen and took hold of the jacket at the shoulder, shook it.

– Can your hear me?

No answer. He smelled alcohol. Not windscreen washer or something from the engine, but liquor.

– Hello, can you hear me?

A faint groan. Axel twisted over to one side and managed to get a finger on the driver's throat.

– Pulse is normal, he shouted to Martin, who was still on the other side. – About ninety, he added.

– Any chance we can get him out?

– The roof is squashed behind the door, we can't get in. The fire brigade should be here any minute.

He shone his torch on the figure behind the wheel, a young man, he could tell by the sideburns. He had a cut on the side of the throat that was bleeding, but it wasn't deep. The smell of alcohol was coming from him.

– He's breathing easily enough. I don't want to touch that neck until I have to.

A rumbling sound from the man behind the wheel.

– Are you awake? called Axel. – Can you hear me?

Again the same sound, concluding with a groan.

– I'm a doctor. We'll soon have you out of there. Were you alone? The man muttered something.

– We'll help you, Axel said soothingly. – It's going to be okay. Suddenly the driver croaked: – Lise . . .

– Were you alone in the car? Axel asked again.

– Lise, shouted the man and tried to raise his head from the wheel.

– Stay calm.

– Lise!

Axel climbed off the bonnet. Sven appeared behind him with a pair of wire-cutters.

– I'm thinking we'd better kill that engine.

– Great. He's almost conscious, but keep a close eye on him. I'll check to see if there might have been a passenger with him.

– Doesn't look like it.

Axel scrambled up on to the road. He could hear sirens in the distance.

– Move your car over to the side! he shouted to a woman who had just stopped. – The fire engine needs to get right up here.

He shone his torch across the dry asphalt. Shards of glass, skid marks. The car had been approaching from the north, from Tangen, not from Dal as he had first thought. He trotted up the side of the road, some way past the last car in the backed-up traffic. A lump of rock was sticking out, and when he shone the light on it, he saw that it was covered with glass and streaks of paint.

He followed the other roadside ditch back towards the crashed vehicle. Ten metres on from the stone he found her. She was lying on her back; she looked relaxed. A young girl. The face pale and unmarked. But the eyes were awash with a thick pale red froth. Not until he bent over to feel for a pulse on her throat did he realise that most of the back of her head was missing.

The helicopter arrived ten minutes later, at a quarter to three. They checked his findings with him. The girl had been killed instantaneously. The driver's thorax was unstable and there was probably internal bleeding. They took him with them. Axel was left standing there, a purse in his hand. It had been found beneath one of the seats. White leather trimmed with fur, two pockets for notes, one for cards. He removed one of the cards, examined it by the interior light of the ambulance. He recognised the name. She was a year older than Tom. Her big sister had been in Daniel's class. Axel had sat on the PTA with her mother.

He turned to the inspector, handed him the card.

– She's from round here, he told him. – They live down in Flaskebekk. The mother's name is Ingrid Brodahl, when you call . .

The policeman trudged towards his car. His shoulders were sunken and he had a slight limp in one leg.

– Hang on, Axel called after him. – I'm driving back through Tangen. I'll talk to them myself.

5

THE BOAT THUDDED into the quayside and several of the passengers who were already standing up toppled into each other. Axel woke with a start and looked at his watch: 7.25. He waited until the exit queue had thinned out before getting unsteadily to his feet, crossing the deck and stepping on to the quay. In the early hours he'd managed an hour, perhaps an hour and a half of sleep. It might have done him good to walk to the office, but he gave in to exhaustion and got into a taxi. Closed his eyes and at once fell into a light sleep. Images from the night flickered across his mind. The car with its rear end up on the road. The girl lying in the ditch more than fifty metres away. Ringing the bell. The light going on in the hallway. The grimy face in the door opening: Lise's father. Axel had met him a few times over the years; he was an engineer, he recalled, repaired ship's engines and was away from home a lot. But today he was home and peering out on to the dark stoop and he still didn't know what kind of messenger he had opened the door to.

Axel looked up and registered that they were just passing Dronning Park. The driver glanced at him in the rear-view mirror. She had heavy bags under her eyes and wore a perfume that smelled like mould.

– Tough start to the day, she said vaguely, not specifying whether she was referring to her own or her passenger's day.

He grunted something or other and closed his eyes again to avoid any further encouragement. Another nine hours and his work day would be over. He would make it through. He'd had his own practice for twelve years. It was like playing the piano. Sometimes he had to improvise, but most of it he knew off by heart, no matter how tired he was. He'd lost count of the number of days he'd worked through with no sleep the night before. He could handle it. But on this morning it was something other than tiredness. Lise's face. Unscathed at first glance, looking almost as though she were sleeping. Like Marlen's face when he crept in in the dark and bent over her. Then shining the light, seeing the eyes . . . Her father had sat bent over on the sofa, staring at the table as Axel explained why he had come. Suddenly he jumped to his feet. *Ingrid, should I wake her?* Yes, Axel thought, it would be best to wake her. And directly afterwards the scream from the floor above that rose and swelled and filled the whole house and would not end. Ingrid Brodahl, whom he knew from parent–teacher evenings and had talked about school breakfasts with, and celebrations for National Day on 17 May, came rushing down the stairs in her pyjamas. She was still howling, and at that instant Axel regretted having gone there.

The taxi braked suddenly and he was thrown towards the front seat. The figure that had by the narrowest of margins avoided being tossed up on to the bonnet of the car skipped on across the road. The driver opened her window and gave the man an earful. From the pavement he turned and glared at her.

– Stop! shouted Axel as the driver started to accelerate through the traffic lights.

– What do you mean? she protested.

– Pull in to the side. Wait here.

He swung the door open, hurried back to the crossing. He saw him making his way down Sporveisgata.

– Brede! he shouted.

The man didn't turn round. Axel started to run. The other man speeded up. There was less than thirty metres between them when he disappeared between two buildings. Axel reached the corner, ran into an empty courtyard. Stood there panting. Calm down, he warned himself. You've had one helluva night. No more now. Just get through it.

6

FOUR PATIENTS WERE sitting in the waiting room when he arrived, half an hour after he was due to see the first of them. He popped his head into the office. Rita was on the phone but put the call on hold and turned to him.

– So you're alive, she exclaimed in the singing tones of her home town in the far north.

– Hard to say, he sighed. – How does it look?

– Alas, no cancellations, you're too popular for that.

She got up, swayed over to where the coffee was simmering, poured a large mug and handed it to him.

– I've told people we're going to be delayed. And I asked Inger Beate to take a couple of your patients before lunch if we're still running late. She gave him a sympathetic maternal pat. – Don't worry, Axel, we'll get you through the day all right.

– What would I do without you? he said, smiling gratefully.

They weren't just empty words. Rita looked after everything. She was firm when she had to be, friendly when she could be. Already he was dreading her going on holiday.

– And don't forget the student, she chirruped.

– Damn, was that today?

Axel had once again agreed to take on a medical student in the practice. He liked being a supervisor, but on this particular morning his patience would probably not extend to pedagogic tribulations.

– I've told her she can use Ola's room; that's going to be vacant the whole time she's here.

– She? Wasn't it a male student?

23

– Apparently they arranged a swap. I left you a note about it yesterday.

He took a swig of coffee. Given the shape he was in, he would have preferred it if it had been a young man.

– Ask her to come in . . . No, give me five minutes and then ask her.

He slumped down into the chair, turned on his computer, stretched the skin of his face as far back as he could. He hadn't seen Brede for twenty years. Didn't even know if he was still alive. It had been weeks, maybe even months, since he'd last thought about him, not until his mother's outburst the day before. It couldn't have been Brede he saw. He'd chased after a guy who looked like him along Sporveisgata . . . He realised how exhausted he was. Maybe he should drop the duty-doctor stuff for a while. They didn't need the money.

The hard disk creaked and whirred and struggled to get going. When the computer's ready then I'll be ready too, he thought. He stuffed the need to sleep into a cupboard, locked the door and threw away the key: I am no longer tired. There was a knock on the door. Damn, he'd forgotten already about the student. He jumped up, slapped his cheeks a few times. *It's show time*, he said to himself in the mirror and called for her to come in.

She shut the door behind her. Her hand was narrow and warm. Miriam was the name. He didn't catch the surname.

– I've met you before, she said.

He frowned.

– Just before the summer holidays. You gave lectures on cancer in general medicine. I spoke to you in several of the breaks.

– That's right, he said. He'd lectured on the importance of being alert, not missing that one among all those who visited the doctor for some trifle or other who was actually seriously ill. – That's right. Now let's see the first patient. You can be a fly on the wall.

He didn't like the expression and wrinkled his nose.

– And in due course, naturally, you'll be working on your own.

He skipped the lunch break but managed to catch up with his appointments; no one had to wait more than half an hour. In the afternoon he had time to discuss some of the cases with the student. He was beyond tiredness by this time and just about running on empty. But he knew there was enough there for him to make it through the rest of the day. Fortunately the student turned out to be calm and relaxed. She was also very knowledgeable, and she asked good questions. She even knew a couple of things about leukaemia that he hadn't caught up with yet, though he was careful not to let her know.

By quarter to four he was ready for the last patient. She'd been given an immediate emergency appointment. He read what Rita had written. *Cecilie Davidsen. Anxious woman with lump in her breast.*

He clicked into her notes. She'd been a patient of his for three years but had only been to the clinic once before, when she had flu and needed a sick note. She was forty-six years old, an air hostess; two grown children and an eight-year-old daughter.

– A woman who doesn't go to the doctor about nothing, he said to the student. – All the more reason to be on the alert.

Cecilie Davidsen was tall and slender, her hair cut short with bleached strips. Axel recalled her at once. She removed her glove, offered him her hand and looked at him with a little smile, as though apologising for bothering him unnecessarily. But somewhere in that look he could see how uneasy she was feeling.

He asked her all the relevant questions, about breastfeeding and menstruation and when she had first noticed something in her breast.

– Let's just have a look, shall we.

She unbuttoned her blouse. He had deliberately not asked her where she had felt the lump so that he could find it for himself. It was on the right-hand side, directly beneath the nipple. It was the size of an almond, irregular in shape and resistant to movement.

– Do you mind if the student feels it?

Though it wasn't hot in the room, Cecilie Davidsen was sweating under the arms.

– Nine times out of ten, lumps in the breast are not malignant, Axel told her as the student carried out her examination. She had clearly done it before, moving her hands slowly and systematically. – But of course we must take every precaution.

– Mammography?

– As soon as practically possible. Something like this needs to be dealt with as quickly as we can.

After the patient had left, he turned to the student.

– Anything to worry about there?

She thought for a moment.

– It didn't seem like it to me, but it was a sizeable lump.

– As a doctor you should always assume the worst, he lectured. – But it isn't necessary to come out and *say* the worst. Not until you definitely know something.

He rubbed his chin.

– I didn't like it. And she had three enlarged lymph glands in her armpit.

He punched out a few lines on the keyboard, printed out a reference to a specialist.

– This'll go in the post today. And I'll call the hospital as well. She'll have been seen before the week is out, I can promise you that.

He glanced at his watch.

– I have to make the four-thirty boat. Tomorrow you can see a couple of patients without me being there.

He usually waited until the second week before suggesting this, but the student – Miriam, was that her name? – seemed to be ready now to see cases on her own. He was rarely wrong in his judgement on this particular matter.

– I've got a car, she said. – If you like, I can drive you there.

He looked at her in surprise.

– Well that's very kind of you. It sounds as if you know where I'm going.

She looked down.

– You said the boat . . . so maybe you live on Nesodden. Or something like that.

She drove with the same calmness as he heard in her voice. Not a single jolt when she changed gear, and he sank back in the seat and closed his eyes. It was as though she expected nothing of him. As though it were not the least bit embarrassing that he couldn't face the thought of talking.

– You're worn out.

Only now did he register what it was he'd been hearing all day: that she spoke with a slight accent. Eastern European maybe. He didn't ask, wanted to know as little as possible about her.

– I had to cover for someone last night, he explained. – It wasn't my turn, but they were in a jam. Something happened, there was an accident . . .

Suddenly he found himself describing it. Lise's face, as though she were lying asleep in the ditch. Her mother, who held on to his arm as he was about to leave and wouldn't let him go.

– She was just a year older than the younger of my boys. He knew her.

The bell on the quay sounded.

– That idiot jammed behind the steering wheel stinking of booze, he exclaimed suddenly. – I could've killed him.

– Your boat, she said.

He didn't move. There wasn't a drop left in his tank. He looked out into the greyness that thickened over the fjord.

– Got things to do?

Without turning, he noticed that she shook her head.

7

Wednesday 26 September

SOLVEIG LUNDWALL PUSHED the half-full shopping trolley in the direction of the frozen goods counter. It was a long way, at least a hundred metres. Rows of kitchen paper and toilet paper to pass. Cat food, dog food. Then the dried food. Porridge oats, muesli, cornflakes, Frosties, Cheerios. She picked up a packet of Honey Corn along the way. When she was little they had Honey Corn every Friday, after dinner. Milk. She must have enough milk. They drank so much milk at home. Four mouths that just drank and drank. A tube of caviar spread maybe, but they already had some. Mackerel in tomato sauce. She had written a list. It was at home somewhere. A man in a grey anorak wearing a cap appeared on her right and swung in front of her. Halted abruptly with his trolley sideways. She wanted to pick up speed and charge into it, stopped herself at the last moment.

– Oh, sorry, he smirked, pretending to be polite, and wheeled his trolley to one side.

She smiled back, as friendly as she could manage. It was stiff, she must have looked pretty strange, but she managed to get past the wrinkled and nicotined face. At the end of the row she reached the milk.

– I must buy enough milk, she muttered. Five litres of semi-skimmed, five litres of skimmed. Ten litres? Back home they drank and drank, you couldn't get them to stop. Per Olav the most, even though Dr Glenne had told him he should drink less milk. Per Olav listened to Dr Glenne. But he loved milk, got up in the middle of the night to drink it. She could see him in her mind's eye, standing there swigging drinking yoghurt straight from the carton. His moustache afterwards,

8

clogged with the stuff. It was better for him than sweet milk, Dr Glenne had said. And Per Olav listened to what Dr Glenne said. Solveig never called him Dr Glenne. Axel when she thought of him, but she never said it so Per Olav could hear her. Glenne, she might say, but not Axel.

The man in the grey anorak appeared by the cheese counter, approaching. He was going to speak to her. Say something that was supposed to be funny. She jerked her trolley the other way, set off full speed in the direction of the crates of mineral water. Wanted to get some Diet Coke but couldn't stop now. Beer. Per Olav had asked her to buy some for dinner because they were having fish, and she grabbed a couple of bottles without noticing what they were. Per Olav wasn't particular. Was it fish today? She was the one who had said so. We'll be having fish for dinner today, she'd announced to Per Olav, standing in the doorway; the kids had already gone out. Fine by me, he'd answered. Fish was fine by Per Olav. She was the one who couldn't stand it. The smell. Worst of all when preparing it. Cutting through the slimy skin and the greyish flesh with the thin streaks of blood, and the brown stuff that ran out of the backbone. Ask for it ready filleted. They didn't have a fish counter at Rema. She'd passed the frozen fish counter. If she turned round, the old man in the grey jacket would be there waiting, stinking of roll-up cigarettes and wanting to chat.

She hurried on towards the checkout. She must have bread. None left in the freezer. She'd written it at the top of the list, in capital letters, with an exclamation mark. Enough for supper and packed lunches. This morning she'd had to send them off with crispbread. It softened inside the wrapping and the kids wouldn't eat it. Came home hungry. And the teachers would be whispering and gossiping about her, that she didn't give them enough food. She grabbed a sack of cat food, two big sacks. They had no cat. The trolley was loaded to the brim. Four people queuing at the checkout. The other tills were closed. She swung into the next row, parked the loaded trolley in front of the sweet shelves. There was a smell of chocolate. Jelly babies and liquorice allsorts. She looked the other way as she slipped through the gated checkout, out into the light.

*　*　*

The tunnel walls whizzed by. There were dark shadows around the reflections in the window. She couldn't see the eyes, but knew the gaze was evil. She turned and looked quickly behind her. The carriage was nearly empty. Just two kids playing truant and a woman in a headscarf with a pram. Must be a Kurd; one of the mothers in the nursery school wore a headscarf just like that, she was a Kurd.

Solveig Lundwall read the poem on the poster next to the door. *If you turn round, you're looking forward*, it said. She didn't want to read any more. There was a little box of pastilles in her pocket. There was a note there too, the shopping list. Bread in capital letters with an exclamation mark. After she'd read it, she couldn't sit still; she dropped it as though she'd burnt herself on it, stood up and hurried to the back of the carriage, sat with her back to the others. There was a newspaper there. *Housing market explodes*. She turned the pages. *Shot down in broad daylight*. Yes, because daylight is broad. He who has eyes to see, let him see. *Killed in car crash*. She stared at the girl's picture. She had long blond hair and big eyes and a mouth with a pained smile. It was holy. – What is it, little angel? Solveig murmured. On the next page she read: *Do you need help?* She turned to the evil face in the window. Yes, Solveig, you need help now. And once she'd realised that, she felt calm. It felt so good she had to laugh. The tears ran until she could taste the salt at the corners of her mouth, but she wasn't crying; she felt the calmness spreading through her chest.

– Thank you, Lord Jesus, she whispered. – Thank you, Lord, for seeing me. Though I wander upon dark ways.

She got off at the Storting. Her jacket was left behind on the seat. She wasn't cold. She wanted to feel light, unencumbered. She stood on the escalator and was raised up into the light. The sky was bright and shining, and from where she was standing, she felt as though the steps would carry her up above the street and over the rooftops.

In Bogstadveien, she stood in front of the clinic door and waited. The tram passed on its way down the road. She stood there a long time before another one came. Solveig, you need help, she told herself again. But it didn't work any more. There was a surging in her chest, but it wasn't calm, more like a jolting. She started making her way up towards Majorstua. There's a fishmonger's there, Solveig; buy five fish and ask to have them filleted. A man on the other side of the road walked by, looking at her. He looked like Pastor Brandberg at the Pentecostal church. Pastor Brandberg is dead, Solveig. She speeded up. The man on the other side of the road did the same. He was wearing a long leather coat, with his hair pulled back and fastened in a ponytail. Pastor Brandberg had baptised her. She remembered his face as she was pulled up out of the water, his eyes as he blessed her. Pastor Brandberg always helped them. He was the one they took her to the first time she got sick. She crossed the road and stood in front of him.

– Can you help me? she asked.

He hurried on without answering, the grey ponytail swaying from side to side on his neck.

She stopped at the pedestrian crossing, held on to the railings. It had started again, and she wouldn't be able to stop it. If a car hit her, the driver would feel bad. But not if it was a bus. It was a bus driver's job to drive around all over town; anything could happen to them. They were protected. The Lord was with bus drivers. They were the instruments of the Lord. Though they wandered upon dark ways. Next time a red bus comes by, you let go, Solveig. She looked up at the sky above Majorstuehuset. The clouds were in sudden motion, pulled apart from each other as though by some mighty hand; the light was unbearably bright. She lowered her gaze. And there, on the steps to the Underground station, enveloped in a blinding white light, stood a man. He had a beard, and his hair was unkempt, his jacket was ragged. The face was turned towards her, and she saw that it was Axel Glenne. *And He shall return, though they shall not know Him.* – But I know him, she murmured. It's not going to happen, not yet. Again the calm surged through her chest, swelling inside her until she trembled in pure joy.

She let go of the railings, turned her back to the bristling stream of cars and started walking back down Bogstadveien.

8

At 12.15, Axel Glenne finished with his last patient before lunch. He made a few notes in the journal, closed it and clicked his computer into hibernation mode.

– Time we had something to eat, he said to Miriam without looking at her. There hadn't been a moment's let-up all morning, and he had barely managed to pass on the odd bit of advice to her in among all the consultations. After what had happened the day before, he felt a bit embarrassed about seeing her today. But she seemed to think it was the most natural thing in the world for the two of them to have sat in her car talking for more than half an hour.

He let her into the break room before him. It was a tight squeeze, though only Rita and Inger Beate were already sitting there. They squashed themselves in around the circular table. Rita's niece had been to see her and Rita had brought along home-made waffles. Inger Beate wanted to discuss a patient with him and brought out a pile of reports from lab tests. She gave him a rundown of the details as she devoured an egg salad, washing it down with coffee. The patient complained of itching, and had lost weight, but otherwise felt fine.

– Before I have a go, let's hear what the student has to say, said Axel, chewing.

Inger Beate Garberg had a strong, bony face with grey hair that hung in waves around her shoulders. She looked at the clock, annoyed, only five minutes of the lunch break left.

Miriam said, – Did you ask if he experiences any discomfort when he drinks alcohol?

Inger Beate glanced over at Axel. He helped himself from the plate of waffles and gave a cautious smile in return. A loaded question there from the student, Inger Beate.

– Of course I asked him that.

– And what was the patient's reply?

– He was vague, she grunted as she closed up the plastic carton containing the rest of her salad. – I'd better ask him again.

It hadn't occurred to her, Axel noted, but he didn't confront her with it. Inger Beate had only recently returned after working for two years among Aids victims in Botswana. She was still struggling to return to everyday life back at home, the parade of patients most of whom were perfectly well and yet still *complained over the slightest thing*. But she was a good colleague, and it would have been no pleasure to catch her out, still less to let a student do so. He knew that she would now take a closer look at the patient to see if there were any other signs of lymphatic cancer. That was what he suspected, after having looked at the lab reports.

– More waffles? Rita said, offering the plate around.

Axel patted his stomach, indicating that he'd had enough.

– I'll take the student with me on my rounds, he said, – in the certain knowledge that you'll hold the fort back here, Rita.

– Don't you worry about that. Actually there's a guy who tried to make an appointment for today. He said he's applied to have you as his family doctor but the papers haven't arrived yet.

– You did tell me we were fully booked today?

– He wondered about tomorrow afternoon instead, and I just mentioned that you always went out on your bike on Thursday afternoons. Was that stupid of me?

Axel furrowed his brow.

– It's none of the patients' business what I get up to in my spare time. Is it so urgent?

– He thought so, but he wouldn't say why.

Back in his office, Axel went over the contents of his doctor's bag with Miriam. Just as he was closing it, Rita called from the front desk.

– Solveig Lundwall is here.

– She doesn't have an appointment today.

– I don't know about that. But she won't go until she's talked to you.

– Tell her I'll call her this afternoon.

He heard Rita saying something at the other end of the phone. Then loud shouting.

– Can you hear that? She's screaming and carrying on.

– All right, send her in.

Moments later the door was flung wide open.

– Sit down, Solveig.

She remained standing and scowled at Miriam.

– We've got a student working in the practice with us. Is it all right if she stays here while we talk?

Solveig Lundwall shook her head vigorously, and Axel motioned to Miriam to leave the room. The moment they were alone Solveig exclaimed:

– It won't do, Axel.

He was taken aback to hear her use his first name.

– What won't do?

She was sitting on the edge of her chair, ready to flare up again.

– She shouldn't be here, she snorted, scowling towards the door.

– You mean the student?

Solveig didn't respond. Axel leant towards her.

– Tell me why you came here, Solveig.

– The whore, she muttered. – The whore of Babylon. She shouldn't be here. I have this against you that you tolerate that woman Jezebel.

Axel had known Solveig for many years; he knew all about her. When she started using biblical turns of phrase, it meant she was about to have another episode.

– I'll help you, Solveig.

– I don't have enough milk, she complained. – They drink and drink and it's never enough. I fill up all the time, it just runs away.

He didn't respond to this. Suddenly her face changed. The despair seeped away and she gave him an agitated look.

– I saw you just now.

He couldn't hide his surprise.

– Majorstuehuset. You were standing at the top of the steps, against the light. Glenne in the forest. You were dressed as a beggar and had a beard, but it was your face and eyes. You were Jesus. Yes, it was you, you were Jesus, Axel Glenne, and you saved me. Had you not shown yourself, I would not have come back.

For a moment he sat there staring at her, unable to say a word.

– In Majorstua? he finally managed to blurt out.

– I saw the picture of that girl in the papers. She can't have been more than sixteen years old. She's watching over me. Something terrible is going to happen, Axel. They have as king over them the angel of the abyss. People are going to die. Pastor Brandberg turns his back and will not see. You are the only one who can prevent it.

He regained his self-possession. She trusted him. She'd come to see him on previous occasions when she was about to collapse. When she talked about death in this way, she was in danger. Twice before she had tried to take her own life.

– I'll call the hospital, he said.

An hour later, he walked Miriam down to the yard, where he had his own parking place.

– What will happen to that last patient of yours? she wanted to know.

He swung out into Bogstadveien, up in the direction of Majorstua.

– Solveig Lundwall? She won't spend too long in hospital. It's usually just a matter of a few weeks.

He stopped for a red light, glanced over towards Majorstuehuset. People were moving up and down the steps, in and out of the Underground station. The person Solveig Lundwall had seen there might have been the creation of her own confused mind. But the description fitted the man he'd chased after himself the day before. The thought of parking the car, going in there and looking . . .

– Solveig is a very capable nursery-school teacher, he said. – She has three children of her own, and I've never had any doubt that she's a good mother to them. Now and then she has psychotic episodes, or goes completely nuts, as she calls it. It's probably three or four years since the last time.

– She evidently trusts you.

– Fortunately. Things nearly went very wrong last time.

– She didn't take all that kindly to me. I think she wanted you all to herself.

He changed lanes and speeded up.

– She's created this ideal image of me. She thought she saw me today by Majorstuehuset. I looked like Jesus.

Miriam didn't laugh, and he was about to go on. About to tell her that he had a twin brother. He glanced over at her. She was in her mid-twenties. At least fifteen years younger than him. But there was this calm about her. And something in her look that made it possible to tell her things. Suddenly he felt an urge to reach out a hand, touch her hair. He turned away and concentrated on his driving.

The students usually liked the home visits. They reminded them of the old idea of the family doctor. Visiting people in their own homes. Sitting at the bedside of an old lady with breathing difficulties. Don't be in a hurry to admit her, first try an increased dose of diuretic. Or a five year old with fever and a rash on the chest; the mother wailing into the receiver that she daren't take him to the surgery, the doctor had to come and see him immediately. The boy started bawling as soon as he saw the doctor's bag, and Axel had to blow into his plastic glove and make a balloon out of it, draw a mouth, nose and ears on it with a ballpoint pen. In a little while the tears stopped and Axel was able to peer into the child's ears and throat and shine a light in his eyes without protest; he even let Miriam look into his eyes as well. He assured the mother that the rash and the fever were the fourth disease of childhood, and that half of the other children at the nursery school were undoubtedly suffering from the same thing. But he let her have his mobile number and said she could call him if she was still worried. When they left, the boy was sitting up playing with the glove balloon and wanting to show Axel a fire engine that he'd hidden under the sofa.

It was approaching 4.30 by the time the round was finished. Axel pulled into a bus bay in Majorstua.

– I'll see you on Monday then, Miriam said, but she carried on sitting in the car.

– Not tomorrow?

– I'm taking the day off tomorrow. And on Fridays we have lectures.

He indicated and pulled back out into Kirkeveien.

– You said you live in Rodeløkka, isn't that right? I might as well drop you off there.

As they waited for the lights to change by Ullevål hospital, he thought about Solveig Lundwall. She was lying in a bare room somewhere in there, almost certainly sleeping, because to help her in the battle against the angel of the abyss that was raging inside her they had probably given her a massive dose of sedative. *Something terrible is going to happen, Axel. People are going to die.*

– I have a brother, he said abruptly as he swung into Helgesens gate. – A twin brother. I haven't seen him in more than twenty years.

Miriam said nothing, but he could feel how she was looking at him.

– I think I probably thought he was dead. Because in a way he has been . . . It might have been him Solveig saw in the street today.

– You can stop here, said Miriam. – I live up there. She pointed to one of the old brick buildings. – Third floor. The attic.

He put the car in neutral, pulled on the handbrake.

– Maybe . . . she began. There was a hint of greenish yellow in her brown eyes. – Would you like a cup of coffee?

He wanted to go with her up into the attic apartment. Sit down in her living room. Feel the calmness that surrounded here. Tell her something or other, he didn't know what. Some people listen, he thought, others wait for the chance to speak. She's a listener.

– If only I could, he said.

Her eyes opened wider.

37

– Sorry, I didn't mean to . . .

He laid his hand on her arm. Let the explanations remain unvoiced. Not a word about Marlen's riding lesson, or that he'd promised to put the rice on to boil.

– Nothing to apologise for, Miriam. He noted that this was the first time he had used her name. – I'll be happy to drink coffee with you another day. Unless you withdraw the invitation.

Outside the car, she turned and smiled quickly.

– I won't do that, she said, and pushed the door shut.

9

AXEL NEVER MADE appointments at the clinic after lunch on Thursdays. With the last one out the door at 12.45, he changed into his cycling gear in the cloakroom and fetched his bike from a storeroom in the cellar. It had been washed and the chain cleaned and oiled after the last ride. Usually he cycled up to Sognsvann and rode on into the surrounding forest, but today he took the bike on the Underground with him up to Frognerseter.

By the time he reached the forest chapel at Nordmarka, it had clouded over. An elderly couple were sitting on a bench by the wall with a flask and a packed lunch. Both were wearing worn anoraks, the man in a peaked blue skiing cap. Axel said hello, unleashing in response a cascade of observations about the weather, the silence in the forest, how to keep your health. He said no thanks to an offer of coffee and a chocolate biscuit, but stood around chatting for a while. The old couple gave him a feeling of having as much time as he could want. The man put down the thermos and laid his hand over his wife's. She had clear grey eyes and laughed with a chuckling sound, like a little stream. Him and Bie sitting like that thirty years from now, he tried to think, but couldn't quite manage it.

He jumped back on to his bike and peered northwards. The clouds were massing. He'd intended to go all the way to Kikut, but he wasn't dressed for rain. Another cyclist came riding up the hill. He was wearing sunglasses and nodded in greeting as he sped by. He was at least ten years younger than Axel, in shiny cycling shorts and a skin-tight top, and for an instant Axel was tempted to get after him and make a race of it, but he dismissed the thought.

On a whim, near Blankvann, he wheeled the bike off the track, locked it and began jogging along a narrow path. Not so fast that he couldn't savour the forest around him. *Listen to Skamndros, he's singing*, Marlen used to exclaim every time they passed a brook in the forest. He was the one who had told her about the Greek river god, and Marlen remembered everything that was said to her. He stopped by a small tarn. One summer, many years ago, he'd brought Bie up here. It was before Marlen was born. They'd bathed. Later, he had lain her down in the heather. She'd complained about the twigs sticking into her, but he'd made her forget about that. Afterwards she called him Pan, and said how dangerous it was to go out into the forest with him. It was less than a year before Marlen's birth, because Bie always claimed that she had been conceived that time in the heather.

He pulled off his cycling vest and plunged into the tarn. Convinced himself that the water was warm for the time of year. He dived under and swam as far as he could. He and Brede had always competed to see who could stay underwater the longest. He'd held out once for almost three minutes. It was on the beach at Oksval. Brede stayed down longer. Four minutes. That was when Axel got scared. He started shouting, waving his arms. Someone ran to fetch the grown-ups. They found Brede over by the jetty, managed to drag him ashore, pumped the water out of him, blew life back into him. Afterwards he could remember nothing; everything just vanished, he said. Several times that summer the brightness in Brede's eyes would suddenly be gone, and for a few seconds at a time he couldn't answer, couldn't hear. Afterwards he would shake his head in confusion, a look of fear on his face. Someone should have realised what was the matter with him, but no one asked. That was the same summer as the thing with Balder, when Brede was sent away.

Axel dried himself off with his cycling jacket, threw his clothes on and carried on running to get his body warmth back. He came across a little trail that led off the path and in behind a thicket. Boot prints in the wet ground heading into the trees. Disappearing by a mossy hillock. He climbed up, hopped down on the other side. Almost fell into a pile of branches. He caught a glimpse of black plastic underneath. A boulder had been placed in front of what looked like an opening. He rolled it to one side, pulled away the plastic and peered inside. Light seeped down through the spruce branches that formed the roof of a small shelter, perhaps two metres in length. On a cardboard box that had once held bananas were a paraffin lamp and two candles waxed on to flat stones. Beside the box he glimpsed a bag and some empty bottles. He couldn't resist and crept further in. The bag contained bread, stale but not mouldy. The bottles smelt of cheap alcohol. In one corner were a rolled-up sleeping bag and two woollen blankets. A book had been tucked beneath them. As he was wriggling out backwards, he pulled it out and looked at it in the grey light of day. It was no more than a pamphlet: *Dhammapada* was the title. A Buddhist text, according to the back cover. The pages were yellowed and stained. Here and there a sentence had been underlined, at one point in red: *He who in his youth has not lived in harmony with himself, and who has not gathered life's real treasures, in later years is like the long-legged old herons that stand sadly by a marshy swamp without fish.*

A movement across his neck, like a breath of wind. He turned, feeling unease at having invaded someone else's life, whoever it might be that was living here. He put the book back where he'd found it, climbed back up the hillock and ran on as hard as he could along the track, felt the warmth creeping back into his body.

Not until he had unlocked his bike and was wheeling it back down to the path did he notice that the rear tyre was flat. He checked the valve. It seemed in order. He got out the pump. When he squeezed the tyre a couple of minutes later, it was still flat.

Approaching Ullevålseter, he saw a woman coming towards him, striding energetically along with walking poles in each hand. There was something familiar about the little figure and the determined face, and Axel greeted her as she passed.

She stopped.

– Is that you? she said.

He tried to remember where he'd seen her before.

– So you're out keeping fit? She looked at the bicycle. – And you've had a puncture.

He recognised the voice. Must have spoken to her on the phone.

– Looks like it, he agreed.

– Sorry I can't help you, she said.

– No, why would you be carrying a puncture repair kit around with you?

She laughed.

– Ask at Ullevålseter, maybe they have something there.

He was about to move on.

– Actually, I was going to ring you, she said. – Funny meeting you of all people. A referral you sent in the other day. An elderly man with problems after a back operation.

The physiotherapist. She was the physiotherapist at the clinic in Majorstua. Any moment now and he'd recall her name. Bie used to go to her.

– I doubt if I can help him much when he's in such pain. But we can talk about it later.

He didn't protest. Rain had begun drizzling from the low cloud, and soon it would be dark. It wasn't every woman who would head off into the forest in the dark, he thought. Bie didn't like walking in the forest alone even in daylight.

– Safe journey home, she chirruped, furrowing her brow sympathetically as she pointed with her stick at the punctured tyre.

10

THE EVENING HAD turned cold, but Axel remained sitting on the terrace with the living-room door ajar behind him. He'd made a fire and put on a pullover. It was now past eleven and he had just gone in to Marlen, who had woken up and called for him. She'd been dreaming that the dead twin had been following her. Before going to bed, she'd come out to see him on the terrace. They'd sat for a while looking at the night sky together, and Axel had told her about the Ethiopian queen Cassiopeia. When she refused to go to bed until he told her one more story, he'd shown her the Twins, Castor and Pollux. He'd told her how strong and brave they were. No one could best Castor when it came to riding and taming horses, nor Pollux in a bare-fist fight. But most of all they were famed for being true to each other. They loved each other more than any other brothers loved, and nothing could part them. Nothing except death. Because the sad thing was that Pollux was the son of the god Zeus and immortal, while Castor was the son of an earthly king. *But weren't they twins?* Marlen protested. *They couldn't have different fathers, could they?* In the world of fairy tales such things are possible, Axel smiled. When Castor was killed in a fight, he had to go to the underworld. Pollux begged Zeus to make him mortal too, so that he too could go down to the kingdom of the dead and be with his beloved brother. But not even Zeus could arrange that. If you're immortal, you're immortal. Then he had an idea, and he fixed things so that the brothers could be together after all. Every other day Pollux could go to the realm of

43

the dead and meet his twin brother, and the other days they could be together up in the sky.

Axel had told the boys the same story, but neither of them had had nightmares afterwards. Before Marlen could get back to sleep, he had to drive the dead twin away. He tucked the duvet tightly around her into a cocoon, and assured her that nobody could get at her now. On top of that, Mikk the mountain lion and Geiki the goat were standing guard around the bed. It all worked, and he heard no more from her.

Before returning to his chair on the terrace Axel had popped downstairs to have a few words with Tom. He stopped outside the door and listened to the reedy voice within. He felt as though he knew the song now, even though he'd only heard it in snatches. When Marlen was going to sleep, Tom had to turn off his amplifier, and his voice sounded even more frail against the almost inaudible chords from the guitar.

Axel had gone back upstairs without knocking. Taken the bottle of cognac and a glass out into the dark with him. Moments later Tom appeared in the doorway asking if he could spend the night at his friend Findus's house, the lad he was going to start a band with. Axel reluctantly agreed. It was better than him sitting on his own in his bedroom all evening. After dinner he'd been on the point of suggesting they might do something together, but he'd waited too long and then it was too late. Daniel was getting to be more and more like a friend the older he got, he thought. Axel could talk about most things with him, and recognised himself in much of what his elder son said. And Marlen could always make him laugh with her strange notions. But there was something about Tom that made him hesitate to approach too close. He didn't know what it was, only that it made him feel shy and clumsy.

He poured himself a glass and sat there inhaling the scent of the golden liquid. He'd bought the bottle on the plane back from Cyprus. They'd spent their Easter holiday there, the last holiday before Daniel moved away from home. Axel had dreaded it. And the sharp white sun and the turquoise sea had heightened his feeling of tristesse. The bus driver who drove them out to the airport was called Andreas. Axel had conversed with him during one of the outings they'd gone on. They were both about the same age. The driver had small eyes and a nose that had been broken and grown back crooked. He watched Bie as she climbed aboard in the short white frock that clung to her thighs and was almost translucent, and Marlen, Tom and Daniel as they followed her into the bus. As Axel passed him, bringing up the rear, he exclaimed: *You must be a very happy man*. He laughed, exposing brown gums. And when Axel sat down in the back of the bus, and Bie pinched his thigh and whispered in his ear that she fancied him, and he put his arm around her and looked at the desolate yellow land gliding by outside, he thought: I must be a very happy man.

The fire had gone out. He poured himself another glass, studied the dying embers as they slowly paled. He thought: I will go up to Miriam's. I'll sit there in her attic apartment in Rodeløkka. Sit there and not do anything but drink the coffee she makes, and talk to her.

He was on his way to the bathroom when he heard a car down in the driveway. He looked out and saw a taxi at the gate. The time was 2.15. Sound of the door being unlocked, Bie's bunch of keys chinking against the glass top of the chest of drawers.

He undressed and stood in his boxers, glanced at himself in the mirror. He still looked like he kept himself in shape, though the line down to the ridge of the hips had acquired a tiny undulation. A few moments later she came into the bathroom and stood behind him.

– Are you still up?

He looked at her in the mirror.

– Unless I'm sleepwalking.

Her hair was unkempt and her eyes were bleary, though the make-up hadn't run. She was wearing a dark green tight-fitting satin dress, with shoulder straps and a plunging neckline. There was a hint of green in her eyeshadow too. When she was made up like that, accentuating the slightly slanting eyes and the high cheekbones, she might be taken for five years younger. Maybe more.

He turned, inhaling. The perfume he usually bought her, the way it smelt hours later, mingling with the smell of her sweat and of other people's cigarettes. A second, foreign perfume was mixed in with the smell of Shalimar; something a man would wear. He could follow the thought, conjure up images of who she'd been sitting with, dancing with. He took her by the arm and pulled her towards him.

– Christ, she murmured as he started to kiss her. – You're hot for it.

Closer and closer it came, the smell of the strange, the thing he didn't know about, that turned her into something other than the person he knew. Her tongue tasted of wine, but vodka too, or gin. It was not often she could be persuaded to drink spirits, and when he lifted her skirt and took hold of her naked buttocks, she groaned and began to pull at his boxer shorts.

He lifted her up on to the rim of the basin, pulled off the translucent string.

– Axel, she scolded him. – Not here, the kids might wake up.

But that was exactly what she wanted, for him to take her right there and then, sitting on the cold porcelain basin, only half undressed, protesting against the damage to her dress when he pulled the shoulder straps down and fastened his mouth to one of her breasts, raised her lower body and pushed himself inside her.

When she came, she swallowed back the sounds. It ended up a long-drawn-out rattle, unlike anything he'd ever heard from her before. He didn't come. When it was over for her, he carried her out of the bathroom.

– Wait, she groaned. – At least let me pee.

He got into bed. Through the open door he heard her flush the toilet, wash her hands, open the cupboard, almost certainly to remove her contact lenses. Then she came padding into him, naked, and closed the door behind her.

– Can't a poor girl get even a few hours' sleep? she complained.

He pulled her down and turned her round. — Oh Axel, she moaned, the way he was used to hearing her. He bent her body at the hips and entered her from behind, lying there without moving, like an insect.

— Tell me where you've been, he whispered as he began to move slowly inside her.

— What is it with you, Axel? she groaned.

— Tell me what you did tonight.

— Lotta and Maren. We ate at Theatrecaféen. Then we went on to Smuget.

— Did you meet anyone?

She twisted her body.

— A whole crowd, she sighed.

— Did you dance?

— Of course.

— With lots of men?

— One especially. A policeman.

He withdrew, then entered her again, quicker and harder.

— He wouldn't take no for an answer. Must have been ten years younger than me. Yes, like that, harder. Oh fuck, yes.

She didn't usually swear; it moved his excitement up another notch. He couldn't face asking any more questions about the policeman, whether they went on anywhere else afterwards, but he could see them in his mind's eye as she put her arm around his neck and pressed up close against him. He surrendered, pushing her down into the mattress, forcing himself up tight against her buttocks. As he came, a face appeared far away inside the darkness. It came closer, veiled in green, looking in at him through an open car door.

11

Saturday 29 September

Axel woke at six o'clock. He wasn't on duty this weekend and could lie in as long as he liked. But he felt himself well rested and swung his feet on to the floor. A few minutes later he was running through the copse, towards the farm lane. It was still only dawn light, the outlines of things flowing into each other. But he could tell that it was going to be a clear autumn day.

By 7.30, he had laid the breakfast table and was sitting fresh from the shower in his boxer shorts and T-shirt, with coffee, orange juice and the *Aftenposten*. He read it back to front, quickly through the sport, lingering over the financial pages. The price of oil was down, in general bad news for those with their money in unit trusts. All the same, as long as there was war and terrorism in the Middle East, prices would stay high. He had some money invested, but not enough to create a dilemma for him. He glanced through the news. Man threatened with a knife in Rosenkranz gate, woman missing in the Nordmarka, electricity prices on the way down after all the rain in the early autumn. He heard someone slipping into the toilet, saw bare feet padding out into the hallway. Marlen popped her head in.

– You sleepyhead, he chided her as he put the newspaper aside. – It's the middle of the day.

She stood there bleary eyed, in a red nightie with a crocodile across the front.

– You're always bragging about how early you get up.

He laughed.

– You want egg and bread, or muesli?

48

She poked out her lip, sat down and gave the question some thought.

– Egg, she decided.

He buttered her a slice of bread with a squeeze of caviar, then turned to her and conjured an egg from her ear.

She pulled a face and stared out of the window, the trees still hidden behind the grey morning mist.

– Get out the wrong side of the bed today?

She turned to him with an exasperated sigh.

– Dad, everyone has the right to be in a bad mood in the morning. For half an hour. At least.

– Quite agree, he conceded. – That is a human right.

– Which came first, the chicken or the egg? she asked.

– The egg?

– Wrong. Because God doesn't lay eggs.

Axel peered into Tom's room and discovered that his son had come home last night after all. He could just make out his shape as he lay under the duvet, his breathing heavy, his face turned towards the wall. There was a close, confined atmosphere there, and the smell of smoke. Axel picked up a shirt that had been tossed over the back of a chair, sniffed at it. He'd seen several of the kids Tom hung out with sitting on the grass behind the centre smoking, but Tom denied that he would ever do anything like that. Axel opened the window, stood a while beside the bed, decided to let the boy sleep on for a while.

Instead, he let himself into the loft. Been putting off for far too long clearing up all the things that had just been tossed in there. He sorted out the sports gear the kids had grown out of, and the clothes he didn't use any more. Suits and shirts that he thought were okay himself, but that Bie had condemned as old fashioned and refused to let him wear. Over the years the Salvation Army had done pretty well out of Bie's aesthetics.

In the furthest corner of the loft, behind the empty suitcases and the drums full of winter clothing, was an old mahogany cupboard.

The key hung from a hook on the ceiling. For the first time in years, he opened it. The two upper drawers contained the few things he had kept after his father's death. A peaked hat. Military paraphernalia. Two pistols: a Spanish one that had been used in the civil war, and a Luger taken when the Germans were disarmed in the final days before the surrender. There was a box containing letters sent to Torstein Glenne by friends being held in the prison camp at Grini. He'd read them all to Axel. Sometimes to Brede as well, but mostly to Axel, to teach him that *freedom has its price*. The maps were in the same box.

On summer evenings, when Colonel Glenne had been sitting long enough in front of the terrace fire with his whisky and his pretzels, he would sometimes allow himself to be persuaded to go up and fetch the maps with all the secret routes inscribed on them. *I probably shouldn't be showing you these, boys*, he'd growl, though twenty-five years had passed since the German surrender. *I might let slip things I've promised on pain of death never to reveal*. And then without further ado he would describe the various hiding places along the Swedish border. Here was where they had hidden out after their actions. After they'd blown factories to smithereens, cut vital telephone wires, helped refugees over the border: Jewish children, Resistance members who had been betrayed, even those occasional oddballs who just panicked and wanted to get out even though the Germans weren't after them.

His father had marked the maps: a cross for each meeting point, dotted lines for the escape routes, circles for the hiding places and communication centres. Afterwards Axel and Brede would play refugees and border guides, and especially Resistance fighters engaging in mortally dangerous sabotage operations. They sank the *Blücher* in the waters off Drøbak, and drove the *Bismarck* and the *Tirpitz* into narrow and treacherous fjords. Above all they blew up the heavy water plant in Vemork. At the very last moment they managed to light the fuse, just before Hitler had finally made his atom bomb; all that was needed was just a few litres of that water, and the Glenne brothers had ruined everything for him. Hitler was furious. He developed an obsessive hatred of them and sent his most dangerous SS men to Norway to capture them. The twins fled to the forest and hid out in the cabins their father had told them about. They sneaked from one to another, dog patrols on their heels, hearing the barking and the shouting of the commandos in German, the most gruesome of all languages. But if one of them was captured, the other would get away, because both had sworn to die rather than inform on his brother.

These games would get Brede so worked up that he could lie awake all night. Sometimes he would even wake Axel to swear the pact all over again: *You will never betray me. I will never betray you.*

Even when they weren't playing, Axel knew he had to look after his brother. That no one else would do it. Every time Brede did something terrible, their parents talked about how they couldn't have him in the house any longer. Axel thought of these as threats meant to get Brede to pull himself together; he never dreamt they might actually mean it. Brede couldn't pull himself together. One week after Balder was shot, they sent him away.

He was sitting on the sofa with Marlen playing Buzz! Jungle when Bie appeared. She stood in the door and watched them. It was 11.30. Axel was still in his boxer shorts and T-shirt, Marlen in her nightie.

– So this is where you are.

– Don't interrupt, Mum, can't you see we're working?

– I see, is that what you're doing?

– Don't you know that playing for children is the same thing as working is for grown-ups?

– Yes, I guess it is. But what about Daddy? He isn't a child, is he, or at least not completely.

– Daddy has a day off. I'm the only one that's working.

Bie stood behind them and followed the game on the TV screen for a while. Then she bent down and put her arms round them, both of them, hugging one against each of her cheeks. Axel put his hand behind her and let it slip up under her dressing gown; she was still naked underneath.

– You're a fine one, she whispered in his ear.

– Stop whispering, Marlen protested.

– I only said to your daddy that he's, er, very fine.

– You're putting him off, she complained. – See, he just lost a life.

– Serves him right. Bie gave up and disappeared into the kitchen. Shortly afterwards she called out:

– Have you read the paper, Axel?

– Sort of.

She was holding it in front of her as she came back into the room again.

– Did you see this about the woman missing in the Nordmarka?

He continued laying waste with the Buzz! control.

– Did you see who it is? she asked. – Hilde Paulsen, my physio.

Only now did he react, jumping to his feet, crossing to her. With narrowed eyes he read the story she was pointing to.

He called the police station, explained what it was about. A woman with a strong Stavanger accent came on the line. Her voice was also unusually loud.

– At what time of the day did you meet her?

Axel thought it over. He'd been up at Blankvann around 4.30. With the puncture it took him perhaps twenty minutes, maybe half an hour, to get down to Ullevålseter. He hadn't checked the time again until he was at Sognsvann, when he noticed it was 6.15.

– And how did she seem? I mean, her mood.

Axel held the receiver well away from his ear.

– Nothing special. Just the usual good mood.

He knew what the policewoman was angling for, but he found it hard to believe that Hilde Paulsen's disappearance had anything to do with her state of mind. A woman in a tracksuit, with walking poles. She'd stopped to discuss a patient with him. An old man with back pain was what was on her mind at that particular juncture. Not suicide.

12

RITA POURED COFFEE for them.

– She was going for a walk in the Nordmarka, she said as she sliced the macaroon cake she'd baked over the weekend. – And since then there's been no sign of her.

Every Friday, and some Mondays, Rita served up *a treat* for lunch. On more than one occasion Inger Beate had taken Axel aside and asked how they could talk to her about it without hurting her feelings, because they couldn't sit there forever stuffing themselves with cake. Axel had a good laugh at her worries and said it was up to each individual how to deal with that particular dilemma.

– Do any of you know who she is?

– Should we? asked Inger Beate, her mouth full of salad. Axel knew there was a case she wanted to discuss with him, but she wouldn't bring it up as long as the student was sitting there. He'd have to call in and talk to her later in the day.

– You know her, both of you.

Inger Beate glanced over at Axel; he was looking the other way.

– About time you told us, Rita, she said, irritated.

– Hilde Paulsen, that physio from Majorstua.

– Really! exclaimed Inger Beate.

Rita held up the plate of macaroon cake and looked from one to the other.

– The police think she's been murdered.

Axel turned abruptly to her.

– How do you know that?

– A friend of mine. Her daughter's a journalist, works for *VG*. They know all that kind of thing there. The police seem to think that Hilde Paulsen met someone while she was out walking, or else someone was waiting for her up in the forest.

She shivered as she said it and nearly dropped the cake plate on to the table.

About four o'clock, Miriam knocked on Axel's door.

– I've written up the journal notes.

He didn't look up.

– The woman who was knocked down from behind, she reminded him. – Question of whiplash.

– I'll have a look at it before I leave.

She didn't move.

– You seem very preoccupied today.

He brushed the hair away from his forehead. Only now did he raise his eyes and look at her.

– Come in and sit down, he said finally.

She closed the door behind her.

– I'm sorry if you . . . he began. – What we were talking about on Wednesday.

Her eyes were bigger than he had remembered them, or was it just the make-up that created that effect. She was wearing a T-shirt under her doctor's coat with big glitter-coated lettering across the chest.

– Is that some secret message on your top? he said, smiling.

She blushed and pulled the coat closed.

– Got it from a friend on my birthday. I didn't have anything else clean.

– Let me see, he said.

Reluctantly she opened her coat. His gaze moved across the twisting letters.

– M-i-r-i-a-m, he read. – Today's a good day, Miriam. For a cup of coffee, I mean.

* * *

Sitting in the back of the taxi he said:

– You're right, I do have a lot on my mind today.

He leaned back into the soft seat.

– That missing woman. I met her the day she disappeared. Maybe I'm the last person to see her alive.

He didn't say any more about it. Not until he was seated on the sofa in her apartment. Beyond the living room was a kitchenette, and in one corner an alcove where he presumed her bed was. While she laid out the cups and saucers, he told her about the meeting with the missing woman up in the Oslomarka. For some reason or other he repeated their conversation verbatim, as far as he could recall it, as well as the thought that had occurred to him: that not all women would dare walk alone in the forest in the evening. After that, he told her about the rest of his day.

Miriam served coffee from a cafetière. He took a sip. Blue Java, if he had to guess.

– This is good coffee. And I reckon I'm a connoisseur.

She was clearly preoccupied with what he had just been telling her.

– Before you met her, she said as she slipped into a chair on the other side of the table, – you took a swim in a tarn deep in the forest, and then you found that shelter made of spruce branches.

– I don't know why I'm telling you all this, Miriam.

– There's nothing to be worried about.

It was as though every little thing interested her. It gave everything he said a slightly different meaning than he gave it himself. At the same instant he thought about taking her up there. To the tarn and the twig shelter. He liked the thought of walking in the forest with her. He was about to say this, but restrained himself. Instead began talking about the life he would soon be going home to. Riding lessons, football practice, family dinners. Marlen and Tom, Daniel who had gone to New York to study, and Bie, who was a journalist on a fashion magazine she'd once edited. He told her all this to release the tension that had been building in him, and he could feel that it helped.

– You're the type of person people open up to, Miriam. Tell you what, if you were in the police, you'd get plenty of confessions.

She looked up through the skylight.

– It's always been like that. The stories I hear live on inside me. They can knock me out of my stride for a long time after.

– How is that going to affect your work as a doctor? You can't let things get to you. If you do, you've no chance.

She blew on to her cup and took a sip.

– I'll have to learn to live with it. Learn how to erect barriers. I think I'm getting better.

– At any rate, I'll spare you the rest of my story, he said, putting down his cup and standing up.

He stopped next to the chair she was sitting in. She looked up. Her face was shadowed in the grey light falling from the window above. That yellowy green he'd noticed in her eyes earlier wasn't visible now. For the first time he sensed that there was something else there, beneath her calm. Had probably noticed it already when she arrived in the morning. He hadn't asked her a single question about her life. It was a matter of avoiding any openings that might turn her into something more than a young student he was in touch with for a few autumn weeks before disappearing from his life for good. He could feel he was almost back in control again and was determined not to let it go this time. All the same, he asked her:

– Has something happened?

She looked away.

– I've got a confession to make, Axel, she answered after a pause. – It was no accident that I got my practical at your clinic. I swapped with someone else. When you lectured us before the summer, I came to see you in the breaks every day. I thought about you afterwards. I was stupid enough to suppose you were thinking about me too. But when I came into your office that first day, you didn't even remember me.

– What did you want from me? he asked.

– I had to talk to you again.

– Talk?

He touched her shoulder. She leaned in towards him.

– I think that's what I wanted.

Her lower lip protruded slightly. He bent down and kissed it.

– I have to go now.

He pulled her up out of the chair. The trousers she was wearing were made of some smooth stuff and were tight across her hips. His hand slid down across the waistband. She stretched up and pressed her lips against his neck.

– This mustn't happen, Miriam.

– All right then, she murmured, – it mustn't happen.

13

FATHER RAYMOND STAYED behind in church after evening prayers. He had to take confession and left the candles burning. The time he sat there waiting and listening in that large space eased his mind. He could approach silence. The sounds of the traffic outside barely penetrated the walls. Then the main door opened. He recognised the figure walking up the central aisle at once.

– Good evening, he said, jocularly formal. – What a pleasant surprise. The young woman took his outstretched hand.

– I won't take too much of your time, Father Raymond.

He brushed this away.

– Dear Miriam, if you only knew what a pleasure it is to see you. It's been months.

He escorted her to a small room next to the sacristy, offered her a seat on the bench beside the door, and sat on a chair opposite her.

– I think of you so often, he said. – Just very recently, in fact.

He remembered at once that it was the day before, in the morning, as he was on his way to the office. He'd thought of her as he was putting the key into the door. He thought of her because she had appeared in his dream the previous night. He didn't tell her this. Instead he asked her how her studies were going. Miriam answered vaguely, and that surprised him, because usually she would respond to such a question in a very detailed manner.

He crossed his legs and sat back, observing her. Her face was what fascinated him most. The sight of a pretty face had always had a stimulating effect on him. Like a good wine, or a well-turned piece of prose. But there was something about Miriam's face. It reminded him of a thought he often returned to. Something by a philosopher who, oddly enough, came from her native country, and whose work he had studied for years: *The trace of Him in the Other's face.*

– I've met someone, she said.

He nodded once or twice, sustaining his silence long enough for her to have no choice but to go on.

– A man.

That much he had gathered. Very slightly he began rocking back and forth in his chair, as though this movement would enable him to put aside everything else that was on his mind and direct his full attention towards her.

– You say this as though it were a problem.

Gone was that slight feeling of dissatisfaction that had taken hold of him earlier in the evening. In its place he felt a quiet joy spreading through him. She was troubled in some way. She had come to him. On another occasion, some time ago now, she had visited him in order to talk about a man. She wanted to end it, but felt sorry for the man and didn't want to cause him any more hurt.

– Have you known him a long time . . . this new one? Father Raymond asked discreetly.

– A week ago tomorrow.

He opened his mouth to say something.

– I know it doesn't sound like long, she added quickly. – But it's as though I've always known him. I can't explain it.

– You are good at explaining, the priest said encouragingly.

She gave him a long look.

– We can't go on meeting . . . He's seventeen years older than me.

– I see.

– He's married with three children. Now I've said it. If you want me to leave, I'll understand.

A smile flitted across Father Raymond's lips.

– I don't believe you can have such a low opinion of me.

She told him more. And yet he still had the feeling she was holding something back. She was troubled, seemed almost afraid, but he didn't push her. When she fell silent, he asked:

– Can people find happiness together knowing that their happiness is built on the destruction of the lives of others?

– I don't think so, Father.

He cleared his throat.

– How involved are you?

– I spoke to him when he lectured us before the holidays. I thought about him all summer. I thought it would pass if I met him again, but it only got worse.

– So you're not being . . . the priest began. – He isn't pressuring you in any way?

– I'm the one who's chased after him, she answered firmly. – I planned it all out beforehand.

Father Raymond had known her for the six years she had lived in Oslo. Even since her first visit to him he had had a soft spot for her, but in a way he felt this was permissible. The weakness was a reminder, an opening back to the man he had once been; in sacrificing the passion that had dominated him formerly, he had rediscovered it at a new level, one where it was ruled not by compulsion but by joy.

– I'll never forget how you helped me that other time, she said suddenly. – It was those conversations with you that gave me the strength to break away from that relationship. It would have destroyed me.

– All I did was pull a few loose ends together for you, he demurred. He didn't want to dwell on this; what she had come to talk to him about now was more important. And, he had to admit to himself, his curiosity was piqued.

– And how far has this relationship gone?

– I haven't been with him in *that* sense. He kissed me. Then he left.

Father Raymond leaned in towards her.

– There are two questions I want you to consider before you leave here. In the first place, what does he want from you?

When she couldn't, or wouldn't, answer, he asked her to tell him what she knew about the man. Afterwards he summarised her reply.

– The picture you paint is of an attractive man, sympathetic and capable, one who does a lot for others. He was a wife and children, and a twin brother whom he hasn't seen for many years. You still haven't answered my question, Miriam, but don't forget it. My second question is the more important: What do *you* want from him?

– I want to be with him, she answered without a moment's hesitation. – In every conceivable way.

Father Raymond lowered his gaze. She went on:

– Only my thoughts tell me it's wrong. Everything else in me wants it. I'll lose everything and be left with nothing. And when I think about it, it's a relief. But he'll never leave his family for my sake. He isn't like that.

– Are you sure that isn't precisely why you want to be with him? Because he is not free to imprison you? Might this be an attempt to gain control of something painful, Miriam?

She looked as though she was thinking over the question but could find no answer. He knew the grief she had been carrying since she was a little girl. But now he was approaching the limits of what he could understand. I know people better than I know men and women, he thought once again.

– I do know something about what you've been through, Miriam. Don't exclude the possibility that I can help you this time too.

The question she was wrestling with had an unambiguous answer. She knew what the right thing to do was, and she had not come to him to hear him say it. He thought he saw in her something of what he himself had once struggled with. And yet she was better equipped to deal with the world than he had been. Or was he judging her wrongly? The way she connected so strongly with others, and connected others so strongly to herself, was that really all to the good? He thought he could see her so clearly. But maybe the shadow was deeper than he realised. Was there something there he didn't want to know about? He had met people who carried around with them a chasm of grief, seen how it trapped and held them like a passion. And how, perhaps even without wanting to, they could turn others into prisoners along with them.

He made her promise to come back. It was all he could do. He could see clearly now how afraid she was. The last thing he wanted to do was turn her away by seeming prejudiced, he thought as he accompanied her back through the church.

As he stood at the altar and watched her walking down the central aisle, he remembered what it was he had dreamt about her last night. He turned at once and went back into the sacristy.

14

AXEL ATE LUNCH in his office and tried to work. He had a pile of documents to get through. A couple of social security forms and four references that had to be sent out in the course of the day. He sat there with the documents and his unopened lunch box on the desk in front of him. Miriam was sick. At least that was what she'd told Rita on the phone. At first he was relieved. It wasn't the first time one of his students had shown a more than professional interest in him. Usually he didn't mind. On the odd occasion he'd been careless enough to encourage it, but he had never before allowed it to develop. Miriam was going to be absent for the remainder of the week. The need to call her crept up on him. He sat with his mobile phone in his hand, put it down again. He should never have touched her. It would not happen again.

He managed only one of the social security forms during his lunch break, and as soon as he was finished with the day's last patient, he put the phone on voicemail and set about the rest of the documents, as well as test results from the last four days. He made a note of the ones requiring further attention. Mostly trifles and probably false readings. Some possibly serious. And one that he sat studying in his hand. Cecilie Davidsen, the results of the biopsy test on that lump in her breast. *Findings consistent with invasive glandular carcinoma stage III. Multiple mitosis, severely atypical and glandular metastasis.* It was less than a week since the patient had come to see him. He had realised at once that the tumour was malignant and that same week had arranged for a mammography. Being on friendly terms with the right people helped, as did a reputation as a good general practitioner.

He opened her notes and found her number, picked up the phone. A child's voice at the other end.

– Is your mother there? he asked.

– Who are you?

– I'm . . . I have a message for her.

The child called for its mother; a little girl, he could tell, about Marlen's age. He replaced the receiver.

In the taxi, the image of Miriam again. She had a tiny freckle on her chin, directly below her ear. And another one just like it on the side of her neck. When she was listening, her eyebrows would rise quickly and quiver a few times before sinking again. He glanced at his watch, not sure whether he would have time to see his mother in the nursing home before catching the boat. *You must always pay your dues, Axel.* For his father, there was only one real sin here in life. Judge Torstein Glenne had come across so many people who had stolen, betrayed, killed. *The only real sin is to lie. Everything else can be forgiven as long as you own up and make amends. When you lie, that's when you're really done for. It puts you on the outside. That is what Brede seems incapable of understanding.*

Axel asked the driver to wait, opened the gate into the garden. The Davidsens had a big garden, with apple trees and a raspberry hedge, and something that looked like clematis covering the whole of the front of the house. He rang the doorbell and heard a dog barking and someone calling inside, then the door was opened and a girl was standing there. She had a thin braid on each side of her head and a small, red, turned-up nose, and he realised this must the girl who had answered the phone twenty minutes earlier. She was holding a cocker spaniel by its collar, not much more than a puppy.

– I'd like to talk to your mother.

She looked at him and seemed afraid. The dog too; it pulled free and ran off.

– You're the person who rang, she said, not releasing him from her gaze.

He nodded.

– You hung up. When Mummy came, there was no one there.

– It was better to come here and talk to her, he said.

Just then Cecilie Davidsen appeared behind her daughter. She was wearing glasses; her hair was browner than last time and combed forward at the temples. It was the fashion, but it didn't suit her. In her hand she was holding a book, an arithmetic primer for nursery school he noted. When she recognised him, her pupils widened and her face seemed to collapse.

– Is it *you* . . . was it you that rang?

He felt clumsy and helpless, and only now realised what a mistake it had been to come in person, bringing this news into her home.

– I've got a visit to make in the neighbourhood. I thought I might just as well call in.

She held the door open for him. All the colour had drained from her face. The girl put her arms around her waist and buried her face in her pullover.

The messenger, thought Axel Glenne as he stepped over the threshold of the large villa in Vindern carrying the results of a test done on a tissue sample full of cells multiplying out of control and spreading death around them. There was a smell of dinner in the hallway, stronger in the living room. Meat and melted cheese, rice perhaps. He waited until the girl had been sent to her room with the puppy and the arithmetic book and a biscuit in her hand.

– It's about your tissue sample, he said, though he could see that the woman sitting opposite him knew exactly why he had come.

15

Thursday 4 October

MARLEN'S FRIENDS HAD been invited for six o'clock. Axel had to drop his bicycle ride; he'd promised to get home early and arrange things. An hour before the party, he went and picked up the fizzy drinks and the pizza. The night before, Bie had baked a chocolate cake, buns, tea cakes and made a jelly. She was on an assignment in Stockholm and wouldn't be back until the celebrations were over. She was happy enough to be missing all the racket and grateful to Axel for standing in. He'd asked Tom to help with the preparations, and his son had grunted something that might have been a yes, but a few moments later Axel had seen the back of his black leather jacket disappearing through the garden gate.

While he laid the table with the paper tablecloth and the paper plates and blew up the balloons, Marlen sat underneath playing with the present he had given her that morning. She wanted a dog, or at least a cat. She couldn't have either because she was allergic. A pig was rejected for the same reason, though from a medicinal point of view, the reasoning was doubtful. So he'd bought her a tortoise. It was good for everybody. It didn't moult, didn't need to go walks every hour of the day and night, was easy to feed and didn't need contraceptive pills or vaccinations, didn't pee on the carpets, and obeyed house rules without making a fuss. Marlen at once announced that it was her best friend. After a few trial baptisms she finally named it Cassiopeia, after another tortoise in a book Axel had read to her, and with that the creature also had its own constellation up in the night sky. Weeks ago Marlen had decided that all the birthday guests should come dressed as some kind of animal. She was going to go as Cassiopeia's big sister, to which end Axel had fastened a brown plastic bowl to her back and pushed all her long hair inside a woollen hat. Now she was lying beneath the table babbling away in tortoise language and waiting for the first guests to arrive.

With the pizza in the oven, Axel sent the twelve little girls in their animal shapes down into the basement, where they could dance to the flashing of disco lights. He went to fetch his mobile phone to see if Bie had been delayed. There was one message. It was from Miriam. He stood out in the hallway, unsure whether or not he should open it. Three days had passed since he had gone up to her flat. He had kissed her. For the rest of that day she had rustled around inside him. Her voice, the smell of her. When she didn't turn up at the office the following day, he had several times picked up his mobile to call her or send a message. But he'd forced himself not to do anything, and it was as though her hold on him was released. Today he had hardly thought about her at all. He had relinquished control and then regained it.

Miriam had written: *I'm better now. See you Monday.* The message was accompanied by a smiley. He knew nothing about her. He didn't want to know. Had made a point of not asking anything that might have led to her talking about herself. Whom she was seeing. Where she was from. Family, friends, former lovers. He had everything to lose.

The alarm from the oven told him that the pizza was ready. He had had fantasies about Miriam. Almost without realising it. Only now did he recognise that in his mind he had started to turn her into something she almost certainly wasn't. Was that why he had been able to go up to the attic flat with her? Was that why it would be possible to see her again? He knew it would happen. Afterwards he would let her go.

Axel had been responsible for most of his sons' birthday parties over the years. Compared to them, girls' birthdays were straightforward enough. Nobody threw slices of pizza around. No one squeezed tomato ketchup across the table. No one put a straw into the ear of the child sitting beside him and blew it full of fizzy lemonade. He could pad about filling glasses for a throng of pink rabbits. There were a few cats too, a couple of ponies, a ladybird and a lugubrious donkey. Natasha, Marlen's best friend, was a lion, apparently, the crown of Afro hair pushed up into a mane and every question answered with an ominous growling. But she laughed until her eyes rolled back in her head when she saw how frightened Axel was, and reassured him that she was really very nice, as long as she got enough pizza.

– My grandad was nearly killed by the Germans, Marlen boasted. – Isn't that so, Daddy?

– That's true enough.

Marlen picked up Cassiopeia and kissed it on the shell.

– Tell about the time Grandad had to escape to Sweden, she said.

Axel declined, didn't want to invite Colonel Glenne to this particular party. He'd hidden bags of sweets in various places around the house and drawn pirate maps with hidden messages showing where they were. But Marlen wouldn't give up.

– Then tell us about Castor and Pollux, she insisted. – The one who had to go into the underworld to visit his dead brother.

She got the support of the other animals for her demand, and Axel saw that there was nothing for it but to tell the story. Even as a child he had always liked to tell stories. If he managed to make them exciting enough, he would have his mother's attention. Astrid Glenne would look at him with her big blue eyes wide open and sit down and listen until he had finished. He considered it particularly successful if he managed to frighten her. When his stories were about Frankenstein and vampires and werewolves, she would be genuinely afraid and hold her hands out in front of her as though she didn't want to hear any more, though more was exactly what she did want. And when he conjured up a picture of Count Dracula sneaking into the bedroom of a half-naked woman, shadowless and driven on by his insatiable lust for blood, then Axel had his mother in the palm of his hand. The more afraid she was, the closer she was to him.

He didn't try to frighten the little girls in their animal costumes with the story of the twins, but wove in new, dramatic episodes that came to him as he was going along. They sat there spellbound. The little one in the donkey outfit, the only one of Marlen's friends whose name he couldn't recall, had black wrinkles painted on her forehead and cheeks and looked like an old lady. Something about her wide eyes made him think of the daughter of the patient he had visited earlier. That feeling of being a messenger of death invading their home in Vindern hit him again. And with it came the thought of Miriam: return her message. Call her. Go there. He had to talk to her.

– You'll find Castor and Pollux if you look up into the night sky, he concluded. – Not too far away from the Ethiopian queen, Cassiopeia.

– Did everyone know Cassiopeia was a queen? shouted Marlen. – We're going out to see if we can find her.

She raced across the room and opened the terrace door with the other animals in tow. Axel followed. The night had cleared, and much of the sky was visible. He pointed out the Twins to them, and Cassiopeia.

– But right next to them is a star you must never look at.

He said no more, and all the girls turned to him.

– What star is that? asked Natasha.

– Its name is Algol; it's in the constellation Perseus, he said. – That's the name the Arabs gave it. It means *the spirit that eats corpses.*

None of the girls said anything; they stood staring up into the dark.

– Sometimes Algol is bright and clear, other times you can hardly see it; it changes all the time. Actually . . . Axel lowered his voice – actually it's Medusa's evil eye we can see up there. It's winking at us. But you don't want to hear any more about that . . .

This was greeted by a chorus of complaints, and Marlen threatened to beat him up if he didn't continue.

– All right then, he said with a heavy sigh. – You leave me with no choice.

He told them about Perseus, the son of the gods who was sent to the land of the Gorgons to capture the terrifying Medusa. He described the monster in minute detail, the snapping snakes that were her hair, the poisonous sulphur gas she breathed out. Lowering his voice to a whisper, he told them the most terrible detail of all: the eyes that were so ugly that anyone who looked into them was turned to stone. A kind of shiver passed through the flock of girls in fancy dress, and that sad little donkey, the one who reminded him of Cecilie Davidsen's daughter, bit her lip and looked as though she was on the verge of tears. Fortunately Axel was able to tell them how Perseus, with the aid of a mirror, managed to cut the monster's head off and squash it down into a sack. The girls sighed with relief.

– The story doesn't end there, he announced. – But I'll spare you the rest.

A new wave of protests, and reluctantly he had to continue the tale of Perseus's triumphs.

– Wherever he went, he took with him the sack with the monster's head inside, and whenever he encountered any wicked enemies, he would pull it out. It was a terrible weapon, because anyone who met the Medusa's gaze, even after she was dead, was turned to stone. And that's the way things are still: no one who looks into the eyes of the Medusa lives to tell the tale.

The girls all glanced at each other. No one said anything.

– Perseus was proclaimed a superhero and he got his own constellation in the sky, Axel said in conclusion. – And in his hand he's holding the head of the Medusa with her evil eye. But of course, I can't show you that.

Bie was seated at the kitchen table with a glass of red wine when he came down from the loft.

– I've been down with Marlen, she said. – She's still awake.

Axel gave a broad smile.

– She's probably not come back down to earth again after the party. But I swear I didn't give them coffee. Not even Coke.

Bie looked at him.

– Marlen said, *This is the best birthday party in my whole life*, imitating her daughter's common-sense delivery, making Axel laugh. – *Not to say the best* day *of my life*.

– Fortunately she says that every time, said Axel and sat down.

Bie poured him a glass of wine.

– You've always been good at playing. Unlike me. She's lucky, Axel. She couldn't have wished for a better father.

He looked up at the ceiling. He experienced a sudden and almost irresistible urge to tell her about Miriam. About being in her flat. At that moment, Marlen called out.

– You stay there, said Bie and stood up. As she passed him, she stroked his hair, then leaned over and kissed his ear.

It was 10.30. Tom was still not home. Axel had sent him a text but got no answer, and it struck him that it was his son he should have spent the evening with. Taken him to the cinema, or a coffee bar.

Bie came back up.

– She wants to talk to you. No one else will do. She just won't give up.

Marlen lay with her head beneath the duvet. He pretended he couldn't find her, felt around on the bed until he came across a foot, which he tickled under the toes.

– Can't you sleep? he asked as she emerged.

– I daren't.

He sat on the edge of the bed.

– What are you afraid of?

– That monster, she whispered. – Medusa. I'm never going to look up into the sky again.

Marlen had a tendency to overdramatise things, but he could hear now that she was genuinely afraid. He'd been too successful in bringing the story of Perseus alive; he hoped her classmates weren't all lying awake in bed too.

– All this about Medusa is just a fairy tale, Marlen. I'll tell you why that star winks at us. Actually there are two stars there. When the weaker one passes in front of the strong one, the light gets cut off.

He demonstrated with his hands how the two stars orbited around each other.

– After a few days, the strong one appears again, and from down here it looks like it's flaring up. The two stars make us believe they are one and the same.

He had to repeat the explanation several times to convince Marlen that it wasn't an evil eye up there looking down at the earth and winking. Eventually she calmed down and went to sleep. The myth of Medusa had released her from its hold.

IT IS THE sixth of October. Not when you hear this but now when I'm speaking to you, it is the sixth of October. I've killed today. I think about it and it makes me feel calm. Then I think of how I'm saying this into the Dictaphone so that you'll hear it and I feel a thrill of expectation. You'll be lying here where I'm sitting now and hearing my voice saying this. You can't move and you can't interrupt me. For the first time you realise it's going to happen to you too.

I didn't plan to kill. Not even when I saw her walking along the forest path towards me. It was nine days ago. I stopped and talked to her. She liked to talk. In the end I had to tell her to shut up. She went rigid and stared at me. Suddenly she turned and began to run back along the track. Then I knew she would die. I caught up with her and grabbed hold of that skinny neck. She started screaming. I was angry as fuck and I closed her shrieking mug. But it wasn't going to happen just yet. She had to know about it for a while first. Same way you'll know about it. I dragged her in among the trees. Had to tape her mouth shut. Tape her hands that kept trying to scratch my face. Found somewhere to tie her up to wait until I could come back and fetch her. It took a couple of hours and by then she was all screamed out. She'd messed herself like a baby in nappies. Didn't weigh much more either, stinking old bag.

I couldn't face taking her clothes off the way I'd planned. But I like to change plans. The best plans are the ones that just come along. Like the way I'm sitting here talking to you. I don't know how it'll be. Nor what'll happen to you. All sorts of eventualities can crop up and get in the way. As I'm recording this, you still don't know that this whole thing is about you. You've done everything you can to forget. But we are joined together. That's what you were trying to say that time you told me about the twins that no one could part. No matter how much you have let me die in your thoughts. You said once that everyone has his own animal. You read that somewhere and wanted me to think about it. We were sitting in the classroom then too, but we weren't alone there. It was just before the lesson began. And when I couldn't think of anything, you said a bear, that was my animal.

PART II

16

DETECTIVE CHIEF INSPECTOR Hans Magnus Viken was standing high above the gully. He'd been there for several minutes. Below him the crime scene was bathed in light from the two large lamps the technicians had rigged up.

He had still not been down there. Not because he dreaded getting a closer look at the deceased, but because first impressions were important. He raised his eyes and looked into the darkness between the pine trees. The actual location in which a body was found always had something to tell. It was usually not possible to describe exactly what it was at first, but it might be useful later, perhaps even crucial. He referred to this to himself as *intuition*, but called it *a gut feeling* in conversation with colleagues. He was convinced that this power to think intuitively was what distinguished an unusually skilled detective from one who was merely competent.

Viken remained standing up there another couple of minutes before climbing down and nodding to the three guys in white coveralls who had completed the first round of examinations of the body and were now searching the surrounding forest floor.

One look at the dead person was enough. The DI was certain this was the missing woman. She was wearing walking gear, Gore-Tex jacket and trousers in some rough fabric. The jacket had been pulled up over the back. She lay with her legs curled under her, in a foetal position. He bent closer, switched on his torch. A gaping wound ran across one side of her neck and up on to her face. It looked almost like deep claw marks, five furrows in the same direction. When he carefully lifted up part of the ripped jacket, a second, similar gash appeared, diagonally down across the back. He peered towards the top of the gorge, where he'd just been standing. A fall on to the stones at the bottom could cause a lot of damage. But these gashes were different. It looked like something done by an animal. Ten days had passed since the woman had been reported missing; she must have been lying there exposed to the elements, and a natural target for scavengers.

One of the technicians shouted. He was standing doubled over at the end of the gorge, where it emerged on to a slope. The others joined him. Viken heard them talking loudly together and climbed closer.

– Found something?

One of them, a raw-boned, grey-haired man he'd known since police college days, beckoned to him.

– Better come and see this for yourself.

Viken shone his torch beam on to the ground, where the moss had been scratched up. Shone it further away; in several places there were similar marks on the forest floor. On a muddy patch of ground distinct tracks were visible. They looked like claw marks.

– Shit, Viken muttered. – They don't exactly look like a dog's prints.

He straightened up.

– How much longer do you need here?

The grey-haired man measured the gully with his gaze.

– Five, six hours to begin with.

Viken thought it over. It was now 8.45. It looked highly unlikely that this was a case for his Violent Crimes section. He had come up here on his own initiative when he heard about the discovery. He was well aware of the fact that not everybody in the Crime Response Unit would be equally pleased at his presence, but having seen the dead woman, he was confident that it had been time well spent. He had seen body parts fished up from the sea. He had entered flats in which corpses had lain rotting and putrefied in the summer heat for weeks. He had seen them disfigured with Sami knives, shot at close range with shotguns. But he had never seen anything resembling these gashes. Carefully he picked his way down the slope, shining the torch on the ground in front of him. A few metres further down he came across two new tracks.

He climbed up above the gully again, pulled the plastic coverings off his shoes and removed a cloth from his pocket. Even when working in terrain like this, he disliked seeing muddy spots on them. Afterwards he stood looking down at the brightly lit scene with the white-clad figures crawling around as they examined the ground around the body. He pulled out his mobile phone, called a number from the address book. A sergeant in the section had at one time been a member of the Hunting and Fishing Regulations committee in the area he came from, somewhere away up in darkest Hedmark. The type of guy who devoted two weeks of his holiday to elk hunting every time autumn came around.

– Hi, Arve, he said when his call was answered. – I know this is a holiday weekend for you, but there's something I want you to see. Are you in town? Good, how quickly can you make it up to Ullevålseter?

Viken stood on the grass with a cup of hot coffee in his hands. The people at Ullevålseter were more than accommodating. The café had closed several hours ago, but they'd offered him something to eat as well. He said coffee was fine, even though his stomach was acid and complaining. In the distance he heard the sound of an engine, and a couple of minutes later a small, light car came up the slope. Sergeant Arve Norbakk, the man he was waiting for, usually drove a big four-by-four, and Viken immediately had a pretty good idea of what was happening.

His hunch turned out to be right. A blond woman he recognised at once jumped out of the passenger door even before the car had come to a halt.

– Well let me tell you, Fredvold, said Viken. – *VG* are usually on the scene long before I've even got my shoes on. I've been here for hours now and not seen hide nor hair of a journalist. No wonder the tabloids are struggling.

The woman was in her thirties, with a jutting lower jaw, and was about a head taller than the detective chief inspector. She wore a leather jacket and boots with heels that gave her another couple of centimetres on him. Tall women always made him feel uneasy.

– Well we'll see about that, she answered. – But finding you here is good news.

Viken grimaced.

– It isn't murder every time I show my face, you know that perfectly well. Did you get permission to drive up here?

– I didn't reckon on meeting any traffic wardens in the middle of the forest, the journalist smiled. Cute as a pike, Viken thought.

A fat little man with an enormous photographer's bag over one shoulder squeezed his way out of the car. The detective chief inspector hadn't seen him before, and when the man approached, clearly intending to shake hands, he turned his back on him, trudged back into the café and refilled his cup. An hour had passed since he'd called Norbakk. He wanted to finish up here and get back down into town as quickly as possible.

Kaja Fredvold and the photographer followed him inside.

– Are you still serving coffee? the journalist exclaimed happily when she saw the steaming pot standing on the counter.

She helped herself and walked over to the table where Viken was now sitting.

– Is the body you've found Hilde Paulsen?

– Looks pretty much like it.

– What happened to her?

Viken drummed on the edge of the table.

– She's lying in a gully, been lying there for a week and a half. Fell, I expect.

– Where?

– Not too far away. Couple of kilometres.

– But this area has been thoroughly combed for days. Dogs and helicopters and an army of volunteers.

– Give us a day or two, Fredvold.

– Us? You mean Violent Crimes?

Viken heard a car outside and stood up.

– Don't try it on. That's all you're getting for now.

They drove up the forest road in Norbakk's SUV, the journalist following them in the little Japanese car.

– Let's hope they get stuck, said Viken.

Arve Norbakk chuckled. He was not much more than thirty, at least twenty years younger than his colleague. He'd joined straight from college and been in the section for eighteen months. Viken, who every semester led a course in investigatory tactics for the students, had personally recommended him to the head of the section. The gut feeling that stood him in such good stead as a detective was every bit as useful when it came to assessing a colleague's personality and qualities. It enabled him to make quick judgements of their weaknesses and strengths, and he had not been mistaken in his opinion of Norbakk. The sergeant might not have been all that quick, but he was thorough and dependable, and smart enough when given the time. And he was someone who thought about what he was going to say before saying it, not the type to shoot his mouth off about anything and everything. The section had enough chattering magpies – an issue on which Viken's tolerance was severely limited.

– You could have forbidden them to drive on any further, Norbakk suggested.

Viken fumbled out a paper hanky and blew into it. Not because he had a cold, but because the smell of the corpse he had been bending over still seemed to be in his nostrils.

– They would have been up there whatever. You know, when the mongrels pick up the scent of blood . . . Apropos mongrels, it was a dog that found the body. A few hundred metres off the track.

Norbakk glanced over at him.

– They've had search lines going across this area several times.

– I know. Our people with tracker dogs, and the army and the Red Cross, with hundreds of volunteers trawling every square inch. No one finds a damned shit. But a retired dentist out walking with his Gordon setter comes across it straight away.

A few minutes later they were stepping over the crime-scene tapes and climbing down into the gully. Norbakk took a quick look at the body.

– Fucking hell, he muttered, and looked up at the top of the gully.

– What do you make of these?

Viken pointed to the deep scratch marks on the back and neck.

– Can't be the result of a fall, Norbakk said. – Must be an animal.

Viken glowered at the journalist and the photographer, who were leaning over the tape and following their every movement. Then he shone his torch on the marks in the moss.

– Bloody hell, Norbakk exclaimed.

– There's a couple more here. We'll need to get the experts on this, but I wanted you to see it first.

Viken shone the torch on the muddy area at the end of the gully.

– What's your guess, Arve?

– Guess? It's a stone-cold certainty.

The three technicians had arrived back by this time. Sergeant Arve Norbakk studied the ground for a little while longer before he raised his gaze and looked from one to another.

– Bear, he said.

17

Monday 8 October

VIKEN WAS IN excellent spirits but for obvious reasons contained himself.

– Are you trying to say that this is not our case? asked Nina Jebsen in her laid-back Bergen drawl. – That this is something for the Hunting and Fishing Regulations people?

Viken rested his gaze on her face. He'd only worked with her a couple of times before. She was in her early thirties, the type most men would undoubtedly have described as pretty, he thought. Meaning a face that was feminine and symmetrical and all that. Not very exciting, perhaps, but she definitely had a woman's body, something the light grey suit with the short cinched jacket did nothing to hide. She just needed to lose about five or six kilos, he said to himself, not for the first time. But all things considered it was best for her to be the way she was. He didn't want any *babe* working next to him, not on the job; that would be bound to cause trouble.

Seen from that perspective, working with the head of the Violent Crimes section, Detective Superintendent Agnes Finckenhagen, was a pretty straightforward business. She was a bag of bones about his own age, with a crooked nose and thin lips. Nina Jebsen's question had been directed at her. Now Finckenhagen's mouth narrowed even further. Viken had long ago worked out that this was a sign she was trying to appear authoritative.

– We've had a wildlife expert up there, she said. – He confirms what we already suspected. She flashed a quick smile at Arve Norbakk, who was sitting directly opposite her round the table. – That is, that the murdered woman, Hilde Sofie Paulsen, has injuries consistent with those inflicted by a bear.

Viken adopted a look of relaxed inscrutability as Finckenhagen spoke. The case had been well handled, and she had praised him before the meeting. Taking Arve Norbakk up to the scene had been a smart move. The sergeant had experience with attaching radio transmitters to bears and was as qualified as any expert to identify the wounds on the deceased and the tracks found nearby. From the moment the body had been found they had been in control of the situation, and they had been firm in dealing with the press. Viken had discreetly reminded Finckenhagen that he was the one who had recommended Norbakk when he applied to join their section and that, probably as a result of this, he had been given the job ahead of people with a longer record of service.

– If it was an animal that did this, then surely we can take responsibility for tracking it down, suggested Inspector Sigmundur Helgarsson with a grin in Norbakk's direction. – There's others can hunt here besides Arve.

– Excellent idea, Sigge, Viken responded tonelessly. – I imagine you grew up hunting polar bears.

– Do they have polar bears in Iceland? Nina Jebsen wanted to know.

Finckenhagen raised both hands.

– Let's drop the macho stuff, shall we. This is a deeply tragic case, it's a very special case, and it's going to be headline stuff all week. We don't yet have a cause of death, but as of this moment there's been no talk of transferring the case formally. Let's hope it goes to the Crime Response Unit and not us.

Viken wasn't all that convinced she really meant what she said. For some reason or other she had already been interviewed in *VG* and *Dagbladet*, and she had an appointment with TV2 later in the day. The uniform she was wearing had been freshly ironed, and if she'd had time she would probably have spent the morning at the hairdresser's having something done about those wisps. None of the higher-ups have any doubt about my qualities as a leader, he thought. Not just on the technical side, but also in dealing with people. Finckenhagen had got the senior post for which they'd both applied for a very different reason. He gave her a disarming smile. Enjoy it while you can, Slinkenhagen.

Arve Norbakk sat up straighter in his chair. His eyes were brown below the fair fringe. They were quite large and round and gave the impression of someone mild and cautious, but Viken knew the sergeant could be tough enough. He'd noticed how Nina Jebsen, and Finckenhagen too for that matter, changed whenever Arve was around. They moved in another way, their voices went up a touch. He didn't object to it at all.

– I'm certain this isn't a matter for Hunting and Fishing, said Norbakk.

– Are you? asked Finckenhagen. – How so?

He looked to be thinking before he continued.

– Those tracks up there, they were reasonably fresh.

– You don't say, Hawkeye? Helgarsson grinned.

– Cut it out, Sigge, warned Viken. – Let Arve finish what he's saying.

– Paulsen has been missing for a week and a half, Norbakk noted. – But the tracks we found aren't as old as that.

– In other words, said Viken, who had already discussed this with Norbakk, – it looks like we aren't done with this case after all.

He went on:

– We've got to keep our eyes on the doughnut and not the hole. And anyway, how many of us here really believe there's a killer bear wandering around up there in the marka?

Finckenhagen blinked a few times.

– Let's wait until we have the pathologist's report, she said.

Viken didn't smirk. He knew she always used phrases like that when she didn't have anything sensible to say.

18

STILL ANOTHER THREE quarters of an hour before the office opened. Axel Glenne usually managed to get a lot of work done in the time before the patients arrived. Go through the mail, finish off the referrals. He turned on the computer. While he waited for it to load up, he looked again at *Aftenposten*. MISSING WOMAN FOUND DEAD was the front-page headline. *Tragic accident*, it said underneath. *Body lay in forest for ten days*.

He put the paper aside. Opened a letter from the surgical department with an appointment for Cecilie Davidsen's operation. They'd been quick; he hadn't needed to send them a reminder. Given what they'd found, there was no time to lose. He remembered that he'd dreamt about her. He'd opened the door of a house he recognised. The villa in Vindern. He hadn't rung, just gone right in. It was dark inside, but he heard sounds coming from the floor above, a woman groaning. I shouldn't be here: the thought flashed through him as he started to climb the stairs. Someone was following him; he sensed a shadow but couldn't turn round.

He looked through his list of patients again. Had to be finished by four. He hadn't visited his mother last week. Hadn't been back since she got him mixed up with Brede.

He found an updated article on whiplash injuries in the online edition of *The Lancet*. He wanted to give Miriam the best possible advice regarding the case she was handling. If she even showed up today . . . Was he hoping she would still be off sick? So he wouldn't have to say anything about the visit to her flat the Monday before? Wouldn't have to joke about it. Or apologise. Maybe that was why she'd stayed away all week.

At 7.40, he heard Rita let herself into the office. A few moments later, he went in.

— New week, new possibilities, she said, without conviction.

— You heard the news, he said.

She nodded.

— It's the most awful thing I ever heard. Imagine that, Axel, a bear.

His eyebrows shot up.

— A bear?

— Didn't you hear? she exclaimed, holding up *VG*. Half the front page was covered with the words: TORN APART BY BEAR IN NORDMARKA. There was an indistinct photograph, white-clad figures stooped over a body on the ground.

— It's just the kind of thing *VG* writes, Rita. It's not possible. Not in the Nordmarka.

— I suggest you read the whole thing. The police say there's no doubt.

He flipped through the ten pages devoted to the case.

— I met her up there. Just before she disappeared.

— My God! Why didn't you mention it before?

He peered out into the waiting room, where the first patient had taken a seat, a retired officer who had known his father.

— There's been so much going on, Rita.

He heard Miriam talking to Rita outside reception. Shortly afterwards, she came along the corridor, past his door, and opened the door to Ola's office. Axel opened the retired lieutenant colonel's notes. Checked the lab tests. His haemoglobin concentration had fallen since the last time it was tested. He heard Miriam's steps approaching again. He looked at some of the patient's other results. There was a knock on the door, which was ajar. He cleared his throat, but before he managed to say anything, she was standing there. He scrolled down to the bottom of the document and looked at the last readings before glancing up. Beneath her coat, she was wearing the top with her name on it.

– Dirty linen basket still full, then? he said, adding, before he had time to wince at his own comment: – So you're feeling better?

She crossed the floor and stood in front of him.

– A bit hoarse, but yes, fine.

He stood up. – Miriam, he said, and put his arm around her. She moved in close to him. He stroked her hair, laid his face against her neck and inhaled. The smell reminded him of something he had forgotten.

The telephone rang. He reached across the table without letting go of her hand.

– Are you ready for your first patient? asked Rita, obviously as a way of reminding him that he was already ten minutes late.

– Send him in. Did you tell him that we have a student here?

– Yes, yes. Another thing, Axel, *VG* just called. I said you were busy.

– *VG*? What did they want?

– A journalist . . . Fredvold, she wanted to talk to you. I said she could try again at lunchtime.

Axel felt suddenly annoyed.

– Listen, Rita, I don't have time to talk to *VG*.

– Okay then, she said, surprised. – What do you want me to say?

– Tell them I'll be busy all day. It's the truth, after all.

19

– This is the closest you get to knowing what it feels like to be a surgeon, said Detective Chief Inspector Viken after he and his sergeant, Arve Norbakk, had pulled on the disposable green capes, with hoods in an almost matching green, and the blue plastic shoe coverings. – And it's plenty close enough for me. I've never yet met one doctor you could trust.

– Right now you look more like a chef, chuckled Norbakk as they entered the sharp light of the mortuary room in the basement of the Rikshospital.

Viken didn't like delay, and he'd taken the trip up to the Institute of Pathology without Finckenhagen knowing anything about it.

– I know it's not long till dinner, he said, wrinkling his nose, – but surely the smell down here doesn't remind you of food?

Two people were already in the room, bent over a steel table. One was a tiny woman in her forties with a heavily made-up doll-like face. Viken knew her well, had worked with Jennifer Plåterud many times. He had quickly discovered that her mind and her tongue were equally sharp and he treated her with a respect that very few others of his acquaintance enjoyed. Viken knew a lot about most of the people he worked with. In his head he kept a catalogue of useful information regarding them, some of which he had even written down. He had tried on several occasions to worm out of Jennifer just what it was that had brought her to Norway. Surely her real reason for leaving Canberra and travelling to the other side of the globe couldn't be that she'd met some farmer from Romerike, the guy she later married? But when it came to her private life Jennifer was a sphinx, and Viken still hadn't got to the bottom of that particular question.

The other person standing there was a man of medium height wearing glasses, with a well-trimmed beard. Viken had never seen him before.

– Frederik Ovesen, the bearded man said, introducing himself with a cough. – Assistant professor at the Zoological Institute.

– Ovesen is their leading expert on beasts of prey, Jennifer announced in perfect Norwegian but with a broad Australian accent. Despite the fact that she was wearing stilettoes under her shoe coverings, she had to stretch to reach across the width of the steel table she was working at.

– How far have you got? asked Viken, with a glance at the body he had last seen in the forest a few kilometres beyond Ullevålseter. The ribcage had been opened up and the heart and both lungs taken out.

– The preliminary autopsy will be ready by tomorrow, Jennifer promised, and Viken couldn't off-hand recall a single time she hadn't kept her word.

– Time of death?

The pathologist pulled on her plastic gloves.

– Four to five days ago. Six at the most.

Viken's eyes narrowed.

– So a week after she went missing. We can only guess what she was doing up there in the marka all that time. Does she look as if she spent four or five days sleeping rough in the forest?

– Not really, Jennifer replied. – But I wouldn't exclude it either. Another thing is that we found large quantities of plaster under her fingernails. Some on the clothes, too. It doesn't necessarily mean anything, but it certainly doesn't come from the forest floor.

– Any signs of sexual assault?

– Doesn't look like it.

Norbakk said:

– I've seen a lot of animals killed by bears. There's no mistaking these gashes across the neck and the back.

Ovesen coughed again.

– I agree. I've never seen a human being who's been attacked, but we do have some archival material. I would say a fully grown adult bear.

– How certain can you be? Viken persisted.

Ovesen opened his mouth, coughed a couple more times; already these glottal eruptions had started to annoy the detective chief inspector.

– We'll send the photos to Edmonton University in Canada, said the zoologist. – They've got documentation there they can use for comparison.

– Would a bear not have ripped open her stomach? Viken wondered.

Ovesen shook his head.

– We humans are not natural prey for a bear. It might gash us, bite, but it's extremely rare that it would attack in order to eat us. Unless we're talking about a seriously undernourished animal.

– Don't rule out that it might help itself to a dead person, said Norbakk. – Old Bruin's a scavenger, after all. And not a particularly fussy one.

– You're right there, said the zoologist. – It might have started gnawing away at the body and been disturbed. Alarmed by something, for example.

Jennifer Plåterud interrupted:

– I can tell you that the deceased was still alive when these wounds were made. There was the hint of a smile about her mouth as she said this.

– So not a scavenger, then, said Norbakk firmly. – But the tracks up there looked fresh enough.

Again the zoologist backed him up.

– Not more than a day or two old. And remember too that it was raining five days ago.

Viken glanced at Norbakk, delighted to have the sergeant along. What do we need experts for, he thought with a grin, when we find all the answers ourselves?

– The preliminary conclusion then will be that all the visible injuries were inflicted by a bear, he announced, looking at Jennifer Plåterud across the partially autopsied body on the table.

– Not that one, Chief Inspector, she said, and pointed with a scalpel.

The smile spread across her face, revealing fine lines that were otherwise hidden by the make-up. She made Viken think of a child that had been working away inside its nose and come up with an enormous bogey. He leant over the body. Four small red pricks were clearly visible on the upper left arm. Jennifer held a magnifying glass to them.

– Injection marks, suggested Norbakk.

– That would be my opinion too, said the pathologist. – There are more of them here. She moved the magnifying glass to two areas on the inside of the thigh. – Moreover, she added, – note the red circles around the wrists.

Viken examined them closely.

– Tape marks?

– I'd guarantee it. There are traces of adhesive on the skin. And the same here. She made a circling motion around the dead woman's mouth.

Four hours after he had left the pathology lab, Viken got a call from Jennifer Plåterud.

– We've got the results of the blood tests, she informed him

Viken grabbed a pen and flipped to an empty page in his notebook. The pathologist wouldn't have taken the trouble to ring unless she had something interesting for him.

– We found large quantities of a substance called thiopental in the blood.

He noted this down.

– What sort of substance is it?

– A so-called barbiturate. It's used in operations and should only be kept in hospitals and by medical suppliers. Some also in veterinary practices.

– Effects?

– A very effective anaesthetic. An overdose can bring on pulmonary and cardiac arrest.

Viken leaned back in his chair. He savoured the fact that earlier in the day Finckenhagen had been so certain that this wasn't a case for the Violent Crimes. He started thinking about who he wanted in his team to continue the investigation.

20

SIGNY BRUSETER PULLED up outside the house on Reinkollen and parked next to the car that was already there. She turned off the engine, abruptly terminating the news broadcast. But letting herself into the house, it felt as though the newsreader's voice was still talking inside her head about what had happened in the forest. Signy had slept badly that night. It was her second day in the new job.

Mette Martin, who was social educator for the three homes that lay round the little clearing, met her in the corridor. Signy was pleased to see her, because Mette Martin was such a self-assured person. Signy hadn't had a job for the past year and eleven months. Throughout the interview she had been convinced that she would never get the job of assistant. Mostly it felt like a relief. But Mette Martin thought that the experience of her years in the nursery made her *interesting*, and that the transition to looking after the mentally handicapped shouldn't be too great. She had called the very next day – to Signy's alarm – and asked when she could begin.

– All quiet here at the moment, said Mette Martin now. – Tora's asleep, and Oswald's sitting in his room. The night shift took care of the morning cleaning. You'll be on your own with them until lunch, then Åse Berit will be here, and there'll be two of you for the rest of the day.

Signy hung up her coat and sat down on the sofa.

– Oswald has to have his medication at nine o'clock, said Mette Martin. – But don't put the radio on. He gets so upset with all this talk about a killer bear being on the loose.

– He's not the only one, exclaimed Signy. – Have you ever heard anything like it? Killed by a bear, a grown woman. And just a few kilometres from Karl Johan and the palace.

– Dreadful, agreed Mette Martin. – Hard to believe, actually.

After she'd left, Signy knocked on Tora's door and went in. They were very particular about that here, always knock on the door, even though Tora couldn't answer and probably had no idea what all the banging was about. Mette Martin had stressed that it was important to show respect for the residents regardless, and Signy approved of her saying that. Tora hadn't exactly been born with a silver spoon in her mouth, Mette Martin said. She had a congenital defect that meant that her brain hadn't developed as it should have done. Remarkable that she was alive at all. Her mother was a drug addict and continued to inject herself even while she was carrying Tora, so it was probably connected with that. In all the time she had been living at Reinkollen, Tora had never had a single visitor. Not a soul beyond these walls cared whether she lived or died. Life hadn't always been easy for Signy either, but when she saw this person whom she dressed and looked after, she felt she had a lot to be thankful for.

When Tora was seated in her chair, freshly washed and groomed, Signy wheeled her out into the corridor and stopped in front of the mirror.

– We care about you here, Tora, she crooned.

Tora moved her jaw as though she was laughing, and made noises down in her throat. Mette Martin had said this meant she was happy, and Signy smiled and stroked her hair, suddenly feeling happy too.

Soon she'd have to see to Oswald. All night she'd been uneasy at the thought of being alone with him. Oswald had Down's syndrome and was nearly thirty years old. Some additional hormonal abnormality meant that he'd ended up a hefty six foot three, broad as a barn door but with a three year old in his head, the main difference being that Oswald didn't have as much language. On several occasions Mette Martin had assured her that he was as gentle as a lamb and had never caused trouble for anyone.

Signy summoned up her courage and opened his door.

– Hi, Oswald, how about coming into the dining room for a bite to eat?

He grunted and stood up so suddenly that she took two steps backward.

– Hold hands, he said, and took hold of hers.

Åse Berit Nytorpet was a big, stocky woman in her sixties with pinched lips and grey hair bunched in a topknot. She arrived at twelve o'clock exactly, took a pair of shaggy slippers from a plastic bag and slid her feet into them.

– Floor in here gets bloody freezing, she said as she waddled into the room.

After giving Tora her bath, the two assistants were able to sit down for a breather.

– Miserable to live here and never even get a visitor, Signy said with a sideways glance at Tora.

Åse Berit snorted.

– Her mother's been on the street for years. You don't expect someone like that to care, do you? But her father's supposed to be a celebrity.

– Really? exclaimed Signy. – D'you know who . . . ?

Åse Berit shrugged her shoulders.

– There are rumours.

Clearly she didn't want to say any more about these rumours. Maybe she was saving them for later. Instead she turned on the radio, but as the time for the news approached Signy had to remind her that Mette Martin had asked them to be sure not to leave it on.

– It's that woman who was killed, she said, lowering her voice. – Mette Martin says Oswald goes completely nuts when he hears about it.

Åse Berit turned the radio off.

– Let them have a taste of it, these city people, she said, pursing her lips. – They've made their own bed, now let them lie in it. Maybe now they'll understand what it's like having wild animals snuffling round the walls of your house. So at least *some* good might come of it.

Signy didn't respond. She couldn't think of any way that what had happened might be good at all. The dead woman was just a few years older than she was herself.

– You should've heard what my old man said when he heard the news yesterday, Åse Berit went on. – Just the year before last we had four pregnant ewes got ripped to pieces. Think it does any good to complain? Oh no, poor old Bruin the Bear has to be left well enough alone, don't you know. Her voice had begun to shake. – Don't touch the wild animals. But people like us who are trying to live off keeping sheep, we're the ones that pay the price.

She pointed demonstratively at her forehead and shook her head.

– Let me tell you something, Signy. She lowered her voice. – When people get angry enough, they can do things they oughtn't to have done.

Signy gaped at her.

– You don't think anyone from round here is involved in it?

Åse Berit pursed her lips and made a zipping motion across them with two fingers. But shortly afterwards she was off again.

– If you only knew how angry some people can be. Things have been brewing for a long time up on the farms around us. Year after year we've had to put up with this. Now things might change. If we're going to have bears, they can roam around wherever they like, and not just up here. We'll soon see how long they put up with *that*.

Suddenly Oswald appeared in the door opening. His lower jaw jutted so profoundly that he drooled from the corners of his mouth.

– Oswald catch bear.

He thumped himself on the chest, and the bitterness in Åse Berit's face dissolved and faded away.

– Yes, you could, Oswald, big and strong as *you* are.

Turning to Signy she said: – He's a lovely lad, is Oswald. But he has his black moments. Best to leave him alone then. It's to do with the way he was brought up.

– What do you mean? Signy wanted to know.

– He didn't have an easy time of it, poor soul, Åse Berit confided.
– Not until he was taken into care. Oswald's father was a nasty piece
of work, right from the word go. And you can trust me, because I
went to primary school with him. You would never catch *me* getting
mixed up with someone like that. There's others'll tell you the same
thing.

She tossed her head.

– He ended up with some city girl that turned up out here. But
then she found someone else and off she went and left him to look
after the kids, and the whole thing just went to pieces. He lost the
farm, had it sold out from underneath his feet. He took the kids
with him and moved out into the woods, to a cabin they owned up
there. Left them to run wild while he sat drinking down in Holtet
with another boozer and drank away what little bit of brains he had
left.

– But wouldn't Oswald have got lost in the woods?

– No, because listen to what his father did. He partitioned off the
cellar under the cabin with a wire fence, and he used to lock Oswald
in there before he went away.

Signy's eyes opened wide. Bad enough hearing about Tora and
her drug addict mother, but this was even worse.

– It's not true, is it? Locked up in the cellar? Like a beast?

– That's why we shouldn't get in his way when he has these
moods. We just don't know what's going on in the heads of people
like that. Do we, Oswald?

Oswald gave a bright smile and continued to beat his chest.

– Oswald catch bear.

21

THE SEAT NEAREST the door in the half-full underground carriage was vacant and Axel was able to lean his cycle up next to him. The weather had cleared, the temperature had risen, and even with the slight damp in the air it felt like summer. Like a gift to those longing for the sun, and a reminder for climate pessimists.

He cycled in the forest every Thursday, switching to skis in the winter months. It was a breathing space in the middle of the week he always looked forward to. But today would be a little different from his usual day off. He avoided thinking about it, took a copy of *Dagbladet* from his rucksack and by the time they reached his station had glanced through it. The bear case continued to dominate the front pages. A couple of days ago it was reported that all witnesses were going to be interviewed again, but so far he had heard nothing. The head of the Violent Crimes section of the Oslo police, Finckenhagen her name was, had made a statement to the press. The case was being given top priority, she told reporters, without making it clear whether or not the police believed a bear was on the loose in the immediate vicinity of the capital. But there was nothing urging people to avoid walking in the marka alone.

Lower down the page there was a fact box. The last confirmed sighting of bears in the Nordmarka had been over fifty years ago, Axel read, although signs had been seen towards the end of the nineties. The maximum life span for a bear in the Scandinavian wilds was in the region of 25 to 30 years. A fully grown bear could reach anywhere between 150 and 280 centimetres in height and weigh between 100 and 350 kilos. Then came a few pointers about what to do when encountering a bear. Don't try to run away from it; the animal is capable of running at 60 kilometres an hour. Turn your back and flee in panic and you'll be taken for prey. Trees don't make a good hiding place; young bears are excellent climbers, older bears can if they have to. Keep calm, move slowly away backwards. Don't try to scare the bear away. Thanks for the advice, Axel grinned, and turned the page.

Interviews with members of the public, questions about whether they were afraid of bears. The paper stressed that life went on as normal in the capital. As though anyone had thought it wouldn't, Axel sighed to himself. The journalist had spent the evening at El Coco's in Rosencrantz' gate, where they were advertising a section of the bar as bear-proof and had installed a sort of mesh screen across the entrance. People could order drinks from the bar with names like Pooh's Honey and Grizzly Killer. Axel rolled the paper up and shoved it down the side of the seat.

She was standing a little way down the platform, wearing cycling shorts and helmet, black jacket and sunglasses.

– Been waiting long? he asked.

A lot of ramblers and cyclists were milling round. They didn't look all that scared by the headlines, or the thought of what might be awaiting them out there in the woods. He gave her a quick squeeze on the arm.

– Cool set of wheels.

She got into the saddle.

– I bought it yesterday.

He waited at the top of Blankvannsbråten. When Miriam joined him, he nodded in the direction of the edge of the forest.

– We'll leave our bikes up there.

– Are you sure it's safe to wander about up here? she asked.

He laughed.

– That bear's miles away, don't worry about that. With everything that's been going on up here, it's been scared halfway up to Valdres or Trøndelag by now. You know how far a brown bear can get in a week?

He took a step towards her, loosened her helmet. Her hair was gathered in two braids and fastened with a grip at the back.

– Unless, that is, there's something else you're afraid of, he added.

By the time they reached the tarn, it had clouded over. He took his rucksack off and put it down next to the little boat lying there with its bow pointing upwards, then took out a white cloth and spread it out, putting a thermos and two cups on it, and a package from Bruun's bakery.

– You brought a cloth?

He gestured expansively.

– A little style, that's all. I stole it from the examination room. It isn't sterile, but I can guarantee it's clean.

She laughed, and he reached out a hand and touched one of her ears, the almost invisible rim of fuzz.

– This is goodbye, he said. – That's why I've invited you out to lunch.

– What do you mean?

– I'll be away next week. Seminar.

He'd forgotten to tell her. Put it at the back of his mind.

– Inger Beate will be looking after you for the rest of your time with us.

He jumped up on to the rock, looked out across the black mirrored surface.

– Last one in is a rotten egg, he called out to her, pulling off his vest, trousers and underpants in one movement and diving in without a moment's hesitation. The water was colder than it had been two weeks earlier. He ducked down and swam a couple of strokes underwater, spun up again and turned round. She was standing by the rock, still looking amazed.

– Don't stand there wondering what day it is, he said to cheer her up.

– I've just had a sore throat.

– All the more reason. This beats an apple a day any time.

She started to pull off her tight shorts. He kept his eyes on her as she took off the rest of her clothes and remained standing there at the water's edge in the sharp grey light. That's not why I brought her here, he thought. But as he stood there in the cold water looking at her naked body, he knew that it would happen soon. Without realising, he had prepared himself for it. There were no barriers left to cross; he was there already. Can't be avoided, he said to himself.

He had a little towel in his rucksack. Handed it to her as she came tripping up on to the bank with small steps. To dry himself he used his vest.

After they had eaten the baguette and drunk some coffee, he said:
– You're still shivering. We need to warm you up.

A few drops of rain showed on the cloth. He pulled her to her feet.

– Five minutes, on the double, he ordered.

He set off running ahead of her, round the tarn and up the hill, and stopped to wait for her there. The drops of rain were bigger now, heavier. She cast an anxious look up into the trees.

– We'd better find somewhere to take cover, he said and took her by the hand.

The little shelter made of spruce branches was still there on the other side of the hill. At first glance everything looked to be much as it had been on his previous visit. Only the empty bottles were gone. He couldn't see the little book of Buddhist scriptures either.

– Is this where you live? she smiled.

He crawled inside.

– When the moon is full I sleep out in the forest, he answered and pulled her inside after him.

– Bed and everything! she exclaimed. – How did you know about this?

He held her close to him.

– Miriam, he said quietly. – I've tried everything. Not even cold showers help.

– Don't help a bit, she echoed.

– I just can't hold out any longer.

– Me neither.

He took off his jacket and vest, bunched them under her; she pulled her shorts off again, kept the little panties on. Pressed her forehead against his and looked into his eyes.

– Did you mean what you just said? That this is goodbye?

Her skin still smelled of the swampy water, mingled with sweat and damp earth and the sap from the pine branches of the roof. He pulled off her panties, noticing that he shook his head as though he were answering her. In the same instant he heard a crack from one of the branches. He twisted round and looked up. Glimpsed a shadow outside. And there, between the pine branches, an eye staring down at them. He tensed himself, pulled away from her and crawled to the entrance.

– What is it, Axel?

He saw no one, listened out among the trees. Then he stretched across the roof of the shelter. A hole had worn through the plastic between the branches; he could look down at her.

– Are you trying to scare me?

There was fear in her voice. And at that moment he saw himself standing there naked, bent over a shelter deep in the heart of the forest. Her fear acted like a signal to him and he reached his arm inside and picked up his clothes.

– It was nothing, he reassured her. – Probably just a bear or something.

It was drizzling as they walked back towards the bicycles. He took her by the hand. If anything more had happened there in the shelter, he thought, if the inevitable had taken place, then we could have been done with it. But now she's closer to me.

– Did I tell you I had a brother? he asked suddenly.

– A twin. You thought it was him your patient saw in the street the other day.

He took a few deep breaths before making up his mind.

– I thought I saw him too. The same morning as you started at the clinic.

He stopped and turned towards her.

– In a manner of speaking Brede didn't exist any more. But these last few weeks he's been cropping up in my thoughts the whole time. Now he won't disappear again. Just then, in that shelter, it was as though I saw him standing there peering down at us. I don't want to involve you in any of this . . .

She moved close to him, put both arms around him.

– I want to be involved. I love everything you tell me about yourself.

He started to walk on, but didn't let go of her.

– It must be twenty years since I last saw Brede. He'd just been thrown out of some dive in town; I happened to be passing by. He couldn't stand upright. I offered to walk him home. Or give him money for a taxi. He lay there on the pavement glaring up at me. *I want fucking nothing from you*, he was screaming. *One day I'll destroy you, the same way you destroyed me.*

22

CECILIE DAVIDSEN DIDN'T go home. She'd walked all the way from the hospital to Vindern. Now she kept on walking up the hill. It had turned dark. For several hours she wandered aimlessly. Ris, Slemdal, all the way up to Voksenåsen, down again to the pond at Holmendammen.

How many other doctors would have taken the trouble to knock on the door and tell her in person? Glenne was the type who cared. The fact that she was going to die mattered to him. *You're not to die, Mummy*. It was nine days ago now. He'd been different from the way he was in the office down in Bogstadveien. Actually she had wanted a female doctor. Or an elderly man. Axel Glenne was younger than her. And yet once she had got used to it, she realised how lucky she had been. He helped her to relax. He was tall and strong and able to deal with anything. But that day last week, when he'd come to her house, he had seemed unsure of himself. Almost confused. He'd come because he wanted to talk to her in person, face to face. He'd come to tell her she was going to die. She had known it. From the moment she realised that the lump had grown. Still she couldn't understand what he was doing standing at her door. Benedicte understood. Before she went to sleep that evening she had said: *You're not to die, Mummy.* And instead of replying, *No, darling, I'm not going to die, not for a long, long time*, she had started to cry. Benedicte did all she could to comfort her, but when Henrik returned home later that evening, she just sat on the sofa, staring, unable to speak. Not daring to speak. Because once she told him, it would be real. The truth of it would dawn on her.

She had been to the hospital that afternoon. Had a long talk with a nurse. Finally the surgeon arrived, the one who was going to do her operation. Are you Cecilie Davidsen? She would so liked to have answered no, told him he was looking for someone else. But there was no way out of it. He was friendly, obviously busy and yet he didn't hurry. But he too knew that it couldn't end well. He didn't say, *You're going to pull through.* He said, *We have to be realistic about this. We'll do everything we can, but the result is uncertain.*

He'd given her a sick note. She regretted agreeing to the idea. Going home to wait. All the thoughts with nowhere to put them. Every time she tried to drive them away, they swarmed over her. Haakon was eighteen. He would be all right. Benedicte was the one she had to think about. The rest of her childhood and all her adolescence without her mother. Would Henrik ask for a less demanding position at work? Would he find another job? Impossible to imagine. He'd ask his mother for help. She was still reasonably fit but didn't have the energy she once had. And he would ask his sister. He would send Benedicte to live there.

The thought of Benedicte growing up with Henrik's sister stopped her in her tracks and she had to support herself against a street lamp. Nausea welled up in her. What if Henrik found someone else? Anything would be better than having Benedicte grow up with her aunt.

She walked over to the wharf and stood there looking out over the dark water. She wanted to cry but couldn't. She hadn't cried since that first evening, when she sat on the edge of Benedicte's bed and stroked her hair. Footsteps in the gravel, away somewhere. Approaching. She couldn't face turning round.

23

Friday 12 October

RITA CALLED HIM at 3.15.

   – You remember I'm leaving early today, Axel?

He'd forgotten.

   – Hasn't Cecilie Davidsen come yet?

   – No, you've got no one waiting. The only one left now is Solveig Lundwall, three thirty.

   – Davidsen didn't call?

   – Not that I know of.

Axel sat there lost in thought. Cecilie Davidsen was due to be operated on at Ullevål hospital next Wednesday. He wanted to see her one last time before she was admitted. Was it because he had called at her home that she hadn't come? Forcing his way into her house with this news. He recalled the daughter's frightened eyes when she opened the door to him.

He shook these thoughts off and wandered out into the corridor. Rita had gone. Inger Beate too. The waiting room was empty. He had an idea and went into Ola's office. At this moment Ola would be at the helm of a sailing boat on his way across the Pacific. Or diving with his sons on a coral reef off the Fiji islands. Holding on tight to the shell of a giant turtle and being pulled along through the water. He'd be travelling for another six months. When Ola gave the best man's speech at Axel's wedding twenty-two years ago, he had said that they each had their own god, he and Axel. He made his offerings to Poseidon, while Axel followed Pan into the forests.

For the time being this was Miriam's office. He thought he could

105

pick up the faint scent of her, even though she hadn't been there for two days. He was attending a seminar after the weekend, and Inger Beate would be her supervisor for the last three days of her practical placement. When they'd parted at Frognerseter the previous day, neither of them had said anything. But Axel had made up his mind that it was the last time he would see her.

He sat down at the desk. Her stethoscope was in the middle drawer, and a couple of her textbooks. He opened one of them. She'd written her name in thick blue ink. He sat a while looking at it.

– You must be a very happy man, Axel, he muttered. – You've been given the lot. There is no more than this.

Beneath the second book he found a stuffed A4 envelope. She'd written her name on this too with the same pen. It wasn't sealed, and when he pulled out the flap he saw that it contained a pile of smaller envelopes. He still knew next to nothing about her, and didn't want to know any more than that either. It was what had enabled him to keep control. It was what made it possible for him to sit there and think that he would never see her again. Let it pass, let her fade away almost to invisibility, and life could go on as before. It was Friday afternoon. He was looking forward to the weekend. Saturday was training with Tom's football team, and Marlen's riding lesson. In the afternoon he was planning a trip to Larkollen. Lay up the boat for the winter. Paint the veranda of the summer cabin. He'd try to get Tom to go along with him. Maybe stay overnight, just the two of them. Apart from that, there was nothing that had to be done. Except paint a few skirting boards, he suddenly remembered, and change the fan belt in Bie's car.

He fumbled down inside the envelope, and was about to pull out the contents when he heard someone calling his name out in the corridor. He threw Miriam's things back into the drawer.

Solveig Lundwall was standing outside the door of his office.

– Hi, Axel, she said as she saw him approaching, and he could tell straight away that she was still not well.

He let her in, asked how the time in the secure wing had been. It had been painful. She'd been strapped down.

– Really? he exclaimed.

She gave him a dark look.

– Do you think I'm lying, Axel?

– Of course not, I'm just surprised.

She sat there in front of him in her dark blue polo-neck pullover and grey skirt, face a little drawn but nicely made up. It wasn't easy to imagine her screaming and foaming at the mouth in a restraining bed.

He checked her blood pressure and wrote out a prescription for her.

– These damn pills make me so fat, she complained. – I wish I could do without.

He could understand. Over the last year she'd put on something like ten kilos.

– Do you feel as though you're in control again, Solveig?

– I'm afraid of going to sleep, because that's when *those* thoughts come back.

– That you have to warn people about something?

– I can't get rid of the thought that something awful is about to happen. There are so many signs.

He ran his hand across his hair.

– But the meaning of signs is dependent on how they're interpreted, he said.

She sat there staring ahead into space.

– Last night I took the tram from Jernebanetorget. The man sitting beside me was reading *VG*. All that stuff about the woman eaten by a bear.

– She wasn't exactly eaten, he reassured her.

– As I was about to get off the tram, this old lady comes over to me. I think she's blind. Her eyes are as dull as pearls and still she's staring directly at me, and then she says, *You've heard it too, I can see it in your eyes*, and she hands me a little piece of paper. And I get so scared, despairing too, but mostly scared. *You have the power*, she whispers before I manage to get off.

Axel could see the pulse beating in her throat.

– What did it say on the piece of paper?

Solveig glanced around the office before answering:

– Rev. 11:7.

He thought for a moment.

– Does it have anything to do with the Bible?

She dug her hand into her bag, drew out a small book and began to flip through it.

– The Book of Revelation.

She found the place and read:

– *When they have finished their testimony, the beast that comes up out of the abyss will make war with them, and overcome them and kill them.*

– I wish old ladies like that would leave you alone, said Axel. Solveig ignored him.

– I've been thinking about it all night. This is a warning, Axel. A number of terrible events are about to take place, and if I, and perhaps a few others, have understood this, then I must deliver a warning. That is what the old woman wanted me to know.

She said it with conviction, and Axel realised he would have to call Ullevål hospital and voice his concern about yet another patient who had been discharged too soon. He knew he ought not to enquire any further. And yet he said:

– Last time you were here . . . You said you'd seen someone up by Majorstuehuset. Someone who looked like me.

She stared down at the floor. It looked as though she hadn't understood the question, and he was glad, at once regretting that he had asked it. Then she raised her eyes and looked at him.

– He hasn't appeared since then, Axel. But he's coming. Once all the evil has happened, he will return. I shall warn you. You will be the first to know, before all others.

As he was about to lock up the office, the phone rang. Not many people had his direct number. Miriam was one of them. An Oslo number showed up on the display. He picked up the receiver and spoke. A male voice at the other end introduced himself as Hendrik Davidsen, clearly accentuating the *d* in his first name.

– My wife is a patient of yours, he explained. – She had an appointment earlier today.

– That's right, Axel said. – Cecilie Davidsen. She never came.

– That's the reason I'm calling. No one has seen her. Not since yesterday afternoon.

Axel sat down in the chair.

– Really? Wasn't she supposed to be at the hospital yesterday for an examination?

– Yes. She left the hospital at quarter past four. There's been no sign of life from her since then. She's never done anything like this before.

Hendrik Davidsen's voice was calm and controlled, but Axel heard the break in it as he said 'sign of life'.

– You've informed the police, presumably?

– They've sent out a missing persons report on her. Not much else they can do. Not at the moment . . .

Axel chose not to ask what 'at the moment' might mean in a situation like this. He informed Davidsen of his wife's condition, but he was already familiar with it. Fortunately he made no mention of Axel's coming to the house with the results of her lab test. But he did ask how his wife had reacted to the news, and Axel was careful not to say anything that might increase his fears. There was still reason to hope that nothing untoward had happened to her. More reason to hope than believe.

24

THE COUPLE TRUDGING across the road by the entrance to Frogner swimming baths were deep into a juicy quarrel. The woman, who was small and round, with Rasta braids, stopped in the middle of the road. She wavered uncertainly on her high-heeled boots, as if she were trying to keep her balance on a pair of stilts.

– Then you can just go on your own, Jørgen, she snuffled. – I say fuck it if you're going to be like that.

A vehicle of some kind swung out from the car park. The man grabbed her by the arm and pulled her to the pavement on the other side. The car swerved around them.

– Bloody hell, Jørgen. I'm not coming with you unless you get yourself thorted out.

– You want me to get *thorted* out? he said, mocking her lisp. He was tall, thin, with a bent neck. – You were the one got us kicked out.

– You're so childish, she said.

He exhaled loudly.

– And where d'you think you're going if you don't come with me?

– What's it got to do with you?

– Fuck, Millie, you're nothing but a shagged-out whore. You've no idea how sick I am of you.

– Same to you. You don't understand *nothing*. Just look at yourself.

– Look at *me*? What's to look at me for?

She didn't answer. A moment later she said:

– Okay then, but get me a taxi.

– I ain't got no readies.

– Think I'm going to walk to Skøyen? In the middle of the night?
He belched. – Then you can sleep in the park.

She stopped in her tracks.

– I mean it, Jørgen, it's past two o'clock.

– It ain't *that* far. I've got a fix. After that you can sleep for the rest of the week.

She groaned, but let him guide her into the alley.

– I need to go to the toilet, she told him.

– Go ahead then.

He stopped and leaned up against a tree trunk, yelling after her as she disappeared down the slope: – You don't need to go half a mile away just to have a piss. There's no one around now, and even if there was, who'd stop just to get a look at your arse?

– Not having a piss, she muttered. – Big job.

– Christ, Millie, you really are fuckin' tasty.

He stood there peering out into the darkness. For an instant it felt as though the huge tree was holding him. He pressed his cheek against the rough bark. Could just make out the high diving board over the baths at the other end of the hollow. He'd jumped from the five-metre board the summer he turned nine. Or ten. He needed a fix. Maybe he'd screw Millie afterwards. If he felt up to it. But she'd have to wash first. Christ. How many women would squat down and do a shite in Frogner Park in the middle of the night? It was always the same with Millie: if she had to do something, didn't matter what it was, then it had to be done at once. No question of hanging on for five minutes.

Her scream was high and long drawn out. She often screamed, but never like this. His first thought was to get out of there. He couldn't take any more bother with that woman. But something in the scream held him, made him move a step or two closer to the slope.

– What's up? he shouted.

He could see her scrambling up the slope. He clambered down a couple of yards and held out his hand. Her jeans were round her thighs, her naked arse shining white in the darkness.

– What the fuck's up with you, Millie? he chided her, but his voice was shaking.

She reached the top and clung on to him.

– Down there, she sobbed. – Something lying down there. I touched it.

25

IT WAS 3.30. DETECTIVE Chief Inspector Hans Magnus Viken stuffed the rest of a slice of Madeira cake into his mouth as he ran a red light in Alexander Kielland's Place. He wasn't hungry, but when he was dragged out of bed in the middle of the night, he had to put something in his stomach to stave off the heartburn. Once it got started it would keep up all morning, sometimes even last the whole day.

As he drove, he got himself ready. Went through his thoughts systematically. What he would do once he reached the crime scene. What he would look for. He was good at that kind of thinking. Keeping a cool head when things got hectic. Because that was what was happening now, he thought as he swallowed the rest of the coffee he had bought at the service station along with the slice of cake. Things were hectic. The press was there, the officer in charge had reported. In force. What else could be expected? A corpse found in the middle of town, so to speak. Judging by the description, he thought it might be related to a missing persons report. The Crime Response Unit had rung on Thursday evening. A call had gone out for a woman who had failed to return to her home in Vindern. She was seriously ill and probably depressed. The family were afraid she might have harmed herself. On the face of it, not a criminal matter. But he had asked to be kept informed of all missing persons reports. After the find up in the marka, he wasn't the only one on edge.

A helicopter was circling above the park. It looked like *VG*, or one of the TV companies. He parked as close as he could to the road. The crowd was even worse than he had imagined. The two biggest newspapers naturally, but also two camera teams, one from

TV2, the other with no visible logo. He pushed his way through and stepped over the crime-scene tape stretched across the end of the car park. There were two stands there, microphones that could pick up conversations a hundred metres away.

– Is it the missing woman who's been found? someone shouted after him.

He raised both arms in dismissal as he walked on across the muddy grass. – All in due course, he grunted over his shoulder.

The first thing that struck him as he made his way down the slippery slope and saw the white-coated technicians moving slowly in the light from the lamps was that it looked as though a scene from a film was being shot. The sight of the twisted body lying among the dead nettles at the edge of the stream, with its face in the water, as though the last thing she had tried to do was crawl there to take a drink, reinforced the impression.

Nina Jebsen came over to him, handed him a pair of blue shoe covers. She was in uniform, he noticed, and her breath smelt of tobacco. A couple of weeks ago she'd announced that she'd finally managed to give up smoking.

– Cecilie Davidsen, said Viken, more as a statement of fact than a query.

– Looks pretty much like it. Hair colour and build are a match. And the clothes still on her fit with the description we have.

– Who found her?

– A couple on their way home. Dodgy types. They're being questioned at Majorstua.

– Any of our people there?

– Arve's in charge. Sigge'll be here before six o'clock.

Viken crossed to the body, shone his torch down. Parts of the back were exposed between the ragged edges of the torn jacket. A broad track consisting of five deep scratches ran from the ribs diagonally up across the neck.

– How the hell? he muttered to himself. – How the hell? His stomach started to churn. He patted his pockets, looking for an antacid, found nothing.

– They're frighteningly similar to the scratch marks on the woman up in the Nordmarka, Nina Jebsen commented from behind him.

He straightened up and took a couple of paces back, stepped into something sticky. He shone the beam downwards. Fresh faeces covered not only the plastic overshoes but also part of the tips of his shoes. He let out a string of curses and looked around for something to clean it off with.

– The technicians have found tracks, Nina Jebsen told him.

Her voice was so studiedly calm that he turned to look at her.

– Tracks?

She pointed in the direction of one of the white coats squatting by the stream a few metres away. The next moment Viken was at his side. The track in the mud was about the length of a child's foot, but much broader, and with clear signs of claw marks. He was no wildlife expert, but he was in no doubt that this track was like the one they had found up in the Nordmarka. He opened his mouth, but what he was about to say stuck in his throat.

The technician shone his torch along the edge of the stream.

– There are more tracks here. They seem to disappear into the water.

Viken's stomach had turned into a burning acid bubble bath. He peered up towards the top of the slope. Heard voices up there, a car starting, someone calling. Maybe they'd picked up what was being said down here with those directional mikes. The helicopter had dropped lower and was circling like a giant bird in the dark sky. He tried to imagine the reaction when news of what he now believed to be the case became known. There would be a storm. A tidal wave. He swallowed down the jet of heartburn that pulsed all the way up into his mouth.

26

By the time Nina Jebsen had finished making out her crime-scene report, the canteen was open. She would have time to pop up there and get a sandwich and a Bonaqua before the meeting began. She took her breakfast back down to the office she shared with Sigmundur Helgarsson. As usual, something or other had delayed him, and she was pleased enough to have the room to herself for a while. She removed the sandwich wrapping, picked up one of the pieces of bread and as best she could scraped off the mayonnaise. There was some left on the lettuce, but she didn't have time to take it to the toilet to wash it off.

As she munched away, she reread what she had typed. It was as though she only now realised what she had seen in Frogner Park the night before. She pushed the half-eaten sandwich to one side, took a few swigs of the mineral water with its sickly raspberry taste, opened *Aftenposten*'s net edition. Main headline: *Found murdered*. She knew this was just the beginning and opened VG Nett to get a better idea of what was in store. *Killer bear tracks in Oslo centre*. She gaped. The photograph had been taken from the helicopter and showed the crime scene by the water, the dead woman, the technicians in white, a figure that might have been herself. The press conference was going to be a lot of fun. It was due to start at ten o'clock. Agnes Finckenhagen and Viken would be there, and someone from the eighth floor, maybe the chief of police himself. Viken had made it clear that there would be *no mercy* for anyone found leaking information in the case. She had to smile at his phrase, like the title of some fifty-year-old Western, but there was no reason to suppose he didn't mean what he said. Viken wasn't as hard to get on with as some people claimed. He was like a reasonably complex machine; it was a question of finding out how it worked. She'd said something along these lines to Sigge Helgarsson one morning after he'd been hauled over the coals, but he didn't seem to share her view. A while back Sigge had started referring to Chief Inspector H. M. Viken as His Master's Voice, abbreviated in due course to just the Voice. Nina Jebsen thought it was a pretty appropriate nickname, but she didn't use it herself.

– We've got one hour before the section leader and I have to leave, Viken announced.

Nina fidgeted with the corner of the report lying in front of her. She thought it was comical, the formal way he always referred to Agnes Finckenhagen as 'section leader'. It was just six months ago that she'd been appointed to the post. There was not much doubt that Viken had been bypassed. A man with thirty years' experience in the job, with a recognised talent as an investigator. When he led a team, there were not many who would cross him, and certainly not those who wished to carry on working in the section. And if you were loyal, he would take you under his wing. It was a safe place to be for a newcomer; she wasn't the only one to have discovered that. He spoke out for them against the higher-ups; *loud and clear*, as he would say himself. And then they had gone and appointed an outsider as section leader. A woman ten years his junior, with little experience of crimes of violence. Viken had contented himself with the observation that it was amazing how far you could get with a few evening classes in Better Leadership at the Business Institute. Especially if you were a woman. And then he kept his mouth shut.

– Do you need to expand the group? asked Jarle Frøen, the police prosecutor who had been put in formal charge of the investigation. A joke, as long as it was Viken who was leading it. Frøen was regarded as one of the weakest of the lawyers. Maybe that was why Viken seemed so pleased to have him along, thought Nina. The lawyer was a tubby man with a pear-shaped head, along the sides of which a few reddish tufts still clung. He wasn't much older than her but looked more like someone in his mid-forties.

Viken seemed to be weighing the pros and cons before answering.

– Let's wait until we know what kinds of skills we're going to need.

– The woman last night, this Davidsen, do we have a cause of death for her? asked Arve Norbakk.

Viken looked over at Nina.

– Know anything about that, Nina?

– I spoke to the woman who's handling the case at the Pathological Institute, a Dr Finnerud . . .

– I think you mean Plåterud, Viken grinned.

Nina Jebsen felt herself going red.

– Correct. She's found a number of hypodermic needle marks on the arms and legs. They also have a provisional result from the blood tests.

– And you didn't tell us until now, Viken interrupted. – Did they find any trace of a narcotic called thiopental?

– Yes, they did.

Viken scratched his thick lower jaw. As usual he was wearing a freshly ironed white shirt. – We haven't told anyone that was what Hilde Paulsen was given an overdose of.

He looked around the table.

– Two women killed in exactly the same way. Let us make this assertion: the perpetrator is the same. Or perpetrators.

He gave them time to digest this. Then he asked:

– What about time of death?

– According to Plåterud, Davidsen had been dead for more than ten hours but less than twenty-four before she was found.

– Less than twenty-four hours, Viken repeated thoughtfully. – I will presume the animal tracks by the water were left at the same time as the body.

He swallowed the rest of his coffee.

– Outside these walls we're going to be as careful as fuck, pardon my French, Nina, you who are so young and unsullied.

She responded with a weary little shake of the head.

– But in here we can be as creative as we like. We damn well need to be. We know that Hilde Sofie Paulsen's body had marks on it indicating an attack by a bear. If we leave out Spitsbergen, then it's extremely rare for anyone to be threatened by a bear in Norway. But now we find a second victim, Cecilie Davidsen, with wounds remarkably similar to those we found on Paulsen, and animal tracks in Frogner Park that are practically identical to those we found up in the Nordmarka. Which of you supposes that a large brown bear is prowling the streets of central Oslo?

He bared his teeth. To Nina it was unclear whether he was smiling or imitating the imagined animal.

– We have to look at other possibilities here. Come on, Sigge, you grew up with polar bears as your next-door neighbours.

The Icelander gave a little laugh, though he obviously didn't think it was particularly funny.

– It might have escaped from somewhere.

– A bear sanctuary? The nearest one is in Hallingdal; that's over a hundred miles away. Think it took the bus?

Helgarsson rolled his eyes, but Nina saw that the corners of Agnes Finckenhagen's mouth were twitching.

– Some people keep animals illegally, she offered.

Viken clicked his tongue a few times.

– I've heard of boa constrictors in bedsits, even Amazonian lizards sticking their heads up out of the next-door neighbour's toilet bowl, but a bear in a bedroom? Any other suggestions? Arve, you know more about wildlife than the rest of us – can we rule out the possibility that there was a bear in Frogner Park, or can we not?

Arve Norbakk looked around, and to Nina it seemed his gaze rested on her a moment.

– Bears avoid people, he told them. – It's unthinkable it might make its way down into a town. Not on its own.

– What do you mean? Could somebody have brought it here and turned it loose?

Norbakk shrugged his shoulders.

– Either that, or the victim has been moved after being ripped by bear claws.

Viken nodded.

– The plaster that was found under Hilde Paulsen's nails might have come from a cellar. Maybe the body was taken out into the marka. But what about the tracks?

Arve Norbakk dotted his pen against a sheet of paper as though sending a signal in Morse code.

– I was wondering about that. The tracks have clearly been made by a bear's paw, but all of them look like marks made by hind paws. So the bear must have been walking upright the entire time.

– Like a circus act, Viken observed.

Norbakk permitted himself a smile.

– A bear will rise up on to its hind legs when faced with a potential danger, he said. – It does so to get a better overview and to pick up the scent of whatever's approaching. It can look as if it's dancing. But if it's going to attack or flee, it quickly gets back down on all fours. Another thing is that the pattern of movement seems odd. There are about twenty metres of tracks before they disappear into the water. But the two paws are much too close together. On top of that, there isn't a single track further down the bank, or on the other side. So where did the animal go?

The question was still hanging in the air when the meeting broke up a couple of minutes later.

Nina scrolled down through the list of witness statements on the subject of Paulsen's disappearance. She carefully read the account given by the man who found the body. Or rather, the man who owned the dog that found the body. Fifteen people had come forward to confirm that they had seen Paulsen in the marka on the day she disappeared. She noted the names down in her notebook. The last confirmed sighting was that made by a doctor, Axel Glenne, who had called them a few days later. She leaned back in her chair, thinking. Something had struck her. She looked out of the window, over the row of hazels and the rooftops down in Grønland. Something she'd read. Her computer had already gone into hibernation and she woke it up and scrolled through the names once again. Found the interview with Cecilie Davidsen's husband. He had attended at Majorstua police station to give his statement. He had raised the alarm after a couple of hours when his wife had failed to return from the hospital and didn't answer her phone. She had just been told she had cancer and would be operated on in a few days' time. The prospects weren't good. He was afraid she might be in shock. At last Nina found what she was looking for: Cecilie Davidsen's doctor. He had been a great help to her, according to the husband. His name was Axel Glenne.

27

IT HAD BEEN snowing since early morning. A total surprise to everyone, even the meteorologists, who had forecast rain.

Signy Bruseter stood on the steps in front of her house and looked out miserably across the fields sloping down towards the village. She didn't like the winter, it was too long already, and now here it was snowing heavily and only the middle of October. Her house lay at the end of a farm track, almost two kilometres from the main road. The farmer who did the snow-clearing for her was reliable, but suppose he was ill? Or if he couldn't get his tractor started and had to take it in for repairs? The thought of being snowed in here at the edge of the forest made her shiver, and she bitterly regretted ever having moved up here. She pulled the shawl tighter around herself, trotted across the yard and opened the garage door. She kept her winter tyres down at the petrol station in Åmoen; she knew the owner and he was always good to her and changed them at short notice. Now it was a question of how to get to the main road and then the seven kilometres to the Esso station.

Luckily the snow was fairly light and hadn't frozen hard yet. All the same, she drove in first gear all the way down. There was more on the news about the murders in Oslo. She couldn't bear hearing about them but couldn't stop herself either. No suspects as yet, they said, and interviewed a female officer. Fincken-something-or-other. *We're following up all the leads we've had so far, we're encouraging anyone who thinks they might be able to help to come forward.* Signy didn't like her voice; it was brittle. *Yes, we do believe it's likely that the two cases are connected. But neither of the victims was killed by a bear.* She sounded arrogant. *No, absolutely not. It would be meaningless under the circumstances to demand that southern Norway be a bear-free area.*

The news continued with a story about a car bomb in Iraq. Signy switched off and stared out at the white flakes that came streaming towards the windscreen. They're not in control, she complained to herself. They've no idea what to do. She'd been lying awake all night. She had hardly any coffee or bread left and hadn't had time to shop. She'd said yes to the offer of an extra shift. Mette Martin was always nice and cheerful, but she evidently expected Signy to cover whenever anyone was sick. That was the way it was when you lived on your own and had no one else to look after. These afternoon shifts were stupid; it meant she didn't get home until about eight, too late to bother making supper. She had a bowl of spinach soup she could heat up. She'd boil a couple of eggs to have with it.

Roger Åheim, who owned the petrol station, was a man Signy wouldn't hesitate to describe as 'warm hearted'. It turned out he was cousin to Åse Berit Nytorpet, whom she worked with at Reinkollen. He always gave Signy a little wink. Though he wasn't far off sixty, he was still a ladies' man. In fact, if what she heard was true, he'd just become a father again. Now, seeing how desperate she was, he put everything else to one side to fix her wheels for her so she could get about.

A young lad Signy knew from before she moved house took over from him behind the counter. Although he couldn't be that young, she thought; it must have been all of twenty years ago when she was his teacher at the primary school in Kongsvinger. Not that *that* was any kind of happy memory; he'd been a right little mischief. Smart enough when it suited him, but that wasn't very often. He was always playing truant, hanging out with boys five or six years older than him and drinking beer. When he went to secondary school, things turned really bad. He'd been in jail apparently, and now he'd ended up here. He was probably still struggling and didn't exactly look a picture of health with his shaven head and tattooed skull. But Signy was the kind of person who cared about people. Every now and then she called in at the petrol station, bought a few small things and had a chat with the lad.

But on this particular morning she sat on the battered sofa in the corner and nervously flipped through the newspaper as Roger Åheim jacked up the car and started work. The last murder victim had a daughter just eight years old. They'd found bear tracks everywhere, all around where she was lying.

Up here we've always had bears, Åse Berit Nytorpet had said a few days earlier when Signy showed her a picture of the first woman to be killed. *Maybe now they'll understand what it's like.*

But there was something else she'd said too, something Signy was still puzzling over.

Some people I know would be prepared to go pretty far to make people down there see sense. Might even drug a bear and drive it down to Oslomarka and let it out there.

– You're surely not saying you know someone who might've done something like that, Signy had protested.

I'm not saying anything. What I'm saying is, it's not out of the question that I know someone with strong views on this business.

That was what had kept Signy awake last night. On several occasions over the past week Åse Berit had hinted that she knew something about what was going on down there in Oslo. And then always that zip-fastener mime across the lips with the two fingers.

By the time Roger Åheim had got the last of the winter tyres on, Signy had made up her mind. She couldn't keep this to herself. She had to tell someone about it.

28

A POWERFULLY BUILT fair-haired man emerged from the lift on the ground floor at police headquarters and walked over to reception.

– Detective Sergeant Norbakk, he said and held out his hand. The handshake wasn't as firm as Axel Glenne had expected, judging by the upper-arm musculature. – Come with me, he added with a nod towards the lift door.

On the way up, Axel looked him over. The sergeant was wearing jeans and a T-shirt and was probably about thirty years old, although that thick curl hanging down over his forehead perhaps made him look younger than he was.

– Probably isn't easy for a doctor to get away from his office in the middle of the afternoon, he observed, most likely as a way of neutralising the tension that arises in a lift when two strange men are standing face to face.

– You're right there, Axel agreed with a friendly smile, though in fact he was attending a three-day seminar on lung disease. He thought better of asking why they had requested that they meet up in person rather than deal with it over the telephone. Actually, he could understand why. The previous evening a female officer had called him and told him who the murdered woman in Frogner Park was. Afterwards he'd spent half the night lying awake, and found it hard to follow what was being said at the seminar in the morning.

They came to a halt on the seventh floor.

– We're going over into the red zone, the sergeant told him.

Axel was led down a corridor with red-painted doors and linoleum in the same colour, with no explanation being offered for the significance of the colour-coding. Presently they came to a door that was slightly ajar. There was a nameplate on it with the sergeant's name. His first name was Arve, Axel registered. He was shown to a chair by the window in the cramped office. It looked out across Grønland and the Plaza Hotel, with Bjørvika and the opera house just visible on the left. The desk was tidy, a pile of documents next to a computer, a couple of copies of the legal code; the shelves were crammed with folders.

– The chief inspector will be here in a moment. Coffee?

Axel nodded and Norbakk disappeared, returning with a thermos and three cups.

– Sugar? Milk?

When Axel declined he said:

– Me too, I don't like junk in my coffee.

Just then the door opened. Axel gave a start and turned round. The man standing there was a little under medium height, wearing suit trousers and a white shirt with the sleeves rolled up. He was thinning on top, and thick grey eyebrows formed a bridge across the powerful crooked nose.

– Viken, he said, sitting down on the chair nearest the door without offering to shake hands. – You've already met Norbakk.

The conversation – Axel preferred to call it that, although *interview* sounded reasonable enough – went on for over an hour. An unnecessarily long time. He had planned to catch the 4.30 boat. It was his turn to make dinner. Marlen had her violin lesson. And he had planned to go over Tom's weekly homework with him, something he overlooked too often and that gave him a guilty conscience. But he was careful to give no indication of his impatience. Said what he was able to say about Cecilie Davidsen. He had never before been in the situation of being interviewed about a dead patient, and he decided to be open about her sickness. Yes, of course the diagnosis had come as a terrible shock to her. No, the prognosis had not been good. Possibly three years to live. It was the young sergeant, Norbakk, who asked about this. He looked up from the computer he was working at and observed Axel with calm, direct eyes. On those

occasions when he did speak, he kept it short and his voice was
relaxed, unlike the chief inspector, who sounded pressured and a
little hoarse. If he had to choose which one of the two to drink
a beer with, thought Axel, it would be Norbakk, no question about
it. As for the other one, Viken, there was an impenetrable sullenness
about him, and he seemed to exude something that filled Axel with
unease. When was the last time Axel had seen Davidsen? he wanted
to know. Axel gave him the date of the visit to her house. Was it
usual to go to patients' houses out of office hours? The chief inspector's delivery was patronising and insistent, but it was the penetrating
stare that irritated Axel most and brought on a sort of reluctance.
He spun it out a bit, didn't tell Viken how he'd stood outside
Davidsen's front door, how the daughter had opened up, the scared
way she'd looked at him. The messenger of death, was what he had
thought. Though not *this* death, the death he was being questioned
about now.

But most of the conversation was about Hilde Paulsen rather than
Cecilie Davidsen. How well had he known her? Did they work
closely together? Had he had any contact with her outside work?
Exactly where was it he had met her that afternoon? Had he met
anyone else? Axel forced his lips into a smile. He was a good observer.
He noticed things, big things, little things. But to remember every
detail of a bike ride nearly three weeks ago was asking a bit much.
He remembered a woman carrying a child in a back frame, three
or four people out jogging. Naturally the elderly couple out at the
Nordmarka chapel; he could give them a detailed description of the
woman's face if they wanted. A cyclist had raced past him, that was
near the chapel too. And after meeting Hilde Paulsen, a steady stream
of keep-fitters and walkers, with and without dogs, on their way to
and from Ullevålseter. Approaching Sognsvann, he'd met three
women in headscarves and long coats, probably Turks or Kurds.
One of them limped and looked as though she had problems with
her hip. Directly behind them a person he recognised from television. A former newsreader for NRK who now had his own talk
show on another channel and was what you might call a celebrity.

And in the car park by the lake, a cyclist with a child-trailer. It was dark by then, and he remembered thinking it was too late to be taking a child out into the forest. Why was he walking when he had the bicycle with him? He told them about the puncture in his rear tyre, then the run and the swim in the tarn. But nothing about the spruce shelter. He didn't know why. Only that the shelter made him think of Brede. Brede had no place in this conversation.

Where were you last Thursday afternoon? the chief inspector wanted to know. When he heard the answer, he observed drily:

– Well, well, the day of your weekly bike ride. And here was me thinking you doctors worked round the clock. Were you with anyone?

Axel had come to tell them what he knew about two women who had been murdered, not to defend anything he himself might have been up to in his private life. He thought it through quickly and came to the conclusion that Miriam had no place in this conversation either.

– No, he replied, and felt himself crossing a threshold as he lied to the chief inspector. – I was alone.

29

DETECTIVE CHIEF INSPECTOR Hans Magnus Viken piled the take-away cartons from China Dragon on to the plate and pushed it to one side as he clicked the remote control. There was a debate programme on TV2: *Should dangerous animals be allowed close to people's homes? What are the limits?* The murder cases weren't mentioned, but the programme was fuelled by the general uncertainty in the air. Viken switched to a travel channel. Pictures of a desert sunset. Looked like Morocco. He watched for a while before getting out the DVD he'd brought home from work with him. Only now did he have time to watch the whole of the Monday press conference, not just the few extracts he'd seen on NRK that same evening. It was useful to watch all TV appearances, which was why they were recorded and handed out to everyone taking part. Learning media skills was as important a part of the job as actual policing skills, they were constantly being told.

The Chief Superintendent led the conference, underlining how important the case had become. As usual he was decidedly pompous, sitting there with his dress uniform and his well-groomed hair, which Viken suspected he dyed to hide any traces of grey. He was rather like the smug chief of police in those children's books about Cardamom Town, and some of the younger officers even referred to him by the fictional chief's name – Bastian.

It was Finckenhagen who had asked Viken to join them. She was another one who just loved the limelight, he'd realised a long time ago. But this was so big that she obviously felt comfortable sharing it with him on this occasion. She didn't look too bad, he had to admit as he watched her taking over after the chief's introduction. Her summary of the case was adequate, and she dealt reasonably well with the questions. On a couple of occasions she handed them over to him. The contrast was evident. He was more concise, and more precise. The way people wanted their police to be, he thought.

The best bit of the press conference came at the end. There were Swedish and Danish journalists there, of course, but also French and Italian, and a team from German TV. No matter how many times they denied that a killer bear was on the rampage in the centre of a European capital, the case continued to attract worldwide attention. The bear prints, and the claw marks on the two dead women, were *gefundenes Fressen* for everyone who had news as their business, and the pictures had already been spread to all parts of the globe. After Finckenhagen had staggered her way through a couple of sentences in primitive English, Viken took over the show. About ten years earlier, he'd taken part in an exchange project and spent a year with the police force in Manchester, and he answered questions from the foreign media in fluent English. Even permitted himself a joke. *Of course, people do call Oslo 'the city of tigers', from the days when people thought it was a dangerous place to be wandering about in at night. But let me state categorically, once and for all: there are no tigers on the prowl here.* He had worked out the joke at the morning briefing, and it turned out to be a hit. Chuckles and grins from the journalists. The chief came up to him afterwards and shook his hand. *Good show, Viken.* A German journalist approached and asked if he could do an interview. As he sat watching the recording, Viken felt well pleased. One–nil, Finckenhagen, he noted, certain that she would have made the same observation.

He switched to NRK in time to catch the evening news. The bear murders, as they were inaccurately known, had been relegated to item number three. The same pictures from Nordmarka and Frogner Park were shown. Then an interview with the chief. Finckenhagen was being kept off stage after a bad mistake on the news the day before. She'd been naïve enough to respond to the proposal to declare southern Norway a bear-free zone. Everyone knew that the politician who had come up with the idea was an incorrigible drunkard who would do or say anything for another fifteen seconds of media fame. Finckenhagen fell for it, and people were saying the chief was not pleased with her. Two–nil, Viken nodded as he peeled a banana he'd bought from a 7-Eleven. They had a calming effect on the stomach, he'd discovered. Every bit as good as the pills his doctor prescribed for him. Despite saying there was nothing the matter with him, the guy still tried to get Viken to stuff himself full of chemicals. *Your stomach is just a touch oversensitive* was his idiotic diagnosis. And in an effort to be funny he added, citing a few crime novels he'd read: *Don't all detectives have upset stomachs?*

There wasn't much the chief could tell the press about the investigation, which made the packaging all the more important. They'd been good from the very beginning and so far no newspaper had commented that for such a dramatic case they seemed to have very little to go on. Was that right? They had backing all the way up the system. Top priority when it came to resources; Finckenhagen could pick and choose as she pleased. So far anyway. They had already received so many tips they had someone doing a rough sorting. And Jennifer Plåterud, the best pathologist Viken had worked with, was calling him daily, hardly able to hide her excitement at all the finds she was making on Cecilie Davidsen. She had been more deeply scratched than the first victim, not just on the back but also on her upper body and face. The same marks as of a hypodermic syringe appeared on her arms and legs. And there were no signs of sexual assault on her either.

The telephone rang. It was headquarters. A colleague from somewhere up in Hedmark wanted to get in touch with Viken. He took a note of the number and made the call. The man who answered introduced himself as Kjell Roar Storaker, sheriff in Åsnes county. Yes, Viken knew where that was, very close to the Swedish border.

– Sorry for ringing so late, it's probably not that important.

– Don't worry about it, Viken reassured him, without shifting his gaze from the TV screen.

– It's about these murders . . . this bear business.

Viken didn't think it was a very good idea to refer to it as the bear business, but he couldn't come up with anything better himself.

– We're getting so many strange calls, you know what people are like.

Viken knew only too well. They'd set up a dedicated phone line for the case. As a joke, he'd suggested they hire a psychiatrist too, since so many of the calls came from people who were clearly in need of that kind of help.

– We sort through them as best we can, the sheriff assured him. – We save you from the worst of it.

– Let's have it, Storaker.

– We received a letter yesterday. Anonymous. The writer says that he, or she, has reason to believe that people from up here might have caught a bear, driven it down to Oslomarka and released it.

Viken turned off the TV.

– Based on what?

– Hard to say. You know, there's a lot of talk of bears up here. Tempers can get heated very quickly. People in the countryside get angry when they feel they're being steamrollered by politicians and so-called environmentalists, the types who tell them they've just got to live with predators while they're miles away from it themselves . . .

– Do you see any reason to take the letter seriously? Viken interrupted him.

– Hm, there's a name mentioned, a woman who keeps sheep, along with her husband. We've had a look, and he has said things to the papers in a way that . . . Well, we don't think this is important. That some kind of activist group has been set up, we can't really see that.

– Fax it down here, we'll have a closer look at it.

Viken reached for the twelve-string guitar on its stand next to the sofa. Began playing a riff. The case was completely different from anything else he'd ever been involved in. Confusion had descended on the city. Even the journalists seemed to have given up their usual hunt for those responsible, in other words, for scapegoats. So far.

The riff he was playing began more and more to resemble the opening of 'Paint It Black'. They had been conducting interviews until late in the evening all week. There was a real danger of the wood drowning in trees. Viken was good at sifting stuff. There were a handful of witness statements that were especially interesting. The retired dentist who had found Paulsen turned out to have good powers of observation. The same could not be said of the two junkies who discovered Davidsen in Frogner Park. They couldn't agree about the vehicle they had seen pulling out of the car park. Was it big or small? Two different answers. Light or dark? A shouting match. Viken recalled what the woman said she'd been doing down the slope by the water. He grimaced at his foot, strummed two chords, the last one in A flat major, and put the guitar away.

He went out to the kitchen to brew more coffee. Knew that he would be sitting up until late. While he waited for enough drops to drip down through the filter paper to make another cup, he called Norbakk. With no apology for the late hour, he related the conversation he had had with the sheriff up in Åsnes.

– You know what it's like in places like that, Arve; d'you think there might be something in it?

He had expected the sergeant to burst out laughing, but he didn't.

– I know a lot of sheep farmers who are desperate, he answered. – Åsnes, did you say? Maybe not such a bad idea to take a trip up there.

– Well then that's settled, Viken said. He already knew who would get the job.

– While we're on it, Arve: that doctor we interviewed today, there was something about him.

– What do you mean?

– Nothing definite. A gut feeling. We'll have him in again in a few days' time.

As Viken was about to end the call, Norbakk said: – By the way, I've found something that might be interesting.

– Out with it then, the chief inspector urged him. He had absolutely no objection to discussing the case with his younger colleague, even if it was well past midnight.

– Those tracks around the victims were definitely made by a bear's paws. But we can't work out how a bear would be wandering around there. He paused.

– Don't keep me on tenterhooks, Viken complained.

– I did a search of stolen property and looked for animal-related things. On the fifth of October, that's to say, two days before Paulsen was found, there was a break-in at a gunsmith's in Lillestrøm. Only a few minor things were taken. But the thief did take a stuffed she-bear that was on a stand just inside the entrance.

– Give over, Arve, Viken protested. – You think we're looking for a killer who drives around with a stuffed bear in the boot of his car?

He heard Norbakk laughing.

– You don't need a whole bear to make a few tracks.

Viken's jaw worked as he thought this over.

– Good to know someone's doing his job, he said finally. – The bear prints are probably some sort of signature.

– Or they contain a message of some kind, Norbakk suggested. – The person who has done this is maybe trying to tell us something.

30

Wednesday 17 October

AFTER HAVING BEEN directed to Nytorpet Farm and established that there was no one home, Nina Jebsen again rang the Åsnes sheriff. He was very helpful and within a couple of minutes had called back with more information. He couldn't get hold of the farm owner, but his wife worked at a home for the mentally handicapped in Reinkollen. Nina groaned inwardly. As though she was supposed to know where *that* was. At the morning briefing, when Viken mentioned the tip that had come in from Åsnes, she hadn't been able to resist a few comments about the bear guerrillas and terrorism among the Hedmark farmers. Viken had responded with a wicked grin before telling her that she was going up there. An exercise in punishment, she'd thought, and swore to keep her mouth shut the next time.

For a girl from Bergen, the landscape in the east of the country could be summed up in one word: forest. And here in the border regions it seemed even thicker than elsewhere. She struggled against a sensation of being locked up inside it. No wonder people got depressed living in places like this, she sighed, without really knowing for sure whether there was any more depression here in the forest depths than there was over in the west. But where she came from, things changed all the time: the light, the smells, the moods, and your own moods with them. She even found herself missing the Bergen rain as she sped on between the rows of spruce with no view of the horizon in any direction.

The sheriff had given her detailed directions how to get to

Reinkollen, but somewhere or other she'd lost the way. She blamed it on her lack of the genes necessary for negotiating a jungle like this. At a village called Åmoen, she pulled in to an Esso station to ask for help. A man who looked to be in his mid-twenties stood lounging in the doorway to a back room. His head was shaven, with a tattoo that appeared to show two crossed swords standing out against the white of his skull. He glanced at her as she approached the counter, then turned and continued to stare at what was presumably a TV screen in the other room. After drumming her fingers and coughing a few times, she lost patience.

– Closed for the day? she said in a voice that startled the young man. He sloped over and scowled at her. Once she had explained her business, he picked up a map book, tossed it on to the counter, flipped through it and pointed.

– You drove past it three kilometres back, here. You can't miss the sign. Even the mongos and halfwits that live up there can find the way.

She stared at him in disbelief. Had to pull herself together as best she was able, but still couldn't resist.

– I see not *all* the halfwits live up there, she murmured.

On her way out she heard him mention a part of her anatomy he almost certainly wished he had himself.

The woman who opened the door to the home was grey haired and slightly built, with a scraggy turkey neck. She had a stoop, and her gaze flickered between Nina and the patrol car parked outside.

– What . . . what is it?

– Does Åse Berit Nytorpet work here?

The woman's jowls wobbled as she gave a slight nod. Nina showed her police ID.

– Nothing's wrong, she added as she saw the frightened look. – I'd just like to ask a few questions.

She was led into the main room. A person of indeterminate age sat in a wheelchair by a table. She was nothing but skin and bone, and her eyes rolled back and forth. A faint sound like a meowing came from her throat.

A tall, stoutly built woman in a knitted cardigan and skirt and wearing shaggy felt slippers stood up.

– Åse Berit Nytorpet?

– That's me, yes.

Nina again introduced herself.

– I'm here in connection with a case we hope you might be able to help us with.

The woman looked to be in her sixties. She wrinkled her brow and didn't seem much friendlier than the woman who'd let her in.

– Is there somewhere we can talk in private? It won't take long.

Åse Berit Nytorpet glanced over towards her companion.

– We can sit out in the kitchen, she decided. – Signy, will you see to Oswald? He could probably do with a little walk to the living room.

The stooping figure with the scrawny neck still looked terrified, and Nina repeated that it was just a few questions, a routine matter.

Out in the kitchen Åse Berit Nytorpet poured a cup of coffee and without a word put it down on the table in front of Nina, who said thank you as politely as she could and continued.

– We're working on a case you may have heard of. The two women found dead in Oslo?

Åse Berit Nytorpet's mouth tightened.

– I know we live out in the country, but we do manage to follow *some* of what's going on.

– Of course. I didn't mean it like that.

Nina sipped the coffee. Boiled, black as pitch.

– Good coffee, she said. – Any chance of a drop of milk in it?

She sloshed some of the brew into the sink to make room for the milk.

– There are rumours around here that someone may have captured a bear and released it in the Oslomarka.

Åse Berit Nytorpet opened her eyes wide.

– Have you come all the way out here to ask *me* about that?

– Why would I come just to ask you?

– Haven't the foggiest.

– Well, we received a tip suggesting that you know something about such a plan.

Åse Berit Nytorp got up from her chair.

– I don't believe you.

– It's the truth, all the same.

She remained standing, scowling at the policewoman.

– That I'm supposed to have something to do with it? Who in the blazes has said that?

– We receive tips. We're not always able to say where they come from. We have noticed that your husband made certain statements to the newspaper.

Nina took out a sheet of paper and unfolded it, a printout from *Glamdålen*'s web edition. Åse Berit Nytorpet took a quick look at it.

– My God, that was years ago . . . You don't actually believe my old man goes about the place trapping bears and sending them off to Oslo?

– I don't believe anything. But we have to look at every possibility, the likely as well as the unlikely. He does express the view here that *someone might just release a bear down there. Maybe it'll take something like that before they realise the seriousness of the position.*

Åse Berit Nytorpet interrupted her: – Have you any idea how much work goes into looking after the sheep? It's our life. Her eyes had darkened. – What do you think it's like to walk out across the pastures in the morning and find dead animals all over the place? No wonder people get upset.

Nina could understand that.

– When you've just arrived back home with a wagonload of dead sheep, you might well say things on the spur of the moment, know what I mean?

Nina agreed that it wasn't a crime for a person to voice their anger.

– Could I have a word with your husband? He wasn't up at the house.

Åse Berit Nytorpet tossed her head irritably.

– He's with my cousin, Roger Åheim.

– Where?

– At a cabin up past Rena. Won't be back down until this evening.

Nina was careful to preserve her polite tone. She didn't want to provoke the woman any more than was absolutely necessary.

– I'm going to give you a few dates and times, and I want you to think carefully before telling me where your husband was on those dates. As far as you're able.

When she came back into the main room, the other woman – Signy – was standing in the doorway to one of the rooms. Abruptly she backed out. Behind her a huge creature came into view. For a moment Nina Jebsen was unsure whether or not the situation was dangerous. The giant strode into the room and stood there glaring from one to the other. Then he took a step in her direction. She jumped. He raised his fist, pounded himself on the chest.

– Oswald get bear, he shouted, spittle drooling from his twisted mouth.

Åse Berit Nytorpet padded across and took him by the hand.

– Now you sit down, Oswald, she said in a honey-sweet voice as she led him over to the sofa.

She turned to the policewoman.

– It's about time you left. Oswald gets upset when strangers come visiting.

31

It was 12.15 when Axel, wearing his cycling gear, emerged from the clinic doors. He'd arranged to have an extra afternoon off that week. Felt like he needed it.

As he headed out into the yard, he heard someone calling his name. He turned. A woman almost as tall as he was, with shoulder-length blond hair, was following him.

– Axel Glenne? she repeated.

He could think of no reason to deny it. The woman said:

– Kaja Fredvold, journalist for *VG*.

She held out her hand, but Axel turned and took the stairs down to the basement door.

– I've tried to call you several times. I'm sure you know what it's about.

– I'm on my way out.

– Off for a run? the journalist asked.

He nodded curtly, unwilling to say anything that might prolong the conversation.

– I've got a couple of questions for you. I'm writing an article about these murders, the bear business . . .

Axel knew he ought to control the irritation he felt brewing inside him. He glanced at her. She was wearing a suit jacket, jeans and boots, and seemed in no doubt at all about her perfect right to pop up anywhere she liked and ask whatever she wanted to.

– I've got nothing to say. Nothing of interest.

– It's amazing what can actually be of interest, she said, giving him a conspiratorial wink, clearly making an effort to seem friendly.

– As far as I can gather, you were the last person to talk to Hilde Paulsen on the day she disappeared.

– Was I?

– And Cecilie Davidsen was one of your patients. We can have a cup of coffee at The Broker. Or something to eat, if you prefer.

Axel sprang up the three steps that led to the basement and stood in front of the journalist.

– Do I look as if I'm on my way to eat lunch?

– No, she smiled. She had an underbite, he noticed. – But it needn't take long. We can do it here if you like.

– Cecilie Davidsen had an eight-year-old daughter. Does it ever even occur to you what it must be like to lose your mother and instead get a picture of a corpse smeared all over the front pages every bloody day?

He was being unreasonable. He was saying things he should never have said. But his irritation had flared up and he could no longer contain it.

– Of course, said the journalist. – We think about these things all the time, but we have other considerations too. People have a right to know . . .

– Bullshit, hissed Axel.

He pulled himself together, managed to get the basement door unlocked.

– This is not necessarily the smartest way of dealing with things, he heard from behind him.

He remained standing down in the dark until he was able to breathe calmly again, still consumed by rage and with no idea where it had come from.

He abandoned the bike ride. An hour and a half later, he walked in through his own front door. Made some coffee and took it out on to the terrace. A cold wind blew up from the fjord. He pulled his jacket tight. Not the smartest way, he repeated to himself. The smartest thing would be to ring the journalist and apologise. Answer the questions politely and willingly, give her enough material for yet another big story. *You'll always do the right thing, Axel.* Call Miriam. Or go over there. Apologise to her for having crossed the limits. Abused his position. Tell her they must never meet again . . .

It wasn't Miriam he should be going to see, it was Brede. If it were even possible to find him. Make up for having betrayed the pact. For having shopped him. As though an apology would be enough. *I want fuck all from you.* They were identical twins; when they were small, it was impossible to tell them apart, until they spoke. Their mother had always said Brede's voice was different. Brede never asked, she maintained, he demanded. That wasn't right, Axel thought. Brede's voice was always full of something that was never allowed to come out. That no one could respond to. Brede was sacrificed, he thought. He had to be sacrificed so that Axel might get on in life. They were one, but something had gone wrong and made them into two, and of the two of them, only one could have a life.

Could he have prevented it? If he hadn't said anything . . . He was fifteen years old when Brede was sent away. Brede had given up playing at being a Resistance saboteur fleeing for the safety of the Swedish border. Now he played Nazi games with the younger kids in the neighbourhood. He was the leader. Called himself HHH: Hitler, Himmler and Heydrich all rolled into one. The kids would arrive home in the evening with swastikas painted in black tar on their chests and refuse to say what they had been up to. Not even when they were caught in the forest near Svennerud, half naked and frenzied, with Brede in the middle waving one of Colonel Glenne's pistols about, did any of them dare to tell on him. But that wasn't when he was sent away. It was later that summer. *That's why I'm asking you, Axel. And I'm only going to ask you once.*

Axel pottered about in the kitchen. Still an hour before Bie was due home with Marlen. He opened the bread bin; there was only a crust left, and he remembered he had promised to shop on his way home. As he was about to take a look in the fridge, his mobile phone rang.

He didn't recognise the number, had no desire to talk to anybody, but steeled himself and took the call.

– Is everything all right, Axel?

He recognised Solveig Lundwall's voice. She had only ever rung him at home once before. It was not a good sign.

– How are you? he said, trying to divert her.

– You must deal with Per Olav, she insisted. – He's drinking even more than before. Litres of it. I know you've told him he should cut down, but he doesn't listen. Just swills it down the moment he gets inside the door. The kids too, but mostly Per Olav. He's up in the night and drinking that damn milk. In the morning it's all gone. I can't put up with it for much longer.

He let her carry on, and when she stopped to draw breath he interjected.

– I'll have a word with Per Olav, Solveig. Make an appointment for him.

She was the one in urgent need of an appointment, and he was about to suggest the following day when she said: – I've seen him. The person you were asking about last time.

– Was I asking about someone?

– You asked if I'd seen that person who looks like you. I saw him. I followed him. No one else knows about him. But the time is near now. You know it too, Axel. The time is near.

– You followed him, you say? Axel responded, wondering whether he ought to contact the hospital straight away.

She didn't reply for a few seconds.

– I'm calling to give you a warning, Axel Glenne.

– It's good of you to worry about me . . .

– Good? This is not good. You must listen to me, not just babble on and always know best.

– I am listening, Solveig.

– Yesterday, she began. – I saw you again yesterday. On the Underground.

He hadn't used the Underground yesterday but didn't interrupt her.

– It was your face, your eyes, your hands. You had long hair and a beard and looked like a tramp, just like that time I saw you at Majorstuehuset. I know you do it so that no one will recognise you, Axel Glenne, not until the right time comes. But I recognised you.

– Where did you say this was?

– On the Underground.

– Which line?

– Frognerseteren. You sat looking out of the window. But it was as though you could see me reflected in the glass. It was creepy, but nice too. It was a church holiday. I meant to get off at Ris, but I couldn't get up from my seat, had to sit there as long as you wanted me to. All the way to the terminus. You got out there and disappeared in the direction of the forest. Understand?

– No, Solveig, I don't understand.

– Then you turned round, and I *wanted* to follow you, I want you to know that, but I couldn't, not yet. And I know Cecilie Davidsen was killed because she was your patient.

She lowered her voice.

– You're the one they're after, Axel. They're after you because you have Jesus in you. You're dangerous to them.

32

HE SWUNG THE car into a parking space along Helgesens gate and turned off the engine. Leaning forward, he could see the window of the attic flat. There was a light on. He still hadn't made the decision to actually go up there. He could turn, head back home, do the shopping on the way as he'd promised. Bie had reminded him of what they needed: bread, mince, toilet paper. The rest he would have to think of himself. Milk, he thought, recalling the conversation with Solveig Lundwall. It wasn't a delusion, what she'd seen on the Underground. It was the interpretation that was psychotic, not the fact that she'd seen someone who looked exactly like him. Is that why you're sitting here, Axel? he thought.

It was 4.30 when he got out of the car. It had been a week since he last saw Miriam. It took her less than ten seconds to open up after he rang the bell. He slipped inside and elbowed the door shut behind him. Without a word she wrapped her arms around him and held him tight.

She leaned towards him and poured him an espresso. She'd been at the gym and was still wearing the white jogging pants and the vest with *Miriam* written across the chest in glittering letters.

The doorbell rang. She gave a startled jump, then disappeared out into the hall, closing the door behind her. He could hear her voice out there, interrupted by another female voice, hoarser and rougher.

He got up and peered into the alcove. There was room for two in the bed, but only a single duvet. Above the bedhead a shelf with bedtime reading: a textbook on orthopaedic surgery, and a few titles in her own language. Next to them a picture of a man about Axel's own age. He was wearing a white uniform. Looked like some kind of naval officer.

When she returned a few minutes later, he was once again seated on the sofa.

– The woman who lives under me, she explained. – She needs someone to talk to. I had to tell her I had a visitor. I'll call in and see her tomorrow, before I go to my lecture.

– Doesn't she have a job to go to?

Miriam was standing in front of him. He picked up the smell of her, thought how a smell could paralyse you.

– Typical doctor's question, she said teasingly. – Do you have a job? Are you on social security?

He could have reached out his hand, let it glide down her back, down to the elastic on her trousers. It was painful to resist.

– You're afraid of being a *typical* doctor, he told her.

– Anita has a doctor who doesn't do enough to help her. He thinks of her as a case.

– Anita, that's the neighbour?

Miriam nodded.

– She's had it rough. Was alone with Victoria and had to work all the time just to make ends meet. Two years ago, someone from the child protection agency turned up and sat with her for a couple of hours. She had no idea what they wanted. A week later they came back and took Victoria.

– I'm sure they must have given the matter a lot of thought.

It was still possible to talk about something, about the neighbour, about anything at all. When the moment came when neither of them said anything else, that was when it would happen.

– They had no reason to do it, Miriam protested. – Someone at the nursery school claimed that Victoria never had any warm clothes on and always seemed hungry. And so off they went. Anita did used to take drugs, but she's been clean ever since Victoria was born.

– Are you certain about that?

– Why would she lie to me?

He had nothing else to say. Took her by the arm and pulled her down on to the sofa.

– How long can you stay, Axel?

She'd taken the slides out of her hair and it flowed down her back. He lifted it to one side and pressed his nose against the nape of her neck. He couldn't stay.

Someone bending over him, staring down into his face. He turns away. Miriam is standing on the bank of the tarn. As he walks over to put his arms around her naked body, she starts to wade out. He follows. The tarn expands until it fills the horizon. Then she dives forward and disappears beneath the water.

He woke up. *What do you want from me, Miriam?* It was quiet in the room. It was morning: 5.30. Daylight coming in from the ceiling window. He'd been sleeping for three and a half hours. He felt rested. He sniffed down from her shoulder to her armpit. The sweat was acrid, herb-like. She lay with her back to him, her hand still around his genitals, and when he removed it she felt for them again, as though unwilling to let go. He pulled one of her arse cheeks aside and wriggled his way in between her thighs.

– What are you doing? she murmured, half asleep, and drew her knee up under her. He had to take hold of it and lift it before he could slip inside her. Then he just lay there, not moving.

– Aren't you asleep? he whispered in her ear as she began to move her backside against his stomach.

– Yes, she grunted. – Don't wake me.

He put a spoonful of strawberry jam on the crispbread, took a mouthful of coffee.

– Axel, she called from the sleeping alcove. – What did you do with my vest?

He finished chewing and swallowed.

– The one with your name on in red glitter? I've taken it. Need something to remind me of you.

The next moment she was standing in the doorway with a towel round her.

– I mean it, I can't find it.

He realised that he was tapping his ring against the coffee cup.

Last time I saw it, you were using it to dry yourself with. Removing any last traces of me.

– I left it on the floor in the alcove; it isn't there any more.

– Were you going to wear it today? With all those stains?

– You idiot, she scolded him. She came over to the table, put her arms around him and slid down on to his lap. – Do you have to go?

– Soon.

She leaned back and looked into his eyes.

– Will you come back?

On his way down the crooked and uneven staircase, he stopped outside the door of the downstairs flat. Miriam had been so upset that the neighbour's daughter wasn't allowed to live there any more. And the memory of that led him to thoughts of his own family. He'd sent a text to Bie. Explained that he'd been asked to cover for someone in Oslo. It was something that happened now and then. *OK*, she'd answered. Just those two letters. He read the hand-painted ceramic nameplate on the neighbour's door: *Anita and Victoria Elvestrand live here*. It struck him that it would always hang there, regardless of whether the words written on it were true or not.

Out on the pavement he stood a moment and inhaled the October air that rushed towards him, dense with cool exhaust fumes. He glanced up at Miriam's window on the fifth floor. Up at the grey-black sky above the rooftops. It was Thursday morning. As he walked towards where his car was parked, he thought: Tonight I must talk to Bie.

THAT SOUND YOU *just heard was yourself sleeping. It's Thursday morning. The time is 6.30. I'm sitting here with the morning paper and a cup of coffee. Like any average person who's got up early and is about to set off for work. It was no more than three hours ago that I made this recording of you. Both of you. Played it back to myself lots of times while I've been sitting here. You've probably got up too. You're tired because you slept badly last night. Lay there muttering and tossing and turning. Your bad conscience getting to you. That would be just like you. Tons of stuff in the papers about the woman they found in Frogner Park. I can just see your face when you found out who it was. The unease that makes you curdle inside. You still don't know what this is about. But you hear a sound in the distance and it's beginning to dawn on you that it's coming closer. You're a good listener. Which makes what you did even worse. There's no way back now. No way back for me either after what I did back then. But now I've done something a lot worse, so it doesn't matter any more.*

She was different from the first one. It took a while for her to get scared. She seemed indifferent when she woke up and found herself taped up. Asked what I wanted with her. I told her straight away. She didn't believe me. Mocked me and tried to make fun of me. But when we got there and I showed her what I had in mind, then she turned into a little child, just like the first one. Emptied all her orifices. Began to scream, too. I let her carry on until she was all screamed out. Then I told her when it was going to happen so she'd know exactly how much time she had left. By the time you hear this, I'll have told you the same thing. How many hours and minutes before it happens.

I lay beside her all through that first night. Removed her stinking clothes. Didn't touch her. Lay there in a semi-doze. Glanced at her now and then. I'd wrapped her in a woollen blanket so she wouldn't get cold. Gave her water too. She wouldn't have any food. She calmed down with me lying there. Started talking. That she was ill and going to have an operation. That she had a child. An eight-year-old daughter who was

149

afraid to sleep alone. Would I let her go so she could get home and tuck in her daughter, who was lying in bed afraid? For a while I let her believe I would. Dried round her mouth with a damp cloth and stroked her cheek. And when she realised I was lying, she began to wail again. But she wasn't angry. I could lie with my face pressed right up against her neck. She wanted me to.

I've killed twice. And still it's not your turn yet. I've chosen the next one. The day has been appointed. I know already how I'm going to get her to come along with me. Know where she'll be found. You'll find her. But not everything will be planned beforehand. I don't like things to be too neat. Chance has to be allowed to play its part. Things can go wrong. And if I'm caught, you'll get away.

PART III

33

Thursday 18 October

NINA JEBSEN WAS at the office by about 7.30. There was a memo
she wanted to have ready for the morning briefing, and a couple of
witnesses she still had to contact, including the former NRK news-
caster who was on the list of people observed on the way to
Ullevålseter on the day Hilde Paulsen disappeared.

Once again she had to give up the attempt to get through to the
TV celebrity. A secretary in the firm he was working for now claimed
he was on holiday in Tanzania. The last time she'd tried, the day
before, she'd been given a different explanation for why the man
wasn't there. Not that it surprised her: the person she was trying to
get hold of belonged to that exclusive group of people who had
acquired the right to be inaccessible, and made use of it.

The trip up to Åsnes in Hedmark the day before hadn't resulted
in much, but Viken might well ask for an account of even insigni-
ficant details and give her a hard time if she couldn't provide it.
She'd be able to describe a visit to the mongoloids at the care home.
The conversation with the bitter old woman over a cup of even
more bitter coffee. Before concluding her memo on the visit to
Reinkollen, she opened the STRASAK database of convicted felons,
ran a search for Roger Åheim, and came up with a hit. He owned
a farm and also ran an Esso station at Åmoen in Åsnes county. In
other words, the place where she'd asked for directions to Reinkollen.
She recalled with distaste the young lout behind the counter, who'd
confirmed every one of her prejudices about backwoods Norway.
She checked the notes and discovered that the owner of the petrol

station had to be the cousin whom Åse Berit Nytorpet's husband had been out with.

She bent closer to the monitor, swiped the page and a list of criminal convictions appeared on the screen. Fifteen years previously this same Roger Åheim had served time for inflicting grievous bodily harm. Lower down the list she found two charges of rape. One was dismissed on the grounds of insufficient evidence. In the other, eleven years ago, a nineteen-year-old woman alleged that she had been abducted by the accused. She'd sustained slight injuries to her face and upper body. Roger Åheim claimed that the girl had gone with him of her own free will. It was one person's word against another and the charge was dropped. Nina scrolled down further and came across a conviction from eight years ago on an environmental charge. Illegal lynx hunting. Roger Åheim insisted he had acted in self-defence, but no one believed he had been attacked by one of these notoriously timid creatures. He had also changed his story several times in the course of the trial.

She heard Viken letting himself into his office. Waited a couple of minutes before knocking and showing him the documents she had printed out from STRASAK. He sat there for a while, his head moving from side to side, the deep furrow prominent over the bridge of his nose. He pulled at his jawline, smoothing out the wrinkles on his cheeks. Presently he said:

– I'll give the sheriff up there a call. He sounds like an okay sort of bloke.

Five minutes later he popped his head round her door.

– Prepare for another trip out into the bush. We'll leave straight after the morning briefing.

Heading north along the E6, she wondered what it was that had persuaded Viken to set aside yet another half-day in following up such a vague lead. He could have left it to the local sheriff's office to take care of. It was becoming more and more obvious to her that Viken was the type who was rarely satisfied with work done by others. A lone wolf who only delegated jobs with reluctance. Not very efficient, she thought, even if the man did have an enormous capacity for work. And why bring her along, and use up a whole day's man-hours? Not that she minded working with him; she handled it better than most of the other detectives. Some, like Sigge Helgarsson, avoided Viken like the plague. No wonder really: Viken had a go at him every chance he got. It was obvious he preferred having Arve Norbakk along when possible. And Arve knew the countryside up there in Hedmark. But today Viken had chosen Nina, and she didn't bother trying to work·out the possible reasons why.

– What are you expecting to get out of this trip? she took a chance and asked.

Viken was a surprisingly careful driver. He was wearing a pair of pilot sunglasses, which he'd taken from the glove compartment, and was sitting back and taking in the open Romerike landscape.

– Not exactly a breakthrough, he said, and didn't sound worried. – Even if this Roger Åheim has been involved in some pretty violent stuff. And the environmental crimes.

She didn't ask why, in that case, they should be spending half a day on it, but he seemed to guess what was on her mind.

– Often you find it's the detours that lead you to the solutions in difficult cases, he told her.

Nina needed a smoke. She sat there trying to summon up the voice of the psychologist who had led the course on how to give up.

– We're struggling because we can't see a motive, she said.

Viken glanced over at her.

– And how often do you find an obvious motive in murder cases?

She thought about it.

– It depends what you mean by motive.

Viken said: – Before I started in Violent Crimes, I worked on white-collar crime. An accountant embezzles money to pay for a holiday home in Spain. An impatient broker doubles his fortune by selling insider information. Clear chain of connection between motive and deed, a calculated risk, possible to work it all out in terms of cost and benefit. But in my twenty years with Violent Crimes, I don't think I've come across a single case of murder where the motive has been easy to understand. And certainly not where it's premeditated.

Several times over the past few weeks Nina had been struck by how unaffected he appeared to be by the gruesome nature of the case they were investigating. This ability to observe things from a distance was probably what made him a top detective.

– The last murder case in Manchester I was involved in was back in '98. The Shipman case.

– That doctor who killed huge numbers of his patients?

– It might have been fifteen or two hundred and fifty, or twice that many, we'll never know. As you'll remember, he hanged himself in jail. So we'll never know either what turned him into a mass killer, even if they write a mile of books about him. There were just a couple of cases where there was even a hint of financial gain in it for him. To understand what drives a man like that, you have to look at the psychological profile.

Not many of his colleagues in Violent Crimes had turned up to hear Viken when he lectured on this subject, but Nina had. Now he glanced at her as though trying to see whether she understood what he was talking about.

– He was probably damaged early on in life, she offered, a little reluctantly. – Abuse of some kind, and then later an extreme need to manipulate the facts of life and death. The control of intolerable pain by inducing it in another.

– That's all very well, he nodded. – Shipman ticked every box. And yet what he did remains incomprehensible. There's something at the heart of every killing that evades any attempt to explain it. If you get too obsessed by motive, you'll often find yourself going astray.

Nina sat back in her seat. Covertly she studied the chief inspector's hands. Not exactly nice, she thought, but fascinating. Narrow and bony, with unusually long fingers.

– So that's why we're on our way to the forests of darkest Hedmark, she said, trying to neutralise the irony with a slightly sing-song childish voice.

Viken burst out laughing. He laughed for a long time – she

couldn't remember ever hearing him laugh so long before – and she felt relieved, and perhaps even a touch of pride too, at having been responsible for it.

– I think maybe you do get the point, he said, the laughter stopping abruptly.

Nina thought about it.

– So you're saying we shouldn't be looking for motives.

– I'm saying that shouldn't be what dominates the investigation in a case like this. Something will start to add up after a while. But never everything. Not even after a full confession and sessions with the shrinks. Especially not then.

– All the same, you sound optimistic, she said.

He drove faster, even though they had left the motorway and were now on a road with only two lanes.

– I don't doubt for a moment that we're going to solve this case, Jebsen. We're hunting a killer who has already told us a lot about who he is. The question is, can we get to him before anything else happens?

A few kilometres past Åmoen, they saw a sign for Åheim. They pulled off the main road and headed north through forest.

– Do you think people are influenced by the landscape they grow up in? Nina wondered aloud, peering at the thick lanes of pine.

Viken seemed to have no special view on the matter. They passed a left turn-off, and he glanced at it before driving on. He had just spoken to the sheriff at Åsnes and been given a detailed description of the route. The sheriff had offered to come along with them, but Viken had rejected the idea. As he explained later, he didn't want local people hanging around while he was working; it would be more of a hindrance than a help.

– I could never live in a place like this, said Nina abruptly. – I'd get claustrophobia after about ten minutes.

Viken ignored her.

– To find the person who's committed these murders, we have to put ourselves in his shoes, he said. – It's not enough to proceed analytically. You've got to take a leap away from your own common sense and morality. Get in tune with that part of yourself that makes it possible for you to follow a human being who doesn't think like a human being.

Nina had heard him say this before, but it had never been clear to her how this could be turned into a method.

– Animals aren't bestial, Viken went on. – An animal can't act like a monster. Only human beings can do that. Anyone who plans a murder has this inside him. It is deviant, but both you and I can find something inside ourselves that enables us to follow this kind of thinking.

– Are you sure we're on the right road? Nina asked. – Surely there can't be a farm this deep in the primeval forest?

– Guess we just have to trust the sheriff, said Viken as he took a right and swung on to an even narrower lane. His lecture continued unabated. – Every murder that has been planned has its own signature. That is the gateway to the sick mind behind it.

– So these bear tracks then, said Nina, increasingly certain that the chief inspector had got the directions wrong.

– And the way the body has been disfigured. As though by a predator. If you combine all the signals from the killer, you can draw a picture of him. It's not too hard. It's harder to get to know the primitive instinct in yourself that makes it possible for you to get inside his skin. See the world through his eyes, move like him, think like him. If you can do that, then you're breathing right down his neck.

Nina glanced again at the dials. They'd driven more than five kilometres now since the last turn-off. It didn't seem to worry Viken.

– From the moment I stood up there in the trees of the Oslomarka and looked down at that dead woman in the gully, I've been working on a profile of him. I can tell you that the man we're looking for is in his thirties, possibly early forties. He is above average intelligence and not necessarily a loner. If he has a family, then he's living a double life, probably has a split personality. He may be educated and hold down a good job. He has not killed before but he has, I would think, a history of abusing women in one way or another. The disfiguring of the victims indicates that. The anger he feels towards these women. He's had a difficult upbringing with a domineering and emotionally cold mother. He feels no regret for what he has done; satisfaction is more likely, and he is capable of killing again.

The forest seemed to be closing ever more tightly around them, and the track became more and more bumpy and rocky. Nina thought briefly of her father, a stubborn old brewery worker who would never ask for directions, and definitely not when he had lost his way. They rounded a sharp bend; beyond it there was a steep rise. There was a barrier at the top of it. Viken sat glaring at it for a few seconds before jumping out and tugging at the padlock.

– Locked, he confirmed, and wiped the mud off his shoes before getting back into the car. – That monkey of a sheriff must have given me the wrong directions.

Nina risked a joke.

– I don't know what to think of you, taking a woman for a ride down a deserted forest track.

Viken wasn't in the mood for it; he was busy trying to worm the car back down the slippery narrow hill. Beyond the bend he had to reverse another several hundred metres before finding a place to turn.

So much for the well-refined instinct, thought Nina, but decided against sharing the observation with the chief inspector. It occurred to her that the investigation might have something in common with this futile trip of theirs.

34

As VIKEN PULLED into the Esso station at Åmoen, he was feeling a little annoyed. He called Sheriff Storaker again but went no further than to say that the route description had not been accurate. It didn't make his mood any better when Storaker insisted that it had been, nor when Storaker then insisted that he would come along to show them the way in person.

– I'll be at Åmoen within fifteen minutes, he assured them. In fact it took seventeen and a half minutes, as Viken pointed out irritably when he did finally turn up.

It would be short-selling him to describe Sheriff Kjell Roar Storaker as a big man. He walked around with his head permanently bent even when there was nothing in the vicinity even remotely at head height, as there wasn't in the car park beside the Esso station. Viken guessed it was doubtless as a result of innumerable encounters with roof beams and door frames. The hand the sheriff offered him was the size of a frying pan.

– Roger Åheim, the man we're looking for, is the owner of the petrol station, he told them.

Viken nodded abruptly. Nina Jebsen had told him this some time ago.

– That's no help to us. The guy isn't here.

Nevertheless the sheriff suggested a cup of coffee and a bun from the counter. Viken couldn't afford to waste any more time and as politely as he could declined the offer, though it was obvious Jebsen was hoping for something to eat. Do her good to wait, he thought with satisfaction as he sat himself behind the wheel. He offered her a sugar-free salt pastille.

As he started the car, she pointed to a male figure emerging from the door of the petrol station, a lanky guy with a shaven head and wearing red overalls covered with paint stains. He started filling the newspaper stands outside the door.

– If you want somebody that gives you the creeps, just have a word with that specimen there.

Viken glanced at her. – You know him?

She started talking about her previous visit, something about this lout here who worked behind the counter, seemed like a complete maniac and immediately picked a quarrel with her, a total stranger. Viken listened with only half an ear.

As they once again turned off at the sign for Åheim, Viken kept close behind the Volvo driven by the sheriff and one of his men. The weekend was approaching, and they were clearly short handed up here, but Storaker seemed happy enough to add another call-out to the budget. It was probably not every day they got the chance to take part in a murder inquiry.

They turned off at the first left. The sheriff never said anything about that, fumed Viken. That was why they had ended up deep in the forest. Wasted almost an hour through his carelessness. He swore and punched the wheel with his fist. Nina said nothing. Just then his mobile phone rang. He put in his earpiece. The woman at the other end forgot to say who she was, but that broad Australian accent was identification enough. People who didn't know the pathologist sometimes wondered if Jennifer Plåterud was American, a suspicion she denied strenuously every time she was confronted with it.

– We haven't found much biological material on Cecilie Davidsen, she told him. – So far everything we've got looks as if it comes either from her or from members of her family.

– In other words, a perpetrator who knows what he's doing, Viken observed.

– However, what we *have* found is dust and traces of plaster beneath the fingernails, and on the clothes.

She was silent for a moment before continuing.

– Most likely the same type of plaster we found on the first victim, Hilde Paulsen. It turns out to be a mixture not much used over the past sixty or seventy years, a high calcium content with added clay. If it was just one of the victims we might think it was a random find. But not when it turns up on both of them.

– That's good, Viken exclaimed. – How about those rips and tears?

– We heard back from Edmonton. They compared our pictures with those from their own archives, including people who have been attacked by bears. They say they're the same.

Viken swerved round a pothole in the road.

– We're asking ourselves if these wounds might have been made by paws cut from a stuffed bear, he said. – In which case, part of the killer's signature, or message if you like. Think that's a possibility?

– Severed bear paws? Well, I'll take a closer look. She added with a little laugh: – Not because I think a dead bear can scratch. At least not that hard.

Viken told Nina what the pathologist had found.

– It shows we're right, she said eagerly. – The victims were dumped where we found them. Both women were probably killed in a cellar.

– In a house built before the war, Viken added. – Or a cabin. It has to be somewhere where people can be kept prisoner for days without anyone finding out.

At last they came to a break in the dense forest, and spied a few patches of cultivated ground. They took another turn off the road and then up towards a farm on the brow of the forest. It consisted of a fairly large barn, the farmhouse itself, and an outhouse. All the buildings looked to be freshly painted. There was a white Mercedes parked outside the outhouse, next to a tractor hooked up to a trailer full of huge plastic containers. Another car was parked behind the garage, a second Mercedes, but this one older and lacking registration plates. Smoke drifted from the chimney of the house.

The sheriff and his assistant had jumped out and stood waiting as Viken and Jebsen walked over.

– Tried to call ahead, Storaker told them. – That Roger Åheim is the type that only answers the phone when he feels like it.

– Wouldn't we all like to be like that, murmured Viken.

The woman who opened the door must have been over eighty. Her white hair was cut short and had recently been permed. It made her look like a sad old poodle, the chief inspector thought. But she was wearing a tracksuit and trainers, and looked in good shape for her age. Sheriff Storaker told her who they were, and she responded that of course she knew who *he* was. She subjected the others to a close scrutiny.

– The reason we're here is we want a word with Roger Åheim, Storaker explained. – That would be your son, if I'm not mistaken. Is he around?

– You just wait a moment, the old woman croaked. – I'll go and see.

She closed the door behind her.

– Funny, said Viken. – When you live somewhere like this, you ought to know who's home and who isn't.

He wandered across the yard to the barn, returning just as the woman opened up again.

– What's it about? she asked, not exactly forthcoming, but the sheriff seemed to be as friendly as he was big, and without raising his voice he said: – Just go and fetch that lad of yours, will you, and then we'll tell you what it's about. Maybe we could come inside for a moment.

Grudgingly the old woman let them into the house.

The man who came down the stairs was in his late fifties. He was wearing tracksuit bottoms too. There was no hair left at the front of his head, but the large pores showed clearly where it had once been. The rest was combed back smoothly. He was wearing a T-shirt and looked like he'd been pumping iron. His skin was so golden-brown that Viken wondered if he'd spent most of the autumn in some kind of banana-ripening facility.

– Well I'll be . . . exclaimed the man.

Storaker beamed good-naturedly.

– No need for me to introduce myself, Åheim. These are my colleagues from the Oslo police.

– Well, well, that's posh.

– I'll get straight to the point, the sheriff continued. – A few years ago you were sentenced for that business of shooting lynx. You were also found guilty of attacking a man with a broken bottle.

Roger Åheim opened his arms. A broad gold chain jangled around his wrist.

– It's about time you let all that stuff go, Kjell Roar.

– There's a lot of rumours floating about the village, Storaker went on, clearly not too happy about being on first-name terms with the owner of the farm.

– Rumours, yeah, plenty of them about. Åheim winked at Nina. – More rumours up here than there are mosquitoes at midsummer.

– Some people say you engage in illegal hunting activities, Storaker persisted.

Åheim came down to the foot of the staircase. Even wearing his clogs, he was half a head shorter than Viken.

– You got nothing better to do than run around listening to gossip?

– It's all part of my job, Storaker said. – But if I suggest to you that people have been hunting bears up here recently, what would you have to say to that?

Åheim shook his head.

– Don't believe a word of it.

Nina Jebsen interrupted.

– Would you know about it?

He let his gaze wander slowly up and down her before turning back to the sheriff.

– Now I'm going to be damned honest with you, Kjell Roar. I keep away from stuff like that. None of my business how other people wipe their arses.

Showing no hint of what he thought of people who announced that they were going to be completely honest, Viken said: – You were quoted in the local newspaper, *Glåmdalen*. He pulled out the printout. – You and one of your relatives, Odd Gunnar Nytorpet . . .

Someone should catch a hungry bear and release it in the woods near Oslo, then we'd see what they said, these bureaucrats and politicians who are so bloody set on taking care of all the predators.

– For Chrissakes, Åheim exclaimed. – That must've been at least ten years ago. You're not trying to tell me you think any of us actually meant it.

No one answered.

– This is a free country. People can say what they like.

Nina Jebsen said: – It's not a bad idea to think before you speak. Especially when what you say is going to end up in a newspaper.

Viken turned as the living-room door opened behind him. A young woman stood there. From southern Asia, somewhere round there, he noted. She was holding a baby in her arms.

– Got a visitor? he asked Åheim.

– Visitor, no, this here is mine.

It wasn't clear whether he meant the woman or the child. Probably both, Viken decided. Sixty years old and he fathers a nipper, good luck with that. He couldn't help wondering how the young woman had ended up out here on this farm. Åheim had probably fetched her back home with him after a trip to Thailand.

– What do you use the barn for? he asked.

Åheim jumped. He took the bundle out of the woman's arms and began to rock it back and forth, though it looked to be already fast asleep.

– The barn? Some hay, pig feed, tools . . . Why d'you ask?

– Come over with us, let's take a look.

Åheim hesitated.

– It's locked.

– I saw that. Monster of a bloody padlock. It's not inconceivable you have the key.

– I rent out part of the barn. I don't have that key.

Viken put on his friendliest grin.

– What can we do about that, Storaker?

The sheriff was already on his way out the door.

– I've got some bolt-cutters in the car. Absolute bloody man-eaters, they are.

– Shit, muttered Åheim, and handed the bundle back to the woman. – I'll have a look, see if I don't have an extra one somewhere.

He disappeared upstairs. The woman flashed them a brilliant smile.

– Bite to eat and a nice cup of coffee, if you feel like it?

Her local accent was so strong that even Viken might have had to change his version of her story.

Roger Åheim let them into the barn through a side door. Storaker had a powerful torch with him. A plough and a small tractor stood in the middle of the vast space. Two hay pens further in.

– I note you've got cables leading out here, said Viken. – What do you use the electricity for?

Roger Åheim wrinkled his nose.

– Machinery. High-pressure hoses. Battery chargers.

– Show us the fuse box.

The farmer hesitated.

– What d'you say your name was?

Viken hadn't introduced himself and wasn't about to do so now.

– You don't need to know that to show us a few bloody fuses.

Åheim turned to the sheriff.

– Little awkward this, Kjell Roar, he murmured. – Got some bits and pieces . . .

He went up to a door, opened it, flipped the light switch. On a table stood an apparatus unmistakably designed for the distilling of alcohol. Four or five white plastic containers. Storaker took the cap off one and sniffed.

– Top quality this, Åheim.

– Personal use only, the farmer assured him.

The sheriff roared with laughter.

– Won't be much left of your liver if you pour this lot down yourself. There's got to be more than fifty litres here.

– Now I'm going to be damned honest with you, Kjell Roar,

Åheim announced once more. – A couple of the lads do come by now and then to pick up a drop. No money changes hands at all.

Viken left it to the sheriff to worry about the farmer's health while he tried to open a cupboard in the corner of the room.

– Is there a single door on this farm that isn't locked? he complained.

Åheim fiddled with his keys.

– Got some stuff in there that has to be kept under lock and key. I've always been the cautious type. Especially with all these kids you get running around up here . . .

– Open it, let's have a look at this stuff of yours.

The three shelves inside the cupboard were filled with cases of solvent and rat poison and tins of treatment for insects and weeds. There were also two small bottles. To his embarrassment, Viken had to get his spectacles out to read the labels.

– What's the ethane for? he murmured.

– I used to keep pigs. Now and then I had to make sure they slept.

Viken stared at Åheim over the rim of his glasses.

– Ethane isn't exactly a sleeping potion.

– Perfectly legal to use it, Åheim responded.

– And what is . . . Zoletil?

The farmer took the bottle and studied it.

– Is that still there? That's from the time when I worked in Farming and Fisheries. Now and then we had to tranquillise some of the larger animals. He handed it back. – People reckon I'm the best shot in the area.

At the back of the shelf, Viken found another two small bottles. He peered at one of the labels.

– Damn, he finally exclaimed, and handed it to Jebsen.

– Pentothal-Natrium, she read, – to be injected, contains thiopental natric. Five hundred milligrams . . .

Viken held the farmer with his eyes and didn't let go.

– Where did you get this stuff from?

Åheim shrugged his shoulders.

– Something I was looking after for the vet. He used it if we had problems with the ordinary tranquillisers. Years since we last needed it. I must have forgotten to give it back.

As they stood outside waiting while the farmer padlocked the door, Viken said:

– Now I want you to show us any cellars you might have, locked or not.

Nina Jebsen put her hand on his arm.

– There's a loft space in there, she exclaimed.

Viken frowned.

– Behind his distillery the roof is sloping, but it's flat at the other end.

– Quite correct, Åheim affirmed as he clicked the lock shut. – Just a lot of junk up there.

– Does that still fit? Viken asked caustically, with a nod at his bunch of keys. – Or does Storaker have to go back to his car and fetch his bolt-cutters?

– How do you get up there? he continued when they were once again standing in the half-darkness.

– I know someone who's in the Oslo police force, Åheim volunteered.

If this was an attempt to distract matters with a bit of small talk, it failed completely. Viken merely turned his back on him.

– Go and fetch us a ladder, Storaker suggested.

– Bit tricky, that, was Åheim's response. But then he gave up and disappeared in the direction of the outhouse. By the time he came back, his mood had sunk a few more degrees.

– There's no need for us to spend the whole bloody day in here.

Storaker positioned the ladder and started climbing up, with the chief inspector holding it.

– Another door up here, he reported after he had reached the platform below the roof.

– That's the bit I rent out, Åheim yelled up to him. – Don't have the key for that.

Storaker gestured to his assistant, who disappeared off out to the car.

— What d'you say his name was, the bloke you rent it out to? he called down to Åheim, who didn't answer.

Within a minute Storaker was finally able to show what his celebrated bolt-cutters were good for. With one tug the padlock was wrenched off, and he shone his torch into the space behind the door.

— Well I'll be . . . he muttered, so loudly that they heard him down on the barn floor.

Viken and Jebsen climbed up. Storaker pointed to a loft space with a little peephole directly under the crest of the roof. Two large freezers stood on the floor.

— Bit of a job to get these up here.

Viken bent double and crept into the space. He opened one of the freezers and pulled out a deep-frozen straw sack, cut it open with a penknife.

— The man is right, he exclaimed as a large, cat-like head came into view. — This here is quite definitely a bit tricky.

35

Anita Elvestrand had put the box of wine back in the fridge; now she had to go and fetch it again. She'd been counting the glasses and stopped at five, but thinking about it she realised that one more wouldn't do any harm. She had a good head for wine. Drinking wine made her feel good, never whingeing or quarrelsome.

They were talking about slimming on the TV. That professor who always wore the bow tie and the stripy jacket and looked like a circus ringmaster was sitting there raving on about what he called health fascism. That was actually a bloody good expression, Anita nodded to him. One of the few professors worth listening to. Wine was good for the heart, researchers had discovered, and even that idiot of a local doctor she'd ended up with had to agree. A little wine each day, he said, but no more than one glass. Yesterday she hadn't drunk a drop, so she was still in credit.

She'd been up and rung on Miriam's bell, wanted to invite her down for a drink, but she wasn't home. She had been talking about going away for the weekend with some friends, but right up until the last minute Anita had hoped she wouldn't go. Miriam was the best person she knew, she thought as she emptied the rest of the glass. She must be careful not to disturb her too often. Mustn't use her up. Even if it wasn't convenient, Miriam never got annoyed when Anita rang on her doorbell. She'd had a visitor yesterday, and Anita knew straight away that it was a man. Even so Miriam gave her a moment and stood chatting with her out in the corridor. Her skin was so soft when she hugged her, it smelt so good. Later in the evening her suspicions about a gentleman caller were confirmed. The ceiling was thin, and you would have to be deaf as a post not to hear what was going on up there. And not just the once either. Anita thought it was odd. Miriam was going to be a doctor, and she was always trying to help. On Sundays she went to some Catholic church or other with nuns and monks. Now and then Anita actually thought of her as being from another world altogether. And then she let herself be had up there, screaming away like any horny girl. But it didn't embarrass Anita to sit and listen to it all. On the contrary, she was so happy for Miriam she almost felt like joining in herself.

Miriam had popped in earlier in the day. Anita asked if she had a boyfriend, because she didn't seem the type for one-night stands. Miriam had been evasive.

– I don't quite know how it's going to work out.

– Are you in love? Anita wanted to know.

– More than that.

– Then what's the problem?

It wasn't just out of curiosity she asked. Miriam didn't look happy. Usually she looked so calm and content, but now there were shadows under her eyes, and her gaze was flickering and anxious.

– He'll never leave his family, she said. – He isn't like that.

– Is it that doctor from where you were doing your practical? Was it him here yesterday?

Her suspicions were confirmed.

– Well then, it's probably not a good idea to get too involved.

Miriam sat staring out of the window for a while before she answered.

– Maybe that's the reason. That I can never have him.

Anita had given up counting the glasses. It didn't much matter. She had the whole of Saturday to recover. On Sunday she would fetch Victoria, hair neatly combed and stone-cold sober. But she might well go out on Saturday night. Never drank much when she was out in town. Over and over again her solicitor had told her how important *that* was. She did have a chance to get Victoria back, but only if she kept her nose really clean.

Someone rang the bell. She jumped. Had Miriam come back after all? She usually knocked.

There was a man standing there she'd never seen before.

– Anita Elvestrand?

She nodded.

– Something's happened.

She stared at him.

– Victoria, he said. – You'd better come at once.

She felt as if she'd been pushed over. She took hold of the door jamb.

– Who are you?

– I'm a doctor, there's been an accident.

– Where? What do you mean?

– Come with me, I'll explain on the way. We tried to call you but you didn't answer.

She was still feeling dizzy as she grabbed her coat, pushed her feet into her boots. He ran down the stairs ahead of her, led her to the end of the block. Heading up the street, he clicked on a key, there was a beep and the lights on one of the parked cars blinked.

He opened the passenger door. Anita wanted to pee and was almost weeping with anxiety.

– Where is Victoria?

– I'll take you there, he said and hopped into the driver's seat.

Abruptly he put an arm around her, pushing her upper body down. She felt him pressing a cloth against her face. It smelt of sharp splinters and opened up a world of memories: corridors and beds, nurses in white coats with masks over their mouths in blinding light.

The smell reached out from the cloth and claimed her.

36

Saturday 20 October

FEET SINKING INTO the mud, he can't see the bottom through the murky water. There's no life down there, he tries to say as he wades out. I can't dive here. Somewhere far away: a telephone. He's never heard that ringtone before, but he knows it's for him. Hears Bie's voice coming from somewhere; he can't answer the call as long as she's there. Disappears back down again into sleep.

When he woke up, she was sitting on the side of the bed. Even through the curtains the sunlight was bright. She stroked his forehead.

— I was almost starting to get worried about you, Axel. You went for a lie-down at about six o'clock last night and you've been out ever since.

He sat up.

— Has anyone rung?

— For you? No, for once the big wide world out there has left you in peace.

Bie put an arm around his waist and pulled him close to her.

— You work too hard, Axel. Weren't you going to start saying no to these night shifts?

He grunted a reply.

— I'd like to hang on to you for a while yet, you know. The way you looked when you came home yesterday . . . You're not twenty any more.

She leant against him, pressing him backwards, laid a thigh across his bare stomach.

– You're the most precious thing I have, you know that, don't you? she murmured, and he couldn't remember the last time she had said something like that.

– What do you know about Brede? he asked suddenly.

She raised herself up on one elbow.

– Brede, your brother? Why are you asking me that?

– What do you know about him, Bie?

She looked searchingly into his face.

– No more than what you've told me. That he destroyed everything he touched. That it was impossible for your parents to have him living at home.

– There's more. Something I didn't tell you. We made this pact never to tell on one another.

She got up and opened the curtain, came back to bed again.

– What's made you think of him now?

He looked up at the ceiling, the throbbing white light mingling with a hint of forget-me-not blue, Bie's favourite colour.

– I saw him in town one day. He was gone before I could get to him.

– Are you certain? You've always been so sure he must be dead.

– He isn't dead. There's a lot you don't know.

– I realise that. She scraped down his chest with her long fingernails. – Don't you think I've noticed how no one in the family has ever talked about him in all the years I've known you.

She bent down and kissed his navel.

– Some things you just have to let lie, Axel. If we spent our lives digging up corpses, we wouldn't have the energy to do anything else.

He twisted round, got to his feet. Found his boxer shorts by the bedside, pulled them on.

– Are you leaving?

From her tone of voice he knew what she had in mind.

– I've got a bladder the size of a nine-month womb, he said with a vague smile. – Just before the waters break.

– You've not forgotten we're invited out tonight?

He let out a groan.
– I thought as much, she said tartly.

Mail from Daniel. He used to write every week, but it was a long time now since they'd heard from him. Normally it would have worried Axel, a twenty-two year old on his own in New York, but these day he had no time to think about it. As he opened the letter, a feeling of missing his elder son came sneaking over him. If he wasn't careful, it might turn into an avalanche.

Daniel had taken his economics exam just the day before and for the past few weeks had been studying round the clock. Again he reassured his parents that New York was one of the safest cities in the world. Not like Oslo. For once there's something about Norway in the *New York Times*. A big article about the two murders. Apparently people are afraid a killer bear is on the loose in the centre of the capital. Can't find anything in the online editions of the Norwegian papers that denies it. What's going on? According to the *NYT* article there's an almost medieval atmosphere. Fears of being attacked by monsters in the dark streets at night. People afraid to go outside (can this be true?), and the journalist writes that it feels like being in a city where the walls were never pulled down. Couldn't have a better advert. Soon you'll be drowning in tourists on the lookout for something exotic and primitive in the heart of what is, after all, a modern capital. I keep having to remind my fellow students that yes, we do have electricity in Norway now, we've even got TV, and – of particular importance to Americans – we have flushing toilets.

Bie had called the family to lunch. Warm baguettes and boiled eggs.
– What are you doing tonight? Axel asked Tom when his son finally appeared.
– Dunno. Going over to Findus's.
– Are you going to rehearse?
Tom shrugged.
– Aren't you going to ask me? Marlen snuffled as she put

Cassiopeia down beside her plate. The tortoise's head and feet disappeared soundlessly inside its shell.

– But of course. What are you doing tonight, Marlen?

She stretched her neck.

– Not telling.

Axel didn't give up.

– Aw, don't be like that. At least give me a clue.

– Nothing *you* need to know about, she pouted as she sneezed across the plate.

The way she said it was so cheeky, Axel thought he might pull her up about it. But then she immediately sneezed again, this time into a serviette Bie managed to stick in front of her nose. Once she'd recovered, she announced:

– Sneezing is the best thing there is. It's like travelling in a space rocket. It tickles and then it's like everything disappears. Is it dangerous?

– You should ask the doctor, was Bie's advice.

– No, not dangerous, Axel reassured her. – Not as long as you come back down to earth again.

37

BIE STAYED DOWN in the hall talking to the birthday boy as the hostess led Axel up the plushly carpeted staircase. As soon as he entered the large room, he caught sight of Ingrid Brodahl and her husband. They were standing alone over by the fireplace, while the other guests were gathered in groups. Ingrid Brodahl, who had clung to his arm, screaming. Images from the night of the accident rose up again. And the feeling of helplessness he didn't know how to deal with. His first thought when he saw them standing there was to turn and go out again, out to the car, drive off somewhere. After the funeral, he had held his hand out to her in the middle of a stream of people offering their condolences. Her features were drawn and strained, but when she realised it was his hand she was shaking she had broken down and her husband had to lead her away. If he spoke to her at this gathering, it might prove too much for her again. Maybe she would always think of him as someone who arrived in the middle of the night bringing news of death.

He stood beside her. Only now did she recognise him. She didn't release his hand as they greeted each other. She looked at him with a glazed stare, saying nothing, but she didn't start to cry. She's boxed it in, he thought.

Axel stood in the darkness at the end of the terrace. The living-room door behind him was ajar, and from within he heard the sounds of Caribbean rhythms. Usually he didn't see much of Bie at parties; neither of them minded letting go of the other for a while. But this evening she had stayed close the whole time. Insisted on dancing with him, held him tight, kissed him with such intensity that they must have looked like a couple who had just fallen in love. He'd danced a few dances with her, cheek to cheek, before withdrawing. *Is something going on, Axel?* she had asked. He had been about to say, *Something is going on, Bie, and I don't know if I can stop it.* But he had shaken his head, and she stroked his neck and told him she understood that he was tired. Stood on tiptoe and whispered in his ear that as far as she was concerned they could go home early.

He took a deep drink from his cognac glass, let it wash around in his mouth. The terrace wasn't west-facing like their own, but faced north, and he could see over to the city on the far side of the fjord. The castle, the town hall, a little to the right Carl Berners Place and then Rodeløkka. He didn't think Miriam was home. She'd said something about going away for the weekend. The relief of knowing she wasn't there, that she'd gone somewhere he couldn't get in touch with her. If he never met her again, how long would it take before he stopped seeing her face in his mind's eye? This was how he must be now: completely passive, not doing anything until she had faded away and it was over.

The sky above him was as clear as dark glass. He found the Twins, then moved slowly on towards the Charioteer and Perseus, holding the head of the Medusa with her evil eye. In the days after her birthday party he'd had to explain repeatedly to Marlen that the star named Algol seemed to pulsate because there were actually two stars that shadowed each other in turn. That had helped. At least she dared to look up into the night sky again. A week ago she'd written a story that she read out to him. About an astronaut who was shot up into space and came close to the terrible double star Algol, the Medusa's eye. He never returned. He had been turned into stone that swirled and circled around up there, away in the outer darkness. Stories too could circle and shadow each other, Axel thought when she had finished reading.

He emptied what was left of the cognac. Thought of something he had seen in a newspaper. An investigation carried out among Italian men. The unfaithful ones were also those who scored highest on the scale of how good they were as family men. The interpretation of this was that feelings of guilt brought out the best in them as fathers. He reached into his pocket, pulled out his mobile phone. *Are you sleeping?* he texted.

As he was sending the message, he heard footsteps on the terrace. When he turned, he saw Ingrid Brodahl standing there. At table they had been seated apart from each other, but he had seen her looking at him several times, and he guessed that she would approach at some point in the evening. Now she was standing there, glass in hand and with a small bag dangling from her arm.

– I saw you come out here, she said.

Her dress glinted in the light from the room when she moved.

– I needed some fresh air, he answered. – Are you back at work?

She had a senior post in a government ministry, he recalled. Possibly the Ministry of Culture.

– I start back on Monday. I don't even have the energy to dread it. Everything seems so remote and distant. Even being here.

She kept her eyes fixed on him.

– I didn't get the chance to say this earlier, I suppose I was a little taken aback, but . . . Thank you for coming.

He presumed she meant the funeral, muttered something about well of course, he had to.

– That night, she continued in a dull monotone. – I realise you could have left it to someone else to come to our house. I can't be grateful for anything. But I do want you to know. It was good that it was you who came.

He looked at her. There had always been something unapproachable about Ingrid Brodahl, he thought. An ironic tone that kept her surroundings at a distance. Now it was as if the world had collapsed on her and torn everything loose with it.

She laid a hand on his arm.

– When you found her. How was she lying?

He took a deep breath, felt the same helplessness as he had done that night.

– Lise . . . she added, almost inaudibly.

Suddenly he started to talk, describing how he hadn't found her in the car and had walked back along the roadside ditch to search. At first it looked as if she was asleep. Ingrid Brodahl tightened her grip on his wrist, and for a moment he was afraid she might lose control. She opened her bag, took out a handkerchief, stood there with it pressed against her nose.

His phone vibrated in his jacket pocket.

– I'll come over one day soon, he said. – We'll talk more about it. If you'd like that.

Without looking up she said: – I'm glad there are people like you. That's probably the reason everything will carry on again. One day.

In the back of the taxi, Bie snuggled up with her head resting on his chest. He put his arm around her, kissed her on the forehead. Her hair smelt of roses and smoke. He stroked her cheek, traced the outline of her lips with a finger. She took it in her mouth and bit it.

– How tired are you actually, Dr Glenne? she asked, undoing a couple of his shirt buttons, slipping a hand in to his bare chest.

– I'm already asleep.

The hand glided down over his stomach and inside the waistband of his trousers.

– Oops. That doesn't appear to be the case with every part of you.

– No, he had to admit. – Some parts just get up and lie down whenever it suits them, no matter how firm I try to be with them.

– Disobedience like that must be punished, she purred.

They had the house to themselves. He got undressed and sat by the little table in the corner of the bedroom, a cognac glass in his hand. Picked up the remote control and turned on some piano music she had left in the player. She came in from the bathroom and stood in front of him. Had left the transparent G-string on.

– When did you start shaving yourself? he wanted to know, still controlling himself.

She raised her chin dismissively, and the movement seemed to release something in him. Suddenly he was on his feet, grabbing hold of her and pulling her over to the bed. They had a pair of handcuffs somewhere; it was a while since they'd used them and he wasn't sure where they were. Instead he snatched up his silk tie and tightened it around her wrists, fastening the other end to the bedpost. As he fiercely pulled her legs apart, she turned and bit him on the shoulder.

– You big rough bastard, she growled.

He fumbles his way along a corridor. It is lit by a strip of small blue lights along the floor. On one of the plates he reads: *Viktor*. The door opens. An interview room within. The detective chief inspector is sitting there, but his name is not Viktor.

We've been waiting for you, Brede.

He opens his mouth to protest. They've got to stop calling him Brede. He refuses to put up with it any more. The chief inspector takes him by the arm, drags him into another room, a large room with a screen pulled down in front of the stage.

We managed to film him. Thanks to you we managed to film him, Brede.

Four or five people sitting in the first row; otherwise it's empty in there. One of them turns, bathed in a greenish light. It's his mother.

I'm proud of you, Axel. Proud of you.

He feels relieved that she recognises him and is about to ask her to explain this business about Brede. *Tell them who I am*, he is on the point of saying, but before he can do so, he is pushed down into one of the seats.

Eighth row. This'll just have to do, it was the best we could get.

Detective Chief Inspector Viktor squeezes in beside him, places a hand on his thigh.

Glenne, you just wait till you see this.

He's got it now, he's not calling him Brede any more.

Viktor turns and snaps his fingers three times. There's an old projector at the back of the room. Rita is there cranking it up. Images appear on the screen. Daybreak. The camera glides between the trees, all the branches bare of needles.

I don't want to see this.

Viktor puts his arm around him, holds him firmly. He tries to pull away, but there's someone sitting on the other side of him too now. Smells of rotting meat. He can't manage to turn his head enough to see who it is.

We're not going to stop until you've seen everything.

The camera approaches a tarn. Someone standing on the bank, a man in a white suit and boots, a bowler hat on his head. He's holding a stone in his hand. In front of him, black hair dipping in the water's edge, lies a naked woman. She is bleeding from the head. A tree trunk gets in the way of the camera.

Watch closely, Glenne, Viktor whispers in his ear. *Watch closely now, and you'll see the Medusa's face.*

The camera moves forward again, zooming in. The man by the tarn turns. His face fills the screen. That evil grin, the laughter that can't be heard.

He mustn't look at the eyes. Tears himself away, heading out, shrieking like an animal as he tries to drown out Viktor's voice: *Do you recognise yourself, Dr Glenne? Now, at last, do you recognise yourself?*

38

AGNES FINCKENHAGEN SAT with a steaming mug of coffee in her hand and *VG* spread out on the table in front of her. The front page was covered with a single headline: POLICE SUSPECT GREEN TERROR. Inside, three pages were devoted to the raid on the barn in Åsnes county in Hedmark, which was presented as the police's most important lead so far in the so-called bear murders. Finckenhagen had just come from a meeting with the Chief Constable and the Chief Superintendent. They wanted to know why they had to learn of important developments from the press. She couldn't give a good answer and had to put up with a roasting that lasted for almost an hour. At the end of it she was given the remainder of the morning to deliver a report on the case.

She rang Viken and asked him to call in and see her. Get here at once, she ought to have said. But Viken was the type you made suggestions to, not gave orders. A man everyone had an opinion on, as she had soon discovered when she joined the section. She got on with him extremely well. To begin with she had had her doubts, not least because he had, after all, applied for the job she had been brought in to do. But he had never shown any opposition or rivalry. On the contrary, from the very first day she had found him loyal, supportive even. You had to respect that, she'd thought. A man whose concern for the job overrode any personal ambition he might have.

She had never heard anyone question Viken's abilities as one of the best detectives in Oslo, and when he spoke, even the most experienced listened. He had led investigations into a number of cases of serial rape, almost all of which had been solved. Influenced by American profilers, he had developed a special understanding of the psychology of people involved in serial criminal activities. He gave lectures on the way technical finds at crime scenes could reveal something about the perpetrator's inner world. Finckenhagen found it very interesting, but discovered that within the section generally, there was little enthusiasm for what he was doing. But she felt sure that developments in the techniques of investigation would presently show him to be right, and she was more than willing to stand up for him if need be. She had seen for herself the almost cruel efficiency with which Viken used his psychological insight to elicit a confession during questioning. As a leader, however, he would have been a disaster for the section, something the people up on the eighth floor had understood only too well. He was the lone-wolf type, someone who found it difficult to delegate responsibilities. What was worse was that he polarised opinion among those around him. People were either strongly for or strongly against him. His supporters appeared willing to do anything for him, it seemed. But even amongst those he was more feared than loved.

Viken knocked twice on the half-open door and walked in. As usual he was wearing a white shirt, open at the neck to reveal a line of thick grey chest hair.

— Are we going to do this sitting down or standing up? he asked with that enigmatic smile Finckenhagen had long puzzled over but in the end found really quite sympathetic.

— Please, do sit down. Have you read *VG*?

— Never miss it.

— Well, what do you make of it?

— They've got hold of more information than we'd like. He didn't appear to be worried in the slightest.

— Where did they get it from? she wanted to know.

He scratched beneath his chin, drew his fingers along his jawline, making the skin taut.

— Possibly from the forest deeps of Hedmark. Possibly from us.

– In which case we have a problem.

He leaned back and stretched his legs out in front of him. The polished toecaps of his shoes glinted.

– I'll take another look at it, Chief. If we find the source, you'll be the first to know. But even so, it could've been worse.

– How d'you mean?

– Journalists are like a wolf pack. If they find a bone, they're all over it. If they don't, they're all over us. That would have done a lot more damage to the investigation.

Finckenhagen wasn't sure she liked the imagery he used.

– The Chief Superintendent is not quite of the same opinion as you. Nor is the Chief Constable.

Viken grinned a rather wolf-like grin himself.

– Let him growl away a bit. That's his job. He doesn't bite.

She had to smile. It was reassuring to have a guy like Viken in the team, someone she could lean on when things got tough.

– Is there anything at all in this story of *VG*'s?

He shook his head firmly.

– Environmental criminality, yes. Hunting and trapping of protected species, sales to foreign countries. But murder and terror? I don't think so. Sure, the guy we've arrested was in possession of the same tranquillising agent as was used in the murders, but I'm inclined to believe him when he says he used it on animals, not people. And anyway, he has alibis for most of the times that interest us.

He added: – Who really believes that here in Norway we've got terrorists who are willing to kill to protest against the government's wildlife conservation policies? We would have known about a group like that a long time ago. But it's enough to keep the press going for a day or two. See how much they got out of that fantasy about a killer beast roaming the streets of the city. No one much above the age of five believes that those women were attacked by a bear, but as you know, people love to read that kind of stuff. If the papers had written that we were looking for a troll with nine heads, they would have sold even more copies.

Finckenhagen had to agree with him.

– I was thinking of suggesting to the Chief Superintendent the possibility of bringing in a psychologist who knows something about profiling. It would give you someone to talk things over with. This case is so special, I think he might go along with the idea. What do you think?

Viken mulled it over.

– In that case we would be saying loud and clear that we suspect a serial killer may be on the loose. It would probably cause as much hysteria as rumours about a killer bear.

– The papers are already speculating along those lines anyway, regardless of what we do. Do we have any use for one of these psychologists?

– We've got a couple up here in the frozen north who think they know something about psychological profiling. What you get from them is a large pile of platitudes and an even larger pile of bills. We'd need to go abroad if we're looking for someone good.

– Think about it. I'm open to suggestions.

– Let's make the most of what we've got for the time being, Viken concluded.

39

Nina Jebsen opened the incident book to see if there was anything of possible significance for the two murder cases. Thirty-five calls had been registered over the weekend, and she gave some of them a closer look. She had lost count of the number of people reported missing after the newspapers began writing about the murders. In most cases they were women who turned up again a few hours later.

Of the three missing-persons reports that were still on file, one was considered interesting enough to send a patrol car to take a closer look. An address in Rodeløkka. A thirty-six-year-old woman who hadn't been seen since Friday afternoon. Former drug addict, Nina saw, noting how this was reflected in the tone of the report. Tempting to suspect the woman had cracked up and gone back to the street; she would probably turn up in a hospital, or at best a hospice, at some point over the next few days. But the neighbour who had reported her missing seemed certain that this wasn't the case. She had returned home Sunday evening to find the missing woman's door half open and the television still on. Nina made a note of the name and continued through the rest of the book.

She was almost done when the phone rang. The switchboard had a caller on the line who insisted on talking to Viken, but Viken was in a meeting. Nina reminded the operator that no phone tips were to be passed on to Violent Crimes without filtering. After Viken had been in the newspapers and on the TV a few times, every Tom, Dick and Hilda who called in insisted it was him they had to talk to. What about those who refused to speak to anyone else? the switchboard operator wanted to know. People who claimed to have vital information about the murders? Nina gave up with a sigh and asked him to put the call through to her.

– Viken? a female voice shouted into her ear.

– Viken is in a meeting, Nina informed her. – Who is this?

– You've got to do something, the woman continued. Already Nina was regretting her indulgence.

– We're always doing something, she said soothingly. – Don't worry about that.

– You're not doing your job, the woman insisted, and Nina glanced at her watch. She'd give this woman thirty seconds before hanging up.

– It's going to happen again. And you're not doing anything.

Suddenly the voice changed. It became deeper and slower:

– You *can't* do anything. It's going to happen anyway.

– Perhaps you'd explain yourself, Nina suggested.

– I will. Don't you worry about that. He who has eyes to see, let him see. As far as I'm concerned, you can go to hell, the lot of you. That's where you're headed. You can't save him.

– Who can't we save?

– There is just one righteous man in this city, and almost no one knows who he really is. And his name shall be blessed for ever. Make a note of that, sweetie, a clearing in the forest, a glen in the wilderness. But he's the one they're after, the killers and the rapists and rope-makers, because if they get him then Sodom and Gomorrah and Jerusalem will fall, and if you understood anything at all inside your heads, you would protect him night and day and twenty-four-seven. The chosen ones will follow him. I've followed him before, all the way to the terminus, the *last* stop, and God knows I will go on following him. Glen in the forest. But his time will soon be up, that's what you don't understand.

The woman hung up. Nina Jebsen remained sitting there looking at the screen for a few moments before opening a document and entering a few lines about the conversation. She asked herself why it was that every lunatic in the world felt drawn towards unsolved murder cases. Like moths to the light.

40

AXEL HURRIED UP the twisting stairway. The yellowy-brown felt carpet was worn down the middle, and the way the stairs sloped to one side gave him a strange sensation of falling. She had sent him a text. *Must talk to you.* He had to talk to her too, one last time.

She opened the door and let him in. Stayed standing in the dimly lit hallway and looked up into his eyes.

– Thank you for coming, she said.

He had brought two bottles of wine with him. They chinked together as he put the plastic bag down.

– I'm afraid, Axel.

He pulled her close, doubting whether he could bring himself to say what he had come to say.

– I wish so much you could stay. Never leave here again.

– What is it you're afraid of? he murmured in her ear.

– Anita's gone missing.

– Anita?

– The woman who lives underneath.

– The one with the daughter who was taken into care?

Miriam nodded.

– When I came home yesterday, her door was wide open. The TV and all the lights were on. I knew straight away something was wrong. I called the police. They've been here.

She took him by the hand, led him into the living room.

– She was supposed to fetch Victoria yesterday afternoon, but she never turned up at the foster parents' home.

– Might she not just have gone off somewhere?

– Without saying anything? When she was finally going to be

allowed to have Victoria stay overnight with her? She was looking forward to it like mad.

Axel didn't say what he was thinking. Former drug addict, suddenly disappears.

– I know something's happened to her. All this that's been going on . . .

Miriam sat on the sofa, wrapped a blanket around herself.

– You're thinking of the two women who were murdered, said Axel. – All that stuff in the papers, warnings about not going out alone.

She bit her lip.

– It's as if it's got something to do with me.

– We always think that way when we're afraid, he reassured her. – There's not a single person in the whole city who isn't affected.

– It's something else . . .

She reached her hand out to him. He leaned over her.

– I want you to lie down beside me, she whispered. – I want you to hold me. As tight as you can.

Lying there on her sofa, in the tiny flat. The feeling of not having to say anything. I like the person she makes me into, he thought. I like the person I am when I'm with her, better than all the other versions of Axel Glenne. And I'm to let him go? Really?

He sent a text message saying he wouldn't be home. No explanation. He couldn't face the thought of making up another lie.

It was 7.30. One of the bottles of red wine was almost empty. Bie had tried to call; he'd put the phone on mute. She'd sent a text: *What is going on, Axel?* The question brought a sense of relief. Now there was no way round it; he would have to talk to her. *Will explain tomorrow*, he wrote back.

– Your father was a war hero, Miriam said suddenly.

Axel shared the last of the wine between them. It didn't surprise him that she had found this out.

– Genuine Norwegian war hero, he confirmed. – There's a phrase for it in Norwegian, *gutta på skauen*, the lads in the forest. For one whole winter he had to stay hidden away in a cabin, completely alone, miles from anyone.

– I've heard a lot about the war in Norway, she said. – Since I came here I've met a lot of people who said it was the brave Norwegians who defeated the Germans. I've even been inside one of those cabins you're talking about, deep in the forest. They had the operations centre in a secret room in the cellar. The grandfather of the person who owns the cabin was a . . . what did he call it . . . was it a border guide?

– That's right.

– He helped refugees over into Sweden. In the end he was caught and sent to a concentration camp.

Axel opened the second bottle.

– It was a very dangerous job, he nodded. – When we were kids, my father plotted in the whole network of cabins and flight routes for us on a map. We imagined walking them with him. I've lost track of how many times he told us about the moment he was just seconds away from being captured by the Gestapo. And every time we were just as scared. Even Brede sat there listening in silence . . . What did you say his name was, this man who was a border guide?

– I don't remember. I can't go around remembering everything. Some things should be forgotten.

It occurred to him that in a subtle way she was trying to involve him. She wanted him to ask more about these things that should be forgotten, tell him stories about her past. Lead him into them as though into a labyrinth. In the end it would be impossible to let her go.

He said: – Are you good at forgetting?

Her eyebrows flew up and quivered a few times. She didn't answer.

– If I asked you to, could you forget what we've shared together? She hugged him tighter.

– You say that as though it was already in the past.

He knew he was getting close to what he was supposed to be saying to her, but then he ducked away. Changed the subject, said something unimportant.

– You left an envelope behind in the office you were using at the clinic.

He didn't mention how close he'd come to opening it, to peering into her life and the things he wanted to know as little about as possible.

– Bring it with you next time you come, she said. – *If* you come.

Again she gave him the chance to say what he had come to say.

Somewhere in the distance a phone is ringing. It's for him, but he can't work out where the sound is coming from. He's lying on a stone floor, he's cold. Brede is walking down a staircase towards him. It isn't Brede. It's Tom, coming down step by step. Never reaching him.

Axel opened his eyes in the dark, sat bolt upright. He heard Miriam's slow breathing. Could just make out the hair that flowed across the pillow by the bedhead. The shapes of the books on the shelf above it became clearer, and the photograph of the officer in naval uniform. The only picture he'd seen at her flat. It had to be her father. He had avoided asking. Suddenly he remembered the last thing he'd said to her before she fell asleep: one day I'll tell you about my twin brother. *One day?* she murmured, half asleep. Next time I come, he said. You will be the first to hear the story. About what happened that summer he was sent away.

It was two minutes to five. He dressed quietly. Out in the hallway he picked up his shoes. There was a smell of something rotting, and it struck him that it was himself he was smelling. He opened the front door slightly and the smell grew stronger. He opened it further. Something was obstructing it. He pushed and managed to get it half open. Suddenly realised what the smell reminded him of: the pathology lab, the smell of an autopsy. He switched on the light. It cast a yellowish cone on to the landing. A hand was lying there, an arm. Ripped and bloody. He hurled himself against the door and stumbled out in his stockinged feet, stepping in something wet and sticky. The body that lay there blocking the doorway was naked. It was a woman. Both legs were missing. The hair was a cake of coagulated blood, the face had been torn open. He couldn't see the eyes. He stepped back inside, into the hallway. The door swung closed.

From the alcove he heard Miriam's voice. She called his name. He staggered in to her.

– Where have you been? What's that smell? Axel, say something. He cleared his throat.

– It's . . . it's happened again.

She jumped out of the alcove.

– What has happened?

His body felt as though it was collapsing; he held on tight to the back of the chair.

– Outside your door.

She was on her way out; he grabbed hold of her.

– Someone's lying there. A woman.

– No!

– She's . . . You mustn't go out there.

– Anita, she whispered.

He let go of her. Tried to keep hold of his thoughts. Managed to hang on to one.

– Wait five minutes, until I'm gone. Then call the police. Lock the door and wait here until they come, don't open up for anyone else.

She looked at him in disbelief.

– Are you going?

– I must talk to Bie. She has to hear this from me . . . that I was here last night. You do understand, Miriam, you must tell the police you were alone. That you couldn't get the door open. That you saw a bloodied arm and didn't dare go out until they arrived.

She was still staring at him, as though she didn't understand what he was talking about.

– Miriam. He took hold of her hair, drew her head away so that he could see her eyes. They looked frozen. – Remember now? Remember to ring?

He held her tight and kissed her on the cheek. Her arms hung slack.

– Don't leave now, Axel, she whispered.

He squeezed out through the door, avoided breathing in the stench. Didn't look down at what was lying there. Staggered down the uneven staircase and out into the back yard. As he put his hand on the gate, someone opened it from the outside. He jumped back a step, stood poised in the half-dark. A man with a cap pulled down over his forehead came in through the opening, pulling a newspaper trolley behind him. For an instant Axel met his gaze.

– Good morning, the man said in heavily accented Norwegian.

Axel dashed past him.

A diffuse band of silver light hung in the eastern sky. He looked at his watch: 5.10. He hurried in the direction of Carl Berners Place before realising he was going in the wrong direction. He turned back. No taxi, he thought. Mustn't let anyone see me. Don't even know where I'm going.

Half an hour later, he rang on a doorbell in Tåsenveien.

41

Tuesday 23 October

VIKEN STOOD ON the top step, breathing unevenly. Not because he was in such bad shape that he was out of breath from climbing a few stairs, but because what he saw was what he had expected to see, and yet so much worse that it left him gasping for air, and the stench from the dead body was almost unendurable.

Nina Jebsen had stopped on the step below him. He had picked her up on the way. An impulse shot through him: shield her from the sight of this. The dead woman – what was left of her – lay with her head twisted to one side, staring towards the stairs they had just ascended, though the eyes were almost caked over with dried blood. Deep rifts, what looked like claw marks, ran from the lower part of the face and down across the shoulder and back. One corner of the mouth had been ripped open, and the tongue lolled through the opening in the cheek.

Viken looked at the constable standing beside the door.

– Is this the neighbour who contacted the switchboard?

The name *Miriam Gaizauskaite* was written on a sign under the doorbell.

– Yes, she called the emergency number about, – the constable glanced at his watch, – fifty-five minutes ago.

– Technical?

– Not here yet.

Something had struck Viken on the way up. He turned and went downstairs to the floor below.

– Jebsen, he called up to her.

Nina came down the twisting staircase. She was pale and held on to the banister as though afraid the timbers would collapse beneath her at any moment.

Viken pointed to the sign on the door: *Anita and Victoria Elvestrand live here*.

– The missing woman, she confirmed.

Viken hurried back up again, over the first reaction now. He borrowed the constable's torch and peered at the floor around the mutilated body. Not much blood; obviously the killing hadn't been done here. The small amount there was came from the severed legs. He could see the clear imprint of a foot in it.

People were talking as they made their way up the stairs. Viken recognised one of the voices, a crime-scene technician. At the same instant he noticed something on the door and the door jamb. He squatted down and shone his torch. A broad marking across the woodwork, five deep downward scratches.

– What's the first thing that hits you when you see this, Jebsen? She squatted down beside him.

– Claws, she said at once. – Marks made by a large paw with claws.

Miriam Gaizauskaite sat on the sofa with her legs curled under her. She was wearing jogging pants and a thick sweater. She sat rocking from side to side and staring in front of her.

– So you didn't hear anything until you tried to open the door? Viken asked again.

She shook her head.

– Listen, Miriam, Viken began, and noticed that Nina Jebsen was watching him. She was probably not used to hearing him address a witness using their first name. – You called the switchboard at seventeen minutes past five. Can you tell us why you were up and about so early?

She glanced at him, then over at Nina. Her pupils were wide open. Is she on something, or is it just the shock? Viken wondered.

– I . . . woke up early. Couldn't sleep. Then I heard someone open the gate, thought it was the paper boy. I got up and went to fetch the paper.

– And you neither saw nor heard anything unusual from the time you went to bed at about twelve until you heard the gate open.

Miriam looked down at the floor.

– I didn't see anything, didn't hear anything.

Half an hour later, Viken made a sign to Nina Jebsen: time to wrap it up.

– We don't know yet who it is lying out there, said Nina, – but we can't exclude the possibility that it's your neighbour.

Miriam began to tremble.

– It is her, she said in a low voice.

– Do you think so?

– Something's very wrong. I've had a feeling about it the whole time.

Viken said: – You know her quite well, I gather. I want to ask something of you. It won't be easy. It isn't easy for us either, if that's any comfort. And you can say no if you don't want to do it.

Miriam released the hold she had around her knees and let her feet drop to the floor. Her phone rang; it was on the coffee table. She picked it up, looked at the display, turned it off.

– It's all right, she said. Her voice was clearer now. – I'll identify the body for you.

The two women went out while Viken had a look round inside the flat. When they came back in again, Nina had an arm around Miriam.

– You're quite certain?

Miriam leaned towards her.

– I recognise the tattoo, she muttered. – On the shoulder. The picture of a naked man.

– Did you have a visitor here yesterday? asked Viken.

Miriam didn't answer.

– There are two wine glasses out in the kitchen. And one empty and a half-full bottle.

– I didn't have visitors. I drank it myself over the last couple of days.

– In other words, you like your wine, said Viken. – Did you drink much yesterday evening?

She closed her eyes.

– A bit too much. I must have fallen asleep.

Before leaving the room, Viken went into the sleeping alcove and lifted the duvet and the two blankets that lay on the bed.

42

At one o'clock on Tuesday afternoon, the investigating team gathered in the meeting room. Four new tactical investigators had joined the group. Agnes Finckenhagen was also present, as was Jarle Frøen, the police prosecutor who was the nominal though far from actual leader of the investigation. The room was divided by sliding doors and there were no windows in the part they were sitting in. Already the air was starting to get heavy and close.

Detective Chief Inspector Viken summed up recent developments.

– We won't get the DNA results today. But there is no doubt that the victim is Anita Elvestrand, the thirty-six year old who was reported missing from her home on Sunday afternoon by her neighbour on the floor above. The same neighbour gave a positive ID of the body.

– What about next of kin? asked Finckenhagen.

Viken nodded to Arve Norbakk.

– Parents dead, the sergeant informed them. – She has a sister living in Spain and a brother who is an oil worker out on the Gullfaks rig. They have been contacted, but neither of them has any imminent plans to come over.

Viken resumed.

– The neighbour's name is Miriam Gaizauskaite, a Lithuanian citizen. She is studying medicine here in Oslo. We'll come back to her. I've had pictures sent over from the pathology lab; let's take a look at those first.

He clicked his way to the file on the computer.

– Jebsen and I were there and saw this abomination. Strong stuff, I warn you . . . One great advantage in your favour: the pictures don't smell.

Sigge Helgarsson seemed to be about to make a comment, but instead tipped back on his chair and said nothing.

Viken pulled down the screen.

– As you will note immediately, the victim exhibits distinctive injuries to the face, neck and down the back.

He clicked through a series of pictures of the ravaged body.

– As you will also note, these wounds are similar to those we have seen on the other recent murder victims. Here, however, is what is left of the lower body. Both legs have been severed, directly below the hip joint.

– For fuck's sake, Helgarsson exclaimed.

– Precisely, Sigge, Viken observed. – I couldn't have put it better myself.

He showed an enlarged image of one of the stumps.

– Does this look like a leg that has been bitten off by an animal?

– It's been sawn off, Norbakk said.

– Dr Plåterud's conclusion precisely. So we are dealing with a perpetrator who goes further each time in the mutilation of his victims. This is a well-known feature of this type of crime.

Viken clicked on, stopped at a picture of an arm, zoomed in. A tattoo of a muscular naked male body appeared.

– I would ask female members of the gathering to avert their eyes, he suggested, after debating with himself how far it was permissible to joke about such things under the circumstances. – It was, by the way, the tattoo that the neighbour recognised.

He zoomed in further still.

– What is this? he asked, pointing to four small dots under the shoulder.

He magnified the image to show a slight swelling under each of them.

– Needle marks, Norbakk volunteered.

– No doubt about it. What do we make of that?

– She takes drugs, suggested one of the new members of the team, a young man with cheeks pitted with acne scars. He was on loan from Majorstua and was hardly likely to contribute anything to the investigation. When Viken had requested more resources, he had been thinking of quality, not making up the numbers. Now he stood swaying back and forth on the soles of his feet, like a teacher savouring the pleasures of correcting a boy who should have known better.

– Apparently gave it up years ago, he informed him. – And this is on the outside of the arm, nowhere near the larger arteries. In addition, no trace of the usual narcotics in the blood. And as you will remember . . . He showed a new picture. – Cecilie Davidsen's upper right arm: three similar pinpricks, five on the thigh. And here, Paulsen: four pricks in the upper left arm, four in each thigh.

– Tranquillisers, the new man from Majorstua corrected himself.

– Precisely, said Viken in an amiable tone. He had no objection to greenhorns, provided they weren't too green. – Dr Plåterud found traces of the same narcotic as was used on the other victims.

– I'm guessing she was subjected to similar treatment, Norbakk ventured. – Tranquillised a few times before being given the fatal overdose.

– Exactly.

Viken clicked up a new picture.

– Someone has left us a footprint in this mess on the floor. The party concerned was wearing a black sock, one hundred per cent cotton, shoe size 47. We've got people examining the fibres to see if there's anything unusual about them.

– How many black socks are there in this town? was Sigge Helgarsson's comment.

– That's for you to find out, Viken grinned. – It'll keep you busy for a while. We also found plenty of skin cells under the victim's fingernails. Let's just hope it wasn't herself she was scratching.

He clicked on and continued.

– Here is the door jamb she was found propped up against.

He magnified the image and pointed.

– Five deeply scored marks across the woodwork, running downwards almost to the threshold.

The recruit from Majorstua exclaimed: – Like scratch marks from a claw.

– What do you think, Arve? Could this have been made by a bear's paw?

– Looks like it. Pretty sick stuff . . .

– I quite agree, Viken said quietly. – Sicker than anything any of us have ever come across before.

He switched off the computer.

– I'll bet a fiver that the neighbour, Miriam Gaizauskaite, had a visitor last night, even though she says not. She doesn't sit up of an evening drinking out of two wine glasses, one with and one without lipstick. I want to find out everything we can about her background.

– Sounds like a lot of spadework for me, said Arve Norbakk. – Just so long as I don't have to go to . . . where was it, Lithuania? he added with a big grin.

Jarle Frøen spoke.

– What about the actual investigation so far?

– Relax, Mr Prosecutor, Viken said patiently. – We're about to get on to that right now. Jebsen, you can start.

Nina looked down at her notes.

– I spoke to the newspaper delivery man. Mehmed Faruq, fifty-three years old, originally from Kurdistan. His papers all appear to be in order. Speaks passable Norwegian. I've got a list of things he noticed in the course of his morning route, from Carl Berners Place and on down. Three, possibly four cars in Helgesens gate. A couple entering a block. A person getting out of a taxi at Sofienberg Park, right next to the scene of the crime. I traced the taxi driver and he confirms the time. He drove past the same place an hour earlier and on that occasion noticed a cyclist with a child-trailer. We'll take a closer look at all these, but the most important thing is this: the delivery man encountered a male as he was passing through the gate at the address where the victim lived.

– Not bad, Nina. Description?

– The person in question is thirty to forty years old, well above medium height, powerfully built, wearing dark clothes, a coat or long jacket, dark hair. This was about ten past five. There was a light in the entrance, so the delivery man got a good look.

– The timing agrees with what the neighbour told us, that she heard someone opening the gate at around five. Have a good look at the delivery man, including his alibis for the other times that are of interest to us.

– Apparently he's just returned from a fortnight in Germany seeing his relatives. Gardermoen airport records confirm that.

– Excellent.

– Some of you may have noted, continued Nina, – an obvious connection with what we have here and witness observations relating to the Paulsen case.

The child-trailer, Norbakk suggested. – You mentioned that a cyclist pulling one of those was seen earlier this morning too.

Nina winked at him.

– No flies on you. It took me a while longer to notice it. We've been assuming that Paulsen was transported from the woods to the place where the body was found. A car on a private forest road would have attracted attention. A child-trailer, on the other hand . . .

Viken noticed that she didn't seem to mind at all that Arve Norbakk was following her with his droopy eyes.

– But that's for transporting small children in, he interrupted.

– In the bigger models there's room for two large children, Nina explained. – And note that this bicycle with the child-trailer was observed right next to the scene of the crime at quarter to four in the morning. Who cycles around with children in the middle of the night?

Sigge Helgarsson woke up.

– Not everyone detaches the trailer every time they go out. Mine is always on, whether the kids are with me or not.

Norbakk offered his support to Nina.

– Hilde Paulsen was 157 centimetres tall and anything but over-weight. She was found with her legs doubled up under her. And Anita Elvestrand's body was partially mutilated.

– My trailer's down in the garage, said Sigge. – We can check it for size.

Nina smiled brightly.

– I saw it not long ago and took the liberty of trying it out myself. There would definitely be room for a small, lightly built woman inside it.

Viken had a witty comment on the tip of his tongue but at the last moment decided against sharing it.

– You've certainly not been wasting your time, Jebsen, he said instead, and almost patted her on the head. – A description of the man at the gate will be released to the media if he has not reported himself to us within, – he glanced at his watch, – precisely five hours from now.

43

AXEL HEARS A phone. He recognises the ringtone but it isn't his. He searches around the room. The sound is getting closer, but he can't find where it's coming from.

He woke with a start and looked around the strange room. It took a few moments for him to realise he was in Rita's apartment in Tåsen. A few moments more before the memory of what had happened fell over him like an avalanche. He sat upright on the leather sofa. The clock on the wall showed 1.45.

His feet felt cold. He'd thrown his socks away in a rubbish bin in Sofienberg Park. He picked up the phone, turned on the sound. A long list of unanswered calls. Four from Bie, three from Miriam. He called her.

– Where are you, Axel? Why aren't you answering your phone?

– I needed to sleep for a few hours. Are the police there?

– They've been here asking all sorts of questions. After that they rang me twice. Some of them are still out there on the landing. They've been in here too, looking all over the place, looking for something. And there's a man standing guard down in the back yard. I just wish I could wake up soon and all this was only a nightmare.

– The woman lying there, was it your neighbour?

He could hear she was crying. Couldn't think of anything to say to comfort her.

– What did you tell them?

She didn't reply at once.

– You didn't tell them I'd been there?

– No, Axel, please . . . but they rang just now and asked if I'd seen a man who went out the gate early this morning. The description fitted you.

– The delivery man. He saw me.

– You've got to go and talk to them, Axel. Straight away.

He called Bie.

– Axel, she cried. – Are you trying to kill me? Have you any idea how many times I've called you? Rita says you're not well but she has no idea where you are. I was just about to start ringing round the hospitals.

– The hospitals? Pull yourself together, Bie.

– You're the one who needs to pull himself together, she screamed. – Don't you know how worried I've been?

He tried to breathe calmly.

– Listen to me, Bie. Don't interrupt. Something's happened. I can't tell you everything yet. I'll talk to you when I get home. I'm not sick, do you hear me, I am *not* sick. There's something I have to sort out first.

– But where are you?

– With friends. They're helping me.

– Can't you come now? she pleaded, her voice suddenly small and frail.

– Brede, he said suddenly. – I must find Brede.

– Brede? Does this have something to do with him? She sounded almost relieved.

– I have to find him. Then I'll come home.

After ending the call, he sat thinking for a while. This idea about Brede was something that had just occurred to him. He couldn't tell her the truth. Not yet. He slumped down into the sofa again.

As he had closed Miriam's door behind him and tottered down that crooked staircase, it had struck him. This is about me. First the physiotherapist up there in the woods. Then Cecilie Davidsen, his patient, whom he'd visited at home. And now the remains of that body lying outside the door. Not until a few minutes later, as he was staggering through Sofienberg Park, did the memory surface, of

Brede raging at him: *One day I'll destroy you, just the same way you destroyed me*. Now, after a few hours' sleep, this was the thought he clung to: This is about me. And Brede. I betrayed him. No one else could hate me this much.

Rita returned at about 4.30.

– Are you still here, Axel? she exclaimed, sounding pleased and shocked in equal measure.

– It's up to you whether you believe your own eyes or not, he answered.

She took off her coat, pushed her feet into a pair of red slippers with plush trimming and took three plastic bags of shopping into the kitchen. She came back in and sat in the easy chair at the end of the table.

– No problem cancelling the appointments?

– In a manner of speaking. They realise that even you can be ill. But now tell me what's going on.

He leaned back in the sofa, let his eyes trace the line of the joints between the ceiling tiles.

– How long have we been working together, Rita?

She thought about it.

– Soon be twelve years.

– Do you think you know me?

– Yes, I would say so.

– Do you trust me?

– Give over, Axel. There aren't that many people I'd let sit by my death bed. But you're one of them.

He gave a quick smile up at the ceiling.

– I hope you feel the same way once you've heard what I'm about to tell you.

Rita had heated up some leftover fish soup.

– You surely can't believe that, Axel, she exclaimed as she placed the steaming pan on the table. – No one would go so far as to kill three defenceless women just to get at you.

– So you think it's coincidental that all the victims have a connection to me?

She ladled out a portion of soup for him.

– It's not up to me to think anything about anything. That's a job for the police.

– You're right. I'll talk to them. But not until tomorrow.

– Are you out of your mind?

He didn't answer immediately. Slurped down some soup; he hadn't eaten anything since yesterday. When he was finished he said:

– I'll talk to them first thing tomorrow. But there's something I have to do first. This evening.

Rita gave a long, demonstrative shake of the head.

– Don't think I haven't noticed how she's been throwing herself at you from the very first day. That student.

– This is not about her.

Rita didn't buy it.

– I get so angry about things like that.

Axel pushed his plate away.

– Three people have been killed, Rita. In some way or other I'm involved. Let's keep Miriam out of this. Do you have a pair of socks I could borrow? And a torch?

44

VIKEN CLICKED HIS way briskly through the net editions of the newspapers. The police hadn't announced that they suspected the same person was responsible for the murders, but the media had no doubt about it. *VG* quickly dubbed him 'the Beast', having suddenly stopped telling its readers that a killer bear was loose in the city. A memo from Finckenhagen dated that same morning had gone out to everyone with instructions in bold type that from now on, all communications with the media were to go via her to the Chief Superintendent. That was fine by Viken, because it would keep her busy for a while and out of the way of the investigation. On the other hand, she had no real overview of what was going on. Viken had seen enough leaders lose their heads when things began to get hectic. As for himself, the more adrenalin that was pumping round the corridors, the calmer he seemed to be. Perhaps the most important quality of all for a leader in our business, he thought as he opened Jebsen's notes to take a closer look at the interview with the newspaper delivery man.

The phone rang. He answered with a grunt and recognised the voice of the girl down in reception whom he thought of as 'the Bimbo'. No, he didn't see people who just turned up on the doorstep, not even if they had something important to tell him. No, not even if they refused to talk to anyone else but him. She should get in touch with central office in the usual way. He didn't have time to keep repeating this every bloody day.

He was harsher than he meant to be, seeing in his mind's eye the Bimbo sitting behind the counter in her bulging blue uniform shirt. Then he heard another female voice in the background. Picked up a name being mentioned.

– What was that somebody just said to you? he asked the Bimbo.

– Oh, are you still there? I thought you'd hung up.

– I asked you what the woman said.

– She said . . . What did you just say? . . . Something you should know before it's too late; it's about someone named Glenne, her doctor.

Viken greeted the visitor as she emerged from the lift. She was above medium height, with reddish hair and a lot of feminine curves. She was dressed in an expensive-looking black outfit with faint grey stripes. The skirt reached to her knees and she wore high-heeled leather boots. She extended a gloved hand towards him as though expecting him to kiss it. Instead he gave it a quick squeeze and introduced himself.

– Solveig Lundwall, the woman responded in a voice he would unhesitatingly have described as mellifluous.

He took her to his office.

– You wanted to speak to me personally, he began.

She removed her gloves and smoothed them out on her knees.

– I've seen in the newspapers that you have been speaking out about these dreadful . . . events. And I have also seen you on the television news. You are a person who instantly inspires confidence.

– Well, said Viken as he leaned back in his office chair. – Our duty is to make the public feel safe. He had always had a weakness for red-haired women. – You wanted to tell me something about a doctor . . .

– Dr Glenne, she said, interrupting. – I delayed as long as I could, but I can no longer keep this to myself.

Viken took a tape recorder out of the bottom drawer. It hadn't been used for several years.

– Do you have any objection to my recording our conversation?

– Absolutely not, Detective Chief Inspector. On the contrary, I would like as many people as possible to know about this.

He puzzled about what she might mean, but let it go.

– Are we talking about a doctor named Axel Glenne, who runs a clinic in Bogstadveien?

– Yes.

– Are you a patient of his?

She confirmed this too.

– What is it you think we should know about him?

She thought for a moment, then said:

– I am not an informer. I don't want anyone to think that.

He pushed the microphone over towards her.

– People who come to us are not informers, they are witnesses. We are completely dependent on people like you to do our job.

She closed her eyes. Emphasising every word, she said:

– Dr Glenne is a good doctor. Very good. But he is not the man people think he is.

She stopped.

– In what way?

– He has taken all the sins of the world upon his shoulders.

Viken moved his head from side to side but said nothing.

– He has saved many. He saved my husband from certain death.

– Your husband is ill?

She muttered something he didn't catch; it sounded like 'milky hell', but he didn't ask, afraid that she might follow up with the medical history of her entire family.

– I'm probably a little slow on the uptake, Mrs Lundwall, he said instead, – but I'm still not clear what it is you've come here to report.

Still she sat with her eyes closed. He saw that her jaw muscles were clenched.

– Dr Glenne has taken it upon himself to save the world from what is to come. I wanted to follow him, but I no longer believe that he is capable of it. I think he is just a human being, the same as you and me.

Viken started scratching his throat.

– He is a *seducer*, she said, opening her eyes again. She looked straight at him, an almost angry expression in her gaze.

– Does this mean, Viken asked, – does this mean that he has transgressed certain boundaries in his relationships with his patients?

She shook her head.

– Not his patients. But the people with whom he consorts are ruffians. And harlots.

Viken found the word quaint.

– You mean prostitutes?

– Call her what you will.

– Her? Are you talking about a particular woman?

Abruptly Solveig Lundwall rose to her feet.

– Now it is said. If you are looking for him, I know where he is to be found.

Viken stood up too, unsure whether to ask her to sit down again.

– Well we're not looking for this Glenne. But there are still a couple of things in your statement . . .

– I have said what there is to say. The money is of no interest to me whatsoever. You may keep it.

Viken was astounded.

– The money?

Solveig Lundwall offered him her hand, and when he reluctantly took it, she bent suddenly towards him and kissed him on the cheek.

– The thirty pieces of silver, Caiaphas, she whispered in his ear.

Viken pulled back, blinking in confusion as he struggled to work out whether she had been mistaking him for someone else the whole time. She smiled, a strange flash in the eyes, and before he could recover himself, she had turned on her heels and was gone from the room.

He remained standing where he was, rubbing his cheek. Not until a couple of minutes later did he turn off the tape and sink down into his chair, still so nonplussed that he wasn't even able to feel annoyed at having allowed a woman who was so obviously stark raving mad to slip through the filters and get all the way up to his office.

45

AXEL FOLLOWED A track at the upper end of Sognsvann. He kept off the marked paths. He didn't know why, but he didn't want anyone to see him. He had just sent two text messages, one to Miriam, one to Bie. Now he turned off his phone.

It had been raining down in town. As he climbed higher through the forest, he saw that it had been falling as snow up there. The footpaths around Blankvann were covered in a thin white carpet that twinkled in the pale light. He picked up the indefinable scent of winter, though small, shrivelled clusters of blueberries still hung in among the heather. He came across a set of fresh tracks; they looked like elk. He'd spotted elk many times. Somewhere not far from here he had undressed Bie, and while he was taking her from behind against an upended pine trunk, a female elk came charging down the slope. It stopped two metres away, stood there swaying and staring, and for a moment looked as though it might attack. Then it turned away and disappeared, two calves following behind. Next day he told Ola what had happened. They'd been sitting in his office having a cup of coffee before the first patient arrived. *Remember what I said in my best man's speech?* Ola had responded, with the most innocent smile in the world. *There's not an animal in the world that will attack you when you're offering your devotions to Pan.* Ola was the best friend he'd ever had. But he had never told even him the story of what had happened with Brede.

He came to a halt by the tarn. A mere two weeks ago he and Miriam had swum here. He could see her in his mind's eye as she emerged from the water. The naked white body coming towards him. Half jokingly she had said she wanted to take him to the place she came from. To a house by the sea, far from the nearest town, which was called Kaunas.

He climbed over the top of the rise and down the other side. Approached the pine-branch shelter from below. Stood a while and studied it. No one there. He switched on the torch and peered in. An empty beer bottle on the rolled-up blanket, an opened packet of frankfurters, a newspaper. He opened it out. *Dagbladet*, two days old. Down at the bottom a picture of the detective chief inspector who had interviewed him: *No new leads in the bear murders case.*

Some distance away, on the far side of the hollow, he sat down in the damp moss, his back against a pine trunk. He sat without moving as the darkness wrapped itself around him. It was wildly unlikely that Brede would show up here, but Axel was absolutely certain that he would. He listened to the autumn evening. The rustling of the treetops. A plane on its way to Gardermoen. Silence afterwards. If anyone approached the shelter, he would hear them coming a long way off.

Half an hour past midnight. A wind had got up in the hollow behind him. The temperature was probably below zero. A half-moon slipped in and out of the clouds. He pulled his jacket tight around him, but it didn't help. A few minutes later he got up and padded down to the shelter. Lay down inside with the mouldy-smelling woollen blanket wrapped around him. Through the rip in the plastic he looked up at a bare patch of black sky. *Brede has been given enough chances to do the right thing, Axel. It doesn't help him at all if you try to excuse what he's done.* Don't send him away, please. He didn't mean it. His father's voice when he answers is controlled, but Axel can hear that there's something smouldering in there, something that will explode if he makes a wrong move, and blow him to smithereens. He daren't say any more. And then his father lays a hand on his shoulder. *I appreciate your wanting to defend him, Axel. You're a fine boy. You'll always do the right thing. But you must understand, some things cannot be forgiven.*

Brede, he thought as he lay there, it wasn't me that wanted it to work out this way. And now as I lie here looking out into the dark, I sense the sheerness of that membrane that divides your life from mine. One more breath could turn me into you with no way back again.

He'd heard nothing; perhaps he'd fallen asleep. Suddenly something covered the gash in the plastic. A face. He jumped up and crawled out backwards. As he straightened up, he heard footsteps moving across the forest floor. Saw a shadow disappearing between the trees.

– Wait! he shouted, running. Stopped by the rise and listened. Heard footsteps some way ahead, in the direction of the tarn. He sprinted as hard as he could, stumbled in the undergrowth, got to his feet again. The figure appeared in front of him, over by the boat that lay upside down, hobbled past it and on up the bank. Axel was gaining on him, caught up with him at last, grabbed him by the shoulder. The person tried to pull himself free. Axel seized him round the waist and threw him to the ground, planted a knee in his chest, pulled the torch from his pocket and switched it on.

– Brede! he screamed into the face below him.

The man pinched his eyes shut against the bright light. He had long grey hair and a beard, and sunken eyes. He looked to be over sixty. He stank of urine.

– What do you want? he whimpered.

Axel bit his lip and swore. Time to pull yourself together, Axel Glenne. Surely you didn't really think it was Brede.

– Are you the person who lives in that shelter?

The old man tried to nod.

– No one else lives there?

Now he shook his head. He had managed to work one arm free and held it up in front of himself like a shield.

– Are you going to kill me now? he murmured.

I am waiting for you. Sitting in the car, leafing through the newspapers. According to some professor or other, they shouldn't be writing about me. Because that is what I want. That the need for attention might make me kill again. If the idiot only knew just how wide of the mark he is. I don't want attention. Don't give a shit what the papers say. This is about you and me. Nobody else.

Finally you show up. I follow you with my eyes as you head down the pavement on the other side of the road. You don't know it yet. But you suspect it. That it's your turn next. Unless chance comes along to save you. The only god that can interfere. I could have planned it in more detail. Tried to control the god of chance. But unpredictability is my nature. I am willing to risk everything. You aren't like that. You always stop in time. Yet we are twin souls. And in that case the bear should be not just my inner animal but yours too.

By the time you hear this, you'll be lying there unable to move. Unable to do anything but listen to my voice. Now you understand what you've done. You feel regret. It doesn't help. Only chance can save you now. As I make this recording, there is still a chance you might escape. Many things can go wrong. You will be given a final warning. Maybe you'll inform on me then and save your own skin. If not, it will be your turn. Three times now I have gone to women and taken them with me. The fourth time things will be different. You will come to me. Your guilty conscience will bring you here. And that is why you are lying in the dark, listening to my voice.

The god of chance is weak now, too weak to interfere. He almost stopped me that day I came for the third woman. When she smelled the cloth and passed out, she vomited and her head banged against the window. A couple with a dog came by but I got her down on to the floor of the car, and it was so dark they couldn't see anything. She was three nights with me. I untied her hands when I was lying beside her. She wanted me. Even though I said I had to kill her, she wanted me. But I didn't exploit her. I'm not like that. Lay next to her the whole of that last night.

Let her hold me and caress me as much as she wanted. It calmed her down and was good for her. We both fell asleep. In the morning I showed her how it would happen. Then I had to tape her up again. I'll show you too. I'll follow every twitch of your face once you realise what's going to happen to you down there in the cellar. Can hardly wait, just thinking about it. To see your eyes then will be the most blissful moment of my life. Afterwards you will be gone, and I will be somewhere there are no other people. What I have done can never be atoned for. They hate me for it. Despise me. There is no way back. That is what it means to be perfectly alone. It never ends. That is what I want.

PART IV

46

Wednesday 24 October

NINA JEBSEN PARKED on the pavement. A constable was still standing in the entrance to the block in Helgesens gate. He was a few years younger than her, tall and muscular, with fair hair. Built like an athlete, she thought. She exchanged a few words with him before heading up to the attic flat. The security tape outside the door had been removed. She rang the bell. It took almost a minute for Miriam Gaizauskaite to open up. Her face was pale and drawn. She tried to smile when she saw Nina.

– I wasn't expecting you just yet, she said.

Nina sat on the sofa and looked around the flat. The walls were painted a peach white; the curtains were red with a motif of tulips. A few plants with drooping heads stood on the windowsill.

Miriam emerged from the kitchen carrying coffee cups and a bowl of fruit. Nina helped herself to an apple. She was hungry, but she could hold out until lunch if she had enough coffee.

– As I mentioned, there are one or two things I'd like to talk to you about. We could have done it on the phone, but we find we often get better results face to face.

– I've already given a statement, Miriam said.

– Yes, you've already helped us a lot, Nina replied encouragingly as she took a bite from the apple. – Don't you have lectures today?

Miriam looked up through the skylight.

– Couldn't face going.

– I understand. But it's probably not such a good idea to sit here thinking too much.

– Two good friends of mine have already called to tell me off. I'll get going again tomorrow.

Nina looked at her. Miriam had large dark eyes and a fine, high forehead on which tiny wrinkles appeared and as suddenly disappeared again. Her nose was quite long, but narrow and straight. She could feel that she liked her, and reminded herself not to let it affect her judgement.

– You said that you heard someone down in the yard on Monday morning. You were lying awake and the time was a couple of minutes past five. Did you hear the gate once or twice?

Miriam thought about it.

– Just once.

– Did you hear anyone talking?

– No.

Nina waited a moment before saying:

– You can trust us, Miriam. Don't be afraid to tell us what you know.

– I've got nothing else to say. Nothing new.

She got up, disappeared out into the kitchen and returned with a cafetière full of coffee.

– Good coffee, Nina said after taking a sip. She added: – You said you were alone all evening yesterday.

Miriam gave a slight nod.

– But that doesn't appear to be the case.

She was startled.

– What do you mean?

– Our technical investigators found a footprint out in the corridor, in the blood on the floor. Where someone stepped in their stockinged feet.

Nina noticed how Miriam was holding on tightly to the arms of her chair.

– They found traces of the same sock in your flat. In the hallway, here in the living room, and over to the alcove.

Without waiting for her reaction, Nina took a sheet of paper from her pocket, unfolded it and laid it on the table in front of Miriam.

– The man delivering the newspapers met someone going out as he was on his way in. He gave us a description, which our artist has used. Look at it carefully, see if you can connect it with someone you might have seen before.

Miriam sat there looking at the drawing. Nina saw a quiver run down her neck, and her pupils grew even wider. Here it comes, she thought, just as Miriam buried her face in her hands and her whole body began to shake.

Viken's office door was ajar. Nina Jebsen burst in, knocking as she closed it behind her. Viken was seated at his computer. He looked up at her over the top of his rectangular glasses.

– Good to see you, Jebsen.

He pointed to the chair on the other side of the desk.

– Just by the way, I have no objection to people knocking on the door *before* they come barging in.

– Of course, I'm sorry. She took out her notebook, flipped through it. – Thought this might interest you. I had another talk with Miriam Gaizauskaite.

– You look like you just won first prize in the office cake lottery.

– Miriam has been on a placement at a clinic this autumn, she said, blushing slightly. Viken felt certain it was because he had mentioned cakes. – Care to guess who her supervisor was?

Viken's jaws began to work.

– You don't mean . . .

She didn't let him finish.

– Dr Axel Glenne. Who we know for sure was the last person to talk to Hilde Paulsen. And was Cecilie Davidsen's doctor. We both agreed that was a little odd in itself.

– A bit tricky, certainly, Viken observed, not quite sure where he had picked up that particular expression.

– But that isn't all.

He was curious now, took off his reading glasses and placed them on the desk.

– Glenne was at Miriam Gaizauskaite's place on Monday night.

– I'll be damned. Are you sure?

– He's spent the night with her twice before, she said triumphantly. – On Tuesday morning he left her flat at about five. According to Miriam, he was the one who found the body outside the door.

Viken let out a long, slow breath, like the sound of air being squeezed from an old rubber mattress.

– The man at the gate, he said. – The description from the newspaper delivery man, it fits. Bloody hell, Jebsen, I think we're beginning to get somewhere here. Let's bring him in.

– I rang the clinic, she told him. – He's off sick and hasn't been there this week.

– Then let's try his home. He turned back to his computer.

– I've rung there too. No one picks up. But his wife answered when I called her on her mobile.

Viken shot a smile at her that was a mixture of surprise and appreciation.

– He hasn't been home since Monday morning. He's called her a couple of times. She says she has no idea where he is.

Viken was on his feet instantly.

– Top marks, Inspector Jebsen. A-plus. I've said all along this has something to do with Dr Glenne.

47

THE WOMAN WHO opened the door was slim and of medium height. She might have been over forty, but she looked younger. Partly because her dark hair was combed forward in a style that seemed very modern to Viken, but above all because of the shape of her face. High cheekbones that kept the skin in place when it might have started to sag.

– Mrs Glenne, I presume? Sorry for disturbing you, he said, surprised at his own instinctive courtesy towards her.

She offered him her hand, and he shook it, surprising himself again. He didn't often shake hands with witnesses he was about to interview.

– Vibeke Frisch Glenne, she said, her handshake firm, with no sign of nervous damp in the palm.

Viken ushered Norbakk forward.

– This is Sergeant Arve Norbakk.

As she greeted his colleague, Viken noticed that her slanting eyes opened wider.

– Eh . . . I believe we've met before, she said, her skin turning a shade darker under the suntan.

– We chatted in town one evening earlier this autumn, Norbakk explained with his boyish smile. – At a club. Smuget, wasn't it?

Viken had a quick think and concluded that it wasn't a disadvantage for his colleague to have met the lady before. If she responded to Norbakk the way most women did, it meant they would both be well received.

Vibeke Glenne led the way into the living room. It was large and bright, with windows facing east and west. Two enormous paintings hung on the wall, neither one of them depicting anything in particular, but the colours were bright, and they looked expensive.

She gestured towards the leather armchairs.

– Do sit down, I'll get some coffee.

A girl of about eight or nine peeked in at them.

– Hello, said Norbakk. – Are you the one called Marlen?

– Blimey, said Viken. – Have you studied the whole family tree already?

– Didn't you see the sign on the door? Norbakk winked.

– You're not wearing uniforms, the little girl stated. She was fair haired, her face round; she didn't look like her mother at all.

– Makes no difference, we're still real, Norbakk countered, producing his badge.

Marlen shuffled over to him and he gave it to her.

– Can you see that's me?

The girl stared at the card, then up at his face. She gave a sudden shy smile, and Viken was surprised to note that Norbakk, who was quiet and reserved , seemed to have a way with children too. All the better, because he himself certainly didn't. What he did have was a sense of where people stood. Interpreting the code developed by each individual. Norbakk's was a touch more encrypted than most, thought Viken. But he was well on the way to cracking it.

Vibeke Glenne returned with a pot of coffee and small gold-rimmed cups on a tray, along with a plate of biscuits that looked home-made.

– Mrs Glenne, as I explained to you on the telephone . . .

She interrupted. – I understand why you're here. But that's about all I understand. Marlen, go down to your room.

– She isn't disturbing us, Viken assured her, registering the little girl's miffed expression. Psychologically speaking it would be an advantage to have the child there, he reasoned.

– She can come up later if there's anything you want to ask her.

Once the daughter had marched out with her haughty princess's neck, Vibeke Glenne added: – I want to protect the children as much as possible. For a moment her voice seemed uncertain. – Though I don't quite know what it is I'm protecting them *from* . . .

She sat upright, looked as though she were making an effort to pull herself together.

– You surely can't believe that Axel has anything to do with these murders.

Viken said, in his most neutral tone: – It's not our job to believe, Mrs Glenne. We leave that to the priests.

It was a phrase he had reeled off many times in the past. A slight movement of her face was enough to assure him that she took his point and was not offended.

– We simply note that nothing has been heard from him. Not to frighten you, Mrs Glenne, but let me remind you that three people have recently gone missing in Oslo. All three were later found dead.

Vibeke Glenne's face turned grey.

– So you have not seen your husband since Sunday?

– Monday morning. He was up even earlier than usual, I think. He was gone by the time I got up, at around seven.

Norbakk made a note.

– How would you describe him? Viken wanted to know.

For a moment she looked surprised.

– Describe?

Viken didn't answer, gave her time.

– He's hard working, clever, a good father. Someone you can trust. I would say he is strong.

Viken was tempted to inform her that this trustworthy man had recently spent the night with a young female student in her flat, but decided not to. He might need to spring the information later as a surprise.

– I'd like to ask you about the Thursday thirteen days ago, he said instead. – Was your husband at home in the afternoon and all through the evening?

She thought about this.

– He goes for a bike ride in the marka every Thursday afternoon. I'll check to see if anything special happened that evening.

She disappeared out into the kitchen, returning straight away with a calendar, flipped back through it.

– He's written 'office work' here. He often stays late at the office in the evenings after he's back from his bike ride. Applications, social security forms, things like that. That's all I know.

– When did he come home?

– I pick Marlen up at the riding school on Thursdays. We're home by eight thirty. I don't think Axel was home by then that Thursday. Why that day in particular?

Viken waited before replying.

– That was the evening one of the victims disappeared. You perhaps know that she was a patient of your husband's?

Vibeke jumped up from her chair.

– But this is insane. Do you know how long I've lived with him? Twenty-three years. If he was mixed up in anything, I would have known it. You can be a hundred per cent certain of that.

Just the same way you can be certain he's a man you can trust, Viken thought with a sour smile on his lips.

– Of course, he said. – We don't doubt that you know him better than anyone else. Can I just use your toilet?

She accompanied him out into the corridor. Viken turned and gave a sign to Norbakk, indicating that he should carry on going through the points they had agreed on earlier in the car.

They came into a large hall with light marble tiling on the floor. Two of the walls were almost covered by mirrors. This must be the hall of mirrors, Viken joked to himself. The toilet was in a corridor leading off it. He locked the door behind him. Having emptied his bladder, he washed his hands. He glanced over at the shelf below the mirror. A tube of toothpaste. Toothbrushes in a mug hanging on the wall. A packet of paracetamol, sticking plasters, some theatrical make-up for kids. The gentry each have their own bathroom, of course, he realised. He sent a text message to Norbakk: *Try to get a look at the other bathroom. Probably upstairs.* On more than one occasion he had lectured younger colleagues on precisely this subject: living rooms show how people want to be seen in the eyes of others;

bathrooms will always tell you something about what lies behind the facade.

As he was letting himself out, he heard a familiar sound coming from a half-open door on the other side of the corridor. He peeked in. A teenager was seated on the edge of his bed, strumming on an electric guitar. A small amplifier stood on the floor in front of him.

– Practising? Viken asked.

The lad didn't seemed surprised to see him standing there. He nodded and carried on plucking away at the strings.

– You play in a band?

Another nod from the lad. He had shoulder-length black hair that looked dyed, and a ring through one eyebrow.

– What kind of music? Viken wanted to know.

The lad glanced up at him, with perhaps just a touch of contempt in his eyes.

– Rock, blues, metal, whatever.

– I play guitar too, the policeman revealed.

– Oh yeah? The lad appeared tolerably interested in this bit of information.

– What's your name?

– Tom.

– Mind if I have a go on your guitar?

Tom hesitated for a few seconds before getting up. He was skinny and rangy, the same height as Viken, with a row of pimples studded across his forehead. He unhooked the strap and handed over the guitar. A Gibson Les Paul. More expensive than any guitar Viken had ever owned. His fingers glided reverently across the strings.

– Get this from your father?

– Birthday present, the lad confirmed. – Dad bought it in England.

Viken strummed a few chords. Even with such a tiny amplifier he could feel the power in the sleek instrument.

– Wish I had one of these, he sighed as he ran through some riffs. – Know this one?

He let his fingers go. Tom watched, his face expressionless.

– Good, he said when Viken had finished. – Heard it before.

– 'Black Magic Woman', Viken said enthusiastically.

– Santana, isn't it?

– Santana nicked it from Fleetwood Mac. The guy who wrote it was called Peter Green. Best white blues guitarist ever. He had a Gibson exactly like yours. In the end he let his nails grow so long he couldn't play any more.

– What did he do that for? Tom asked.

– He thought it might cure him of having to play the blues.

– Crazy.

Viken handed the guitar back.

– Your turn.

Tom hung the guitar round his neck, turned up the amp a few notches. Viken didn't recognise the riff, but it was powerful; the lad could play, there was no doubt about it. Suddenly a hoarse, reedy sound emerged from his throat. Viken leaned in the doorway, surprised. The lad sat there with eyes closed, suddenly deep inside his own, vulnerable world, with no thought of the stranger standing there watching him.

When he was finished, Viken exclaimed: – That's powerful stuff, Tom.

The boy could hear that he meant it and smiled quickly, then turned and put the guitar on its stand next to the bed.

– Do *you* play in a band? he asked, clearly to deflect his embarrassment.

– Long time ago now, said Viken.

– What was it called?

Viken grinned. – We called ourselves the Graveyard Dancers. Actually came quite close to getting a recording contract.

– Cool name, Tom nodded.

Viken took his chance.

– Why isn't your father home?

Tom shrugged his shoulders. – He rang Ma yesterday. It has something to do with his brother.

– Your father's brother?

– Yep, twin brother.

Viken was careful not to show too much interest.

– So your father has a twin brother. What's his name?

– Brede.

– Are they completely identical?

– Dunno. Never met him.

At that moment Vibeke Glenne appeared.

– Are you in here?

Viken winked at Tom.

– Couldn't pass up the chance to try that guitar. I've never played on anything as good. Get yourself a Peter Green album, hear what he gets out of a Gibson.

– Album? Tom echoed in surprise.

– Er, I'm sure you can download the tracks, the chief inspector hurriedly corrected himself.

– Your son tells me that Axel has a twin brother.

Vibeke Glenne refilled their coffee cups.

– There hasn't been any contact for years. Brede is an alcoholic, or a junkie, or I don't know what. Been in and out of institutions all his life.

– The lad says he's never met him.

She stared off into space.

– Neither have I actually.

Viken looked at her in astonishment.

– In twenty-three years?

– They lost touch when they were in their teens. Brede wouldn't see Axel any more. Jealousy and all the rest of it. Axel has managed to make something out of his life. Brede didn't care about anything.

Viken sat thinking about this as Norbakk wrote something in his notebook.

– So you don't actually know if they resemble each other?

– They're identical. I've seen photos of them when they were children. It's impossible to tell the difference between them.

– Can you show me some of those photographs?

– Childhood photographs? Now listen here, I've still not even been told why you . . .

She broke off, got up and went into the next room. Viken heard her opening drawers. She returned with three or four photo albums in her arms.

– Here. I'm sure you'll understand if I say I'm not in the mood to sit here reminiscing with you.

– That's perfectly all right.

The photographs were from the early days of colour film. The colours were dull and had acquired a yellowish patina. Days by the seaside, celebrations of National Day in May. A woman with blond hair gathered in a braid, and a much older man whom Viken seemed to recognise.

– Axel's parents, I presume.

Vibeke Glenne leaned over the table.

– That's right. He was twenty years older than her. Famous for being in the Resistance; later became a supreme court advocate.

– Torstein Glenne? exclaimed Viken, astonished that the connection hadn't occurred to him earlier. – Is your husband Torstein Glenne's son?

He composed himself and flipped on through the album, stopping at a page with a number of swimming scenes. Fjord, smooth sloping rocks.

– Where were these taken?

Vibeke Glenne cast a quick glance.

– At the cabin. The summer place down in Larkollen. We've still got it.

Viken's eyes narrowed.

– Summer place? Does it have a basement?

– A creep-in basement. Why on earth do you want to know that?

Viken didn't answer.

– How old is the cabin? he wanted to know.

Vibeke Glenne raised her chin, obviously a mannerism of hers when she was thinking about something.

– It's been in the family for a long time. From when Torstein was a child, I should think. From about the twenties or thirties.

– Is this Axel or Brede?

Viken held the album up so she could see.

– Axel, she decided.

– Show me a picture of Brede.

She pointed lower down on the page.

– But they're absolutely identical, Viken protested, – even got the same swimming trunks. How can you be sure?

– Axel told me who was who.

Viken flipped on. Father, mother and one of the twins.

– Are there no pictures of them together? he wondered.

– What do you mean?

Viken searched back through all three albums.

– Dozens of pictures of twin brothers, but not a single one of them both together.

Vibeke Glenne looked exasperated.

– And what's supposed to be the significance of that?

Viken mulled it over.

– You tell me. Probably none. Who have you talked to about Brede?

– Talked to? Actually, no one other than Axel.

– Are you telling me that you have never heard his parents or other members of the family say anything else at all about this twin brother?

She said: – Brede was sent away from home when he was fifteen. According to Axel, it was impossible for him to go on living there. He was beyond control. It was something that was never talked about in the family. Brede was, and is, taboo. Axel said I wasn't to mention him to other people.

– So the parents sent their fifteen-year-old son away and never wanted to see him again?

– Axel's family are a *little* unusual, Vibeke Glenne confirmed. – Not exactly awash with love and affection. I've never known my mother-in-law, Astrid, to care in the slightest about anyone other than herself. Not even her grandchildren. And old Torstein was, of course, a god. Remote and severe.

After a short pause she added: – Axel never talks about it, but I have noticed that he is still preoccupied with his twin brother. When he called yesterday, he mumbled something about finding him. It's almost certainly got something to do with what happened when Brede was sent away.

– And what did happen?

She leaned back in the chair, crossed one leg over the other. Norbakk stood up before she began to speak.

– Afraid I'll have to use your toilet too. No, don't get up, I can find my own way.

– GET ANYTHING OUT of your visit to the toilet? asked Viken once they were seated in the car again.

Norbakk swung the vehicle down towards the gate and out on to the road.

– Mostly just the usual stuff, he said. – I presume you don't want the brand names of a lot of shampoos and hairsprays and skin creams.

– Could probably use a few tips, said Viken. – What about medicines?

– Paracetomol, ibuprofen, stuff like that. A couple of things I didn't recognise; I'll check them when we get back.

– Doctors want to stuff us full of chemicals for the slightest thing, Viken observed. – But when it comes to their own family, they shut up shop. You said *mostly* the usual stuff?

Norbakk accelerated out of the roundabout.

– Well, not all parents with a family of young kids have a pair of handcuffs hidden away at the back of the wardrobe in the bedroom.

– Handcuffs? And in the bedroom?

– I got mixed up with all the doors and by happenstance ended up in the wrong room.

– I didn't hear that, Arve, Viken grinned. When the sergeant was still wet behind the ears, he was the one who had taught him the use of the word *happenstance*. It had served him well many times himself.

He sat there scratching his jaw.

– So Axel Glenne allegedly has a twin brother, he said after a while.

– Allegedly?

Viken started humming a melody. Even the most fervent Stones fan might have had difficulty in recognising 'Under My Thumb'.

– I have very clear memories of a case we worked on when I was in Manchester. Chap who had been knocked down and stabbed, had his credit card and all his ID stolen. He didn't know who the attacker was, but he was able to give a very detailed description of him.

He carried on humming, possibly the same song. Norbakk glanced over at him.

– Was the case solved?

– Indeed it was. The description fitted the victim himself so well that some bright spark thought of checking it out. And it matched.

– He'd stabbed himself and stolen his own ID?

– Exactly. But it was impossible to get him to see it. He's still walking around believing he was attacked. If, that is, the shrinks haven't managed to get his head sorted out. And now I'm going to reveal to you why I'm telling you this entertaining little tale. Imagine a man in his forties. He has a twin brother no one in his family has ever seen hide nor hair of.

– His brother hates him.

– All right. But there is not one damn picture of the two of them together.

– Chance is what rules almost everything that happens in the world.

Viken gestured with his arm.

– Don't get me wrong, Arve. I'm not the type that takes the long way round. The simplest answers are always the best. But this business about the twin . . .

– Was he thrown out of the house? I didn't hear the whole story.

Viken took a box of pills out of his pocket and tapped out a couple.

– Acid indigestion, he explained. – Bananas are just as good, but I can't go around looking like a starving ape.

He found a bottle of dead fizzy water in the glove compartment.

– The Glenne family hardly sounds like the best family in the world to have grown up in. But everyone has some sort of cross to bear. You know about the father. One of the heroes in the Resistance, and after that, a big cheese in the supreme court for years. They still called him Colonel there, long after the war ended. And the mother, according to Vibeke Glenne, was an immature and self-centred upper-class woman. But there again, it's by no means certain a daughter-in-law is the most objective person to provide that kind of description. The older Mrs Glenne apparently didn't want children. And when she suddenly found herself with two, that was at least one too many. It was worse for the twin who was disciplined according to Old Testament principles. Naturally he grew up to be the terror of the neighbourhood. The good twin, Axel, always tried to defend him – this is still according to the younger Mrs Glenne – but the whole thing exploded the summer they turned fifteen.

He put the tablets in his mouth, swallowed them down with a swig of water, and made a face.

– Would have been better off using wiper fluid, he groaned.

– What happened that summer?

Viken started chewing on a salt pastille. He noted with satisfaction that his story about the twins had captured Norbakk's full attention.

– Vibeke Glenne says that at one time old Torstein had a dog. Apparently he was more devoted to it and treated it better than his wife *or* his kids. It wouldn't surprise me if that was true. I was fortunate enough to meet Colonel Glenne on several occasions before he retired. The rumours I had heard were by no means exaggerated: he was not the sort of man you messed about with, if I can put it like that.

He looked out across the fields, up to a copse under the bright evening sky.

– Quite nice out here, he mused.

– What about the dog?

Viken turned towards Norbakk.

– You want to hear the end of the tale? Short version, Brede got pissed off with the animal, almost certainly with good reason. He shot it with one of the colonel's own guns. Axel pleaded for him, his wife says, but his pleas fell on deaf ears and the lad was packed off to what used to be called in those days an approved school. He never came back home.

They drove over the crest of a hill. On the other side, at the edge of the road, a number of floral bouquets were gathered, a few small lighted candles beside them.

– Accident black spot, said Norbakk. – This stretch here is supposed to be highly dangerous.

Viken didn't hear what he said. He continued on his own train of thought.

– My idea goes something like this: imagine this twin has not merely disappeared, but never even existed in the first place.

– That ought to be easy enough to find out, Norbakk countered.

– Probably. A run through births, marriages and deaths ought to do it, even if he changed his name.

– What about asking the mother? Isn't she still alive?

– I gather she's senile, yodelling away in some posh rest home somewhere in the west end of town.

Norbakk appeared to be thinking about this.

– The three killings we're working with are unlike anything else I've ever come across in this country before, said Viken. – We've been offered a profiler if we want one. But it won't do any harm if we think along psychological lines without having so-called experts breathing down our necks. You remember the profile I made of the perpetrator after the first two murders? A highly educated man in a well-paid job, a family man with a split personality, someone who grew up with a cold and unemotional mother who tyrannised him. When you've got a serial killer, be sure to take a very good look at the relationship he had with his mother. That's where you'll find the skeleton in the cupboard.

– Are you trying to say that this doctor, Glenne, has an imaginary twin brother who carries out sick stuff like this for him?

– I'm not saying anything, Arve, but there's no law against thinking out loud. Often very necessary, in fact. When Norbakk didn't respond, he added: – System is alpha and omega in our kind of work, I've been telling you that ever since you left school. But at the same time it's important not to overlook your gut feeling. In the end, most cases are solved by the gut, Arve, whether we like it or not.

He laid a hand on his own, rumbling and growling like a leaden sky on a late summer's day. Maybe it was protesting about the part it had been given to play.

49

FOR THE SECOND day in succession, Axel woke up on Rita's sofa. He looked at his wristwatch. Thought it had stopped, but the clock on the wall showed the same time, and afternoon sunlight streamed in through the living-room window.

He hadn't told Rita he would be coming back, but when he peered into the kitchen he saw that the table was laid for him. There was a note next to the plate: *You'll find what you need in the fridge and in the cupboard on the right.*

He swigged down two glasses of cold orange juice, made himself a muesli mix and started the coffee machine going as he waited for the muesli to swell. Glanced through *Aftenposten. Police have important leads in bear-murder cases.* On page 4 was an identikit drawing of a person they wanted to talk to, a man seen near the scene of the crime that morning. – Is that what I look like? he murmured. Wide face and curly hair flopping over his forehead.

He took his coffee into the living room, sat back down on the sofa, turned on his mobile. No message from Miriam. Three from Bie. He listened to the first of them . . . *And the police have been here looking for you. Asking where you were when your patient went missing. They looked through the photo album and asked all sorts of things about Brede, wondered if he existed at all. It was horrible. Please come home, Axel. Now.*

He sent a text in reply: *Be home this evening.* Couldn't face the thought of what it would be like. An unfaithful husband. A father wanted by the police. *You're a good boy, Axel. You'll always do the right thing.* He'd reached some kind of limit. If he went any further, he'd end up losing everything he had. Was that why he was still sitting there? Did he want to give everything up? Want Bie to be so crushed that she wouldn't have him back? Want her to do what he wasn't capable of doing himself, breaking up? *You must be a very happy man.*

He waited another half-hour before ringing Miriam. Was about to disconnect when she finally answered.

– I miss you, he said.

She said nothing.

– Miriam?

– Why did you disappear yesterday?

There was a note in her voice he hadn't heard before.

– Couldn't you have stayed and talked to the police?

She was right. He had been cowardly.

– They found out someone had been here, Axel. I had to tell them it was you.

He looked out of the window. In the next-door garden there was a climbing frame with a swing and an orange plastic slide.

– You've got every right to be angry with me.

– I'm not angry, Axel, I'm afraid.

– I understand that.

– No, you don't understand.

Between the rooftops he could make out the trees in the Nordre cemetery, and a chimney sticking up from Ullevål hospital. The sky was pale grey, with a hint of yellow.

Without knowing why, he said: – Is it me you're afraid of?

He heard her draw breath.

– You must go to the police.

If he didn't turn himself in, they'd soon be publishing his name and his photograph. But he sat there listening to her voice, and he couldn't bring himself to regret any of it.

– I want to see you one more time, he said. – Then I'll go to the police.

– It's my fault.

– What is your fault, Miriam?

– If it hadn't been for me, none of this would have happened.

She's the one regretting it, he thought. I can't bear to hear her saying that.

– I must see you.

– I'll call you this evening, she muttered.

– Are you at home now?

She hesitated before saying: – I'm at a friend's house. Slept here last night. I have to pull myself together and go back home soon.

– I'll come over.

– No, Axel. I daren't.

She ended the call. He rang her again, but she didn't answer.

Rita arrived at 5.45. He was still sitting on the sofa, looking out at the evening sky. It had turned a dark yellow.

– Are you still sitting here, Axel? she exclaimed. – You're becoming a fixture.

He smiled feebly.

– Don't worry, Rita, I'm not moving in.

She carried in some bags of shopping.

– I didn't mean it like that. Have you spoken to the police yet?

He didn't answer.

– Axel, for God's sake. They're all over the place looking for you. I had to tell a little white lie at the office. Actually, it was more dark grey.

She was getting in trouble too because of him.

– You've got no call to be in hiding. What's the matter with you?

She sat down in a chair.

– Is it that student? Miriam?

He leaned his head back.

– I don't expect you to understand it, Rita. I don't understand it myself. I turn my back on Bie and the kids, spend the night with a student seventeen years younger than me. I stumble over a dead woman and run off. Last night I was wandering about up in the Nordmarka and terrified the life out of some old tramp.

Rita leaned towards him, put a hand on his arm.

– Sounds like the worst kind of mid-life crisis to me. Maybe you'd better pick up the pieces before it's too late.

He had to smile. Just for a moment he felt he was standing on something firm that wouldn't give way beneath him. A place where it was possible to take a decision. Doubt is what makes you crack up, he thought. You've never been the brooding type. You've always acted. Always moved on.

– You're right, Rita. Time to get things straightened up. I'll go to the police. But there's one thing I have to do first.

He could see that she very much wanted to know what that might be, but he didn't give her the chance to ask.

50

NINA JEBSEN POPPED a piece of Nicorette into her mouth and again tried to get into the register of residents site. When she got the same message again, that the server was down, she reached for the phone to call Viken, and remembered in the same instant that he was in a meeting. She considered postponing the search, but then had a better idea. The chief inspector had popped in to see her after returning from Nesodden. She had rarely seen him looking more pleased. He congratulated her once again for establishing that Axel Glenne had been at the student's flat in Rodeløkka. Nina had no objection to being praised by Viken, and she was encouraged to continue her search for Axel Glenne's twin, even though she was unable to access the register of residents. Even when Viken was at his most provoking, she found herself inspired to try her hardest. It was by no means everyone's reaction. Sigge Helgarsson, for example, responded to Viken's style in the opposite way, becoming reluctant, passive, inclined to do no more than the bare minimum.

She called the Rikshospital. Was informed that the departmental head was the only one able to give permission to divulge information from the maternity ward, even when the information was over forty years old. The head had gone home for the day, but would be back tomorrow. Nina looked at the pile of documents on her desk, thought things over. Viken had said Glenne was born in Oslo, but not where in Oslo. She could try the other hospitals, but reasoned that the same rules of access would apply there. She decided that Axel Glenne's twin brother could wait another day. *If he exists*, as Viken had commented, with that rascally smile of his.

For a man like Axel Glenne, a successful doctor and father of three, to have invented a twin brother and persuaded even those closest to him that he was out there somewhere seemed a little far-fetched, to put it mildly. Even more so that it all had something to do with the murders of three women. It was no secret that Viken had a weakness for convoluted psychology. He had persuaded her to read books by John Douglas and other writers on the subject of the psychological profiling of killers, and he was apparently still in regular contact with a profiling expert he had got to know during his much-vaunted period with the CID in Manchester. Not long ago he had given a lunch-hour lecture on split personalities. But he had no respect at all for the opinions of Norwegian psychologists and psychiatrists on such matters, know-alls and phoneys that they were, every last one of them.

Nina had already managed to assemble a fair amount of information on Glenne and his family. The wife, Vibeke Frisch Glenne, known as Bie, had studied theatre and art history. In the eighties and nineties she had been editor of the Norwegian edition of *Anais*, later working as a freelancer for a number of other women's magazines. She wrote about literature, travel, sex, fashion, and of course about health. Nina had found images of her on the net, from which it was obvious that she was an attractive woman. The Glennes' joint income was of a size she could only dream about, and they had enough in the bank to keep them in style for the rest of their lives. Axel Glenne had been in practice for sixteen years and there had never been any complaints against him. He had three tickets for speeding and a conviction for driving while under the influence of alcohol that was over twenty years old. Not a lot that could be used against him.

She read through the memorandum Arve had written about Miriam Gaizauskaite. As usual, he had done a thorough job and had come up with a lot of stuff. Miriam hailed from a small country town in the south of Lithuania. Catholic family. Oldest of four children. Mother a doctor. Father a naval officer in the former Soviet Union who died in a submarine accident in the Barents Sea when Miriam was eight years old. Miriam came to Norway six years ago to take up a place at the faculty of medicine in the University of

Oslo. From there on the information was a little sparse, and Nina reflected that for once, she could have done a better job than Arve. She also noted a few errors.

It was gone 6.30. Her stomach was rumbling. All she'd had to eat since lunchtime was a piece of crispbread. Convenient to have so much to do that she had no time to think about food, but it was going to be a long evening, and she ought to eat something to keep her concentration levels up. She could probably allow herself a little more now, seeing as she'd missed dinner. Arve Norbakk was also going to be working late, and she had nothing against a visit to a local café in his company.

He glanced up when she popped her head in.

– Busy?

He thought about it. Didn't exactly seem open to invitations.

– I'm trying to find out whether old Mrs Glenne gave birth to one or two children all those years ago, she told him.

– Probably no point in asking the woman herself, he observed with a show of interest.

– I called the home where she's living. According to the carer I spoke to, she denies ever having had any children at all.

– Like that, is it, he grinned absently, but Nina was not going to give up that easily.

– Actually, I've just been looking through that memorandum you wrote about the medical student.

As she had expected, this interested him more.

– I was just sitting here thinking about her, he said. – Do you think it's enough with only one man on guard up there?

Nina had been wondering the same thing.

– She was given the offer of a personal alarm but said no. So there's nothing more we can do.

He looked as if he was considering the matter.

– I guess you're right at that. And something's going to happen pretty soon now.

– An arrest? asked Nina. – Glenne?

Arve Norbakk leaned back in his chair.

– Bet your bottom dollar.

– But do we have enough? It all seems a bit thin.

He looked up into her eyes, and she wanted to sit down on the desk, right next to his hand.

– Viken's made up his mind, he said. – Show me the police prosecutor in Oslo who could say no. Certainly not Jarle Frøen.

She understood what he meant.

– What I was going to say about your memo, she said, resuming her thread, – is that it contains one big mistake plus one *major* oversight.

Her ironic tone was supposed to convey that she was exaggerating, but it couldn't be *too* obvious, not if she was to succeed in arousing his interest. From the look he gave her, she guessed she had succeeded. She suspected him of being more ambitious than most of the others, and she felt certain that this oversight she was teasing him about was the result not of carelessness but of the fact that he took on more work than everyone else.

– Let's hear it then, he encouraged her.

It had often struck her that Arve Norbakk had a chance of going far in the business, and she didn't think any the less of him for it.

– The mistake first. Miriam hasn't been in Norway six years, it's seven years. She told me she spent a year in school here before she began studying medicine.

He let out an exaggerated sigh of relief.

– So that's it then? he smiled, and at once turned serious. – Thanks, Nina, a bit too much haste rather than speed at the moment. Great having a colleague who gives you the chance to correct your mistakes.

She saw her chance and took it.

– Fancy coming out for a bite to eat? Then I'll tell you about the other thing, the oversight.

His mobile phone rang; he picked it up and looked at the display.

– Sorry, I have to take this. Can we do it tomorrow?

Maybe he was just saying it to avoid the invitation, but Nina decided that he really would like to have that cup of coffee with her.

– Deal, she said. – I'll come and pick you up.

51

WHEN EVENING PRAYERS were over, Father Raymond went to his office and tidied away a few documents on his desk. He felt restless, and that was always when he worked best. As though the Lord had given him the gift of restlessness so that he would not fall for the temptations of passive self-satisfaction but make use of the abilities he had been blessed with. He began work on the lecture he was going to give at Saturday's instructions seminar. It had started to rain, and a fierce wind rattled the house. He liked the sensation, how vulnerable it made him feel as a human being. And with it that sense of being held tight.

After he had been working for a while, he heard a knock on the door, and for a moment he struggled against a feeling of irritation at the interruption.

– Miriam, he exclaimed when he saw who it was standing there. Her hair hung down over her eyes. – But you're soaking wet.

He found a towel in the cupboard and she dried her face.

– I forgot my umbrella, she explained. – Not that it would have been much help in this wind.

She was not just wet, he noticed. There were shadows below her eyes, and her hair was unkempt. Beneath her coat she wore a thin blouse with the top button undone. He couldn't see the cross she usually wore on a gold chain around her neck.

– I rang at the sub-prior's office, she burst out. – He said I would find you here.

Father Raymond had often thought of her after her last visit. What she had told him of the relationship with this man who was married with children had worried him. Most of all because she seemed to have got so deeply involved. She had been so tormented, and now obviously things had got even worse.

– What can I do for you, Miriam?

She looked as though she was struggling to find the words.

– That business you were talking about last time, he said to encourage her. – Have you managed to get any closer to making a decision?

She looked down at the floor.

– I haven't seen him for a couple of days.

He gave her time to continue.

– I'm afraid, Father.

The priest coughed. He felt a powerful desire to sit down beside her.

– My neighbour has been murdered . . . She was lying outside my door . . . She has a little daughter.

She burst into tears. Father Raymond got up and went over to her. He touched the collar of her coat with two fingers. Miriam bent her neck; it looked so slender and vulnerable.

– This is a terrible story, he comforted her. – And for you to be mixed up in it. It's so meaningless.

She turned her face up to him.

– It's as if it's had something to do with me the whole time, Father.

She was pale, and her mascara had run. Now, seeing this face so naked and helpless, he felt even more powerfully than before this sensation for which there were no words. The trace of Him in another's face.

Miriam picked up the towel and dried around her swollen eyes.

– Something happened, she snuffled. – Just before I came here.

He began to rock back and forth on his feet, almost imperceptibly. It helped focus his attention.

– Can you tell me about it?

She hesitated.

– I don't know. I don't want to get you in trouble.

– Dearest Miriam, you know you can tell me everything. There is not a single thing you could tell me that I could not bear to hear.

She grabbed his hand and squeezed it quickly. He closed his eyes.

– Dearest Miriam, he said again.

– There was something in the letter box. An envelope with some . . . really hideous pictures.

– What kind of pictures?

She began to shake, and he put his arm round her shoulders.

– If it is something criminal, you must go to the police.

– Not until I know, she said in a low voice. – If I'm wrong, it would destroy him.

– Him?

He held her gaze.

– Is this the man you have a . . . have had a relationship with?

She swallowed twice.

– Is he threatening you, Miriam? Because you refuse to see him any more? You must not take any chances.

She straightened up. A firmness had appeared in her eyes.

– It always helps to come here, Father. When I talk to you, I know what the right thing to do is. I must be completely certain first. I can't bear the thought of going through the rest of my life ashamed. I've already hurt him so much. If I'm wrong, it could destroy everything for him . . . First I have to hear what he says. I must give him the chance to explain. Can I come to see you again tomorrow? Or Friday?

– Dearest Miriam, come whenever you want to.

Again she took hold of his hand, and this time she kept hold of it.

– I don't know what I would have done without you.

Father Raymond felt a warmth spreading through his whole body.

– But you must promise not to say a word about this to anyone, she said.

He was taken aback.

– I have a duty of confidentiality, Miriam, as you well know. But if you believe yourself to be in danger, in any way . . .

She released his hand.

– I don't know if I can let you go, he protested. – Not until I know what this is about, what you're telling me.

She attempted a smile.

– Dear Father, will you have me cloistered? Lock me up with the nuns in Karina priory?

Father Raymond had to abandon his attempt to finish writing the lecture that evening. After Miriam had gone, he sat there listening to the rain lashing against the window. He had no doubt that she meant what she said. He was bound by his oath of silence, but not where life and limb were in danger. He made up his mind to visit the prior to discuss the matter.

52

VIKEN RESTED HIS gaze on Jarle Frøen, the police prosecutor. Beneath Frøen's thin red hair an irregular array of freckles was scattered across his scalp. It looked as though he might have stood beneath the ladder where a particularly clumsy painter was at work. The little splashes continued down on to a pale face that had a rather doughy consistency. As though it would never quite stop collapsing.

Viken enjoyed the feeling of being in control of the situation and did not let himself be provoked by Frøen's surprising obstinacy. On the contrary, he found it stimulating. He didn't even have to look at Finckenhagen to know where he had her, and that the result of the meeting was a foregone conclusion.

— We must keep our nerve, Frøen objected, and Viken smiled a friendly and obliging smile. It was, after all, the prosecutor's job to sit there and cast doubt on whether they had enough evidence to make an arrest. — I note that this Glenne has a connection to all the victims, a distant one to be sure, but in and of itself striking. I note that he disappeared from the scene where Elvestrand's body was found. Perhaps not surprising that he didn't want to be caught with his trousers down, so to speak.

Frøen chuckled at his own little joke.

— I note also that he has not reported to us, despite our efforts to get in touch with him. I note that he has not been home since Monday. All more than a little suspicious, I grant you, Viken. But do you honestly think it's enough to warrant holding him in custody? I'll tell you what the court will want to know. One: is there the least bit of technical evidence that actually links the accused to the case? Two: where the bloody hell is the motive?

Viken let him ramble on and didn't waste time with interruptions that would only have encouraged him. When Frøen did finally stop, he even permitted himself a question: – Any further objections? He was careful to sound encouraging rather than sarcastic, and cast a glance in Finckenhagen's direction, though she wasn't the one he had asked.

– I'm certainly not going to lecture you about the due processes of law, he said to Frøen, once the prosecutor had declined the invitation to continue. And thinking that a touch of flattery never did any harm, he added: – It's good to have you on the team, Jarle. A relief to have people around who really know their stuff. Who can separate the wheat from the chaff. If we put enough effort into it and find Glenne in the course of the evening, that gives us effectively twenty-four hours before we need to make a formal application for remand. Plenty of time to go over every inch of his office, both the cars, the villa with garage and outhouses, the summer place down in Larkollen, and anywhere else you like. As for technical evidence, you can bet your boots we'll have some by this time tomorrow. As you know, we have DNA traces from the victims. The most interesting were those found under Anita Elvestrand's fingernails. I've just been talking to the pathologists. They had a preliminary DNA analysis of this material. Dr Plåterud said it was *very* interesting.

– In what way? Frøen wanted to know.

– Some peculiarity or other they need to take a closer look at . . . Viken prised a piece of paper out of his breast pocket and put his glasses on. – She called it *translocation*. People with such genes need not necessarily be visibly different, but it is not unlikely that someone in the immediate family might in some way deviate from the norm. It would be absolutely *spiffing* to get a little peek at this Dr Glenne's molecules.

From the corner of his eye he could see Finckenhagen smiling.

– And I'll use stronger language if we haven't got something out of this chap before we get that far. I'll use the time well, you can rely on it. We'll drive him as hard as we can the whole night. You asked about motive. Well, as you know, I am of the considered opinion that the whole concept of motive is too narrow to encompass murders of this kind.

He left a short pause before continuing.

– This won't be so much about motive as about a psyche so twisted that we have difficulty in comprehending it.

– Do you have any reason to believe that Glenne is so deranged? I mean, to all intents and purposes the chap seems completely functional.

Viken leaned across the table and gave a detailed account of the story of the twin brother whom no one had ever seen. Frøen did not look impressed.

– Someone born in the middle of Oslo in the sixties must be registered.

Viken couldn't agree more.

– I've got Jebsen trying to trace him. But if she'd found him in births, marriages and deaths then she would have let us know long ago. Anyway, whether he exists or not, this whole business with the twin is so odd that the shrinks are going to be on it like vultures.

– What about the claw marks on the victims? Do you have anything connecting Glenne to that? I mean, apart from the fact that the man obviously likes riding his bike out in the woods?

This latter was said with what Viken would call a sly look, but he didn't let it put him off his stride.

– I've had Plåterud look at these marks again, he answered, and pointed to a document on the table in front of him. – The slashes on the victims aren't particularly deep; they could well have been made using claws from a severed bear's paw. Even the rip on the cheek, if the claws had been sharpened. I have a theory as to why the killer does this. Apart from that, you're probably also aware of the fact that Glenne doesn't have a watertight alibi for any of the relevant periods of time.

Still in the same acid tone Frøen said: – I see you suggest that he may even have risen in the middle of the night, driven to a premises in Lillestrøm, stolen a stuffed bear and then returned to his bed before his wife woke up.

– That may be what happened, Viken confirmed stoically. – He might also have got hold of a bear's paw in some other way. And I'll bet my bottom dollar that several pieces of this puzzle fall into place when we interview him. If we don't get started now, I'm afraid these pieces may elude us for good.

Frøen shrugged his shoulders.

– We can still bring him in on a voluntary basis and get a DNA sample, he protested, addressing Finckenhagen.

– In principle, she observed.

Viken nodded, as though again giving the idea serious consideration.

– Always supposing that we get hold of the bloke, and he says don't mind if I do when we politely ask him to accompany us. On the other hand, he's been playing hide-and-seek with us for two and half days now. Even so, Jarle, this is not the thing we've really got to worry about. He disliked addressing the prosecutor by his first name, but the situation required it.

– No?

Frøen was clearly feeling ill at ease, despite his uncharacteristically tough tone. A large oval patch of sweat had formed between his prominent nipples. His whole fat, doughy body would slump to the floor if the chair wasn't there to keep it up, thought Viken as he played the card he had been saving till last, even though everyone knew he held it.

– How would you like to wake up early tomorrow morning and read the following story in *VG*? He held an imaginary newspaper up in front of him and pointed to the screaming headline: – *Wild beast claims its fourth victim. Police helpless.*

Frøen's nostrils flared, and he started clicking the point of his Biro in and out.

– Can we pick him up tonight? Suddenly his major worry seemed to be that the arrest wouldn't happen quickly enough.

Viken raised his hand, and for a moment it looked as though he was about to swear an oath.

– Just give us the sign, Jarle, he said warmly, – and we'll have Dr Glenne next time he turns on his mobile phone.

53

THE WIND SWEPT down from Slemdalsveien as he crossed the road, the little drops of rain stinging against his forehead and cheeks. He was glad it was rainy and blustery. He wished he could open his head and let the wind stream through it. He was on his way to talk to the police. And home after that. It would be late when he got there. The children would be asleep. Probably Bie too, unless she was too restless. He imagined himself sneaking into the bedroom, sitting down on the side of the bed. Waking her by placing a still-wet hand on her cheek.

He stopped on the steps up to Majorstuehuset, turned on his mobile and scrolled down to Miriam's name. It was the fourth time in half an hour he'd called her. Even so he waited for the answering machine to come on. He had no message for her.

He heard a train come jangling into the station as he bought his ticket from the machine. He had no small change, used his credit card. Didn't hurry, ambled down on to the platform as the last carriage disappeared into the tunnel. If he never went home again, what would he miss? Sitting on the terrace with a glass of cognac. Looking up into the bright, fathomless sky above the fjord. Or sitting with Marlen at the kitchen table. She's telling a story she's made up, a journey somewhere, out beyond the Milky Way. She's drawn the fabulous creatures she encountered there . . . Standing outside Tom's room, hearing him play on his electric guitar. All he said when he got it was *Thanks*, sullen as ever, but Axel could see how thrilled he was, and understood that this guitar would bring them closer together.

After the next train had arrived and he was settled in a window seat, he looked up and saw flashing blue lights on the street outside. Two or three cars pulled up on to the pavement. It reminded him with a jolt of where he was going. Now that he was actually on his way, the feeling of repugnance at the thought of handing himself in for interrogation grew even stronger . But he couldn't put it off any longer.

The train stopped in the middle of the tunnel, stayed there. There was no announcement. He looked around the half-full carriage. At an angle to one side of him a boy of about Daniel's age was reading a magazine and listening to music through earphones, the leg on the seat shaking, possibly in time to the music. Maybe Daniel would be the one who would feel most betrayed, even if he had left home. Daniel had always reached out to him. Three seats further down, two girls of African appearance were tapping in messages on their mobiles. On the seat behind them was a woman in a hijab. She was looking out of the window into the dark tunnel wall. Bie and the children. To be with them and feel no shame. The way things used to be. It sounded like something from another time zone altogether. From the time before Brede reappeared in his thoughts. Axel had kept him at bay all these years. Locked him in a dark room and ignored the shouts coming from inside. Discovered a kind of peace in not hearing them any more. But Brede had managed to get out anyway. The day his mother mistook Axel for him. The train set off again. He knew it wasn't possible to close that door again. Could no longer rid himself of the thought of what had happened that summer.

Police on the platform at the National Theatre station. He counted four or five. One of them with a dog. He still hadn't realised why they were there. Not even when a couple of them burst into the carriage and ordered everyone to stay in their seats. Not until one of them stopped in front of him and yelled at him to hold out his hands did it dawn on him. But he had never been able to relate to orders screamed into his face, so he did nothing. At the same moment he felt a violent tugging at his shoulders, his arms were pinioned behind his back and he was pushed forward head first, his forehead and nose thudding on to the floor. A knee was forced into his neck, his wrists manacled together.

– Stay completely still! a voice bellowed into his ear.

He twisted in order to be able to breathe and was hit on the jaw. Heard another voice, further away: – Suspect apprehended at National Theatre station. Situation under control.

A response through a crackling transmitter: – Definite identification?

– Driver's licence and Visa card. It's him.

He couldn't tell how long he lay there. Five minutes, maybe ten. The other passengers were told to leave. At last the pressure on his neck was relieved.

– On your feet.

He stood up, blood in his mouth. One of them at least was wearing a holstered pistol, he noticed. Am I *that* dangerous?

Outside, by the fountain, a car was waiting. He was led towards it. Halfway across the square a figure jumped out in front of him. The flash cut through the semi-darkness and tore it wide open. Twice, three times, until he was pushed in through the passenger door.

In his student days Axel had made a bit of pocket money at the weekend by doing blood tests on suspected drunk-drivers. He knew what a holding cell looked like. But he had never been inside one behind a locked door. He sat with his head resting against the wall, legs stretched out in front of him across the floor. His neck was aching, over the shoulder and down the ribcage on one side. He was certain at least one rib was broken. He had a swelling above his right eye and was still bleeding inside his mouth. An eye tooth had come loose.

A little earlier, he had heard sounds from one of the neighbouring cells. An elderly man, it sounded like. Pretty drunk, but sober enough to reel off a few verses: *If you've sunshine in your heart, then the whole wide world is yours.* And *When the chestnuts bloom on Bygdøy Allé . . .*

It helped, hearing him sing out his joy like that. Axel could imagine what he looked like. See the days when the old man had first learned the songs, of which only these carefree fragments now remained. Think of some explanation for why he had ended up under arrest. That way he could keep the other thoughts at bay. But at some point the old man had been let out. It must have been an hour ago, maybe two. Naturally they'd taken his watch, along with his mobile phone, his wallet, belt and shoes. Now all was silent in the other cells. He was left at the mercy of his own thoughts between the sallow green stone walls, under the bright strips of neon lighting. These were the thoughts he would be living with for every moment that was left to him.

Bie had once shown him a picture in a magazine. A Buddhist monk walking through a valley flushed with red and gold leaves, sunlight streaming down through the branches. Beneath the picture it said: *Not one single thought disrupts this walk*. But the monk hadn't got where he was by pushing thoughts away. He must have accepted them so completely that there was nothing left of them at all. Suddenly Axel thought of how he used to imagine his old age would be. Strolling along a beach. Sitting on a rock and looking out over the sea. A feeling of everything being calm and settled, of everything having been done, and now all that remained was to wait. Lying in that cell, staring into the wall, he knew he would never reach that beach.

54

THE RECTANGULAR ROOM he was taken to was inward facing. It had no windows and was lit by strips of neon lighting in the ceiling. The walls were grey, as was the wall-to-wall carpet. A video camera was suspended above the door, and he realised that the interview was going to be filmed, that someone would perhaps be sitting and following the proceedings on a screen.

A table and three armchairs by the further wall. He at once recognised the men sitting there. They were the same two who had interviewed him about a week earlier. It felt more like a month to him, maybe longer.

The younger one stood up. He was about the same height as Axel, powerfully built, with dark eyes beneath his light fringe.

– Sit down, Axel, he said and pointed to the vacant chair.

Axel understood that he was being addressed by his first name for a reason. But this man seemed a sympathetic type, and he was relieved to think that he would be present throughout the questioning.

– As you might remember, my name is Norbakk. And this is Detective Chief Inspector Viken.

The chief inspector directed his cold gaze on Axel and gave not the slightest sign of recognition. He was wearing a white shirt, obviously freshly ironed.

Norbakk said: – We've decided to charge you with the murders of three people. Hilde Sophie Paulsen, Cecilie Davidsen and Anita Elvestrand. This gives you certain legal rights. Among other things you have the right to see all documents relating to the case. And within twenty-four hours at the latest, a lawyer of your own choosing will be appointed to defend you, or else we can choose one for you.

You have the right to have your lawyer with you during all questioning, but it may take some time for him or her to arrive. So we propose to make a start now. It means we can cut down on the amount of time you spend in the holding cell. Not a very cosy place to spend a night.

This was said with a sort of empathic undertone. Evidently the two men were to play different roles. This Norbakk was to be the friendly, understanding one. Axel hadn't the slightest idea what his own role was supposed to be. He recalled suddenly a dream he had had several times. Stepping out on to a large stage, glimpsing a room full of people, the sense of their anticipation. Silence falls, everyone awaits his opening line. That's when he realises he hasn't learnt a single one of them.

– Fair enough, he heard himself say. – Let's begin.

Down in the cell he had wondered whether he should ask for a lawyer, but had decided that the arrest was a misunderstanding he would quickly manage to clear up on his own. Not even the words *charge you with the murders of three people* altered his view. He had been on his way here to hand himself in. Voluntarily submit to questioning. Had given a blood sample without protesting.

– That's good, said Norbakk as he sat down again. – You're a cooperative type of person, we appreciate that.

Axel looked over at Viken, who had still not yet said a word, and who had kept his gaze on Axel's face throughout. It looked as though he were scrutinising his every pore. Below the bushy grey eyebrows the detective chief inspector's eyes were red rimmed, Axel noted. Lack of sleep, or an allergy maybe. He met the gaze, couldn't face holding it, fixed instead on a point on the wall while he waited for Viken to speak. A long time passed, maybe as much as a minute, before he did so.

– Have you ever paid for sex with a prostitute?

Axel was startled. The voice was low and intense. But it was the content of the question that surprised him. On his way from the cell, in the lift, he had thought about what they might ask him. His whereabouts. Why he hadn't handed himself in. His relationship to the dead women. But this was something else.

– I'll repeat my question. Ever had sex with a whore?

In that instant he knew he shouldn't say anything else without his lawyer being present. But this was not the time to show weakness. He had nothing to hide. Bought sex? He'd been to a brothel once, in Amsterdam. In his second year as a student, a trip abroad with the so-called Brass Band Orchestra, in which he did his feeble best with a tuba. He was the only one with the lungs for it, and his lack of musical ability was of no consequence to the orchestra. The visit to the brothel had been the result of a bet made over an almost empty bottle of whisky.

– We note that it is taking some time for the question to be answered, Viken commented tonelessly.

Axel pulled himself together. – No, I've never done that.

He saw a tightening at the corner of the detective chief inspector's mouth, as though he were registering a small victory, and it struck Axel that they had information about what had happened that night in Amsterdam over twenty years ago.

– Have you ever had a homosexual relationship?

Abruptly it felt as though the floor his chair was standing on was uneven. He knew he shouldn't ask what the question had to do with the case. Or what was meant by a homosexual relationship. Whether nudity and intimate touching among teenagers counted. He must not on any account get involved in a sort of struggle over limits with the dour man on the other side of the table.

– No.

– Children?

– What are you asking about?

– I'm asking if you've ever had sex with children or minors?

– Of course not.

– Have you ever felt any attraction in that direction?

– No.

– Sadomasochistic sex?

Not once had the chief inspector's voice deviated from that same low and intense delivery. Axel shook his head.

– Does that mean no?

– Yes . . . it means no.

He glanced across at the other man. Norbakk nodded to him with something that might have been an encouraging smile playing around his lips.

– And yet, Viken continued, lowering his head a fraction, – and yet we found, in the bedroom you share with your wife, at the back of a cupboard, a certain item.

Axel knew at once what he was talking about. Suddenly in all its enormity it dawned on him that his status as the accused gave the law the right to enter his home, trample through his bathroom, kitchen, bedroom, through his children's rooms. He felt himself stripped naked, exposed to public view in the marketplace. Felt an urge to ask for a towel to hold in front of him.

– A pair of handcuffs, he said. – My wife and I . . . we bought them for a laugh. It was a long time ago.

– Who did you say bought them?

Axel thought back.

– It was me.

– And who usually wears them?

– Well, I've tried them too, yes.

Detective Chief Inspector Viken's face remained as expressionless as a mask. But there was a hint in the eyes that he was enjoying himself.

– How did you meet Miriam Gaizauskaite?

Finally, a question Axel had been expecting.

– I was her supervisor during her practical training in general medicine.

– Supervisor? Is that all?

– We've been together.

– What does that mean?

– We had a relationship. A couple of weeks.

– Sexual?

– Yes.

– And your wife, does she know about this?

– Not yet.

– And you think it's okay to deceive her?
– No.
Here Norbakk interrupted.
– You say you *had* a relationship.
Axel felt relieved at being asked the question.
– It can't go on, he said.
– Nonetheless, you've rung her twelve times in just the last twenty-four hours, Viken countered. – That doesn't sound as if you're completely finished with the young lady yet.

Without a pause he continued: – When did you last see your twin brother?

Now Axel tried to hold the chief inspector's gaze.
– Years ago. Don't exactly remember when. Ten, maybe twelve.

Before he had time to think any more about it, Viken was at him again.

– In the photo albums from your childhood, there is not a single picture of you and Brede together. Not one fucking photo. That bothers us, Glenne. Anything like that, where we don't understand shit, that bothers us.

Axel looked up at the video camera, then at the wall, then at the table between them.

– Brede isn't in any of the pictures in those albums, he said. – All the pictures are of me.

A low growling sound emanated from Viken's throat.

– You'd better explain that to us, he insisted.
– There's nothing to explain. Brede was sent away to a kind of institution. All his possessions were given away. All the photos with him in them were removed.

– Removed? Who did that?
– My mother, I suppose. Nothing was ever said about it.

Viken looked to be chewing this over.

– You told your wife that several of the photos in the album are of Brede.

Axel struggled to know what to say.

– Give us the name of one person who knows him, Viken suddenly

263

asked. – Somebody we can get in touch with who can confirm that this twin brother really existed.

A space seemed to open up. A cold wind blew in through it, and Axel heard his father's voice: *You must always pay your dues, Axel.*

– I want my lawyer, he said as firmly as he could. – Before we go any further.

Now there was no doubt about it: the detective chief inspector's lips moved.

Enough to show a small amount of pink gum.

Axel knew several lawyers. Just four days earlier, he'd been at the fiftieth birthday celebrations of one of them. He'd been standing in the dark out on the terrace and looking up into a starry sky. That was in the days when he still believed he could choose how the rest of his life would be.

He couldn't face the thought of involving someone he knew. At this stage someone chosen by the authorities would be good enough. At this stage? He was still thinking it would all be over by nightfall, or at the latest the following day. He'd thought he would be going to work. With patients to look after. Then home afterwards. Dimly he became aware that this was not how it was going to be.

The defence lawyer's name was Elton. A skinny little guy about his own age, with square designer glasses and a slim-fit shirt that would have suited someone twenty years younger. His voice was slim fit too. Axel had thought that what he needed was someone who could steer a boat. That way he could lie down in the bottom and not look over the railings until they were in the harbour. Elton didn't look like a skipper at all, but he'd got hold of the documents relating to the case and glanced through them. Afterwards he announced confidently: – Let's hope this is all they have, Axel. I think they're taking a flyer here. And if that's the case, you'll be a free man very soon.

When the interrogation resumed, Norbakk had been replaced by a young woman. She had a Bergen accent and was quite pretty, both factors that had a calming effect on Axel. There was something about the pitch of her voice that he liked. She'd taken over the part of the helpful and friendly one, read him his rights as an accused person all over again. He didn't catch her name.

Viken picked up where he had left off a couple of hours earlier. Why had the twin brother been expelled from the family? Why had Axel not managed to get in touch with him all these years? Who could confirm that he actually existed? None of these questions excited any particular reaction from Elton, but he wanted to know why the investigators hadn't managed to trace the twin brother using public records. Once he had been given the explanation, he advised his client to answer as fully as possible.

Axel had managed to think things over during the break. Prepare what he intended to say about Brede. Not a version based on lies, but one that avoided essentials. All these questions about his twin brother confirmed something he had had only a strange and inexplicable hunch about: that Brede was involved in the murders of the three women. Yet it merely left him still more confused, and when he was asked what he'd been doing wandering about in the Oslo forests for almost a whole day and night after he'd stumbled across Anita Elvestrand's body, he had trouble answering. Viken leaned towards him like a hound picking up the scent of its prey. Had anyone seen him up there? He had met a tramp. Could he describe him? Wasn't it odd that he kept on going back up into the woods? That he always seemed to be up there at roughly the times when the murders were committed? Again and again Viken came back to this business of *What were you doing up there?* And each time it became more and more difficult to avoid giving an answer.

Viken said: – Now let me help you, Glenne. I'll run through the case for you. It's hard to start talking. But once you're over the first hurdle, you'll feel as though a great burden has been lifted from your shoulders.

His voice had taken on a more conciliatory tone, as though he wanted to be a friend, an intimate friend.

– Let's start with Thursday September twenty-seventh.

In detail he went over what Axel had told them about the bike ride in the forest. The swim in the tarn, the puncture.

– On your way back, you meet someone you know. She's a physiotherapist, and you've worked with her on several occasions over the years. Let's halt there for a moment. We'll come back to it later. But first a bit about your family background, Axel Glenne.

Viken started talking about his father. Portrayed a man who always demanded the utmost of himself and of others. Someone whose demands his son did everything he could to live up to, but could never quite meet. A remote, punitive, god-like figure of whom Axel was terrified. But it was the mother Viken really wanted to talk about. He described her as *an insensitive and superficial woman who always put her own needs above those of others.* Someone who had bullied her son and made him feel like a nothing. Axel, becoming increasingly confused, did not interrupt. Where had Viken got all this about his parents from?

– You might well have needed a brother. Someone to carry the burden of the suffering you endured at home. Because you were a lonely child, weren't you, Axel? So lonely you had to invent a twin brother, since you didn't have one.

Axel almost burst out laughing, but he was just too tired. It stuck in his throat like a ball. Viken carried on a while longer, talking about Axel's life, the expectations, the rejections, the punishments, the emotional coldness. Then abruptly he was back in the Nordmarka again.

– You see that woman standing there, Axel. What takes place inside you at that precise moment?

Axel was still completely bewildered by the man on the other side of the table. Viken was obviously playing a game, but one that was becoming more and more difficult to understand. All Axel knew was that the rules changed the whole time.

– Nothing special, he choked out. – I hardly knew her.

– Hardly knew her. And yet all the same, that rage flared up inside you. Rage because she was an older woman. Because here she was, standing directly in front of you, blocking your way, so to speak.

Things start to get thick, dense. Things start to happen you have no control over. You grab hold of her, drag her off the path and into the trees.

– No!

He heard his own voice. He should not have shouted. He should have answered calmly. Or else shaken his head with a weary smile. But he shouted because suddenly he felt an urge to say, *Yes, that's what happened*. A temptation to assume the blame, to be so weighted down with blame he might sink to the very bottom, to a place where it was not possible to go any lower. He shouted because, in spite of it all, he did not wish to drown.

– What are you doing? he groaned. He turned to Elton, but the lawyer sat with his eyes looking straight ahead, clearly having no objections to the chief inspector's methods.

– Let's put it like this, Axel, Viken said in an understanding way. – Let's say it wasn't you who did it. Let's imagine it was someone else who showed up at just that moment and dragged Hilde Paulsen off into the trees. Can you visualise that?

Axel bit his split lip.

– I'm certain that with an imagination like yours you can see it. It isn't you who does this, it's someone else. He looks like you, he's your double. Your twin. The evil shadow that has followed you ever since you were a child. The person who suddenly takes over and does things you would never have done yourself. Things so terrible you can't bear to think about them, things you would have stopped happening had you been able to. Let us call him Brede.

Axel stared at him in astonishment. Viken's eyebrows were like hairy larvae, coiling and arching, not going anywhere.

– It is Brede who drags Hilde Paulsen off into the trees with him. He ties her up, hides her. A few hours later he comes back with a child-trailer, the thing kids sit in. He takes her to a place that only he knows about. Keeps her prisoner for several days in a cellar. Sedates her using a product that is familiar to you as a doctor, Axel. It's called thiopental. Brede feels all-powerful as he stands there over the defenceless body. He can decide exactly how much longer she has to live. To the second when she is to die. He picks up a bear's paw he has lying there. He's no longer human now. He's a powerful animal. He is God. He slashes her skin with the sharp claws, many times, uttering the kind of sounds an animal would make. Then he kills her. Pushes the hypodermic into her thigh. The final dose.

Viken never once took his eyes off Axel. Axel avoided them.

– After that, he takes her back into the wood, not too far away from the place where he first met her. He uses the same child-trailer. She's a small woman and there's plenty of room for her when he folds her over. Is it possible for you, Axel, to imagine that that is exactly how it happened?

He couldn't bring himself to respond. Viken continued with his story. Now it was about Cecilie Davidsen. Axel goes to see her at the house in Vindern with the results of a test. His normal practice is to give patients this type of information at the clinic. Unless it was Brede who suddenly thought of visiting her at home? A few days later, Thursday October the eleventh, he follows his patient through the evening darkness. He attacks her, sedates her, drags her into his car. He kills her in the same way as he killed Hilde Paulsen. But he goes further this time, rips up more skin with the bear claws. Then he dumps the body in Frogner Park. It's spectacular. The whole of Oslo is talking about it. It's inconceivable, it's evil, it's as though someone or something very powerful is behind it all.

Then it's Anita Elvestrand's turn. She's the neighbour of the beautiful young woman Axel has started spending his nights with. That's why he chooses her. A sign to his twin brother. I'm close, Axel, I'm with you, following you, like a shadow. Even when you're in bed with your student. He visits her on the night of Friday October the nineteenth. Somehow or other he persuades her to go out to his car with him. She gets in, and she's already on her way to the place where the two other women lost their lives. A remote cabin perhaps. Or a summer place in Larkollen. Axel spends Monday night with his student. He gets her drunk on red wine. And while she's asleep, that's when it happens. The remains of Anita Elvestrand are brought in through the gate, probably using the same child-trailer that was used for Hilde Paulsen. She is carried upstairs and dumped in front of the door to the flat where the student and Axel are sleeping. – Because that's what you're doing, isn't it, Axel? Or maybe you weren't sleeping in her bed after all? Were you helping Brede carry a body?

Viken paused for a long time. A minute passed without anything being said. Maybe two minutes. Axel understood why that time was there. It was there for him to start talking in. And in the middle of this absurd game, he was pained at the thought of once again being asked to betray Brede.

The silence was broken by Elton's feminine but surprisingly authoritative voice.

– Time to wrap this up, he said, tapping on his D&G watch with his index finger.

It was now five o'clock in the morning. But Viken had been given both time added on and extra time. He was back in his role as the tenacious Rottweiler that never lets go. Axel was still managing to keep it together, but it took him longer and longer to come up with answers to even the most simple questions. Why did he still have a child-trailer in the bike shed? Wasn't his daughter nine years old? When was the last time it had been used? And where were the socks he was wearing when he found the dead woman outside the door?

It was light outside by the time he was taken back down to the holding cell in the basement. He had been lying in the bottom of a boat being sailed by others. Now it had capsized, and this murky green prison cell was the beach on which he had been washed ashore. He felt as though he had lost everything.

55

Thursday 25 October

NINA JEBSEN WAS the first to arrive at the meeting. After two and a half hours' sleep on a sofa in one of the offices, she had managed to shower and put on her make-up, but she had no clean clothes to change into. She popped the day's first Nicorette into her mouth. It tasted like the rubbers she used to chew into little pieces when she was at primary school. Fortunately the coffee was freshly brewed and she had an unopened pack of chewing tobacco in her jacket pocket. She'd make it through to lunch without eating.

Sigge Helgarsson arrived and sat down beside her.

– Our oldest girl was up all night being sick, he said by way of apology. – And Vala was on duty at the nursing home. Did I miss anything?

Nina moved her chair away from the potential source of infection.

– Don't think anyone noticed you weren't here. It's been non-stop since yesterday afternoon.

Sigge gave a sigh of relief.

– I know someone tried to call me, but I had to turn off the phone to grab a few hours' sleep early this morning. It was hell at home. Hope it wasn't His Majesty's Viken, the Voice himself.

Nina couldn't stand any more of the chewing gum and wrapped it neatly in a serviette, which she tossed on to the table.

– Viken's got other things to think about apart from you and your sick kids. Just be sure you don't stick your pretty neck out too far today. If you don't want your head chopped off.

– Bad as that, was it?

Nina yawned.

– We've been talking to Glenne for over twelve hours.

– Anything that nails him to the murders?

– Nails him? Not even a piece of Sellotape. Oh shit!

She sat up abruptly.

– The maternity ward, she muttered.

– Forgotten something? Are you pregnant?

At that moment Norbakk entered with Jarle Frøen, followed by the lad from Majorstua and a couple of the other newcomers. Nina was on her way out of the door when she bumped into Viken.

– We're starting now, he said gruffly. – You can go to the toilet in the break.

Viken looked as though he hadn't had a moment's sleep. He was unshaven and his eyes were even more red rimmed than usual. But, as ever, he was wearing a freshly ironed white shirt. It occurred to Nina that he must have a cupboard full of them in his office.

– We'll deal with the interrogations first, he began. – A number of interesting pieces of information have emerged. We can confirm that Glenne has no proper alibis for any of the times we're interested in. He's vague about a number of things and his answers are shifty. That confirms the impression we have generally of an evasive personality.

He stopped briefly. Jarle Frøen interjected rapidly.

– I've read the report, Viken. There isn't much there that is going to impress a court.

– Yes, but we're not finished with him yet, barked Viken, and the prosecutor decided not to pursue it.

– Admittedly the opening round has not given us the results we had been hoping for, the detective chief inspector continued, his voice a little calmer.

He addressed himself to Norbakk.

– You've talked to the people at the lab?

– Just before I came here, yes, Norbakk nodded. – They've been through Glenne's villa on Nesodden with a fine-tooth comb, as well as the clinic and offices in Bogstadveien, and both cars. We've also got people looking at the summer place in Larkollen.

– The child-trailer?

– That too, of course. And they're working on the hard disks of both his computers.

– And?

– There's a huge amount of material to go through . . .

– But so far?

Norbakk rubbed his neck.

– First impression: not much. Not counting the pair of handcuffs found in a cupboard in the bedroom.

He gave Viken a little smile as he said this, but the chief inspector turned abruptly to Nina. She knew what was coming and steeled herself for it.

– What about this twin that no one else knows anything about, not even the wife he's been married to for twenty-three years?

She looked out through the window.

– I did make another attempt to find out about it, she began.

– Attempt?

– The site is still down. Partly, that is.

– Down? Impossible.

– It's very rare, but . . .

– Don't tell me, Jebsen, Viken interrupted, – that you've been sitting around twiddling your thumbs while some dolt of a computer engineer is down there scratching his head?

Fortunately that was not the case.

– I've been in touch with the maternity ward at the Rikshospital. The section head there is the only one who can give permission for access to information in patients' notes. I was supposed to call back . . .

– I don't believe it! thundered Viken. – You mean all you did was telephone?

He looked at her, his eyes narrowed. Nina felt herself shrinking in her seat. Maybe I'll end up the size of a pepperpot, she thought suddenly, and laughed nervously at the strange thought.

– I have had rather a lot to do, she managed.

– Yes, but for Christ's sake, you might have taken the trouble to actually go along there. Do I need to remind you that we are dealing with a perverted and deranged person who has *so far* taken the lives of three women? If we're going to stop him, everyone needs to pull their finger out and do exactly what they've been asked to do. And I mean *everyone*.

His mobile phone rang; he glanced down at the display.

– It's the pathology lab, he said. – We'll take a ten-minute break.

He disappeared out into the corridor.

– Whooph, Sigge gasped. – Glad that wasn't me.

– He's under a lot of pressure, said Nina.

Sigge rolled his eyes.

– As if he's the only one who's noticed things are hotting up.

Nina didn't answer. She picked up her phone and withdrew to a corner of the room. A minute later she had the section head at the Rikshospital on the line. She told him what it was about, stressed how vital the information was to the investigation, that it was a matter of urgency. He promised to look into it.

When the meeting resumed, she noticed that Viken had used the break to calm himself down.

– Sorry about the interruption, he began, and for a moment Nina wondered whether he was going to apologise for the outburst against her. He didn't. – The call was from Dr Plåterud, he said. – She has really pulled out all the stops. She's got Glenne's DNA profile ready and waiting for us.

It was obvious to all what the results were.

– No match with the material found under Anita Elvestrand's fingernails.

Jarle Frøen placed both fists on the table. They were so ugly Nina couldn't help staring at them. Big and pale, with scattered tufts of red hair along the backs of the fingers, and as freckled as his face and his bald head.

– The court is in session at six this evening, he informed them.

– I postponed it for as long as possible. The question now is should we abandon it and drop the charges?

Viken glowered at him. Nina could see him struggling to maintain the calm he had achieved during the break.

– The DNA result needn't necessarily mean anything at all, he asserted. – There's a great deal of material still to be analysed. Last night I spoke to a former colleague in Manchester. An expert in the field of psychological profiling. He thinks what we have is extremely interesting. He agrees that this business of the bear prints is some kind of message. Same thing with the method of killing, making it look as though the victims have been savaged by a bear. His advice is to listen to this message, find out what it is the killer is trying to tell us, and wind it in from there. I asked him about this theory of a split personality. He says it's not unlikely that what we're dealing with is a person with two or more personalities. Several factors actually point in this direction. Among other things, the very short interludes between each killing. As you know, my hypothesis is that this twin brother of Glenne's doesn't exist . . .

Nina's phone rang.

– This looks like the hospital, she said and stood up. – They promised me a quick answer.

She grabbed her pen and notebook and let herself out into the corridor. A woman named Astrid Glenne *had* given birth at the Rikshospital. The senior consultant himself had personally gone to the trouble of searching the archives to track down the notes. Nina was too tense to thank him. She had to concentrate fully to stop her pen from shaking as she wrote down what he said.

The buzz of voices stilled as she appeared in the doorway. She could feel every gaze following her as she made her way back to her seat.

– That was the Rikshospital about the birth record.

She looked at Viken. He half closed his eyes.

– About bloody time, he murmured.

– The senior consultant called me in person; he'd made it his number one priority.

– Get to the point, Viken interrupted.

Nina swallowed her irritation.

– Astrid Glenne gave birth to two boys on the night of the seventh of September 1964. The first birth was unproblematic. The second child got stuck and had to be delivered with forceps. He wasn't breathing, had to be resuscitated, and lay in an incubator for more than three weeks, but he survived. He suffered from convulsions of some kind . . .

– Yes yes yes, said Viken gruffly . – We don't need to hear the whole of the midwife's report.

Sigge Helgarsson couldn't resist it: – So goodbye, Mr Hyde. That leaves us with just Dr Glenne.

Viken gave him an angry look.

– What matters is not whether or not this twin actually exists. You can say what you like about Icelanders, but they're not the brightest tool in the shed.

Sigge gaped.

– *You're* the one who needs to get it together, he burst out. – If you'd said that about someone with black skin, you'd get yourself a reputation as a racist.

Viken brushed this aside.

– Racist, did you say? Before the Americans were allowed to use the base at Keflavik, they had to bloody well sign an agreement saying that not one black soldier would be stationed there. You Icelanders were terrified they might get your women pregnant. At least that way you wouldn't be as milky white as you are now.

Nina Jebsen looked at him in astonishment. Sigge flushed to the roots of his hair.

– Complete crap, he growled. – Fifty-year-old rumours.

Viken shrugged.

– Pal of mine worked up there for a long time, he knows all about it. But we don't have time for this nonsense.

– You're damned right there, Viken. Jarle Frøen grinned as he got to his feet. – I'll have a word with the district court.

56

THERE WERE ONLY two other customers at the Asylum Café. They took a window seat with a view over to the multi-storey car park and Grønland Square. When Nina had popped her head into Arve Norbakk's office fifteen minutes earlier, it was clear that he had forgotten their arrangement to have coffee, and when she dropped a hint about it, he seemed to be so busy that she thought he would back out again. But as soon as he had picked up the hint, he was on his feet: that was a great idea, they needed to talk.

– Not a day of celebration for the team, he observed as they sat studying the menu. – All the more reason to treat ourselves to something nice to eat.

Nina agreed, but contented herself with a salad and bread on the side; it was too early for lunch.

– Sigge says he's heard rumours that Finckenhagen wants to take Viken off the case, she said.

Arve Norbakk looked straight at her. He had the darkest brown eyes she had ever seen, at least in someone whose hair was so fair.

– Finckenhagen, he spluttered. – She wouldn't dare. Even if Viken has made a fool of himself.

– He's got tunnel vision about this, Nina announced. – The most elementary beginner's mistake. These last few days he's been interested in nothing but this doctor.

– Are you so sure it's all been a waste of time?

She glanced at him.

– Sounds as if you still think Glenne is the one we're looking for.

– I'm only saying it's a good idea to keep an eye on him, said Arve.

– Should we really have been using such a huge amount of resources keeping a tail on him, as Viken insisted?

Arve answered without looking up from the menu.

– Maybe. The most obvious trails still begin and end there.

Once they'd ordered, Nina said: – One thing I've been thinking about. The ages of the three victims. Hilde Paulsen was fifty-six, Cecilie Davidsen forty-six, Anita Elvestrand thirty-six.

Arve raised an eyebrow.

– You're right. Ten years younger every time.

– Probably just chance, she said, – but it does seem odd.

– If it isn't just chance, and it happens again, then the next victim should be a woman of twenty-six.

– Don't say that, she exclaimed as she finessed the plug of chewing tobacco out of her mouth and wrapped it in a serviette. She washed her mouth out with Pepsi Max. – I'm not sure we're taking good enough care of this medical student.

Their food came. She'd ended up with spaghetti bolognese after all.

– Viken asked me to stay in touch with her, Arve reassured her. – I talked to her earlier today. She can call me whenever she likes. If she's not interested, that's all we can do, you know that as well as I do.

Nina wrapped spaghetti round her fork and realised that she'd made a mistake. Spaghetti was fine for kids, and a couple who'd known each other for a while. But first time out in a café with a man sitting opposite and watching you? Tacos were the only thing worse, she groaned to herself as she reached for a serviette. Fortunately Arve tactfully lowered his gaze to the rib steak on his own plate.

Once she'd eaten as much of the spaghetti as she thought she could allow herself, it was time to turn the conversation to matters outside the investigation.

– How did you end up in the police, Arve?

He laughed slightly and poured more beer into his glass. He was a guy who could fix car engines, mend things, cut down trees. His hands were broad and thick, with marks and scars he must have got working with machines and tools. She tried to imagine what it would feel like to be touched by them, held tight by them.

– Probably because I figured it was somewhere I could actually *do* something, he said. – Started studying law, but I always had to get a pal to wake me up during the lectures. Dropped out and spent a couple of years at folk high school, mountain climbing and rafting and camping out in cracks in glaciers. That was probably when it dawned on me that I needed a more active life than just swotting up on points of law. Something more unpredictable. I've always been someone who likes doing something. How about you?

She pushed the plate of half-eaten spaghetti to one side. She hadn't the slightest objection to telling him the story of her life. What it was like to grow up in a high-rise in Fyllingsdalen. The friends who got pregnant as soon as they were done with high school, then moved out of the family apartment and into the block opposite. She'd always known she had to get out of there. Arve carried on eating and listening, didn't say anything.

– What was that other thing, by the way? he suddenly asked.

– Other thing?

– You said yesterday you'd found one mistake and one omission in my notes about the medical student. You gave me the mistake straight away, I was supposed to get the omission for dessert.

Nina wiped thoroughly around her mouth. Registered that the serviette was still showing signs of tomato sauce.

– You dashed that report off pretty quickly, she said, and risked a teasing smile.

– You're right, I had to prioritise. Aren't you going to tell me?

Nina leant back in her chair. She'd managed to change into a light silk blouse she'd bought earlier in the day. It clung tightly across her breasts.

– According to Miriam herself, she doesn't have a large circle of friends. She's got two or three close ones, and she has some contact with the Catholic church in Majorstua.

– Well I got all that, didn't I? Arve protested.

– Yes, but not that she's been engaged.

His eyebrows shot up.

– Really? Here in Norway?

She gave a triumphant laugh.

– For two years.

– Well, you got me there all right, Nina.

She liked the way he said her name, putting equal stress on both syllables.

– Honestly, he continued, – I'm glad it was you who noticed. There are enough people who like to exploit others' mistakes. Did she say who to?

– I didn't ask; that wasn't the most important thing right then. She said she broke up with him some years ago. I still don't know whether it's of any importance at all . . .

Arve scratched the tip of his chin with two fingers. He sat for a while staring thoughtfully into the air, straight past her.

– It might well be important, Nina, he said at last. – I guess Viken's not the only one who's been suffering from tunnel vision these last few days.

57

AXEL STUMBLED THROUGH the park outside the police station where he'd spent most of the last twenty-four hours. He stopped under one of the huge hazels. It was still raining, but not as much as the day before, and the wind had subsided.

He had a large swelling above one eye, and his lower lip was still swollen. He had hardly slept for the past few days, nor washed nor even run a comb through his hair. The bristles on his chin itched, and he could smell the body odour seeping up from his armpits. The physical degeneration felt like a temptation to sink further down into it.

It was dark by the time he slanted across the street to a café on the other side. In a stand outside the door a few last copies of the morning's papers were still on display. The entire front page of *VG* carried a picture of a man being restrained by two police officers. The features of the face had been disguised, but anyone who knew him would have been in no doubt about who it was. The caption read: *Doctor arrested – suspected of murders.*

He needed something to drink. Most of all he needed to empty his bladder. The man behind the bar stopped him as he was on his way to the toilet.

– Are you going to buy something? The toilet is for customers only.

– A cognac.

– Can you pay?

The man gave him a lingering scrutiny. That's the way it is now, thought Axel. This is the reception you'll be getting from now on.

– You'll just have to wait and see, he muttered as he walked into the strong smell of filthy urinal.

Afterwards he took a table in an inner recess of the darkened room. The first glass disappeared in one. It wasn't cognac, but the colour wasn't unlike. He signalled to the barman and had a second. For a brief moment waving a credit card had changed his status. He took his time over the third glass. He couldn't quite come to terms with the thought that at some point or other he would have to get up and leave the place.

His phone vibrated in his jacket pocket. He didn't know how long he'd been sitting there staring down at the table. It struck him that if he didn't answer the phone now, he would never answer it again. A distant sense of relief when he saw that it was Rita. She was the only person he could face talking to right now.

– Axel, I don't believe you. What a pickle you've got yourself into now.

He tried to make a joke about pickle but it didn't work out. Instead she got him to tell her about the last twenty-four hours. Afterwards she said: – What are you going to do now?

He drained his glass.

– Didn't you say you started working for me twelve years ago, Rita? Not many people know me better than you do.

He fell silent. She said: – I don't believe for one moment that you . . . Not for one moment, Axel, do you hear me? But you were incredibly stupid to let yourself get mixed up with that . . .

Axel interrupted before she could use a word he didn't want to hear.

– It isn't her fault. Save the criticism for me.

– She rang yesterday, by the way.

– Miriam?

– Isn't that who we're talking about?

– What did she want?

– Apparently she left an envelope behind in the desk drawer in Ola's office. She said she'd come in and fetch it, but I never saw her.

Axel could feel himself waking up.

– When was this?

– Yesterday afternoon. And then she said something very odd.

– What did she say?

– That if she didn't turn up, I was to deliver it to you as soon as possible. She said it was important. Seemed really upset.

He checked his unanswered calls. Over thirty of them. Lots from Bie. One from Tom. And directly below it on the list: Miriam. Yesterday evening, 6.55. He called his voicemail. Twenty-three messages. The first was from Bie. Then a journalist from *VG*. Then several others he didn't know. He clicked his way through them. On the sixth he heard an indistinct sound, a car engine probably, above it a pop song he'd heard a few times, and someone whistling in the background. He was about to click forward to the next one. Then he heard her voice: *Where are we going?* Miriam: the name shot through him. An indistinct male voice answered her. Axel couldn't stay seated; he had to get to his feet. He clamped the phone to one ear, pressed a finger in the other. Miriam's voice: *The cabin? Are you mad?* Suddenly the man's voice was more prominent. *What the hell have you got there? Give it to me!* Some rustling sounds. Then her scream. Rising and ending in a shout: *Axel.* Then silence.

Axel stumbled to the toilet. Played the message over again. There was something familiar about the man's voice. He couldn't place it. It was drowned out by Miriam's scream. She was calling for him. She was frightened.

He ran to the door.

– Hey there! yelled the bartender and raced after him. – You're a helluva cheeky bastard.

Axel raised both hands submissively.

– Sorry, got a message, I have to leave. Of course I'll pay.

The bartender glowered at him. Not even a big tip sweetened his mood.

Outside the café he ran into a woman in a black coat.

– The very person I'm looking for, she said as he hurried on.

He turned round.

– Kaja Fredvold, *VG*, the woman informed him. – We've met before. I'd like to interview you.

A swarm of thoughts buzzed through Axel's head. Miriam. She had been afraid when he called her the previous afternoon. Afraid when he visited her that last time. He hadn't understood what it was. Hadn't wanted to understand.

– I don't have time for people like you, he said as calmly as he could.

The journalist grabbed him by the sleeve of his jacket. When she smiled, her jaw jutted forward, making her underbite even more prominent.

– We're going to run a story on you anyway, Glenne. You'll find it pays to play along.

A man emerged from a car parked half up on the pavement. He was fat and grunted like a sumo wrestler. He was holding a camera.

– This is Villy, he works with me. We'll drive you home and we can talk on the way.

Axel turned and was about to walk on. The journalist still had hold of him.

– Or we can just do it in here in the café, she suggested. – Looks like you've been enjoying yourself there.

Axel pulled himself free and pushed her. She staggered back a few paces and somehow or other managed to trip over a kerbstone. As Axel rounded the corner, he heard her shouting something to the photographer.

He asked the taxi driver to stop at the bus bay in Helgesens gate and continued on foot. The gate was half open; he slipped through and let it swing shut behind him.

On the landing outside her doorway, there was no sign of the mangled corpse that had been lying there when he'd left the flat two days earlier. A bouquet of flowers hung from the door handle. He'd sent them himself, before his arrest. He rang the bell, tried the handle at the same time. The door wasn't locked.

Her smell in the hallway. Her perfume. Faint smell of damp from the bathroom. All the lights in the living room were on. The bed was made. He lifted the blanket; a T-shirt on the pillow. Surgical textbook on the shelf above. And the photo of the man in naval uniform. The coffee machine in the kitchen was on, the glass jug half full. On the table, a dish with a packet of lasagne, ready for heating, and a piece of crispbread with a bite taken out. Next to it was a white A5 envelope. He picked it up. There were photos inside. Four of them. The first showed the terrified face of Hilde Paulsen, the physiotherapist. She was lying on the floor, up against a stone wall. On the back of the photo the number 1 had been written with a black marker pen. The second picture showed the face of a dead person, with bloody scratches running from the jaw down over the neck. He recognised Cecilie Davidsen. She lay propped up against what had to be the same stone wall. On the reverse the number 2, again written with a black marker pen. The third photograph: the head of a woman with fair hair. He was in no doubt that this must be Anita Elvestrand. The eyes stared at him – he could tell that she was still alive – but the mouth had been ripped open at one side and the tongue protruded from the gash. On the back, the number 3.

The fourth picture was of Miriam. She was smiling and looked happy. Bright sunlight caused her to peer into the camera, and her hair was shorter than it was now. The photo was taken standing against a creosoted wall. Half of it had been cut off. Someone was standing next to her; a bit of the hand holding her shoulder was still visible. On the back, in the same felt-tip writing: *And the fourth will be . . .*

He dropped the pictures on to the table and stumbled out into the corridor and down the twisted staircase without closing the door behind him.

58

AXEL WAS RUNNING through Sofienberg Park. Suddenly he stopped and pulled out his phone, punched in the police station number. He couldn't face the thought of talking to Viken so instead asked for the young sergeant, whose name, he now recalled, was Norbakk.

– I'll put you through to the operational leader, the woman at the other end told him.

– I want to talk to Sergeant Norbakk, Glenne insisted. – Nobody else. Call him and tell him that Axel Glenne is trying to get in touch with him.

Within half a minute his call was returned.

– Glenne? Where are you calling from?

Axel recognised Norbakk's voice.

– It's about Miriam Gaizauskaite. You know who that is? He carried on walking through the park.

– What about her?

– I think she's been abducted. She left a message on my voicemail.

– Message?

– She was screaming, calling for help. Someone attacked her. It must have been last night. In her flat there's an envelope with photographs of the dead women. Do you understand what I'm saying to you?

– I understand. We'll send a car up there. Can you come to the station and make a statement?

– I've got nothing else to say.

He terminated the call, switched off his mobile.

Rita stood in the doorway and stared at him, her eyes wide.

– What do you look like? Has someone beaten you up?

He tried to smile through his swollen lip.

– You'd make a pretty convincing tramp.

– The envelope, he said.

Rita pulled her dressing gown tight around her.

– What is it, Axel? Aren't you well?

He was neither well nor ill. Fear had made him alert, cleared his head. He explained the situation in a few words.

– That is the sickest thing I've ever heard, Rita declared. – You know what, now, for the first time, I really do feel afraid.

– Where is that envelope Miriam rang you about?

– It's still in the drawer in Ola's office.

– Can I borrow your car?

– Yes, but have something to eat first. You stink of alcohol. It can't be all that urgent now you've told the police.

He allowed himself to be persuaded. While he waited, he sat at her computer and logged on. He was the lead story in all the online editions. *Police release accused*, he read in *Aftenposten*; *43-year-old doctor is still suspect*. *VG* ran with a different story: *Furious suspect attacks journalist*. He had to read it through twice before he realised what it was about. Beneath the headline, a photograph of himself. An old one that Bie had taken at Liseberg. He was standing by a merry-go-round, laughing. The light in the room seemed to change as he looked at it, becoming brownish and dreamlike, the shadows deepening. He was losing everything. He thought of Bie. The children. Mostly of Daniel. This is your father, Daniel. Miriam's voice came to him: *If I close my eyes in the dark, Axel, I see your face.* He stood up, went out to the bathroom. Pulled off his jacket and vest and stuck his head under the shower. You've got to wake up now, he growled. Axel Glenne, you've got to wake up.

Rita put a plate of chicken breast in mushroom sauce on the table. She glanced at the computer screen.

– So proud I know such a famous person, she remarked drily.

Axel managed a brief laugh.

– How about the patients? he wanted to know.

– Not a single one of them believes you're capable of anything like that. Not one, take my word for it. Quite a few have called in just to say so. A couple have cancelled their appointments, but only for practical reasons. Not more than three or four.

– Have you heard anything from Solveig Lundwall?

– Come and sit down and eat. You look like death warmed up standing there.

He did as he was told.

– Her husband called. Solveig's been sectioned.

Axel tore off a piece of chicken.

– Good news.

– Apparently it was quite dramatic. She was going to hang herself from a tree. She's got some idea that somehow she has betrayed you. That it's because of her you wound up in jail.

– She's in a terrible state, he said, chewing away. – They must be quite sure they don't release her until she's been given the help she needs.

Rita said: – By the way, *Seen and Heard* called me last night. They want to do a feature on you.

– That rag. He glanced across at her. Nothing surprised him now.

– They said they'd give it a positive spin. Something people would enjoy reading, in spite of all the terrible things.

– What did you tell them?

– I told them to go to hell and take their enjoyment with them to spread it where it's needed.

He put his hand over hers.

– Without you that's where I'd be too.

He would have liked to say more, but instead he stood up and turned to the window, looking out at the night sky shaded with hints of orange.

59

RITA HAD TIDIED his office after the search, but it was still chaotic. The computer had not yet been returned. Some of his books and folders were still missing. He let himself into Ola's room. It didn't look as though the police had been in there.

The envelope lay in the middle desk drawer, where he had seen it earlier. He opened the flap, pulled out the pile of smaller envelopes. All were stamped and addressed to Miriam. There was also a single sheet of paper. He unfolded it, recognising her handwriting. It looked like the beginning of a letter.

I received your most recent letter today. Yes, I've met someone else! It's horrible of you to spy on me, but I'm not going to let you spoil things. No matter what you do, I'll never tell him about you. You don't exist when I'm with him. Not even in my thoughts.

Are you trying to scare me? I thought you'd understood. I don't wish you any harm. You've suffered enough as it is. I wish you well. But I can't do any more for you. Not after what happened in the cabin that time. You told me about your family; I know I'm the only one you've dared to talk to about them. I've thought a lot about what you told me. Your grandfather, who helped so many refugees to freedom during the war, how he was arrested by the Gestapo and sent to a concentration camp. When he got back he was a wreck, but never a word of thanks for all the lives he'd saved. And your father, the best father in the world, you said, but he drank and kept you both locked up in the cellar. I remember as though it were yesterday when you told me about it. We were sitting on the steps outside the cabin, and I didn't understand how you could think such a thing, that it was all your mother's fault because she left you, and that your father always meant well by what he did. I was stupid enough to say what I thought of him, and then you seemed to turn into another person completely. I can't forget it, even though I want to. I'll always see your eyes the way they were that night in the cellar. You hated me then, you wanted to destroy me. A thousand apologies can't make up for something that has been crushed. I know you trusted me more than any other girl you've ever met. And that was why you told me about your family. I can understand you and forgive you, but I can never trust you again. You must go to a

That was obviously as far as she'd got. He looked through the envelopes. The last one was stamped 27 September this year. It contained a folded sheet of paper.

This is the last letter I'll write to you. Don't know if you'll read it. Makes no difference. I've started talking to you instead. Have found a way to get you to listen to what I have to say. Get you to listen to every fucking word. With no chance to get away. I waited for you yesterday. You said back then that you needed time before you were ready. Now that time has passed. I wanted to surprise you. You came out and got into a car with a man. Drove to Aker Brygge. You sat half a bloody hour in that car. Today he drove you home, and as you were about to get out, he took a sniff at you and then I knew what was going on. He's forty-three. Seventeen years older than you. He earns eight hundred and fifty thousand a year and has seven million in the bank. He's married and has three kids. I guess that's all okay by you. And then I think how I should never have let you out of the cellar in the cabin that time, that the one night you spent down there wasn't enough. That maybe I'll come and fetch you from your bed one night when you think you're safe and take you back to that cellar, and who knows whether you'll ever get out again.

Axel sat there looking at the letter. It had been typed on a computer and wasn't signed. No sender's name on the envelope. Posted the day after she started her training with him. Several times Miriam had wanted to tell him about something that had happened to her. Something she was afraid of. Each time she'd got close to it she'd pulled away. That last night he'd spent with her, she had said something about a cellar in a cabin she'd been in. Close to the Swedish border. What were you doing out there? he should have asked her. But he hadn't. He'd guessed it had to do with a man. He didn't want to know anything about her past. About the men before him. What the two of them had together existed on a tiny island in the present moment. Both past and future could wipe it out at any time. But he had wanted to talk about himself. Something from his own past. Had he been using her? He saw her in his mind's eye. The way she looked when she was listening. She took it all in, didn't try to change anything.

The next letter he opened was more than two years old.

When you left, it was allegedly because you needed time to think, but more than a year has passed now and I think you were lying. It's not a good idea to lie to me. I know you thought it was horrible to be left sitting down there in that cellar, but I didn't know what I was doing. When you come, you'll see that I've changed. You didn't believe me when I told you that you were the first girl I'd ever been with properly. There have always been women I could have had; I got plenty of offers but I was never interested. After that first night in Sandane when we walked along by the fjord, I told you it was you I wanted. Nobody else. And you said that made you happy. You said a lot of other things too. That there was nobody else you wanted either. That you would stay with me for ever. That we were twin spirits, and all that kind of girl talk. That you liked having sex with me. That it was the best you'd ever had. Killing someone is no worse than giving them something and then suddenly taking it away again.

Dated 19 August last year:

I know you saw me today. You walked right past the car. You saw me and then pretended you hadn't seen me and crossed over the road with your friend. You took the Metro down to the Storting and then walked to Alexis's. You spent an hour there and then you went home. There was a light on in your window until ten past eleven. Then it was dark. You were sleeping. Or else lying there thinking. I've been off work all this week. There hasn't been a single second of the day when I haven't known where you are or what you're doing.

On 9 June:

If you can just manage to forget what happened, this is my plan. I'll sell the cabin and borrow from the bank and buy a place in town. Big enough for two. Please forget what happened. I made a mistake and I've really learned my lesson.

He flipped back through the bundle of letters. Flipping his way back through a relationship he didn't want to know about. He knew that what he was reading could tell him what had happened to her. Suddenly it dawned on him that it might also tell him something about where she was. He recalled what she had said about the cabin she'd been in. Had to be the same one that was mentioned in the letters. A cellar that had been used during the war. The former owner of it had been a border guide, she'd told him. The grandfather of someone she knew.

As he read back through the letters, more and more of them were written in an untidy scrawl. The tone of them changed too, the threats disappearing as he reached a time before what must have been the break-up. He opened an envelope stamped 16 July, five years ago:

I'm still sitting here on the steps and looking down at the path. Then I look at the finger with the ring I got from you. Engaged.

Imagine if you'd got the weekend off and decided to come out here again. Surprise! You like to surprise me. What you wanted to do the night before you had to leave, I never would have believed it . . .

Axel skimmed ahead.

I knew you'd like it out here in the forest. Best cabin in all Hedmark. We can stay up here for months and years with no one ever disturbing us. Maybe we should move out here, settle down, go hunting, live off the forest. The way my father did. Leave the rest of the world behind.

There was a photo with the letter. Axel held it under the light from the desk lamp. It was the same picture that had been in the envelope in her kitchen, only this one wasn't cut in half. She was standing in front of the creosoted cabin. The person with his arm around her looked to be twenty or thirty centimetres taller than her. From his features it was clear he had Down's syndrome. On the ground in front of them was the shadow of a head and a hand. Thrown by whoever was taking the picture. On the back of the photo was written: *Oswald doesn't have the words to say so, but he likes you too.*

Axel tore the letter out of the envelope that was date-stamped four weeks before the last one he had read.

Pottering about here and counting the days until you come. Looking forward to showing you the real me. I know of a great place to swim that nobody else knows about. A tarn not too far away. Then we can head on towards the border, and I'll show you a bear's hide. Maybe the mummy bear herself will be there. Saw the tracks of a female and two cubs not long ago. You say the bear is my inner animal. Yours too, if you ask me. Have fixed the car and will pick you up at the station as planned. But that old bus isn't reliable. If it breaks down on the timber road, you'll have to take the bus to Åmoen. The cabin is nearly ten kilometres further north and deep in the forest, so don't try getting there by yourself. Ask one of the

guys at the Esso station to drive you up here. I worked there every
school holiday when I was a kid. Ask for Roger Åheim and say
hello from me.

He read through the last lines again. She's in that cabin, he thought
with a jolt. And in the same instant: I know how I can find it.

It was just after midnight. After the phone had rung for the seventh
time, he began to doubt whether anyone would answer. Another ten
rings and he was about to give up. Then he heard a grunt at the
other end.

– Tom? It's Dad.

No answer, but he could hear his son's breathing. Imagined him
standing there in the dark in his boxers and T-shirt, trying to figure
out what was going on.

– Dad, he muttered. – Christ . . .

His hair would be dangling down over his eyes as he stood there,
thin and pale, shivering with cold. When was the last time Axel had
felt the need to put his arms around his son? Hold him close, hold
him tight so that he wouldn't disappear.

– What is it?

The voice was distant; the boy had regained his composure.

– Tom, you've got a thousand questions you want to ask me. I'll
give you answers to all of them in just a little while. All the answers
I can. But right now I need you to help me with something very
urgent. Can you do that?

A grunt from the other end.

– You know Grandad's old maps, the ones up in the loft? We
used to look at them together, you and me and Daniel.

– That stuff from the war?

– That's exactly what I'm talking about. I want you to go up to
the loft and get them.

– You mean now?

– I mean now.

– What d'you want them for?

As calmly as he could, Axel said: – A woman has gone missing.
I have to find her. Before it's too late.

– Are you and Mum going to get divorced?

– I need you to do as I ask, Axel said, pulling hard at his cheek.
– Go up to the cupboard behind the suitcases and the boxes with
the winter gear. Take your phone with you. Don't wake anyone.

He heard Tom opening the door of his room. Moving through
the house. Axel imagined himself walking along beside him. The
smells from the kitchen, the bathroom and toilet, of unwashed
clothes, soap, perfume, bread, leftover food. The smell of the house
itself, layered in the walls, contained his whole history within it.
And the smells of the sleeping, those who meant more to him than
anything in the world. If the door was slightly ajar, he could stop
outside, listen out for Bie's breathing in the dark.

He heard Tom open the door to the loft and pulled himself
together. Thought about what he was looking for. The box on the
second shelf down of the cupboard.

– Have you found them, Tom?

– Yes.

– I want you to fax them to me. But you have to be quiet, don't
wake your mother.

– Don't think these'll go in the fax.

– You'll have to cut them up and send them in smaller sections.

– You want me to ruin them?

– We can tape them together if we need them later.

He explained to Tom what to do. Shortly afterwards, the fax
machine in the photocopying room next to the office whirred into
life. Once he had satisfied himself the maps were legible, he
asked:

– How is Marlen?

Tom didn't know. – She's started sleeping with Mum. Why have
I never met Brede when he's my uncle?

Axel glanced at his watch. It was 12.55.

– He refuses to see me.

– Mum says he's an idiot.

– She's never met him either. Brede was treated badly. He was angry because I had all the advantages.

Tom said: – If you're Daniel, then I'm Brede.

Axel felt his heart sink.

– That's not true, Tom. I love you very much indeed.

– You're in all the newspapers and on TV. Everyone I meet talks about you the moment my back is turned. Calling you a bloody killer.

– They're wrong. He buried his face in his hands, rubbed hard up and down.

– Are you going to be moving out?

– I don't know, Tom. All I know is that this will soon be over.

He spread the pages out across the desk. The maps were from the 1940s. Routes taken by refugees over the border into Sweden drawn by the old Resistance hero Torstein Glenne for his sons. Circles around the places where there were cabins that could be used as hideouts. Which Axel, many years later, had pointed out to his own sons, using the same words about the price of freedom as his father had.

From the internet he printed out a map of Åsnes county, located Åmoen. *Nearly ten kilometres further north*, it said in the letter. He searched with his fingers across his father's map: Fallsjøen, Åmoen, a farm track leading north, a timber road branching off from it. He checked the distance. It coincided with one of the places Torstein Glenne had circled.

– That's where you're keeping her, you bastard, he muttered. But I've got you now.

Sergeant Norbakk answered at once. Axel said: – I know where she is.

– What the hell are you talking about? Miriam?

Axel described what he had found in the letters. He had expected scepticism, but the sergeant appeared to take him seriously.

– Were the letters signed? he wanted to know.

– No, but there is a name mentioned in one. Axel took out the photo. – Oswald, it says. That must be the person in the picture with Miriam. A very tall man who appears to have Down's syndrome.

– Excellent, I've got all that. Anything else?

– The letter-writer says he used to work at an Esso station at a place called Åmoen.

Norbakk expelled a long, slow gush of air.

– We'll get in touch with the owner. Maybe the guy still works there. He added: – You've made more progress in one evening than the police have in four weeks.

Axel didn't know quite how to take this. Maybe it was meant as an apology.

– We'll get people out there straight away, Norbakk said. – Give me a route description while I call the operational centre.

– You turn off a couple of kilometres past Åmoen. Axel described the route up through the forest.

Norbakk said: – I've got a map on my screen; are there any place names after you turn off the A road?

Axel checked his own map.

– It says Åheim at the end of the first side road. You drive on. Turn off east quite a way after that.

Norbakk asked him to repeat his description of the route. – Good, he said. – We'll take someone with us who knows the area. We'll also need people from the Emergency Response Unit. I'll call you if we need to check anything else.

– I'm going myself, said Axel.

Silence from the other end.

I must find her, he thought. Maybe I'll never see her again after this. But I must find her, or I'll lose everything.

– D'you think that's such a good idea? said Norbakk at last. – This is an armed operation.

– I'll take the map and the letters with me, Axel replied.

After ending the call, he felt a peculiar calm. A few raindrops came spinning through the night and splattered in a pattern on the window. It felt as though layers of dross had suddenly been cleared away from his mind.

– I'm going myself, he repeated aloud as he let himself out of the office.

LAST NIGHT WE *sat in the car after I'd taped your mouth. I didn't say a word. Only now, when you're lying in bed, are you going to hear what I have to say. Summer three years ago was the last time we lay in this bed together. We will lie here again tonight. Maybe I'll free your hands, so you can touch me. I didn't touch any of the others. I'm not like that. Just lay there beside them so they wouldn't feel too alone. But you belong to me. I want you one last time before I take you down into the cellar. You've been there before. If only you knew how much pleasure it has given me to think of your beautiful eyes the moment you realise the way this is going to happen. You told that story about the twins who were inseparable. One of them had to go to the kingdom of the dead. Maybe I'll join you down there soon so we can be together. The god of chance decides when it will be.*

You're the only one there's any urgency about. Soon they'll know you're missing. I asked you to bring the pictures I put in your letter box. You left them behind. Maybe I'll have time before I go to work tomorrow. Maybe I'll let someone else find them. I've been leaving clues for them to follow the whole way. Scores of opportunities to get to me before I took you. If they'd done their job properly down at the police station, this would never have happened. Not to you or any of the others. It's all their own bloody fault.

I told you once that unfaithfulness is the worst of all sins. Actually, the only one. I said it on one of the first days at the school. We bunked off and took a walk along the fjord. You said you felt the same way. I thought you realised that I meant it. You pretended to understand. You should have listened to me. You did what you should never have done. I don't care a damn who he is. He's just anybody at all. Now it's too late. I'm coming to you now, Miriam.

PART V

60

It was 1.45 when Axel passed Kongsvinger. The fuel gauge was dipping down into the red but he didn't want to stop yet.

As he emerged from the valley around the River Glomma, the landscape changed. The road cut its way through kilometre after kilometre of thick pine forest. If he found her, what would their future be? He knew the answer, but couldn't bear the thought. If you want to go on living with yourself, then you must *do the right thing*, he told himself, and it was as though the words came to him in his father's voice. More than anything else Torstein Glenne had despised people who failed to do the right thing. Who ran off leaving others to face the music. The way he thought Brede always did. *You must never be that kind of person.* His mother's voice: *Axel is his father's son all right.*

He drove past a lake that had to be Fallsjøen. Reached the village of Åmoen, swung in at the Esso station. It wasn't a twenty-four-hour station and he stopped in front of the pump with the credit card slot. This is where you used to work, he thought as he flipped open the petrol cap and started to fill the tank. Maybe you still do work here. I'm right behind you and you don't even know it.

He was thirsty. He found a tap on the wall at the rear of the building, slurped water from it. A waste bin stood on the corner. He picked out a container that had held windscreen cleaner, rinsed it out and filled it, got back into the car and looked again at the map. And the photo of the creosoted wall of the cabin that was up there in the forest somewhere. Driving on, he counted the farm tracks, turned off at the third. *Åheim*, it said on the sign.

He glanced down at the mileage. He'd driven nearly five kilometres since Åmoen. A forest track appeared on his right. It continued north-east and disappeared between the spruces. He followed the stony and pitted road for fifteen minutes. It made a sharp turn and climbed steeply. At the top of the rise the way was blocked by a barrier. He could see that it was firmly padlocked. He reversed down the hill. A couple of hundred metres before he reached a place where he could leave the car. He found the torch that Rita had put back in the glove compartment after he had borrowed it last time. Jogged back up to the barrier. If the police had been there before him they would have cut the lock. He called Sergeant Norbakk, got no answer, debated whether to wait for them. Miriam, he thought, and dismissed the idea.

The slope was even steeper on the other side of the barrier. At the top, the track swung round a small tarn. The sound of his footsteps against the soft ground broke the silence. And his breathing. His heartbeat. The cabin was behind a rise. He could only just see the outline, but he knew that was the place. When he reached it, he recognised the wall she'd been standing in front of in the photo, the brown-creosoted horizontal planking.

The door was locked. He switched on the torch and walked round the cabin. A couple of small windows on the sheltered side. He looked round for something to break one of them with. There was a small shed on the other side of the clearing. That was locked too, but the hasp holding the padlock was rusty and loose. He grabbed hold of it, managed to wrench it off, toppled backwards when it eventually gave. He shone the light into the darkness inside, saw a tall pile of logs and pulled one out. The pile started to collapse, something fell from the top of it. He twisted away, was hit by something big and heavy, tried to hurl himself out of the shed.

When he looked inside again, a dark shape was lying on the floor. He kicked at it. It didn't move. A large, lifeless animal. A bear, he could see now. The eyes were glassy, the jaws open revealing sharp yellow teeth. The animal was stuffed and nailed to a stand. Two of the paws had been cut off. He pushed it to one side and picked up the log that had caused the woodpile to collapse. As he was about to go outside again, he noticed a trailer standing directly inside the door. It was collapsible, a child-trailer. It looked new, he registered as he hung the door back in place.

He broke a window in two places, opened the hasp, crawled inside, stood there and sniffed. Dust and resin, but mostly the odour of rotting food. He shone the torch around. Braided mats on the floor. It looked freshly varnished. Firewood piled in the fireplace. Pictures on two of the walls: a tarn, a sunset between the trees. A door leading into a small kitchen stood half open. A fridge that was closed but not turned on. A couple of cartons of sour milk on the shelves. No sign of any rotting food. By the back door he found a fuse box. It must mean the place had its own generator.

On the table in the main room was a map of the area and an envelope. It contained photos. He took them out, shone his torch on the top one. Miriam walking along a street in town. Next, one of the flat where she lived, taken looking up towards her window. The one after that showed a woman in a dark coat on her way out of a house. The woman was Cecilie Davidsen, the house the villa in Vindern. He flipped quickly through the rest. One of Miriam's car with two people inside, the Nesodden ferry in the background. Then one of himself getting out of the car. The last one in the pile had been taken in a dark room. He could just make out his own face, in a bed. Next to him Miriam's dark hair against a pillow. He threw the photos down on to the table.

Beyond the fireplace he found two doors. The nearer led to a bedroom with bunk beds. A cupboard in the corner stacked with woollen blankets. The second door was locked. There was something white lying in front of it. A vest. He straightened it out, recognised it at once, her name with the pink glitter lettering over the chest. It was covered in stiff yellowish patches.

He hurled himself against the locked door. It didn't move.

– Miriam, he shouted into the gap. Pressed his ear to it and listened. No sound from within.

He took his mobile phone out again, again tried the sergeant's number. He heard a phone ringing in the kitchen. Grabbing hold of the log he had placed on the table, he crept out, overwhelmed with a feeling he was on the point of being able to put into words. Then something happened behind him, a wave breaking, splintering the darkness and hurling him into a storm of light.

61

NINA JEBSEN OPENED the office door. It was only 7.15. She had had a restless night and woken early. After an hour of tossing and turning she had decided to get up and make better use of the time.

She spat out the day's first Nicorette. The waste bin hadn't been emptied and yesterday's sticky deposits still clung to the plastic liner inside. She punched in her password and logged on. Here we go again, she thought in frustration. With the charge against Glenne dropped, they would now have to go through all the witness statements and documentation again. It reminded her of the snakes and ladders they used to play as children. Just before you reached home, you could trip and slide all the way back down to square one. She tried not to think of how many thousands of pages of documents relating to the case they had amassed thus far. Memories of the visit to the café yesterday afternoon kept coming back to her. This was what had kept her awake in the night. *See you later, Arve*, she'd said as they stood in front of the garage at the station, sounding more like an invitation than a salutation. He'd stepped closer to her and brushed the backs of his fingers against her cheek. Twice, while looking into her eyes. At that moment she had thought, *Now it's going to happen*. Then he said, *See you* and headed for the garage door, leaving her standing there with her insides on fire. But at the last minute he'd turned round and suggested they go out together again *one of these days*. Maybe have a drink or two.

Nina picked up a pen and wrote on a memo pad: *Arve*. Sat there looking at the name. She had always had neat handwriting. It suited his name. She opened a pack of chewing tobacco and navigated to the file on Miriam Gaizauskaite. She recalled something they had talked about yesterday. The victims' ages. Paulsen fifty-six, Davidsen forty-six, Elvestrand thirty-six. Miriam had turned twenty-six three months earlier. Her stomach rumbled. She'd had no breakfast. In the desk drawer she found an apple and took a bite through the leathery skin. It was mealy inside, but she didn't care . . . There was something else too. The first victim had been found in the Oslo marka, the second in Frogner Park, the third outside Miriam's door. It was as if something was getting closer. She carefully read through Arve's report again, noting with a smile that he had corrected the mistake she had alerted him to. *Lived seven years in Norway*, it now read. That first year she'd been at the folk high school near Sandane, in Nordfjord.

She closed the report and looked over the notes she had made herself since starting on the case. There was a vague feeling of having missed something. A piece of information, something she'd heard but not properly understood. She navigated to the report on the visit to the Reinkollen collective, not necessarily expecting to find it there. She heard footsteps out in the corridor and recognised them, spat out the tobacco and pushed the unsightly waste bin out of sight below the table. Arve always came early to work. If you twisted her arm, she would probably have admitted there were other reasons for her getting here before everyone else today, because she was most definitely not a morning person.

His office was a little further down the corridor, meaning he had to pass her door. It was ajar, but to make certain he knew she was there, she kicked at the waste bin and then swore. The steps stopped outside. There was a knock. She swivelled round in her chair.

– Hi, Nina. Having trouble?

– Not really, I just . . . tripped.

She didn't say what it was she might have tripped over, sitting there at her desk like that.

– Yesterday was fun, he smiled.

The way he said it made her cheeks glow. He must have noticed.
– Really enjoyed it, he added.

– Me too, she managed to say.

She pulled herself together, indicated his hand.

– Cut yourself, Arve?

He turned it over, saw what she was pointing to, on the outside of his wrist.

– Damn, I thought I'd wiped it all off. Had to clean a fuel injector in the car. He winked at her. – Not to worry, I'll survive.

He looked paler than usual, drawn around the eyes.

– Sleep well? she asked solicitously.

– I wouldn't say that. Feel as though my phone's been ringing all night.

– Anything important?

He rubbed his bristly chin. The beard was much darker than the hair, she noticed.

– Among other things, several calls from a certain Axel Glenne. Nina was curious.

– What did he want?

– Hard to say. He was babbling on about this medical student, something about letters someone had sent her. I think he's playing a game with us. I had to convince him we were on our way with everything we had. I'll tell you the rest at the morning briefing.

Don't go yet, she thought, and it seemed to help, because he took a step closer.

– What are you up to, by the way? I never thought of you as an early bird.

He glanced at her screen.

– Åsnes county? I never heard any more about your trip up there.

She crossed one leg over the other. Again she was wearing the tight-fitting blouse. She noticed how his gaze passed over her breasts.

– Amazing number of trees, she sighed. – You've probably got no idea what a nightmare it is for a girl from Bergen to get lost in a place like that. You from the depths of the deep dark forest up there.

He smiled at her turn of phrase. Maybe he was thinking about sitting on her desk, close enough for her to touch his thigh through the trousers.

– Two expeditions in two weeks, she said brightly as she cleared away some papers. – Viken got lost and drove us up some dark little cul-de-sac. We came to a barrier and couldn't turn round. Imagine it: alone with Viken in a deserted forest. Pretty scary, I can tell you. Felt like Little Red Riding Hood on her way to Grandmama. And the first trip was even worse. I ended up at some place called Reinvollen . . .

– Reinkollen.

– Yeah, that was it. Residential home for extraterrestrials suffering from mysterious illnesses.

He didn't respond and it make her feel nervous. She began describing the trip in detail, talking about the old ladies who worked there, and that wizened creature in the wheelchair, an Egyptian mummy of indeterminate age. She told the story well, she noticed, and Arve smiled a couple of times in the course of her narrative.

– At one point I nearly jumped out of my skin. An enormous mongoloid giant suddenly appeared in the doorway. He stood in the middle of the floor and beat himself on the chest and bellowed: *Oswald catch bear, Oswald catch bear.* She imitated his performance. – But the old ladies didn't seem bothered in the slightest. They sat down on the sofa with him and petted him and he quietened down after that.

Arve Norbakk nodded.

– They're very good with him.

She pushed her chair back.

– Do you know . . . ? Have you been there?

He looked at her for a long time. The expression in his eyes changed; they seemed to harden, and then open again. He leaned against the desk and smiled.

– Oswald is my brother, he said.

62

Nina struggled to stay focused. She scrolled down through the report from the visit to Reinkollen, and then, again, the interview with Miriam Gaizauskaite. Arve had gone to his office, and no one else had arrived in the meantime. As she tried to read through the documents, she kept hearing herself making fun of Oswald. She bit her lip. She hadn't felt so stupid for a long time. She'd apologised several times. Arve tried to laugh it off. Assured her that he didn't take it personally. Enjoyed a good story. Things a lot worse than that got said and done. That it was ignorance, not malice. Are you sure you're not mad at me? she'd asked repeatedly. Before he left, he stroked her hair. To reassure her, perhaps. Or for some other reason.

Before she could make up her mind about that, the phone rang. It was reception.

– I've got someone on the line who wants to talk to you. Says he's a Catholic priest at a church here in Oslo.

Miriam, thought Nina. Without further ado she asked for him to be put through. The man introduced himself as Father Raymond Ugelstad, a Dominican friar.

– This is about Miriam, she said at once.

– Yes, said the priest. – She mentioned your name when she was here the other day. I believe you've spoken to her.

The voice was light and nasal. She imagined a stout elderly man, a monk in a brown habit.

– I'm ringing because I'm worried. Quite frankly, I think something might have happened to her . . .

Two minutes later, Nina knocked on Arve Norbakk's door. It was a relief to get the chance to talk to him about what the priest had said. It would ease the embarrassment of their last conversation, might even remove it completely.

– I've just had a phone call. About Miriam.

She explained.

– We'd better check it out immediately, Arve responded. – I just tried to call her but she didn't answer.

The door to Miriam Gaizauskaite's flat was ajar. There was a bunch of flowers hanging on the door handle. Nina opened the little card that was tied to it with gold thread. *When this is over* . . . she read. She showed it to Arve, who had to lean against her to read the handwriting.

– I don't like this, she murmured as she pushed the door open with the toe of her shoe. – Miriam?

Arve was standing right behind her.

– We ought to call for backup before we go in, Nina.

– We don't have time for that. She had no objection to showing him that she could be decisive. – Backup in case of what? You think there's a giant bear in there?

He laughed. – I can see you're not the nervous type.

Nina peered into the living room. It looked pretty much as it had done the last time she was there. A few Pepsi bottles on the table, a pile of books. The alcove was empty, the bed made but the duvet rumpled.

– Miriam? she said again as she headed towards the kitchen.

Not there either. Washing-up was piled on the worktop. A plate on the table. Beside it an opened envelope and some photographs. She picked one of them up. It was Miriam. It had been cut in half, she noted as she turned it over. *And the fourth will be* . . . she read on the back.

Viken drummed on the tabletop. He was freshly shaved and his aftershave smelled different from the one he usually used. The neatly ironed white shirt was buttoned up well past the declivity in his neck. Nina knew that Finckenhagen and Jarle Frøen were being carpeted by the Chief Constable now that the charges against Glenne had been dropped. They were the ones who had to take the rap.

More than anything the chief disliked it when people tried to shove the responsibility down through the ranks. And as soon as he was done with Finckenhagen, she had called Viken in and given him a carpeting of her own, which was a lot softer to stand on and didn't seem to have made any particular impression on him. Viken was if anything even more obstinate, and what Nina and Arve had just told him about the finds at Miriam's flat seemed to leave him more convinced than ever that he had been right. He put Nina in mind of a dog that never lets go once it has sunk its teeth into something.

– This is no time for being wise after the event, he said in a voice that seemed to leave the matter open to doubt. – I assure you that Finckenhagen knows exactly what I think. I asked for a man to be left on guard outside Miriam's flat. I asked that a minimum of resources be left available to keep an eye on Glenne after we let him go. My words fell on deaf ears.

He glared, but Nina saw a glint of satisfaction in the grey eyes.

– You were supposed to be keeping an eye on her, he said, addressing himself to Arve Norbakk.

The sergeant was leaning in the doorway.

– I called her last night. Everything seemed to be in order. I asked her to keep my number handy and to get in touch instantly if something happened.

Viken raised a hand.

– You did what you could, Arve. I'm glad somebody knows what we're trying to do here.

Norbakk's response to being praised was inscrutable.

– And another thing, he said. – I had Glenne on the phone to me twice last night.

Viken raised his eyebrows.

– What did he want?

– He called the station the first time at about eleven, asked to speak to me personally. When I rang back, he told me what shits we were. I made the mistake of calling without blocking my number, and a few hours later he was there again, muttering away about Miriam. Still having a go at us. He didn't sound completely sober.

Or maybe he was on something else. He called another couple of times, but I passed up the chance to hear any more of his crap.

– Perfectly understandable, was Viken's response. – Nina, I'm putting you in charge of the search for Miriam. Are all our reports on her up to date?

Arve Norbakk cast a glance in her direction.

– Just a couple of things I have to add, he said quickly. – I'll do it straight away. Give me a couple of minutes and I'll get a printout from her mobile phone. And Glenne's.

– Good. Jebsen, you find out when that bunch of flowers was sent, and by whom. I have my suspicions. Where's Sigge?

– He called in, said Nina. – He's at home, one of his kids is sick. Unless it was both of them. He's going to try to get in later.

Viken's bushy eyebrows reared up and faced each other like two hairy snakes about to copulate.

– What's the matter with that bloke? he growled. – Hasn't he got a wife?

The flowers had been sent from Flower Power in Majorstua on Wednesday evening at 6.40. Nina spoke to the florist on the phone. He thought he could remember the man who had made the purchase, a bouquet of nine long-stemmed roses. The description was vague, but it fitted Glenne.

Nina entered the information and thought about it. The delivery man had been there Wednesday evening. When no one answered, he had hung the flowers on the door. They were still there on Friday morning. But according to Arve, Miriam had been home when he called her yesterday evening. So why hadn't she taken them inside?

Again she looked at what Arve had written about Miriam. There was something she hadn't quite understood, and she knew it had to do with this report. Something Arve had said. She still couldn't think what it was . . . She noticed that he hadn't added the information about the engagement. She sat there, staring at the screen. Miriam had mentioned that the man she had been engaged to was someone she met in her first year in Norway. In other words, when she was attending the folk high school in Nordfjord. It would be possible to check the list of former pupils, but it was by no means certain that the fiancé had gone to the same school as her. It would be easier to ask someone who actually knew her.

During her interview Miriam had named two other students as her closest friends. Nina had made a note of their names. She looked them up in her notebook. Thought she should let Arve have them. Didn't want him thinking she was taking over his job. That she thought he wasn't doing it well enough. On the other hand, he had undertaken to check a mass of mobile phone calls and would have enough to be getting on with. He would thank her for it. Then she could remind her of their agreement. To have a drink together. Or two.

She was about to call directory enquiries when Viken burst in.

– Now we've got him, he trumpeted.

Nina had never seen him looking so elated.

– The photos you and Arve found in Miriam's flat. They were covered in big juicy fingerprints. Want to guess whose?

It wasn't hard to guess, but she didn't want to spoil his surprise.

– Glenne, Viken said as calmly as he could. – Dr Axel Glenne.

Nina had the feeling of climbing aboard a merry-go-round that was already in full swing.

– He might be the one who sent them to her, she offered tentatively.

Viken drummed away on the door frame.

– I called Frøen. Nina, even he realises what this means.

Across his face were written the words: *What did I tell you?* All the more important, then, for her to tell him what she had found out.

– Miriam had a lengthy relationship after she arrived in Norway. She was engaged. I'm just trying to find out who the man was.

Viken gestured to her.

– That'll have to wait. I need you for something else. We don't have much bloody time. We're going after Glenne now, with everything we've got.

313

63

Oswald had been restless all morning. He paced back and forth in the room making deep growling noises, and paid no attention to Signy Bruseter when she spoke to him. He hadn't eaten, and she hadn't been able to wash him. According to the night shift he'd been the same all night, wandering around restlessly, not getting a minute's sleep. And of course, it affected Tora too. She sat there in her chair and never stopped whimpering. Several times Signy had been on the point of calling Mette Martin and warning her, but she decided to hang on until Åse Berit showed up. Åse Berit always managed to calm Oswald down, no matter how upset he was.

At a quarter past eleven, Signy heard the front door open and gave a sigh of relief. It wasn't Åse Berit Nytorpet who came into the room, however, but a much older woman. A tiny, skinny little thing with permed silver hair and thick glasses.

– I heard things were a bit upside down here today so I came in earlier, she said.

Signy stared at her in surprise.

– Isn't Åse Berit coming?

– Åse Berit's off sick.

The old woman held out a withered, scrawny hand.

– I'm Ingeborg, she said. Ingeborg Damhaug. I used to work here before, worked here for years.

Signy smiled bravely. Åse Berit was so big and buxom you could take shelter behind her when Oswald was upset. But what use would this little bag of bones be?

– What's the matter with Åse Berit?

The old woman sighed.

– It's all just got too much for her. The police have been up there and turned their farm inside out. Even taken up the floor. Åse Berit's nerves couldn't stand it.

Signy looked down at her feet.

– Apparently there's someone sneaking around the village telling tales on folk, Ingeborg sniffed with contempt. – Now, Oswald, what's all this, walking up and down and not eating anything?

– Oswald catch bear.

– Right you are, cooed Ingebord. – I'm sure you can, but now you just come and sit down.

She put an arm around the giant resident and led him over to the dining table.

– Ingeborg catch bear, Oswald shouted, and the old woman burst out laughing.

– Yes, that'll be the day, she chortled, wiping away the tears, and it looked as though Oswald was joining in her laughter.

She put milk on the table and Oswald drank it down in one gulp. She refilled the glass and buttered some bread, and he ate with a hearty appetite.

– Oswald and I are old chums, hummed Ingeborg. – Isn't that right, Oswald?

– Oswald drive bus, he rumbled, his mouth full of bread and liver pâté.

After his meal, she took him by the hand and led him into his room.

– Now you just have a nice little lie-down, Oswald, you've been up and about all night.

– I've known Oswald since he was seven or eight years old, Ingeborg explained later as they sat at the table. – Oh, it breaks my heart to think about him, that lad.

Signy sipped at her coffee.

– Åse Berit told me his father used to lock him up in the cellar when he was a little boy. Surely that can't be true?

Ingeborg shook her head and stared in front of her. Tora had fallen asleep in her chair, her head hanging down at an angle, drooling at the mouth. Ingeborg got up and wiped her face, placed a pillow under the bony chin.

— It's true all right, she said. — I was working in child care at the time. It was a terrible business.

— But the father must have been a complete madman. Didn't anyone say anything?

Ingeborg shot Signy a bleak look.

— That's the thing that bothers me most of all, that we didn't act sooner. We got several messages saying things were going to pieces up at old Norbakk's, but it wasn't until a member of the family rang and said we'd better get ourselves up there as fast as possible . . .

She bit at the pale strip of her underlip.

— It's over twenty years ago now, but I'll tell you this, Signy, it's a sight I will never forget. Never.

— What happened?

Ingeborg sat for a while with her eyes closed. To Signy her eyelids seemed as sheer as tissue paper. It was as though the old woman were looking straight through them at her.

— We went to the cabin, up in the forest, she said at length, the eyes expressionless when she opened them again. — And what a mess when we got up there. Bottles everywhere, filthy clothes and unwashed dishes, a broken window so it was freezing cold inside. First off we couldn't find the boys anywhere. Not until we went down into the cellar. They were locked inside, both of them. And there was Arve with his arms around Oswald, trying to keep him warm.

— Arve? wondered Signy.

Ingeborg took out a handkerchief and blew into it.

— Oswald's older brother. They'd been sitting down there for days. The father had given them a bottle of water and tossed them a few crusts of bread before he took off.

— So then you did something?

— Oh yes. Young Arve was fostered with some people down in Lillestrøm. Oswald was taken into institutional care, and now he's never had it so good. But we waited too long before doing anything . . . Well, the father was sentenced for child neglect. Served a few months. When he got out, he lived like an animal up in that cabin. Drank himself to death in the end.

Suddenly Ingeborg's wizened face lit up.

– But I'll tell you this, Signy, that Arve Norbakk is what they call a real superkid. It's amazing how well he's managed. Before we found foster parents for him, he was living with us, and I've been following his progress ever since.

She exposed a line of pearly white teeth that looked completely genuine.

– Always bright and positive, that Arve. The only thing that upset him was if someone said something bad about his father. Then he'd scream and carry on. If the police hadn't locked his father up, according to Arve, he would never have drunk himself to death. He hated the police more than anything else. Not counting his mother, who'd left them. I was so worried about him. But then he calmed down, and he never spoke about either one of them again.

– My God, Signy exclaimed. – What could make a child say something like that?

Ingeborg sighed and looked at her watch.

– Well well, Signy, I suppose we'd better go in and wake Oswald, or he'll be up all night again.

Signy jumped to her feet.

– Just you sit there.

She opened the door to Oswald's room. A blast of wind struck her from the wide-open window. The bed was empty.

64

Not until she'd started the car and Viken had jumped in beside her did Nina get round to asking where they were going.

Viken said: — Arve checked the list of calls to Glenne's mobile phone. Somebody called him from a landline in Tåsenveien at three minutes past nine yesterday evening. The owner of the house is a Rita Jentoft.

— Jentoft? I've heard that name somewhere before . . . We interviewed her. I think it was Sigge.

— Correct. Fifty-two-year-old woman, born in Gravdal in Vestvågøy county, lived in Oslo for twenty-five years. Widowed for the last eight. Trained medical secretary. Now works at a certain clinic in Bogstadveien. No previous convictions. Want her income tax details?

— I get it, said Nina. — His secretary.

She stopped at the entrance to the driveway. A patrol had already arrived. Viken jumped out even before she turned the engine off. Two constables in uniform stood on the steps.

— No one answered when we rang the bell, one of them said. — The door isn't locked but we were given orders to wait for you.

— The back, barked Viken.

— We've got a man there.

— Good. Then let's go in.

He opened the door.

— Police! he shouted from the hallway.

Ten minutes later, they had established that the house was empty, from basement to loft.

* * *

The waiting room at the Bogstadveien medical centre was packed. A woman wheeled a pram back and forth in front of the reception desk. The child inside screeched and howled. The telephone ringing behind the counter sounded almost as angry, but there was no one there to take the call. Viken opened the glass side door and let Nina in front of him into a corridor. On the right was a door to a storage room with shelves full of hypodermic syringes and other items and equipment. Another door had Axel Glenne's name on it. It was unlocked, the office within dark and empty. On the next door the sign read *Inger Beate Garberg*. Viken knocked and stepped inside in the same moment. A woman in a white coat turned towards him. Her long greyish hair hung in a braid down her back. On a bench behind her was a man with his legs drawn up. He was naked from the waist down.

– What's going on here? the doctor shouted, pointing at Viken with her plastic-gloved finger. – You've no right to come barging in like this.

Viken mumbled a sort of apology. – Police, he explained. – Can we have a word with you? Now.

Dr Garberg came out into the corridor with them. She was half a head taller than Viken, and he looked a little ill at ease.

– Where is Rita Jentoft? asked Nina.

Dr Garberg rolled her eyes.

– In reception, I presume, or gone to the toilet, I have no idea.

– Have you seen Axel Glenne since yesterday evening? Viken wanted to know.

– No, the doctor seethed, – I have not seen him, and it's about time you left that man alone. You've done enough as it is. How is he supposed to deal with all that stuff you've released to the newspapers about him? It's the most disgraceful thing I've ever come across.

She was incandescent with rage, and Viken took a couple of paces back. He almost collided with a small, stout woman who emerged from the door behind him.

– What's all the shouting about? she wondered.

Ignoring her, Dr Garberg continued her tirade. She peeled off the plastic glove, crumpled it and tossed it to the floor. Now it was about the patients' archives, which the police had been interfering with without her permission.

– I'll deal with this, Inger Beate, said the stout woman, and led them into Glenne's office.

Viken nudged Nina.

– Our female medical friend is suffering from hysteria, he diagnosed. – Recommended treatment, half a bottle of red wine and a roll in the hay.

Rita Jentoft had what Nina would call shock-bleached hair. Not really suitable for a woman past forty. But she was smart, and friendly, and she gave precise answers to all their questions.

– Are you sure about that? Nina repeated. – Did Glenne say that he had told the police about what he had found in Miriam Gaizauskaite's flat?

– I've told you twice, and I'll tell you twice more if you like, Rita Jentoft answered. – Axel was in a state of shock over what he'd found. He was terrified something might have happened to that *student*. She almost spat the last word out. – That was why it was life and death for him to get down here to find that envelope.

– What envelope?

The secretary didn't mind telling them.

On their way back out to the car, Nina said: – What she says seems credible enough. It would explain how Glenne's fingerprints ended up on the photos.

Viken grunted. – I'll admit it's probable the woman believes it herself, he conceded. – She seems the naïve type. It won't surprise anyone to learn that Glenne is a world champion manipulator of other people.

His mobile phone rang. He took the call and listened for a few seconds before saying:

– Aker Brygge? You've warned Central? Good, we'll be there in a couple of minutes. By the way, Nina tells me that this Miriam was

engaged; obviously we need to find out more about that too . . . Got
that?

He nodded briskly as the caller finished what he had to say.

– Great work, Arve.

He ran down the remainder of the steps and jumped into the car.
As Nina got in, he opened the window and placed the blue light on
the roof, turned on the siren. As they sped down Bogstadveien, he
gave her the news in a sharp burst: – Call registered on Glenne's
phone four or five minutes ago. He's at Aker Brygge or very close
to. At least *someone* is doing their job.

Nina tightened her seat belt. On an emergency call-out she would
much rather drive herself than be Viken's passenger.

– What about this man Miriam was engaged to?

– Arve checked that out a long time ago, it says so in the report.
A guy she met at a school somewhere or other in the west country.
At the moment he's living in Brazil.

– Is that definite?

– Of course, he said with a heavy sigh. – Arve's double-checked it.

He threaded his way through the traffic. His phone rang again.
He pulled a hands-free set out of the glove compartment and fitted
the earpiece into his ear.

– Yes, he answered irritably, but his tone changed at once.
– Thanks for ringing, but can it wait? . . . Okay, let's do it now then.

He spun through the red light at the crossroads and then up along
Slotts Park, now and then grunting into the phone.

– Thank you very much, he said finally. – I'll call you back.

He pulled the earpiece out as they sped down Henrik Ibsen's
gate.

– That was Plåterud. About the fibres found under Elvestrand's
fingernails. They confirm what they suspected about the DNA
profile. They come from a man who *may* have a close family relative
with some kind of chromosomal abnormality. Such as Down's
syndrome. Not much help. The woman might have scratched any
man in town. But there's something else Plåterud says we ought to
take a closer look at.

Nina didn't dare distract his attention from the driving by asking questions, but Viken went on:

– They found traces of saliva in Elvestrand's hair and analysed it.

– And it wasn't the same profile? Nina hazarded.

Viken accelerated down Løkkeveien.

– That's a pretty safe bet. Not from a human being at all.

Nina held on tight to her seat. She felt as though they were playing a game of join-the-dots and getting it all wrong.

– A fucking bear, Viken added to himself.

65

AXEL WOKE TO the stink of rotting meat. He lay there without moving. The smell was a warning. Carefully he opened his eyes to darkness. Am I blind now? The thought shot through him. He tried to lift a hand, felt a burning pain in his upper arm as though from a bad wasp sting. His hands wouldn't move. They were twisted over each other and tied to something behind him. He turned his head slowly to one side, then the other. Finally he located a pale strip of light, diagonally up from him. I can see, he muttered as he tried to sit upright. There was a flash in his head, and then he collapsed and was gone again.

– What happened, Axel?

His father's voice is cold and without a trace of anger. It makes Axel more afraid than his anger does.

– I don't know.

He looks down, but notices his father slowly shaking his head.

– Do you think I'm an idiot, Axel?

– No, Father.

– You were there. The two of you were the only ones there. I'm asking you to tell me what happened.

Axel stares at his father's shoes. They glow a reddish brown in the light falling from the living-room window. He and Brede have made a pact. If he breaks it, there will be no one left to defend his brother.

– Ask Brede, he manages to say.

– I *have* asked Brede. He maintains that it wasn't him, but he refuses to say any more. Brede always denies everything, you know that. He's the type who just doesn't know how to do the right thing. He's been given several chances to confess, but he simply goes berserk.

His father takes a few heavy breaths.

– I know that you and Brede will never tell on each other. That's good.

His tone of voice is friendly now, which makes it even worse. When that friendliness is there, you have everything. When it's gone, you lose everything.

– But you're going to have to make an exception here. Killing a dog is as bad as killing a human. That's why I'm asking you, Axel. And I'm only going to ask you this once: was it Brede?

– Yes, Father.

He was sitting with his back wedged up against something hard and round; a pipe, perhaps. His body was stiff; he must have been sitting in the same position for hours. His hands were cuffed, he could feel that, and he tried to understand what had happened. I was attacked. He was here. Waiting for me inside the cabin. The police didn't come. The cellar . . . I'm a prisoner in that cellar.

– Miriam, he whispered.

He heard the echo of breathing somewhere in the dark. To his left. Not an echo. Someone else's breathing, slower and more powerful than his own. The stink of something rotten was so acrid that it had woken him up. He had been present once when the police broke into an apartment belonging to an old woman who hadn't been seen for over a fortnight. The stench invading his senses now was even worse than that. He breathed through his mouth as slowly as he could to try to control it. Fought against the urge to howl up at the ceiling. Forced himself to sit still. My only hope, he thought, without knowing why. Stay calm. Miriam's only chance.

66

He was woken by a sound. The strip of light was gone. It had to be evening, or night. Footsteps directly above his head. A door closing. Footsteps back across the floor, stopping. Something being moved, a piece of furniture. Directly afterwards, a trapdoor opening. Bright light, burning his eyes. He had to shut them tight again. Heard steps coming down a ladder, a kick on his foot. He raised an eyelid. The torchlight was playing directly into his face. Behind it a form bending to him.

– Right, so you're awake.

He still couldn't see who the figure was. But he knew at once.

– Got something for you to drink.

A plastic bottle was pressed against his lips. There was no smell from it and he took a couple of swigs.

– What do you want from me, Norbakk? he murmured.

The cone of light moved away from his eyes.

– What do *you* want from *me*? You're the one who broke in here.

Axel breathed as deeply as he could.

– Miriam . . .

It sounded as if the other man laughed.

– You mustn't harm her, Axel groaned. – I'm the one who got her involved in all this.

– Shut up, Norbakk hissed. – I know everything that's been going on, understand? Every last thing the two of you have been up to. When you screwed up in the pine shelter, and at home in her bed. She wanted you. Don't try to defend her, it might make me angry with you too.

Again he directed the torch beam into Axel's face.

– I've got nothing against you, Glenne, he said, calmer now. – No objection to you screwing Miriam. That's okay by me. I let you do it. You're not a bad guy. If you hadn't come out here, you would have escaped.

– Escaped what? Axel managed to ask.

Norbakk didn't reply. A few moments later he said: – That day you were riding in the forest. I was standing there watching when you swam in the tarn. Would have been a piece of cake to take you then. Standing there bollock naked and looking round. But that would have been too easy. So I just messed with your bicycle.

He made a noise like the sound of air escaping from a tyre.

– It was when I saw you stop to have a chat with that old biddy that I knew what was going to happen. It was a great moment. Other people might have had the same idea, but how many of them would have managed to carry it through?

He whistled a snatch of melody.

– This wasn't about you. You just happened to get in the way. He leaned down towards him. – Not your fault, Christ, no. I like you, Glenne. You're a good doctor, a great father to your kids. She's the one who stirred up all this shit. She promised me everything. And then off she went. Did she say that you were her twin, did she tell you that too?

Axel couldn't answer.

– What do you think we should do with these women who promise us everything and then run off?

This time he didn't wait for a reply.

– I gave her some idea of what was going to happen. Made her feel it was getting closer without letting her quite realise what it was. One . . . two . . . three. And the fourth will be . . . Those other old biddies, that was just chance, same as you.

He laughed.

– She felt sorry for me, Glenne, she couldn't bring herself to do anything that might get me into worse trouble. She had to be a hundred per cent sure first. Poor girl. Who should we feel sorry for now? What d'you think?

– I like you, Norbakk repeated when Axel still did not respond.
– It's too fucking bad you had to come out here.

– They'll find us, Axel coughed. – I used my mobile phone up here.

Norbakk clucked his tongue.

– Sorry to have to tell you this, but those calls are my department. And the last call registered from Axel Glenne's telephone was made from Aker Brygge. Full call-out. I'll leave you to guess who made it. Now your phone is lying at the bottom of the fjord just off the end of the quay.

Axel tried again: – There's a lot of people know you and Miriam were a couple. Sooner or later . . .

– Maybe they will find out, Norbakk interrupted. – And maybe they won't. In any case, it'll be too late.

– What d'you mean?

– I've just had an idea. Now I can see how this all works out in the end. It's actually quite beautiful. Norbakk sounded as if he was talking to a close friend. – You'll be found tomorrow. Together. Someone will discover your bodies in the boss's garage under the police station. You'll be lying with your arms around each other, as though you're embracing . . . There's a logic to it. It'll be big. Like planting a huge bomb under the place.

Axel tried to make sense of what he was hearing but couldn't manage it.

– If they shape up a bit, they'll find out who put you there, Norbakk mused. – That's the way I want it to end. They could have guessed a long time ago. If Viken had been a little bit smarter and a little bit less self-centred, he would have known about Miriam and me weeks ago.

Suddenly he sounded frustrated and annoyed.

– I've given them something to work with all along, helped put them on the right track. If they'd done their job properly, none of this would have happened. But now it's happened anyway.

Axel tried to turn.

– Where is she?

Norbakk coughed.

– You want to know?

– Yes.

– She's lying in bed in a room up there. Had to lock her in. She's fine now. I'd just finished putting the covers over her when you came barging in.

Axel shook the handcuffs.

– If you release me, I'll help you.

Norbakk laughed loudly.

– You're lying there and you're going to help me? Don't make promises you can't keep, Glenne. I like you, remember. Don't disappoint me. We mustn't lie to each other, you and I.

He squatted down and added confidentially: – I'll let you out of those handcuffs soon.

He picked up a syringe and held it in the light from the torch.

– I'll give you something that'll help you sleep. When you wake up, the cuffs will be unlocked. I'll give you a chance. I'm not a monster.

– A chance?

Norbakk played the light in an arc around the cellar. The room was almost big enough for him to stand upright in. It was partitioned by a gate.

– You ought to be curious about this place, Glenne. Your father must have been here many times when he was with the Resistance. My grandfather helped him escape. It was just before he was caught himself. I can well imagine they were friends. They had a transmitter here. Even a printing press. But no prisoners. That came later. Long after the war. It was my father who put that partition in.

He shone the light into a corner. A huge dark hulk lay there. It was breathing slowly and deeply.

– What the hell is that?

– Not so loud, Glenne, unless you want to wake him up.

Norbakk played the torch back and forth over the sleeping shape a few times.

– Not too hard to trap one of these when you know how they

328

live. And where. How they react when you put out bait for them and cover it up with branches and soil. All you have to do then is lie there and wait. But a giant like this one, I would never have managed to get him here all on my own . . . You should meet my brother, Glenne.

Axel's eyes were wide open. He couldn't believe what they were seeing.

– It's had the same medicine as you're going to get. It'll sleep for a while yet. And now *you're* going to sleep. In an hour's time, when you wake up, you'll be in there, with the animal.

He leaned forward and pushed the syringe into Axel's upper arm.

– What's the matter, Glenne? Don't you like teddy bears?

67

ONCE MORE THE darkness had coiled itself around him. He lay and swim in it. Felt far away, drugged. *I found you, Axel*. Somewhere up there he sees her face. Miriam, he says. *Do you regret it, Axel?* No, you were the one I was looking for. Was always looking for. She smiles down at him. *I want you to live*. With one finger she closes his eyes. A crowd of people come up the hill, in through the door. They're carrying candles. They gather round and look at him lying there. Daniel leans forward and lays a flower on his chest. A rose. Tom is crying. His whole face is open wide. I tried to be good enough, Tom. Tried to get close to you. Bie is wearing a little black hat with a veil across her face. She's holding Marlen close to her. Her eyes are hard and dark blue, resembling a certain kind of jewel, the name of which escapes him.

He sat up abruptly. The cuffs dangled loose from one wrist, his hands were free. The stench was as powerful as before. He picked up another smell too. Wetter, stronger. Blowing in a steady rhythmic stream against his face. Each time accompanied by a small gurgling sound. He was sitting with his back against the partition. Locked in, he thought in panic. With the animal. He fumbled around, touched something, picked it up and gripped it to see if it could be used as a weapon. Dropped it again as soon as he recognised what it was. The remains of a leg and a foot.

– Norbakk, he shouted as he got to his feet, tearing at the gate.

In the corner to his left, a rustling sound. Something happening in that furry pile. An animal, waking up. He backed away as far as he could. The trapdoor opened, light spread across the ceiling and down to where he stood. Then Norbakk was climbing down.

– Slept well, Glenne?

The voice was bright and cheerful.

– Now I realise you mean what you say, Axel shouted. – Open this bloody gate, the animal's waking up.

– That's right, Norbakk whispered. – He's waking up. Now we'll see, right?

He shone his torch on the pile of fur lying by the wall. Two black eyes visible.

– The big fella hasn't suffered down here. I believe in treating animals well. But he hasn't really had all that much to eat. The first two I had down here, I let him scratch them a bit and then doped him again. The last one had to sacrifice her legs. So now he's had a little taste, no wonder he wants more. It'll soon be time for him to go into hibernation.

He hung the torch from a hook in the ceiling, turned it so that most of the cellar was illuminated.

– Need enough light for us to see what's going on.

He lowered his voice.

– Usually these beasts are pretty groggy when they come round after sedation, but not this one. He's mean and keen. Probably scared, too, just like you.

Axel grabbed hold of the padlock and rattled it.

– What do you want? Tell me what you want me to do. Is there anything you want?

Norbakk reached up through the trapdoor, picked up something from the floor of the room above.

– That's what's so fucking awful, Glenne. You've got nothing I want. Not any more. You've got money, but I'm not interested in that. And you've got a cute, hot wife. Spent a whole evening getting it on with her.

Axel heard him grin.

– Met her at Smuget. She picked the winning number that night all right. She might've ended up here too, but she's the wrong age. The god of chance held his protecting hand over her.

He walked over to the gate, pointed a video camera at Axel.

– Tell me what it was like, he said. – Tell me what it was like screwing Miriam, then I'll tell you what your wife was like.

– Jesus, Axel shouted, struggling with the free end of the handcuffs.

– Tell me, then I'll let you out. Did she get you to do the same things as me?

He held the camera up into Axel's face.

– I always did like you, Axel, he murmured, putting his hand through the bars, squeezing his arm. – I would love to hear you describe . . .

With a jerk Axel had the cuff fastened around his wrist.

– Axel, now that really wasn't very clever. Norbakk's voice was lower. – Not very clever at all.

A growling noise came from the corner, the sound of claws against the stone floor. Norbakk tried to pull his arm free, but Axel leaned forward with all his weight.

– Okay, shouted Norbakk. – I'll unlock the gate. Then you can let go of my fucking arm.

He fumbled with the padlock. Lost his camera on the floor. Axel heard the padlock being opened, removed. At that moment there was a rattling sound as the animal approached through the half-dark. He felt its breath hit him, the smell of its guts. He pulled himself round, dragging Norbakk's arm with him. The rattle turned into a roar in the animal's throat, and then it opened its jaws.

Norbakk screamed. The animal had taken hold of his arm and was jerking its head from side to side, its eyes bloodshot and bulging. Axel tried to hold on to the gate but was dragged away. With a ripping sound, Norbakk's arm was torn off. The great jaws let go their hold, the animal lifted its head, lowered it again, raised its snout. Axel managed to half turn away. Pain ripped up through his skull, down across his face. The iron gate flew open. He was hurled backwards, and tumbled to the floor outside. As though through water he heard Norbakk's screaming close to his ear. A hand grabbed him by the hair; he drove his elbow backwards and hit something soft that gave way. He rolled over and managed to catch hold of the ladder, climbed up one step, then another, dragged himself up on to the floor of the room above, crawled away from the opening. He felt as though half his face had been burnt away. He could see, but only through one eye. Beneath him Norbakk's screaming ended abruptly.

Axel hobbled over to the bedroom door. Still locked.

– Miriam, are you there?

He turned and ran for the front door. The sounds he could hear coming from the cellar were unendurable.

It was dark outside. A thin white layer of snow on the ground. Light from a half-moon shining through the trees. He made his way round the side of the cabin. Which window? he thought feverishly. Which window? He stopped at the first one. Something was dangling from his wrist. The stub of an arm still held in the cuffs. It wasn't his. He grabbed hold of it and smashed it against the window, took hold of the hasp and opened it. Didn't notice that he cut himself as he hoisted himself inside and tumbled down on to the floor.

In the pale moonlight he saw the outline of her head against the pillow, the hair flowing around it.

– Miriam . . .

He took a step towards the bed. Moving through a smell he refused to breathe in. Still saying her name. As though it could drive that smell away, out of that dark room. He pulled the blanket off. Couldn't see what the body lying there looked like. But he could no longer will away the stench and he staggered backwards and dived out through the window. Lay trembling on the ground. When he looked up, he saw the animal appearing round the corner of the cabin. He dragged himself to his feet. *Stand still, Axel, don't run. You mustn't run now.* The beast raised itself on its hind legs. Turned its head and looked sideways into his eyes.

He yelled. Everything inside him went into that yell. He howled himself empty, screaming into the bear's face. It stayed up on its hind legs for a few seconds, about as tall as he was. Then it lowered its upper body, took a few paces backwards, raised its snout and sniffed the air. At last it turned, and with a growling noise sidled away towards the forest, where the moon was slowly disappearing behind the tallest trees.

Sitting in the car, he came to his senses again. The key was in the ignition. He started the engine and let the car trundle down on to the forest track. Hoarse noises were still escaping from his throat, coming in bursts, he didn't know where from, or how to stop them. The car moved slowly down the track in first gear. Sergeant Norbakk's arm still dangled across his lap.

Round a bend a figure approached into the beams of the headlights. Axel braked. He still couldn't see out of his right eye. The figure leaned across the bonnet and stared in through the windscreen. A broad distorted face with slanting eyes and open mouth, shouting at him.

He pressed the horn down hard.

– Catch bear, the man seemed to be saying. – Oswald catch bear.

Axel put his foot down. The huge body slid off the bonnet and down into the ditch. In the rear-view mirror he saw it climb back up on to the track and continue on up the hill behind him.

68

QUARTER OF AN hour to closing time. The young man behind the counter at the Esso station in Åmoen had made a start on cashing up for the day. Everything seemed to be in order. At least half an hour since the last customer. Someone he knew, the old woman who'd been his teacher back in primary school. Couldn't sell her a drop of petrol; all she wanted was a newspaper and some sweets. But what Signy Bruseter really wanted was a natter. As usual she asked a load of questions about what he was up to, what his plans were for the future, all that kind of stuff. And she wanted to tell someone about what had happened at the place where she worked, one of the inmates who'd run off. Signy's nattering could drive you nuts. He imagined himself picking up the biggest pair of pliers in the place and smashing them over her head; that would get him a bit of peace. Instead he told her there was something he had to do out in the workshop, and in the end she'd gone.

He leaned up against the door to the back room and watched the TV screen hanging up on the wall in there. Jackie Chan's face grinning down at him. He'd seen the film before and knew there was a good bit coming up soon. He tossed a hamburger into the microwave. Thought about eating it before he left but then decided to take it home. Enjoy it in peace and quiet with another film. He took it out and stuck it into a plastic bag along with the local paper and a Red Bull.

Just then a car turned on to the forecourt. Looked like a Nissan Micra in the colour they called Old Lady's White. It rolled past the pumps and came to a halt. A guy tumbled out on the driver's side and came staggering over towards the door, opened it and stood swaying in the entrance. It was a sight the young man behind the counter would never forget as long as he lived. A big man with half his face torn away, from the hairline down. Something that must have been an eye dangled against his cheek. His light jacket was drenched in blood. He supported himself against the newspaper rack, seemed to be trying to say something, but the sounds that came from the bloodied mouth were incomprehensible. Then he raised his arm. Something was dangling from it, attached by a handcuff. Something that looked like a hand with a bit of the lower arm.

The lad backed away into the room behind him, slammed the door shut and turned the key in the lock. With trembling hands he took his mobile phone from his top pocket and punched in the emergency number.

69

AT 1.10 A.M., ARMED police mounted an operation in Åsnes county in Hedmark. Members of the Emergency Response Unit went into action, surrounding a cabin in the forest north of Åmoen owned by Sergeant Arve Norbakk of the Oslo City Police. Snipers were put on alert and a dog team was also on the scene.

The door and the windows on two of the walls were wide open. Through a megaphone the operational leader ordered everyone inside the cabin to come out immediately. There was no reaction, nor was there when the command was repeated. At 2.23 the cabin was bathed in light from mobile floodlights and a combined assault was mounted on three fronts. The first man through the door shouted a warning; again there was no answer.

– I'm hearing sounds, he reported through his radio headset. – Like a child whimpering.

They were given the go-ahead and went in. The smell of rotting meat hit them. The front room was empty. The kitchen too, and one of the bedrooms. Another door was locked and secured. An open trapdoor was found. Obviously where the sounds were coming from. One of the three officers who had entered the premises got down on the floor and wriggled his way over to it. The stench here was even stronger. From the ceiling below him a torch shed a faint light on what lay beneath. It struck him that the cellar was much larger than it appeared to be from the outside. A metal gate divided the room in two. He leaned further forward, shone his own torch around. In one corner, behind the ladder leading down, sat a bent form with its back to him. Now it turned towards the light. The sergeant stared down into the pale, wide face. It looked as though tears were falling from the slanting eyes. The man sat cradling something in his arms. It looked to be about the size of a doll. Behind him lay the twisted shape of a human body.

– What are you doing down there?

He got no answer. One of the others joined him.

– I'll go down. The guy's mentally retarded. Looks like there's someone else there too. Probably not conscious.

He jumped down into the semi-darkness, pistol in one hand, torch in the other.

– You can't sit there like that, he said. – What's that you've got there?

He shone his torch on the thing the man was holding in his arms. At first he couldn't tell what it was. Then abruptly he staggered back and supported himself against the ladder. The light from the torch was shining directly on to the face of a severed head.

At 4.15, the remains of the two bodies were carried outside and placed in the clearing in front of the cabin. A pile of excrement was found by one of the cellar walls. The wildlife expert was in no doubt about the kind of animal it came from, and tracks found in and around the cabin confirmed this. Along with the injuries sustained by the two bodies, this seemed a clear indication of the cause of death. As soon as it was light enough, four teams of hunters were sent out into the forest. It would take three days before they managed to track down the bear they believed to be the one that had been kept in the cellar beneath the cabin. It was shot and dissected. In its stomach the hunters found partially digested remains that they were immediately able to identify as human.

At 12.00, a press conference was held in a fifth-floor meeting room at Oslo police station. The room was packed with journalists, over a third of them from foreign media. Representing the police were the Chief Constable, the Deputy Chief Constable and the Assistant Chief Constable, as well as the head of the Violent Crimes unit,

Superintendent Agnes Finckenhagen, who briefed the gathering on the so-called bear murders. She announced that the case could now be considered solved, and assured members of the press that they would be kept up to date on any further developments. She also asked for their understanding on this difficult day. It was an appalling tragedy for the victims and their families, and one in which the Oslo police too had suffered.

As soon as questions were invited, all hell broke loose in the room, and it took some time for things to calm down enough for the questions to be heard. Finckenhagen sat there pale and drawn, the make-up cracking around her eyes, and struggled to control her voice. It was obvious that many of the journalists had been unable to take on board the extraordinary details that had emerged from the briefing, and the questions they asked were relatively straight-forward to answer. *VG*, on the other hand, seemed to be particularly well informed. The female reporter immediately asked about Sergeant Arve Norbakk, his role in the investigation, and his relationship to one of the murdered women.

– When a serial killer involved in the investigation of his own crimes has clearly influenced the direction of that investigation, what are the consequences for the police? she added.

Finckenhagen was taken completely by surprise. She had expressed herself in very general terms about *an employee in the Oslo city police force*. She turned to the Chief Constable, and in his eyes thought she could see what the ultimate consequences of this question would be. She felt dizzy.

– There will be a full inquiry into personnel and leadership routines, she heard him reply. – Obviously it's much too early to say what the results of that inquiry will be. We can however confirm that things have happened here that should not have happened in the matter of employment practices and follow-up routines.

Detective Chief Inspector Hans Magnus Viken and the rest of the team followed the press conference on the screen in the meeting room. Nina Jebsen sat leaning forward, chewing away intensely at something, while Sigge Helgarsson tipped his chair back against the wall and lounged there, a bemused smirk on his face.

– Heads will roll, he predicted, evidently not realising that his language was a trifle inappropriate under the circumstances. – It's on days like this you realise how lucky you are not to be one of the bosses.

For once Viken didn't turn on him with a sarcastic riposte. He stood by the wall, arms folded, expressionless and silent. Images from the previous night were still etched across the light cells of his retinas. Arve Norbakk's cabin, the bed containing the remains of the missing woman, Miriam Gaizauskaite. He had also been down in the cellar . . . The smells were even more persistent, he noticed. He shook them away, grabbed his coffee cup and emptied it, felt the acid bubbling and boiling down in his stomach. The burning grew worse when he thought about Arve Norbakk. He'd given himself a day, two at the most, to put these thoughts behind him. He'd spent all night trying to come up with an alternative explanation. In some way or other Arve had to be a victim too. In the minutes before Axel Glenne was wheeled into the operating theatre at Ullevål hospital, Viken had been allowed to ask him some questions. A few of his worst suspicions were confirmed, but shreds of doubt remained.

Not until about ten o'clock had he been able to sit down with the letters from Glenne's car, and a Dictaphone they found at the cabin. A video camera had also been found there. Viken ran the first clip, from which he understood that the sufferings of the victims in the cellar had been thoroughly documented. He decided that the rest of the clips could wait for another day.

By the time he had read the letters and listened to the recordings made on the Dictaphone, all the pieces had fallen into place and there was no hiding place left for his doubt. Arve Norbakk had been one step ahead all the way. He'd led them on and played with them. Offered them explanations for the bear tracks and the claw marks. Advised Viken to send people to Åsnes. Had them looking in an area close to the cabin where the victims had been held prisoner.

And he had deceived them. Information about Miriam Gaizauskaite had been withheld or altered. The identity of the former fiancé fabricated.

Viken glanced at the piece of paper on which he had jotted down a number of timelines. Miriam had been abducted on Wednesday evening, at some point after leaving the Catholic church in Majorstua at 6.15. Norbakk could not have managed to drive out to the cabin with her and be back again by nine o'clock, when the interview with Glenne began. Viken realised that she had probably lain bound and drugged in the back of Norbakk's car while Norbakk was taking part in the interrogation. That meant she had been in the police's own garage, a few floors below where they were sitting. According to the pathologist's report, she hadn't been killed until Thursday night, more than twenty-four hours later.

Viken didn't waste time in self-recriminations. Even as he was reading the letters, he was working out how something he had understood much too late might in fact be turned to his advantage. He managed to catch Finckenhagen just before she was called in to see the Chief Constable about preparations for the press conference, and showed her the letters.

Not long afterwards, Kaja Fredvold from *VG* had called. Suddenly Viken knew the best way to play his cards. He skipped down the stairs, got into his car and returned her call.

Nina was the first to get up and leave the meeting room once the press conference was over. Viken saw from the movements in her neck and back that she needed to be alone. But when he passed her door a few minutes later, she called to him. Full of trepidation, he stopped in the doorway. She was sitting in front of her computer and waved him over.

– Look at this.

Viken peered over her shoulder. Nina's hair smelled of some kind of fruit, and he leaned so far forward that his arm brushed against her back. She was looking at the web edition of *VG*. The headline filled most of the screen: *Infidelity, jealousy and bestial murder*. Beneath was a picture of Miriam. She was standing smiling outside the cabin.

A giant of a man, obviously with Down's syndrome, had an arm around her. Viken had seen him earlier when two detectives led him up from the cellar and out of the cabin.

Viken wrinkled his bushy eyebrows and made a supreme effort to appear surprised.

– How the hell did they get hold of that story? he exclaimed, as Nina clicked on a link that said: *Read all about the bear murders and the Oslo police scandal*.

70

AXEL HEARS A phone ringing far away. He gets out of bed. The sound is coming from somewhere outside the frosted window. He tries to open it, but there are no hinges. *I can't answer you, Miriam. I don't know where it's ringing.* He raises his fist to break the window.

He was held by several pairs of hands.

– Take it easy now, Axel, the dark voice above him said. – Take it easy and everything will be fine.

He opened his eyes. Could see through only one. Three faces above him.

– Who are you?

– I'm the person who operated on you.

– Miriam's trying to call me!

One of the others, a woman in small round glasses, said:

– You didn't have a phone with you, but if someone rings we'll make sure you get a message.

– What have you given me?

– You're on a morphine drip.

Axel sank back on to the bed. They let go of him.

– I can only see through one eye.

The surgeon sat on the edge of the bed.

– You only have one eye to see with, Axel. But there's nothing wrong with that one. You'll see as well as a one-eyed eagle.

The smile was fixed around his mouth.

– The operation was a success. Our only problem is all these damned journalists. But we're doing what we can to keep them away.

– Who's that ringing?

The woman in glasses bent over him again. The smell of carbolic soap and mackerel from her mouth.

– It's quiet here, Axel. No one's ringing.

He takes hold of the mobile phone on the bedside table and presses it to his ear. He's picked up the wrong phone again; the ringing is still there. The glass in the window is frosted, opaque, but he can see a bright light burning on the other side. Shadows moving. *Time to do the right thing, Axel.* Yes, Father, I will do the right thing. But first I have to take this call. Miriam's calling, she's the one I want to tell. *Don't try it on, Axel. Do the right thing. Now.*

Two boys standing outside on the steps. It's summer, and the sun is almost white. They're skinny and bare chested, their arms pink. One of the first really warm days of the summer holidays.

– Let's ride to Oksvalstranda, Brede suggests.

– My bike's still got a flat, Axel says. – And anyway, we promised to look after Balder.

– You can sit behind me. Balder can come with us.

– Not with his paw, Axel protests. – It'll make the infection worse. You heard what Father said this morning. He'll kill you if you do it.

Brede laughs. The kind of laugh that seems to come from some completely different place than his thin neck.

– Suppose Balder did get really ill and die, that would serve the old man right. He loves that dog more than he loves any of us.

Axel weighs it up. Brede says: – If you don't believe me, we can always shoot the dog and then you'll see if I'm not right.

Balder raises his great head and looks at them from the shadows at the corner of the house.

– See, he's laughing at you, says Axel.

Brede ambles over, bends to the dog and scratches behind his ear.

– You're not doing that, are you, Balder? You're not laughing at me.

The dog's tail swishes across the grass like a great bushy snake.

– You shouldn't say things like that, Axel says, suddenly angry.

– Like what?

– What you said about the old man.

Brede looks at him with narrowed eyes. The look makes Axel even angrier. He pulls open the door, runs into the house and up to the first floor, then on up into the loft. Comes back down with a leather pouch in his hand.

Brede has got up and is standing beside Balder.

– What are you going to do with that?

– You always act so bloody tough, Axel hisses. – Now let's see how tough you really are.

He opens the pouch and pulls out the polished black weapon, holds it out to his brother. Brede looks at him, half grins. He takes the gun and releases the safety catch.

– It isn't even loaded, he says and hands it back. – Talk about being tough. You're the biggest yellow-belly round here. You never dare do anything yourself, always get someone else to do it.

Axel puffs out his cheeks in contempt. He takes aim with the pistol, circling round. Points it at Brede's temple.

– Want to bet it isn't loaded?

Brede is still grinning, but the grin has stiffened.

– Why don't you find out, he says in a low voice. – See if you dare.

Axel squeezes the trigger. It's hard and smooth, and the movement of his finger can no longer be stopped. It can be slowed, but not stopped. He turns his hand round and down towards the dog as the gun goes off.

The nurse with the round glasses bent over him. She still smelt of mackerel, and he opened his mouth to ask her if she would mind not getting so close.

– Are you up to seeing visitors? she breathed into his face.

He tried to turn away.

– Brede? he asked.

– Your family's here. Is that his name, your son?

Marlen slipped into the room and stopped just inside the door. Tom pushed her to one side and opened the door all the way. Then Bie appeared and closed it behind them. She was wearing her short jacket. The black leather looked soft.

Marlen ventured closer. She peered up at Axel's face, dropped a bouquet of flowers on to the bed. She put something else there too, a sheet of paper, before taking a few steps back.

– Is it true that you fought with that bear? she whispered.

He moved his head carefully, tried to nod.

– I've done a drawing for you.

He picked it up. Animal shapes against a dark blue background, and a little yellow sun with something bright green in the middle of it.

– This is your eye in the sky, she explained, still whispering. – It's a new star now. Right next to Cassiopeia.

– Come here, he said as distinctly as he could. – You too, Tom.

They stood by his bed. Tom had his arm around his little sister, as though making sure she didn't run off.

– Daniel will be here soon, he said. – His plane lands in an hour. It was me who rang and asked him to come over.

Axel took his hand. He felt a burning sensation where his eye had been.

Bie still stood there, a little behind them. Her eyes were as hard as tiny sapphires.

– I'll do the right thing, he said.